"THRILLING!"

"WONDERFUL!"

"WELL-PLOTTED AND EXCITING!"

ELIZABETH PETERS
THE GOLDEN ONE

By Elizabeth Peters

ELIZABETH PETERS

THE
GOLDEN ONE

A NOVEL OF SUSPENSE

AVON BOOKS
An Imprint of HarperCollinsPublishers

This is a work of fiction. Names, characters, places, and incidents are products of the author's imagination or are used fictitiously and are not to be construed as real. Any resemblance to actual events, locales, organizations, or persons, living or dead, is entirely coincidental.

AVON BOOKS
An Imprint of HarperCollins*Publishers*
10 East 53rd Street
New York, New York 10022-5299

First Avon Books paperback printing: April 2003
First William Morrow hardcover printing: May 2002

Avon Trademark Reg. U.S. Pat. Off. and in Other Countries, Marca Registrada, Hecho en U.S.A.
HarperCollins® is a registered trademark of HarperCollins Publishers Inc.

Printed in the U.S.A.

10 9 8 7 6 5 4 3 2 1

To Tracey

We praise the Golden One,
the Lady of Heaven, Lady of Fragrance,
Eye of the Sun, the Great Goddess,
Mistress of All the Gods,
Lady of Turquoise, Mistress of Joy, Mistress of Music . . .
that she may give us fine children,
happiness, and a good husband.

—Epithets of Hathor,
compiled from various sources

Acknowledgments

To err is human, and I am and I do, despite the fact that I go to considerable effort to get even small details right. I do not scruple to make use of my friends in this endeavor; several of them have read all or part of the manuscript and made suggestions. I am particularly indebted to Tim Hardman and Ann Crispin, for setting me straight on the (to me) esoteric subject of horses and cavalry. Catharine Roehrig, one of the few Egyptologists who have visited the area of the south-west wadis, was good enough to tell me where I went wrong in my initial description. Donald Ryan, one of the few others, also corrected mistakes in his usual tactful manner. Dennis Forbes, George Johnson, and Kristen Whitbread read the entire bulky manuscript and offered advice. If errors remain, they are mine, and not those of my advisers.

Preface

The Editor is pleased to present another of the journals of Mrs. Amelia Peabody Emerson, Egyptologist, adventurer, wife, and mother. (She would, the Editor believes, approve that order.) Editing her prose is no easy task, for the original text contains some misinformation, a great deal of repetition, and certain omissions. In order to repair the latter fault, the Editor has, as before, inserted sections from Manuscript H, begun by Ramses Emerson at approximately the age of sixteen, and continued by him and his wife after their marriage. This manuscript describes events at which Mrs. Emerson was not present, and gives a viewpoint differing in significant ways from hers. She was an extremely opinionated lady.

The rest of the Emerson papers are still being studied, collated, and edited. Material from these sources has appeared in earlier volumes (and may appear in the future), but none of it adds anything relevant to the present volume.

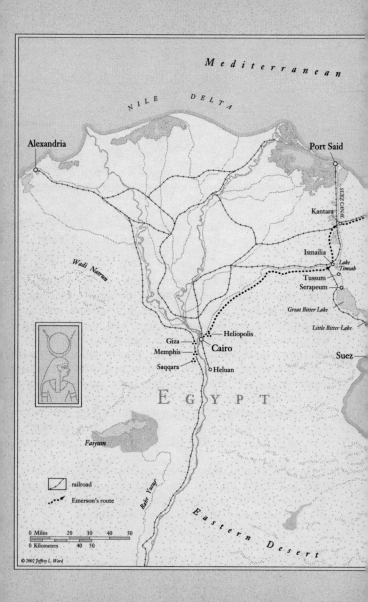

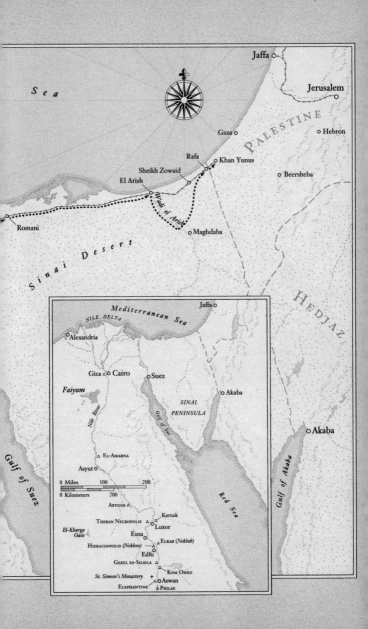

THE
GOLDEN ONE

PART ONE

· ·

The Cemetery
of the Monkeys

One

When I am in one of my philosophical moods, I am inclined to wonder whether all families are as difficult as mine.

I was in such a mood as I dressed for dinner on the penultimate evening of our voyage. We would dock at Alexandria in two days, unless, of course, the ship was sunk by a German torpedo. A winter voyage from England to Egypt is never comfortable; but in that fateful December of 1916, after more than two years of war, the possibility of submarine attack had been added to the perils of rough seas and stormy weather.

I was not thinking of that danger—for I make it a habit never to worry about matters that are beyond my control—nor of the difficulty of trying to keep my footing while the floor of the cabin rose and fell and the oil lamps swung wildly on their brackets—for mine is the sort of mind that rises above such things—but perhaps these considerations did affect me more than I realized, giving a pessimistic cast to my normally cheerful reflections.

Mind you, I had no legitimate grounds for complaint about my immediate family. My husband, Radcliffe Emerson, is the most distinguished Egyptologist of this or any other era. His sapphirine-blue eyes, the cleft, or dimple, in his strong chin, his thick sable hair, and muscular but sym-

metrical frame are additional attractions to me and, I regret
to say, to innumerable other females.

He has a few minor eccentricities: his command of invec-
tive, which has earned him the Egyptian sobriquet of Father
of Curses, his explosive temper, his autocratic, arbitrary
method of dealing with the authorities of the Service des
Antiquités, which had led in the past to our being barred
from most of the interesting sites in Egypt . . .

Well, but no proud mother could have asked for a better
son than mine. Ramses had been named for his Uncle Walter, but everyone called him by the nickname given him by
his father in infancy. He was as handsome and intellectually
gifted as his father, idealistic, kind, and courageous . . . A
little too courageous, perhaps? He had been one of the most
infuriating children I have ever had the misfortune to encounter, and his reckless disregard for danger, when he believed the cause he supported to be morally right, was one
trait that I had been unable to eradicate. The most terrifying
of his adventures had occurred during the winter of
1914–15, when he had taken on a secret assignment for the
War Office. He and his best friend, David, had completed
their mission successfully, but both had been seriously injured, and Ramses's true identity had been exposed to agents
of the Central Powers. I had hoped his marriage would sober
him, but although he was as passionately attached to his
beautiful wife as Emerson was to my humble self, Nefret
had not been the calming influence for which I had hoped.
She would have thrown herself in front of a charging lion if
Ramses were its destined prey, but what I wanted was someone who would prevent him from provoking lions in the first
place.

Nefret had been our ward, dear as a daughter, before she
married our son. As a firm believer in the equality of the female gender, I could only approve the determination with
which she had achieved against considerable odds her goal
of qualifying as a surgeon. As a person of high moral principles I could only commend her for spending part of her large

fortune in establishing in Cairo a hospital for women that served even the lowest and most despised members of that sex. If only she would consent to settle down—devote her ardent energies to medicine and to archaeology, and to Ramses—and perhaps . . .

The boat gave a great lurch and I dropped the earring I was endeavoring to insert. With a muttered "Curse it" I lowered myself to hands and knees and began feeling about on the floor—without, I hardly need say, losing the track of my mental musing.

Honesty compels me to admit that the propensity of my son and daughter to become engaged with individuals who desired to wreak grave bodily harm upon them was not entirely their fault. Emerson and I tended to attract such individuals too. Over the years we had dealt—effectively, I hardly need add—with murderers, forgers, tomb robbers, and criminals of various sorts. Several of them had been related to us.

As I crawled under the dressing table in pursuit of the elusive earring, I remembered something Emerson had said about my side of the family, to the effect that not one of them had any redeeming qualities whatever. This was rude, but undeniably correct. One of my nephews had been—I am happy to employ the past tense—a thoroughly repellent human being. Sennia, his little daughter by a Cairo prostitute, who had been callously abandoned by her father, was now part of our family.

The boat bounced again and the top of my head came into painful contact with the underside of the dressing table. Since I was alone, with no one to overhear, I permitted myself a few expletives. I do not approve of bad language, but everybody else in the family employs it freely. It is Emerson's fault. He cannot or will not restrain himself and of course the children emulate him. There are times when Nefret's language . . .

The cursed earring continued to elude me, but I endeavored, as is my habit, to look on the bright side. Emerson's kin were exemplary human beings: his brother Walter, a true scholar and gentle man; Walter's wife, my close friend Evelyn; and their fine brood of children, in which category I must include the husband of their daughter Lia. David, a talented artist and trained Egyptologist, and Ramses's best friend, was the grandson of our dear departed reis Abdullah. We had missed him terribly the year before, in both his professional and personal capacities.

However, there was Emerson's other brother.

The door burst open and Emerson staggered in. Observing my position, he let out a bellow of alarm, seized me round the waist, and lifted me to my feet—and off them. "Did you fall, sweetheart? The cursed boat is bouncing like a rubber ball. Speak to me, Peabody."

I was touched by his use of my maiden name, which he employs as a term of approbation and endearment, and by his tender concern, but discomfort compelled me to utter a mild complaint. "I cannot breathe, Emerson, you are squeezing me too tightly."

"Oh." Emerson removed one arm and caught hold of the doorframe.

"I dropped an earring," I explained, after drawing a long breath. "Pray put me down, my dear. I don't want to lose it, it was one of the pair you gave me last Christmas."

"I will find it." Emerson deposited me on the bed and began crawling round the floor. "Stay still or you will brain yourself. Ah—here you are, my love."

The gem winked and sparkled in his big brown hand. As a general rule I do not care for diamonds—an antique scarab or a string of mummy beads is much more to my taste—but Emerson had selected the stones and designed the settings. Having observed that other women seemed to like diamonds—it had only taken him thirty years to notice this—he had decided I should have some, too.

"Why have you got yourself up so formally?" he demanded. "No one will dress for dinner tonight, the sea is too rough."

"It is necessary to keep up appearances, especially in times such as these. Have you forgotten the date?"

"Yes," said Emerson, in—I could only suppose—a desperate attempt to forestall my suggestion that he assume evening dress. Emerson dislikes the confinement of tightly fitting garments, and I would be the first to admit that his impressive form never shows to better advantage than when he is attired in the wrinkled flannels and open-necked shirts he wears on the dig. I felt obliged to persevere, however.

"It is December the thirty-first, Emerson. We must toast the New Year and pray that 1917 will bring better hopes."

"Bah," said Emerson. "It is an artificial distinction with no meaning. The only significance of January the first is that we will be one day closer to Alexandria. You are fine enough for both of us. That gown becomes you, my love. Is it new?"

It was not, and he knew it—at least I think he did—it is difficult to be certain with Emerson, since he remains happily oblivious to things one expects him to notice, and sees things one hopes he will not.

A glance in the mirror gave me little in the way of confirmation of his compliment, for my image was distorted by movement and shadow. However, I know my own appearance well enough—a form perhaps slightly more rounded than in the distant past, a rather too prominent chin, eyes of steely gray, and black hair that is long and thick but not sleekly shining, despite the hundred strokes of a brush it receives each evening. (In the pages of my private journal I will confess that its color owes a little something to art rather than to nature. Emerson is unaware of this small deception and I have seen no reason to enlighten him.) In short, beautiful I am not—except in the eyes of my husband.

Softened by this touching thought, I smiled affectionately at him. "No, Emerson, you would be the only person not in evening dress. On this occasion especially it is necessary to display a stiff upper lip and—"

"Damnation!" Emerson shouted.

With my assistance and a good deal of grumbling, he did

as he was told. He then offered me his arm, and the remnants of his ill humor vanished as I clung tightly to it. Emerson likes me to cling to him. I do not do it often, but I doubt I could have kept my footing that night without his support.

We had not seen much of our fellow passengers, of whom there were far fewer than in the happy past. The inclement weather had kept most persons in their bunks. Thanks to the judicious application of whiskey and soda, which is, among other things, an excellent remedy for mal de mer, we had been unaffected, but there was little pleasure in walking the deck in a howling gale.

More people than usual were at dinner that evening. The celebration of the New Year was no doubt the occasion, but few of them looked as if they were in a mood to celebrate. The tightly curtained windows of the dining salon were a silent reminder of war, and the ship kept rolling about in a disconcerting fashion. Perhaps, I thought hopefully, submarines do not sail in bad weather. I must remember to ask someone.

The others were already at our table; as we wove a somewhat erratic path toward them, Ramses rose, balancing lightly with a hand on the back of his chair. I was pleased to see that he was properly attired in black tie and that Nefret looked particularly lovely in the soft shade of blue that matched her eyes and set off her red-gold hair. The fifth member of the party was tightly wedged between them, in order to prevent her from flying off her chair. Sennia should have been in her cabin with Basima, her nurserymaid, for the hour was late for a seven-year-old, but Basima did not feel well, and Sennia had wanted to be with Ramses on this special occasion—and she had got her own way, as she often did.

It was not surprising that many people believed my nephew's child to be Ramses's illegitimate daughter, for she had my dark gray eyes and his coloring. Ramses had always looked more like an Egyptian than an English person: wavy black hair, black eyes and thick lashes, skin several shades darker than is common in our island. (I cannot explain this, and I see no reason why I should be obliged to do so.) His looks are very pleasing, and I assure the reader that his fond mother has not been the only female to think so.

He seated himself somewhat hastily and caught Sennia as she slipped sideways. She let out a high-pitched laugh, which sounded very loud in the subdued air of the salon. Several persons looked and smiled; several others frowned disapprovingly; but that peal of childish laughter had unquestionably relieved some of the tension that filled the room.

"Enjoying this, Little Bird?" Emerson inquired fondly.

"Oh, yes, it's great fun bouncing up and down. And if I spill soup in my lap Aunt Amelia cannot say it is my fault." She gave me a cheeky grin, and I smiled back at her, glad she was too young to share the uneasiness that affected the rest of us. We had thought long and hard about exposing her to the perils of the voyage instead of leaving her in the tender care of Walter and Evelyn; but Sennia had not thought about it at all, she had simply assumed she would come along, and any attempt to prevent her would have led to consequences that were loud and unpleasant. Emerson could not bear to see her cry, and the little witch knew it. She had come into our lives under circumstances that were painful to recall even now, but what a joy she was to us all! She was quite like a grandchild . . . the only one . . . thus far . . .

Nefret caught me staring at her and the color in her face deepened. "Yes, Mother?" she inquired. "Is there a smudge on my nose?"

"Why, no, my dear. I was just thinking how that shade of blue becomes you."

The subject was one into which no person of sensibility could properly probe, and I felt certain I would be the first to be informed.

After Ramses, of course.

A great deal of soup was spilled, and not only by Sennia. Most of the diners stuck it out until the end, however, and after Sennia had finished the light meal which was all I allowed her, she began to fidget and look round. How she had got to know so many of the other passengers I could not imagine, since we had never let her out of our sight, but her waves and smiles were acknowledged by several persons. One was a tall gray-haired gentleman whom I had seen once or twice on deck; his forbidding face broke into a smile and he waved back. Sennia received an even more energetic response from a man seated at the captain's table. He had a round face, as red and wrinkled as a well-preserved winter apple, and he bobbed up and down in his chair, waving, until the young man next to him put a restraining hand on his arm. He was as stiff as the older man—his father?—was friendly. Eyeglasses gave him a scholarly look, but he was dressed with foppish elegance, every hair in place.

"Who are they?" I asked Sennia.

"They are Americans. Can I have an ice?"

"May I have an ice. Yes, you may."

"Is the lady his wife?" Nefret asked. "Goodness, look at that frock, *and* the diamonds, *and* the rubies."

"Vulgarly large," I said with a sniff.

"I think they are very beautiful," said Miss Sennia. "She let me look at them one day—it was in the salon—but only because Mr. Albion told her to. She is not as nice as he is, and their son is not nice at all." She took firm hold of the bowl and dug her spoon into the pink mound. "Mr. Albion wanted to meet you, but I told him you did not meet people."

"Good girl," said Emerson approvingly.

Between bites Sennia told us about the gray-haired gentleman, who was going out to join a firm in Alexandria, and about several of the other passengers. The storm began to subside, the howls of the wind were not so loud, the motion not quite so violent; but I believe we were all relieved when the attendants came round with champagne and the captain rose to propose a toast. It was somewhat long-winded. I remember only the end.

"To the health of His gracious Majesty and to victory in 1917!"

Somehow I was not surprised to hear a familiar voice amend the statement. "To peace," said Ramses. We drank to that.

As it turned out, we reached Alexandria without being torpedoed, and were met by Selim and Daoud. Selim had replaced his father Abdullah as our reis, or foreman; he and his Uncle Daoud, like Abdullah's other relations, were as close as family, and valued assistants in all our endeavors. They assisted us in resuscitating poor Basima and Gargery, our butler, who had suffered horribly from seasickness the entire time, and Sennia's cat, who had not been seasick but whose normally bad temper was even more strained by long confinement in a room that was in constant motion. It would have been impossible to leave the nasty beast behind because Sennia, and, to a lesser degree, Nefret, were the only persons who could control him. Horus was the only cat with us that year. Seshat, Ramses's erstwhile companion and guardian, had given up a professional career for domesticity. Perhaps she felt she could now trust Nefret to look after him.

Basima brightened as soon as she set foot on dry land, and Gargery, though still unsteady, went off with Daoud to see about the luggage. We had a great deal more than usual this time, for we had reached a momentous decision. Ordinarily we left for Egypt in the autumn and ended our excavation season before the summer heat set in; but this time we had come for an indefinite stay. Emerson, who does not fear man nor beast nor demon of the night on his own account, had declared his nerves were unequal to having the rest of us travel back and forth as long as the submarine menace remained.

"It will get worse before it gets better, mark my words," he had declared. "I don't mind people shooting at us or shutting us up in pyramids or trying to brain us with heavy objects—that is to say, I don't much like it, but I have become accustomed to it. Having a bloody ship sunk under us by a bloody U-boat is something else again. Call me a coward if you will . . ."

None of us did; as Ramses remarked, there was not a man alive who would have dared. I knew how Emerson felt, for I have the same fear of air raids. We had, all of us, been in deadly peril on more than one occasion, and felt quite comfortable about our ability to deal with ordinary human adversaries. To be sure, there were human beings at the control of aeroplanes and submarines, but since one never saw them, one was inclined to think of the machine itself as the enemy—a remote mechanical menace.

Nor for worlds would I have questioned Emerson's motives in proposing the scheme, but he had always yearned to work year-round in Egypt instead of having to close down the dig in March or April, sometimes when the excavation was at its most interesting. For the past several seasons our archaeological activities had been even more constrained by family matters and by Ramses's undercover work for the War Office. This season Emerson had been awarded the firman for a site in Luxor. It was of all places in Egypt the one we loved best—the scene of several of our greatest discoveries, our home for many happy years, and the home as well of our dear friends the Vandergelts, who were even then settling in for a long season of excavation.

There was only one objection I could think of to such a splendid prospect. I do not refer to the blistering heat of Luxor in summer—an objection that would never have occurred to Emerson, who has the constitution of a camel—but to the fact that we would leave behind for Heaven knew how long our beloved family. The Reader will be cognizant, after my earlier remarks on the subject, that I was not thinking of the members of my side of the family.

"Nonsense," said Emerson, when I mentioned this. "You are hopelessly given to melodrama, Peabody. We are not bidding anyone a final farewell, only prolonging the separation a trifle. Circumstances may change; we will not be completely cut off."

He had readily agreed that we must spend Christmas with our loved ones and we did our best to make a merry time of it, for the sake of the children—Sennia, and Lia and David's little Dolly, who was just old enough to toddle about. All our surviving nieces and nephews were there: Raddie and his new wife, the widow of a friend who had died in France; Margaret, newly engaged to a young officer; even Willie, on leave from France, who tried, dear lad, to make twice as many jokes to compensate for the absence of his twin brother, Johnny, who had been killed in action the year before. There were tears as well as laughter; the war was too much with us; but we carried it off, I think, and there was one moment of genuine hilarity when Emerson asked David if he had considered coming out later in the season.

"Up to you, of course," he added hastily. "But little Dolly is fit and healthy, and Lia—"

"She is doing very well," said Nefret. "All things considered."

She smiled at David, whose candid countenance betrayed his relief at her intervention. He had difficulty in refusing Emerson anything, and he had not known how to break the news.

I, of course, had known the moment I set eyes on Lia.

Emerson's jaw dropped. "Oh, good Gad!" he shouted. "Not again! Just like her mother! It must be a hereditary—"

"Emerson!" I exclaimed.

The reminder was sufficient, for Emerson is really the kindest of men. He managed to choke out a few words of congratulatory import, but everyone had heard his bellow and most of them knew what had occasioned it. Even Evelyn, who had not laughed a great deal since Johnny's death, had to retreat behind the Christmas tree to conceal her mirth. She was well aware that Emerson had never entirely forgiven her for abandoning a promising career as a copier of Egyptian scenes in favor of motherhood.

We would miss David and Lia, and not only for their affectionate companionship; David was one of the best artists and epigraphers in the field and Lia had learned enough about Egyptology to have become a valued assistant. Their absence would leave us somewhat shorthanded that season. I did not allow that to worry me. We would manage somehow. As I stood on the dock at Alexandria, the old joy of being back in Egypt pervaded every atom of my being. We got ourselves and our baggage onto the train for Cairo with only the usual confusion, which was compounded by the presence of the cat. Horus had to sit between Sennia and Nefret, since he refused to tolerate anyone else.

Other members of our Egyptian family awaited us at the station in Cairo. We were soon the center of a shouting, cheering mob, which included not only our friends but practically every Egyptian who happened to be there, all greeting us by our Egyptian names. Emerson disliked formal titles and would not allow our workers to address him as Effendi, but he rather reveled in his well-deserved sobriquet of the Father of Curses. Many Egyptians still called me Sitt Hakim, though a lady doctor I was not; however, in my early days in Egypt, when medical services for the fellahin were practically nonexistent, even my limited medical skills were appreciated. The title should have been Nefret's, but she had long been known as Nur Misur, "Light of Egypt"; and Ramses was Brother of Demons—a tribute to his supposedly supernatural powers.

Emerson was soon so enveloped by well-wishers that only his head (hatless, as usual) showed above the crowd, some of whom attempted to embrace him while others knelt for his blessing (and baksheesh).

All at once Emerson's voice rose in a vehement swearword. "Stop him!" he shouted, spinning round in a circle and swatting his admirers away with wide sweeps of his arms. "Where did he go?"

"Why, Emerson, what is the matter?" I demanded, hastening to his side.

Red-faced and shaking with rage, Emerson invoked the Creator in a manner of which I thoroughly disapprove. "He was here a second ago. Dressed in rags, smelling like a camel, squatting at my feet . . . Where is he?"

"Vanished," I said, as the crowd again closed in. "Did he speak to you?"

"Oh, yes, he spoke. 'Welcome back, brother! And thank you.'" Said Emerson, between clenched teeth, "I had just given him fifty piastres."

Emerson's other brother. Strictly speaking, he was a half brother, the son of Emerson's father and a lady who had had the misfortune not to be married to that gentleman. Only recently had we discovered the true identity of the man who had been for many years our most formidable opponent, a master of disguise and the head of a ring of criminals that specialized in tomb robbing and antiquities fraud; and the additional, equally astonishing fact that Sethos, as he chose to be called, was one of Britain's most valued secret agents. These revelations had forced us to reevaluate a relationship that had been marked by considerable acrimony. As I pointed out to Emerson, one cannot wholly despise a man who has risked his life for us and for his country.

I made the point again as my seething spouse spun round and round in a vain attempt to locate the insolent beggar. Ramses and Nefret hastened to us, demanding to know what had happened. A few brief sentences of explanation sufficed; they were only too well acquainted with Sethos's skill at disguise and bizarre sense of humor. Ramses's enigmatic countenance remained unmoved except for a faint line between his brows, but Nefret's dimples were very much in evidence. She had a certain weakness for the man. Most women did, and Sethos was not above exploiting it for his own advantage.

There was nothing to be done about locating him in that mob, so, with the assistance of the children, I forced Emerson into a carriage and persuaded him to delay discussion of the matter until we had got ourselves settled into the hotel.

Although he was anxious to get on to Luxor, Emerson had agreed to spend a few days in Cairo catching up on the news. Press censorship was so strict, we had only the faintest idea of what had been going on in our part of the world. We were staying at Shepheard's; and it was with a sense of agreeable nostalgia that I found myself once again in the ambience that had provided the prelude to so many remarkable experiences. The villain Vincey (and his cat) searching our luggage in the bedroom; the Master Criminal, aka Sethos, aka (had I but known) my brother-in-law, slipping a sleeping potion into my wine in the dining salon . . .

"What's he up to now?" Emerson demanded, as the servants carried in our bags and the manager advanced to welcome us.

"Do stop shouting, Emerson," I implored. "Wait until we are in private."

We had been given our old rooms on the third floor. By the time we had got everyone settled in and I had convinced Sennia that she must have an early supper with Basima instead of joining us for dinner, the sky was darkening and the lights of Cairo were twinkling through the dusk. The private discussion I had promised Emerson would have to wait a little longer; Gargery was not to be got rid of. Fully recovered and officious as usual, he was determined to carry out the duties of a valet. Emerson did not employ a valet, nor should the Reader suppose that under ordinary circumstances we would have taken a servant as useless as a butler with us to an archaeological dig. Gargery was something more and perhaps something less than a butler, however; he had taken part in several of our criminal investigations and had proved himself ready and willing to employ any methods he deemed necessary to protect us—and most particularly, Sennia.

I completed my toilette and retired to the sitting room, where I found that the sufragi had delivered a number of messages and letters. I glanced through them, entertained by the growls and curses coming from the dressing room. Finally Emerson emerged, looking sullen but very handsome in black tie, and after admiring his handiwork and requesting my approval, Gargery retired.

Emerson said, "Now, Peabody, curse it—"

"No, my dear, not now. We will want to hear what the children have to say about this."

Nefret and Ramses were late in joining us in the dining salon, so I took advantage of the interlude to see if there was anyone present from whom I could extract useful information. Pickings, as Emerson remarked, appeared to be slim. Many of our fellow archaeologists had left Egypt for war duties. I had hoped to see Howard Carter, who led a peripatetic existence, running back and forth between Luxor, where he excavated in a rather random manner, and Cairo, where he carried out certain mysterious activities on behalf of the War Office. However, he was not there.

There was one familiar face among those present—one I would rather not have seen. He was looking directly at me, and I was not quick enough to avoid meeting his eyes; the thin lips compressed between a pointed nose and chin parted in a smile and he rose to his feet.

"Curse it!" said Emerson. "It's that bastard Smith."

"That is only his nom d'espionnage, Emerson."

"His what?"

"You know what I mean. I thought it a rather clever term."

Emerson's expression indicated that he did not agree. "His name is Boisgirdle-Bracedragon," I added. "Or is it Bracegirdle-Boisdragon? The reason I have difficulty in remembering is, of course, because I dislike the fellow so thoroughly. It is a well-known psychological—"

"Don't talk psychology to me, Peabody. It is a damned ridiculous name in any case. If we must refer to him at all, Smith is good enough. He isn't going to have the infernal gall to speak to us, is he?"

If Smith had intended to do so, Emerson's concentrated scowl made him think better of it. He sank back into his chair. I kept an unobtrusive eye on him, though, and when Ramses and Nefret joined us a few minutes later, he again rose, and this time, he bowed in our direction.

Ramses misses very little, and this overture would have been difficult to overlook. His bland expression did not change, but Nefret let out a muffled swearword. She looked very beautiful in her favorite cornflower blue, with pearls and sapphires as her ornaments and her gold-red hair coiled into a coronet around her head; but her pretty face had assumed a scowl almost as forbidding as that of Emerson.

"What's he doing here?" she demanded.

"One must suppose he is dining," said Ramses coolly.

"Here?"

Nefret had a point. Shepheard's was no longer the hotel favored by the smart set of Cairo. "Smith" was a member of that group of silly women and pompous officials, the majority of whom were probably unaware of his intelligence activities, believing him to be an official of the Department of Public Works. He was dining alone that evening.

It would not have been difficult for interested parties to learn the date of our arrival and the name of the hotel where we had booked rooms. Some of those interested parties were in London, and I did not doubt that their particular interest was in my son. At the behest of his superiors, Smith had tried once before to recruit Ramses for a dangerous mission. Would he try again? Or—the idea had just occurred to me— did his presence have something to do with the reappearance of Emerson's brother? Sethos had been connected in some way with the group Smith directed, whatever it may have been. Secretiveness is second nature to such persons; they may and do claim it is necessary, but in my opinion they revel in being mysterious.

I did not mention this conjecture to Emerson, for that would have inflamed his temper even more.

"The devil with Smith," he declared. "What I want to know is—confound it, young man, what are you doing?"

"Serving the next course," I said, as the youth fumbled

with the plates. "That is his job, Emerson. Stop terrorizing him."

"Oh. Well. Sorry, my boy," he added, addressing the waiter, who went pale with horror.

I groaned. "And don't apologize to him!"

It has proved impossible to train Emerson in the proper ways of dealing with servants. He treats prince and peasant, basket carrier and archaeologist the same—that is, he shouts at them when he is out of temper and begs their pardon when he has been unjust. The waiter ought to have been trained in the proper way of dealing with Emerson, whose peculiarities are well known to the staff at Shepheard's, but he was very young and apparently he had not taken the warnings to heart.

With the assistance of the headwaiter he managed to get the soup plates off the table and the fish course served, and Emerson, who was unaware of having done anything unusual, resumed where he had left off. "What's Sethos doing in Cairo? What was the point of that impertinent encounter? Was it a challenge or a warning or—"

"Why should it have been either?" Nefret asked. "We haven't heard from him for months, and he knows we have good reason to be concerned about him. Perhaps it was only his way of telling us he is alive and well."

"Bah," said Emerson.

Nefret laughed, and I said, "Now, Emerson, you mustn't hold a grudge, my dear."

"Grudge! It is petty-minded, no doubt, to resent a man because he tried to kill me and seduce my wife and steal my antiquities."

"That was all in the past. The services he has rendered us and his country in the past few years attest to the sincerity of his reformation, and his recent—er—arrangement with another lady should be sufficient assurance of his abandonment of an attachment that was, I do not doubt, occasioned as much by his resentment of you as by his interest in me."

I paused to draw a deep breath, and Emerson, who had

been stabbing at his fish, placed his fork on the table. "Peabody," he said mildly, "that was even more pompous and pedantic than your usual declarations. Do not suppose that the complexity of your syntax can conceal the inaccuracy of your conclusions. He has not reformed. He as good as said so last year. As for his arrangement with Miss Minton, for all you know that came to an end almost as soon as it began. Your attempts to communicate with the lady this past summer were unsuccessful, weren't they? Don't deny that you tried, for I know you did."

At this point *he* had to pause in order to breathe. "Ha!" I exclaimed. "You did the same. And you learned, as did I, that after being incommunicado for several months she had been accredited as a war correspondent and was in France. You also tried to get information about him from the War Office—without success, as you ought to have anticipated. Why won't you admit that you care about the man? After all, he is—"

"Mother, please!" Nefret said. "You are becoming heated. And so are you, Father. Perhaps you might allow someone else to offer an opinion."

"Well?" Emerson demanded of his daughter. "What have you to say?"

"Nothing, really."

"Ah," said Emerson. "Ramses?"

He had remained silent, only smiling faintly as he looked from one speaker (Emerson) to the other (me). Now he shrugged. "Speculation about the motives of my uncle are surely a waste of time. One never knows what he will do until he does it." Reddening, Emerson started to speak. Ramses raised his voice a trifle. "Thus far, all he has done is greet you. An encounter of that sort would appeal to his peculiar sense of humor, and he couldn't risk a face-to-face meeting, not if he is still working undercover."

"I don't give a curse about that," Emerson declared forcibly, if not entirely accurately. "What I want to know is whether he is still in the antiquities game. Ramses, suppos-

ing you and I make the rounds of the cafés tonight and interrogate the dealers. If 'the Master' is back in business—"

"They won't tell *you*," I said.

"No," Nefret agreed. After the waiter had removed the
plates without incident (Emerson's attention being otherwise engaged), she planted her elbows on the table and
leaned forward, her blue eyes sparkling. "Your methods are
too direct, Father. Do you remember Ali the Rat and his—
er—young friend?"

Emerson choked on a sip of wine, and I said uneasily,
"Ramses can't be Ali the Rat again, Nefret. His masquerade
was discovered."

"But the people who knew of it are dead," Nefret argued.
"And I made a very pretty boy, didn't I, Ramses?"

She turned to look him squarely in the eyes. He did not respond at once. Then he said equably, "Very pretty. I'd prefer
not to risk Ali, in case some of the old crowd are still hanging about, but we might try a variation of the same thing."

I had been afraid of this, though I had not expected matters would come to a head quite so soon. Nefret was as
courageous and capable as any man, and utterly devoted to
her husband. He was equally devoted to her, and I could
only imagine what a struggle it must have been for him to
admit she had the right to share his adventures and his danger. Naturally I was in full agreement with her demand for
equality; had I not demanded and (more or less) received the
same from Emerson? That did not mean I liked Nefret's doing it. Principles do not hold up well when they are challenged by personal affection.

To my relief, Ramses went on, "Not tonight, though. It
will take me a while to collect the appropriate disguises."

"Certainly not tonight," I said. "It has been a long day. We
should retire early."

"An excellent suggestion," said Emerson, cheering up.

"Yes, Mother," said Ramses.

We had a little private conversation, Emerson and I, sitting cozily side by side before the dying fire in the sitting

room and sipping a last whiskey and soda. I summed it up by saying, "So it is agreed that we leave Cairo as soon as possible?"

Emerson nodded emphatic agreement. "It is worrisome enough having Ramses prowling the suks and the coffeeshops looking for criminals, without her going with him."

"Not so worrisome as having him take on another filthy job from the War Office. Smith's presence this evening was highly suspicious, Emerson."

"Nonsense," said Emerson. "However . . . Good Gad, what with the intelligence services and my devious brother, Cairo is no place for a family of harmless archaeologists. But you are worrying unnecessarily, my love. There is no way on earth Ramses could be persuaded to take on another assignment."

Emerson's tender affection did not miss the slight shiver that ran through my limbs. "Damnation, Peabody," he snarled, "if you are having one of your famous forebodings, I don't want to hear about it! Come to bed at once."

While we breakfasted in our rooms, Emerson looked through the post (distractions of various kinds having prevented him from doing so earlier) and came upon a letter from Cyrus Vandergelt that aroused such indignation he leaped to his feet, rushed to the door, and would have bolted out in his dressing gown had I not caught hold of him.

"For pity's sake, Emerson, where are you going?"

Emerson waved the close-written pages at me. "They're at it again. Another tomb. Looted. The artifacts already at the Luxor dealers. Damnation! Ramses—"

"If you want to share this with Ramses," I said, interpreting his incoherent comments with the skill of long experience, "I will send the sufragi to invite him and Nefret to join us. Sit down, Emerson, or, if you prefer, put on your clothes. A few more minutes' delay cannot worsen a situation which—"

"Curse it," said Emerson, heading for the dressing room.

He took the letter with him. Being accustomed to my husband's impetuous behavior, I dispatched the sufragi on his errand and went on with my breakfast.

The children must have been already up and dressed, for they came almost at once. "Is something wrong?" Ramses asked.

"Why should you suppose that?" I replied, over the cries of outrage from the adjoining room. Some of them had to do with his inability to find his shirts, whose location (in the second drawer of the bureau) I had pointed out to him the previous night.

"A summons at such an early hour—"

Emerson came charging out of the dressing room, attired in trousers and shirt. "Ah, there you are. Good. Just listen to this."

"Finish your breakfast, Emerson," I said, deftly removing the crumpled pages from his clenched fist and handing them to Ramses.

I will summarize the account, which Ramses, at my request, read aloud.

A few months earlier, rumors had spread that a hitherto unknown tomb had been discovered by the indefatigable thieves of Luxor. It had contained objects of rare value and distinction: royal diadems, vessels of stone and precious metal, and jewelry of all kinds. For once, the rumors were correct. Cyrus, who had heard the tales shortly after he arrived on the scene in November, had gone straight to the shop of our old acquaintance Mohammed Mohassib, who had been dealing in antiquities for thirty years. The canny old scoundrel, looking as pious as only a Luxor dealer can, had denied any knowledge of the reputed treasure. He always did, though it was well known that he had handled many of the big finds. There was nothing anybody could do about it, since he never kept the valuables in his own house, but distributed them among his various relations, and when he was in the process of marketing the goods he conducted private negotiations with interested parties who were not inclined to turn him in because they wanted the artifacts themselves.

Knowing this habit of dear old Mohassib's, Cyrus had persisted until Mohassib finally remarked that he had just happened to have acquired an interesting object—not from a tomb robber, of course! It proved to be a heavy gold bar approximately two inches long, set with five small figures of reclining cats, two of which were missing; the surviving three were of gold and carnelian. Cyrus knew his antiquities too well to remain long in doubt as to the meaning of what he saw. "The gold spacer was part of a woman's armlet," he had written. "Had to be a female's because of the cats. It had the cartouches of Thutmose III. They're saying there were three burials in the tomb, folks—queens or princesses related to Thutmose III."

Attempting (in vain, if I knew Cyrus) to conceal his excitement, he had immediately made Mohassib an offer. The old gentleman had regretfully declined. Another party had expressed interest, and he was obliged to give him the first chance. What else could a man of honor do?

"That's how it stands," Cyrus ended his letter. "I'm pretty sure the 'other party' is Howard Carter, acting as agent for Carnarvon or some gol-durned museum. Mohassib is trying to raise the price by playing the bidders off against each other. You better get down here and talk to Mohassib, Emerson; he's a wily old skunk and you're the only one he's scared of."

"We are leaving Cairo at once," Emerson declared.

Ramses exchanged glances with his wife. "Excuse me, Father, but I don't see the need for such haste. The tomb has been cleared and Mohassib isn't going to admit anything, even to you. It would make better sense to talk with Carter. Isn't he working for the War Office? He may be in Cairo even now."

"Hmph," said Emerson thoughtfully.

"We cannot leave immediately," Nefret said. "I must go to the hospital. I've been out of touch for months, and there are a number of matters I must settle with Sophia before I go away again."

"Hmph," said Emerson again. Emerson's grunts are quite expressive, to those who have learned to differentiate them. This one expressed disagreement and protest. The hospital Nefret had founded for the fallen women of Cairo was in a particularly vile part of the city; as she had pointed out, the unhappy creatures she wanted to help would not have dared venture into a respectable neighborhood.

"It's all right, Father," Ramses said. "You don't suppose I would allow my helpless, timid little wife to go alone to el-Wasa?"

Nefret put out her tongue at Ramses. She had never entirely abandoned such childish gestures. This one appeared to amuse Ramses a great deal.

"Ah," said Emerson, brightening. "Good. What about you, Peabody? Are you going with them?"

"I have other plans," I said, folding my napkin.

Emerson's eyes narrowed into sapphirine slits. "Oh, no, you don't, Peabody. You are coming with me. Or," he added, "to put it another way, I am going with you."

The children left us and I sent Emerson off to finish dressing. I knew the process would take him some time, so I went to see how Sennia and her entourage were getting on. She and Basima and Gargery—and the cat—were still at breakfast. Sennia had a perfectly astonishing appetite for so small a person. When she saw me, she dropped her slice of toast—jelly-side down—and ran to throw her arms round me, demanding to know where we were going that day.

"You and Gargery and Basima will have to amuse yourselves today," I replied, in the tone that brooked no argument. "The rest of us have errands. I suggest a visit to the Museum, or perhaps you would like to hire a carriage and go out to Giza."

"I do not believe that is a good plan, madam," said Gargery, winking furiously and wrinkling up his face in a most alarming manner. "After what happened last year—"

"That was last year, Gargery. The people responsible for that incident are no longer a threat to us."

"But, madam! She will want to take the da——the cat with us."

He scowled at Horus, who was sitting by Sennia's chair cleaning his whiskers. Horus left off long enough to sneer at Gargery. All cats can sneer, but Horus did it better than most. He had a very large head and the dark stripes on his face reminded one of a gargoyle.

"Shall we go to Atiyeh?" Basima asked. "Others of the family will want to see the Little Bird."

"And you will want to see them," I said, realizing I ought to have thought of it. Basima was a devoted and dedicated woman who seldom asked anything for herself. In fact, it was an admirable idea; the village near Cairo where the northern branch of Abdullah's family lived was not far off, and Sennia would be under the close supervision of dozens of affectionate friends who would prevent her from getting into mischief. I expressed my approval, and Gargery was pleased to agree. Nobody asked Horus for his opinion.

"Where is Ramses going?" demanded Sennia, who was nothing if not persistent.

"Somewhere you cannot go. We will be back in time for tea."

I left her pouting and Gargery fingering some object in his pocket which I hoped was not a pistol, though I feared it was. He took his duties as Sennia's guard very seriously.

After I had collected Emerson and made him put on a waistcoat and tie, and had changed my blouse, which bore several sticky handprints, we left the hotel and strolled along the Muski, waving away offers from cabdrivers.

"Where are we going?" I asked.

"Don't be coy with me, Peabody," said Emerson amiably. "You are going to the suk, aren't you, to bully, harass, and interrogate antiquities dealers about Sethos."

"I thought I might ask a few questions of a few people, yes. Wouldn't that be preferable to having the children prowling about the city after nightfall, with Nefret decked out as Ramses's—er—his—um—"

Emerson shuddered. "Good Gad, yes. But—but she didn't mean it, did she?"

"She meant it."

It is a nice healthy stroll from Shepheard's to the Khan el Khalili, along the Muski and through the old Fatimite city with its mosques and gateways. Yet how the character of the city had changed! Motorcars and motorbicycles wove hazardous paths among horse-drawn cabs and donkey-drawn carts and caravans of camels. Uniforms were everywhere, the men who wore them as diverse as their insignia: tall rangy Australians and bearded Sikhs, dark-skinned Nubians and pink-cheeked boys fresh from the English countryside.

It was a depressing sight. These men, now so bright-eyed and cheerful, were destined for the battlefields of Palestine and Europe, from which most would never return.

The Khan el Khalili at least had not changed—the same narrow lanes, covered with matting and lined with small shops selling every variety of goods from silks to carpets to silver. Peddlers and sellers of sweetmeats wended their way through the crowds; a waiter, carrying aloft a tray with small cups of Turkish coffee, hastened to the shopkeeper who had ordered it.

Not far from the mosque of the venerated Saint Hosein is the area given over to the stalls of the booksellers, and it was here I hoped to rid myself of the amiable but inconvenient presence of my spouse. Somewhat to my surprise he did not put up much of an argument.

"You are calling on Aslimi, I suppose," he said.

"And perhaps a few others."

"Very well." Emerson took out his watch. "I will give you three hours, Peabody. If you aren't back by then, I will come looking for you."

"Anything but that!" I exclaimed jestingly.

Emerson grinned. "Quite. Enjoy yourself, my love, and don't buy any fakes."

Aslimi did deal in fake antiquities, as had his father, who had met a very ugly death in his own shop some years before. At first I did not recognize him. He had gained an enormous amount of weight and was almost as fat as his father had been. Seated on the mastaba bench outside his shop, he was importuning passersby in the traditional fashion and in a mixture of languages: "Oh, Howadji, I have beautiful antiquities! Monsieur et madame, écoutez-vous!" and so on. When he saw me he broke off with a gurgle and began wriggling, trying to stand.

"Good morning, Aslimi," I said. "Stay where you are."

Aslimi swallowed. "The Father of Curses—"

"Is not with me."

"Ah." Aslimi put his hands on the approximate region of his waist and sighed heavily. "He gives me pains in the stomach, Sitt Hakim."

"It is as God wills," I said piously. Aslimi shot me a look that indicated he was more inclined to put the blame on Emerson than on Allah, but he rallied enough to go through the prescribed gestures of hospitality, offering me coffee or tea and a seat on the mastaba. Then we got down to business.

I left the shop an hour and a half later, with several parcels. Bargaining takes quite a long time, and the subtle interrogation at which I excel takes even longer. Since I had time to spare, I stopped at a few more stalls, learning little more than I had from Aslimi, but purchasing a number of items that would be needed in our new home: a set of handsome copper cooking vessels, thirty yards of blue-and-silver Damascus silk, and two elegant carpets, all of which I directed to be sent to the hotel.

I found Emerson surrounded by loosely bound volumes and piles of manuscripts and several of the more learned booksellers, with whom he was engaged in heated argument. I had begun to suspect that they enjoyed egging him on, for his views on religion—all varieties of religion—were unorthodox and eloquently expressed. The discussion ended when I appeared, and after an exchange of compliments all round, I led Emerson away.

"Why do you do that?" I scolded. "It is very rude to criticize another individual's religious beliefs, and there is not the slightest possibility that you will convert them."

"Who wants to convert them?" Emerson demanded in surprise. "Islam is as good a religion as any other. I don't approve of Christianity or Judaism or Buddhism either."

"I am well aware of that, Emerson. I don't suppose you learned anything of interest?"

"It was very interesting. I raised several unanswerable points . . ." He noticed my parcels and took them from me. "What have you got there?"

"Don't unwrap them here," I cautioned, for Emerson was, in his impetuous fashion, tugging at the strings. "While you were wasting your time debating theology, I went about the business for which we came to the Khan. Aslimi showed me some remarkable things, Emerson. He told me he had never known the supply of merchandise to be so great. He is getting objects from all over Egypt, including Luxor."

"What the devil!" Emerson came to a dead stop in the middle of the road. He began to unwrap the largest parcel, ignoring the camel advancing ponderously toward him. The driver, recognizing Emerson, managed to stop the recalcitrant animal before it ran into my equally recalcitrant spouse. He turned an outraged glare on the camel, which responded with its usual look of utter disgust. I stifled my laughter, for Emerson would not have found anything amusing about his attempt to stare down a camel.

Somehow the driver got the beast past Emerson, who had not stirred an inch. I took the parcel from him.

"It is not like you to be so careless, Emerson," I said severely. "Careless with antiquities, I mean. Come out of the middle of the road and let me undo the wrappings enough to give you a peep."

Care was necessary, since there were two objects in the wrappings, both of them breakable—or at least, chippable. The one I showed Emerson was an alabaster disk with a thin band of gold around the rim.

"No hieroglyphs," he muttered. "Beautiful piece of work, though. It's the lid of a pot or jar."

"A very expensive pot," I amended. "I have the pot as well—an exquisitely shaped alabaster container, most probably for cosmetics. Now shall we go back to the hotel where we can examine it in private?"

"Hmmm, yes, certainly." Emerson watched me rewrap the lid. "I beg your pardon, my dear. You were quite right to scold me. What else have you got?"

"Nothing so exciting as the cosmetic jar," I said, "but I believe they are all from the same tomb—the one Cyrus told us about."

"So Mohassib didn't get everything." Emerson strode along beside me, his hands in his pockets. "How did Aslimi come by these?"

"Not from Sethos."

"You asked him point-blank, I suppose," Emerson grumbled. "Aslimi is a congenital liar, Peabody. How do you know he was telling you the truth?"

"He turned pea-green at the very mention of 'the Master.' It would have been rather amusing if he had not been in such a state of abject terror; he kept wringing his hands and saying, 'But he is dead. He is dead, surely. Tell me he is really dead this time, Sitt!' "

"Hmmm," said Emerson.

"Now don't get any ideas about pretending *you* are 'the Master,' Emerson."

"I don't see why I shouldn't," said Emerson sulkily. "You are always telling me I cannot disguise myself effectively. It is cursed insulting. So—from whom did Aslimi acquire these objects?"

"He claimed the man was someone he'd never seen before."

"I trust you extracted a description?"

"Certainly. Tall, heavyset, black beard and mustache."

"That's no help. Even if it was true."

"Aslimi would not lie to *me*. Emerson, please don't walk so fast."

"Ha," said Emerson. But he slowed his steps and gave me his arm. We had emerged onto the Muski, with its roaring traffic and European shops. "We'll just have time to tidy up before luncheon," he added. "Do you suppose the children are back?"

"One never knows. I only hope they haven't got themselves in trouble."

"Why should you suppose that?"

"They usually do."

From Manuscript H

The infamous Red Blind district of Cairo was centered in an area embarrassingly close to the Ezbekieh and the luxury hotels. In the brothels of el-Wasa, Egyptian, Nubian, and Sudanese women plied their trade under conditions of abject squalor. In theory they were under government medical supervision, but the government's only concern was the control of venereal disease. There had been no place for the women who had suffered beatings or botched abortions or illnesses of other kinds. Even more difficult to control were the brothels in the adjoining area of Wagh el-Birka, which were populated by European women and run by European entrepreneurs. They were foreigners and therefore subject only to the authority of their consuls. Ramses had heard Thomas Russell, the assistant commander of the Cairo police, cursing the restrictions that prevented him from closing down the establishments.

The alleys of el-Wasa were fairly quiet at that early hour. The stench was permanent; even a hard rain only stirred up the garbage of the streets and gathered it in oily pools, where it settled again once the water had evaporated. There were no drains. Ramses glanced at his wife, who walked briskly through the filth, giving it no more attention than was necessary to avoid the worst bits, and not for the first time he wondered how she could bear it. To his eyes she was always radiant, but in this setting she glowed like a fallen star, her golden-red hair gathered into a knot at the back of her head and her brow unclouded.

Initially the clinic had been regarded with suspicion and dislike by the denizens of the Red Blind district, and Nefret and her doctor friend Sophia had deemed it advisable not to advertise its presence. Now it was under the protection of the Cairo police. Russell sent patrols around frequently and came down hard on anyone who tried to make trouble. Emerson had also come down hard on a few offenders who had not known that the person in charge was the daughter of the famed Father of Curses. They knew now. Nefret had found another, unexpected supporter in Ibrahim el-Gharbi, the Nubian transvestite who controlled the brothels of el-Wasa, so the expanded building now proclaimed its mission in polished bronze letters over the door, and the area around it was regularly cleaned of trash and dead animals.

"I'll not come in this time," Ramses said, when they reached the house.

Nefret gave him a provocative smile. "You don't like trailing round after me and Sophia, do you?"

He didn't, especially; he felt useless and ineffective, and only too often, wrung with pity for misery he was helpless to relieve. This time he had a valid excuse.

"I saw someone I want to talk with," he explained. "I'll join you in a bit."

"All right." She didn't ask who; her mind was already inside the building, anticipating the duties that awaited her.

He went back along the lane, kicking a dead rat out of his path and trying to avoid the deeper pools of slime. The man he had seen was sitting on a bench outside one of the more pretentious cribs. He was asleep, his head fallen back and his mouth open. The flies crawling across his face did not disturb his slumber; he was used to them. Ramses nudged him and he looked up, blinking.

"Salaam aleikhum, Brother of Demons. So you are back, and it is true what they say—that the Brother of Demons appears out of thin air, without warning."

Ramses didn't point out that Musa had been sound asleep when he approached; his reputation for being on intimate terms with demons stood him in good stead with the more superstitious Egyptians. "You have come down in the world since I last saw you, Musa. Did el-Gharbi dismiss you?"

"Have you not heard?" The man's dull eyes brightened a little. It was a matter of pride to be the first to impart information, bad or good, and he would expect to be rewarded. He looked as if he could use money. As a favorite of el-Gharbi he had been sleek and plump and elegantly dressed. The rags he wore now barely covered his slender limbs.

"I will tell you," he went on. "Sit down, sit down."

He shifted over to make room for Ramses. The latter declined with thanks. Flies were not the only insects infesting Musa and his clothes.

"We knew the cursed British were raiding the houses and putting the women into prison," Musa began. "They set up a camp at Hilmiya. But my master only laughed. He had too many friends in high places, he said. No one could touch him. And no one did—until one night there came two men sent by the mudir of the police himself, and they took my master away, still in his beautiful white garments. They say that when Harvey Pasha saw him, he was very angry and called him rude names."

"I'm not surprised," Ramses murmured. Harvey Pasha, commander of the Cairo police, was honest, extremely straitlaced, and rather stupid. He probably hadn't even been aware of el-Gharbi's existence until someone—Russell?—pointed out to him that he had missed the biggest catch of all. Ramses could only imagine the look on Harvey's face when el-Gharbi waddled in, draped in women's robes and glittering with jewels.

Musa captured a flea and cracked it expertly between his thumbnails. "He is now in Hilmiya, my poor master, and I, his poor servant, have come to this. The world is a hard place, Brother of Demons."

Even harder for the women whose only crime had been to do the bidding of their pimps and their clients—many of them British and Empire soldiers. Ramses couldn't honestly say he was sorry for el-Gharbi, but he was unhappily aware that the situation had probably worsened since the procurer had been arrested. El-Gharbi had ruled the Red Blind district with an iron hand and his women had been reasonably well treated; he had undoubtedly been replaced by a number of smaller businessmen whose methods were less humane. The filthy trade could never be completely repressed.

"My master wishes to talk with you," Musa said. "Do you have a cigarette?"

So Musa had been on the lookout for him, and had put himself deliberately in Ramses's way. Somewhat abstractedly Ramses offered the tin. Musa took it, extracted a cigarette, and calmly tucked the tin away in the folds of his robe.

"How am I supposed to manage that?" Ramses demanded.

"Surely you have only to ask Harvey Pasha."

"I have no influence with Harvey Pasha, and if I did, I wouldn't be inclined to spend it on favors for el-Gharbi. Does he want to ask me to arrange his release?"

"I do not know. Have you another cigarette?"

"You took all I had," Ramses said.

"Ah. Would you like one?" He extracted the tin and offered it.

"Thank you, no. Keep them," he added.

The irony was wasted on Musa, who thanked him effusively, and held out a suggestive hand. "What shall I tell my master?"

Ramses dropped a few coins into the outstretched palm, and cut short Musa's pleas for more. "That I can't do anything for him. Let el-Gharbi sweat it out in the camp for a few months. He's too fat anyhow. And if I know him, he has his circle of supporters and servants even in Hilmiya, and methods of getting whatever he wants. How did he communicate with you?"

"There are ways," Musa murmured.

"I'm sure there are. Well, give him my . . ." He tried to think of the right word. The only ones that came to mind were too friendly or too courteous. On the other hand, the procurer had been a useful source of information in the past, and might be again. "Tell him you saw me and that I asked after him."

He added a few more coins and went back to the hospital. Dr. Sophia greeted him with her usual smiling reserve. Ramses admired her enormously, but never felt completely at ease with her, though he realized there was probably nothing personal in her lack of warmth. She had to deal every day with the ugly results of male exploitation of women. It would not be surprising if she had a jaundiced view of all men.

He met the new surgeon, a stocky, gray-haired American woman, who measured him with cool brown eyes before offering a handclasp as hard as that of most men. Ramses had heard Nefret congratulating herself on finding Dr. Ferguson. There weren't many women being trained in surgery. On the other hand, there weren't many positions open to women surgeons. Ferguson had worked in the slums of Boston, Massachusetts, and according to Nefret she had expressed herself as more concerned with saving abused women than men who were fool enough to go out and get themselves shot. She and Sophia ought to get along.

As Ramses had rather expected, Nefret decided to spend the rest of the day at the hospital. She was in her element, with two women who shared her skills and her beliefs, and Ramses felt a faint, unreasonable stir of jealousy. He kissed her good-bye and saw her eyes widen with surprise and pleasure; as a rule he didn't express affection in public. It had been a demonstration of possessiveness, he supposed.

Walking back toward the hotel, head bent and hands in his pockets, he examined his feelings and despised himself for selfishness. At least he hadn't insisted she wait for him to escort her back to the hotel. She'd have resented that. No one in el-Wasa would have dared lay a hand on her, but it made him sick to think of her walking alone through those noisome alleys, at a time of day when the houses would be opening for business and the women would be screaming obscene invitations at the men who leered at them through the open windows.

His parents were already at the hotel, and when he saw what his mother had found that morning, he forgot his grievances for a while. The little ointment jar was in almost perfect condition, and he was inclined to agree with her that the scraps of jewelry—beads, half of a gold-hinged bracelet, and an exquisitely inlaid uraeus serpent—had come from the same Eighteenth Dynasty tomb Cyrus had told them about.

"Aslimi claimed the seller was unknown to him?" he asked. "That's rather odd. He has his usual sources and would surely be suspicious of strangers."

"Aslimi would not dare lie to *me*," his mother declared. She gave her husband a challenging glance. Emerson did not venture to contradict her. He had something else on his mind.

"Er—I trust you and Nefret have given up the idea of visiting the coffeeshops?"

"I wasn't keen on the idea in the first place," Ramses said.

"Well. No need for such an expedition now; your mother questioned the dealers and none of them had heard of the Master's return. Be ready to take the train tomorrow, eh?"

"That depends on Nefret. She may not want to leave so soon."

"Oh. Yes, quite. Is she still at the hospital? You arranged to fetch her home, I presume."

"No, sir, I didn't."

Emerson's brows drew together, but before he could comment his wife said, "Is there something unusual about that ointment jar, Ramses?"

He had been holding it, turning it in his hands, running his fingers along the curved sides. He gave her a smile that acknowledged both her tactful intervention and her perceptiveness. "There's a rough section, here on the shoulder. The rest of it is as smooth as satin."

"Let me see." Emerson took it from him and carried it to the window, where the light was stronger. "By Gad, you're right," he said, in obvious chagrin. "Don't know how I could have missed it. Something has been rubbed off. A name? An inscription?"

"The space is about the right size for a cartouche," Ramses said.

"Can you see anything?"

"A few vague scratches." Direct sunlight shimmered in the depths of the pale translucent stone. "It looks as if someone has carefully removed the owner's name."

"Not the thief, surely," his mother said, squinting at the pot. "An inscribed piece would bring a higher price."

"True." Emerson rubbed his chin. "Well, we've seen such things before. An enemy, wishing to condemn the owner to the final death that befalls the nameless, or an ancient thief, who intended to replace the name with his own and never got round to it."

Having settled the matter to his satisfaction, he was free to worry about Nefret. He didn't criticize Ramses aloud, but he kept looking at his watch and muttering. Fortunately she returned before Emerson got too worked up.

"I hope I'm not late for tea," she said breezily. "Have I time to change?"

"You had better," Ramses said, inspecting her. Not even Nefret could pass through the streets of el-Wasa without carrying away some of its atmosphere. "How did it go?"

"Just fine. I'll tell you about it later."

She rather monopolized the conversation at tea, which they took on the terrace. Even Sennia found it difficult to get a word in.

⋮

I could tell Ramses was perturbed about something and I suspected it had to do with the hospital; yet nothing Nefret said indicated that she was unhappy about the arrangements. Unlike my son, Nefret does not conceal her feelings. Her eyes shone and her cheeks were prettily flushed as she talked, and when Sennia said pensively, "I would like to come and help you take care of the sick ladies, Aunt Nefret," she laughed and patted the child's cheek.

"Someday, Little Bird. When you are older."

"Tomorrow I will be older," Sennia pointed out.

"Not old enough," Emerson said, trying to conceal his consternation. "Anyhow, we must be on our way to Luxor shortly. Nefret, when can you be ready?"

"Not tomorrow, Father. Perhaps the following day."

She went on to explain that she had arranged to dine with Dr. Sophia and the new surgeon, Miss Ferguson. A flicker of emotion crossed my son's enigmatic countenance when she indicated she would like him to be present. He nodded in mute acquiescence, but Emerson firmly declined the invitation. The idea of spending the evening with three such determined ladies, discussing loathsome diseases and gruesome injuries, did not greatly appeal to him.

So we had an early dinner with Sennia, which pleased her a great deal. It did not please Horus, who had to be shut in Sennia's room, where (as I was later informed by the sufragi) he howled like a jackal the entire time. As we left the dining salon, we were hailed by an individual I recognized as the apple-cheeked gentleman who had been one of our fellow passengers. His wife was even more resplendent in jewels and satin. Sennia would have stopped, but Emerson hustled her on past, and the gentleman, encumbered by the large menu and even larger napkin, was not quick enough to intercept us.

"Curse it," said my spouse, "who are those people? No, don't tell me, I don't want to know."

After returning Sennia to Basima, who had taken refuge from Horus in the servants' dining hall, I settled down with a nice book—but I kept an eye on Emerson. I can always tell when he is up to something. Sure enough, after pretending to read for fifteen minutes, he got up and declared his intention of taking a little stroll.

"Don't disturb yourself, my dear," he said. "You look very comfortable."

And out he went, without giving me time to reply.

I waited a quarter of an hour before closing my book. A further delay ensued when I attempted to get out of my evening frock, which buttoned down the back; however, I was not in a hurry. I knew where Emerson was going, and I fancied it would take him a while to get there. After squirming out of the garment I assumed my working costume of trousers, boots, and amply pocketed coat, took up my parasol, left the hotel, and hailed a cab.

I assumed Emerson would have gone on foot and kept a sharp eye out for that unmistakable form, but there was no sign of him. When we reached the Khan el Khalili I told the driver to wait and plunged into the narrow lanes of the suk.

Aslimi was not happy to see me. He informed me that he was about to close. I informed him that I had no objection, entered the shop, and took a chair.

Aslimi waddled about, closing and locking the shutters, before he seated himself in a huge armchair of Empire style, its arms and legs ornately gilded, and stared hopelessly at me. "I told you all I know, Sitt. What do you want now?"

"Are you expecting someone, Aslimi?"

"No, Sitt, I swear."

"I am. He will be here soon, I expect."

We sat in silence. The sweat began to pour down Aslimi's face. It shone like polished amber. I was about to offer him my handkerchief when there was a soft sound from behind the closed door at the back of the shop.

Aslimi kept his most valuable antiquities in the back room, which opened onto a narrow slit of a passage next to the shop. His eyes opened so wide I could see the whites all round the dark pupils. For an instant cowardice struggled with greed. Greed won out; with a grunt he heaved himself to his feet. By the time he accomplished this feat, I had burst through the door, parasol in hand.

Facing me was the intruder. There was enough light from the open door behind me to show his tall, heavyset form and his black beard and mustache. It was the man Aslimi had described that afternoon! The seller of stolen antiquities had returned! Aslimi screamed and thudded to the floor in a dead faint. I twisted the handle of my parasol, releasing the sword blade concealed therein.

"Stop where you are!" I exclaimed in Arabic.

With a sudden sweep of his arm, the man knocked the blade aside and seized me in a bruising grip.

Two

"**H**ow many times have I told you not to attack an opponent with that damned parasol?" Emerson demanded.

"I did not attack you. You attacked me!"

Emerson handed me into the cab and got in beside me. He was still wearing the beard and clothing he had borrowed from Ramses's collection of disguises.

"It was self-defense, Peabody. I can never predict what you are likely to do when you are in one of your combative moods. You didn't recognize me, did you?"

"I certainly would not have gone on the attack without provocation," I retorted.

"Come, Peabody, be a sport. Admit you didn't know me."

"I knew you the moment you took hold of me."

"I should hope so!" He put his arm round me, which I permitted; but when his face approached mine I turned my head.

"That is a very prickly beard, Emerson."

"Well, curse it, I can't just peel it off; this adhesive won't come loose unless it is soaked in water." Emerson was still in a high good humor and rather inclined, in my opinion, to rub it in. "I told you Aslimi had lied to you."

"Was that why you went disguised as the man he had described?"

"No, I did that because I wanted to," said Emerson,

chuckling. "The description I finally pried out of him was the exact opposite of the one he gave you: medium height, slim, young."

"But unknown to Aslimi."

"It doesn't fit any of the thieves or go-betweens known to me either. We must accept it, however."

The beard assumed a particularly arrogant angle. I was forced to agree with him. After I had restored Aslimi from his faint, he could not quite get it straight in his head who the intruder was: a thief bent on robbing and murdering him; or the Father of Curses, bent on something equally unpleasant; or both in the same body. He was certainly too confused and terrified to lie.

We reached the hotel without anything of interest happening, to find that the children had not yet returned from dinner. Emerson had removed the turban and caftan, but the beard and mustache occasioned a certain hesitation in the desk clerk; had it been anyone but me asking for the key, he might have questioned the identity of the fellow I was taking with me to my suite.

"He didn't recognize me either," Emerson declared smugly.

"Ha," I said.

Emerson was sitting with his chin and mouth in a basin of water, breathing through his nose, and I was enjoying a restorative whiskey and soda when there was a tap on the door. I responded, and Nefret put her head in. "We only stopped by to say . . ." she began; catching sight of Emerson, she flung the door wide and hurried to his side. "Father! Are you hurt?"

"No," said Emerson, gurgling. He spat out a mouthful of water.

Ramses's face twitched in a frantic attempt to control his amusement. "It's the beard," he got out.

"I think that's done the job," Emerson said. He peeled the thing off and gave Nefret a cheerful smile.

"Hold it over the basin, Emerson," I said, as water streamed from the bedraggled object onto the carpet.

"What? Oh." Chagrin wrinkled his brow, and he attempted to wring the water out of the beard. "Hope I haven't spoiled it, my boy. I would have asked you for the loan of it, but you see, the idea came to me after you left, and I had to act at once."

"That's quite all right, sir," said Ramses. "Might one ask . . ."

"Certainly, certainly. I will tell you all about it. Make yourselves comfortable."

It was evident that he planned to revel in every detail, so the children followed his suggestion, settling themselves on the sofa side by side and listening with interest. Neither of them interrupted until Emerson, with great gusto, told of my pulling out the sword.

"Good God, Mother!" Ramses exclaimed. "How many times have I told you—"

"She didn't know me, you see," Emerson said, beaming. "She won't admit it, but she didn't."

"I did not recognize you immediately," I admitted. "But the room was dark and Aslimi was shrieking in alarm, and I didn't expect you would come that way. Nefret, my dear, are you laughing?"

"I'm sorry. I was picturing the two of you scuffling in Aslimi's back room. Neither of you was hurt?"

"No," I said, while Emerson grinned in a particularly annoying fashion. "It may take Aslimi a while to recover, though."

"He admitted that his original description was false in every particular," Emerson said smugly. "The seller was bearded, of course—most Egyptians are—but he was young, slender, and of medium height."

Ramses could not come up with a name to match the new description either. "Someone new to the business," he said thoughtfully.

"Someone who has been in Luxor recently," Emerson added. "Assuming, that is, that the artifacts did come from the tomb of the princesses. He must have got them direct from one of the robbers, who had withheld them from the rest of the loot. Those scoundrels cheat even one another."

"I suppose you are now even more on fire to go on to Luxor and track down the thieves," Nefret said, tucking her feet under her and leaning against Ramses.

"You would like a few more days at the hospital, wouldn't you?" Emerson asked.

"Well, yes; but I wouldn't want you to change your plans on my account."

I must give my dear Emerson credit; he was too forthright to pretend he was doing it on her account. "The tomb has already been robbed and the loot dispersed," he explained. "And I expect everyone knows the identity of the thieves—the Abd er Rassuls, or one of the other Gurneh families who specialize in such activities. It is strange, though, to have some of the objects turn up in Cairo. The local boys usually work with Mohassib or another of the Luxor dealers. Ramses, are you certain that ointment vessel is Eighteenth Dynasty?"

"No, of course not," Ramses said, somewhat defensively. "I'm not an expert on hard stone vessels. The same forms and materials were used over a long period of time. If you think it's important, we might pay a visit to the Museum and see what examples they have."

"If we can find them," Emerson muttered. "The way that place is arranged is a damned disgrace."

Emerson always complained about the Museum and about almost everything else that was not under his direct supervision. I pointed out that Mr. Quibell, the director, was doing the best he could under difficult circumstances. Emerson nodded grudgingly.

"No doubt. I suppose we ought to call on him. Or we might have one of your little archaeological dinner parties,

Peabody. The Quibells, and Daressy, and anyone else you can collect."

My dinner parties, celebrating our return to Egypt, had been very popular. For the past few years I had been loath to hold them; it was too painful to see the diminished company and reflect on the fates of those who were no longer with us: our German and Austrian colleagues departed, the ranks of the French and English Egyptologists depleted by death or military service. However, I had already been in receipt of friendly messages from those who were still in Cairo—the news of our arrival had, of course, immediately become known. Emerson's proposal solved the difficulty of how I was to respond to these greetings and invitations, and astonished me not a little, for he was never inclined toward social engagements, and he had been insistent on leaving Cairo as soon as was possible.

A brief period of reflection explained his change of heart. The letter from Cyrus and the discovery of the artifacts at Aslimi's had whetted his curiosity; Cyrus's mention of Howard Carter being in some manner involved aroused an understandable desire to question that individual. There was another reason for his willingness to stay on in Cairo; he was hoping for a further communication from his brother. He had made a point of looking through the messages every day and his disappointment at finding nothing of the sort was evident to me at least. I confess I was also somewhat exasperated with Sethos. What had been the point of that brief encounter?

Unfortunately I was unable to locate the archaeologist whom Emerson had hoped to interrogate. Howard Carter was not in Cairo. No one knew where he was. However, when the sadly diminished group met next evening, he was the chief topic of conversation. Owing to the short notice, the Quibells were the only ones who had been able to accept my invitation.

"You just missed him," Annie Quibell said. "He got back

from Luxor a few days ago, and went off again without any of us seeing him. James was furious."

She smiled at her husband, whose equable temper was well known, and who said calmly, "I presume his duties for the War Office called him away, but I had hoped to hear more about his recent work in Luxor."

"And his dealings with Mohassib?" Emerson inquired, motioning the waiter to refill James's wineglass.

"Who told you that?"

"Cyrus Vandergelt," I replied. "Is it true?"

James shrugged. "I've heard the rumor too, but I doubt Carter would admit it to me, even if it were true. He spent several months out in the southwest wadis, where the princesses' tomb was found; when he was in Cairo for a few days early in December, he gave me a brief report. Did you hear about his finding another tomb of Hatshepsut's? This one was made for her when she was queen, before she assumed kingly titles. It was empty except for a sarcophagus." He picked up his glass and sipped his wine appreciatively.

"Where?" Emerson asked.

"High in a cleft in the cliffs, in one of the western wadis," Annie said. She and her husband were not great admirers of Howard; after his falling-out with the Service, he had begun dealing in antiquities, and this did not make him popular with his professional colleagues. She added, with a distinct and amusing touch of malice, "He didn't find Hatshepsut's tomb, James. Some of the Gurnawis did. He only followed them."

"Bah," said Emerson vehemently. "I wonder what else he did?"

"So do I," said James.

Having failed to locate Howard, Emerson was ready to leave for Luxor at once. However, it was not to be. We were finishing breakfast en famille in our sitting room when a messenger arrived with a letter for Emerson. It was a delightful little domestic scene, with Sennia badgering Ramses to give her a lesson in hieroglyphs and Horus snarling at Gargery and Emerson reading the *Egyptian Gazette* and smoking his pipe, while Nefret told me about the new arrangements at the hospital. When I saw the envelope, with its official seal, it was as if the sun had gone behind a cloud.

"Whom is it from?" I demanded.

Emerson frowned over the epistle, which he was holding so I couldn't read over his shoulder. "Wingate. He would like me to come to his office at my earliest convenience."

"Sir Reginald Wingate? What does the Sirdar of the Sudan want with you?"

"He replaced MacMahon as high commissioner last month," Emerson replied. "He doesn't say what he wants."

We had all fallen silent except for Sennia, who had no idea who the high commissioner was and cared even less. Emerson looked at his son. "Er—Ramses . . ."

"Yes, sir. When?"

"Later. He says 'at our convenience.' It is not convenient for me at present."

Sennia understood that. "Ramses will have time to give me my lesson," she announced firmly. Sennia was in the habit of making pronouncements instead of asking questions; it usually worked.

Ramses rose, smiling. "A short lesson, then. Let's go to your room where we won't be distracted."

The door closed behind them—and Horus, who went wherever Sennia went unless forcibly prevented from doing so. Having got Sennia out of the way, Emerson turned stern blue eyes on Gargery, who stood with arms folded and feet slightly apart, exuding stubbornness. "Go away, Gargery," Emerson said.

"Sir—"

"I said, go away."

"But sir—"

"If there is anything you need to know, Gargery, I will tell you about it at the proper time," I interrupted. "That will be all."

Gargery stamped out, slamming the door, and Nefret said quietly, "Do you want me to leave too?"

"No, of course not." Emerson leaned back in his chair. "It isn't the military or the secret service this time, Nefret. Wingate probably wants us for some tedious office job."

"Are you going to accept?"

"That depends." Emerson got to his feet and began pacing. "Like it or not, and God knows we don't, we cannot ignore the fact that there is a bloody war going on. They won't let me carry a rifle, and Ramses won't carry one, but there are other things we can do, and we have no right to refuse."

"You and Ramses," Nefret repeated, with a curl of her lip. "Men. Never women."

"You offered your services as a surgeon, didn't you?"

"Yes." Nefret's eyes flashed. "The military isn't accepting women physicians. But that would have been saving lives, not—"

"There are other ways of saving lives, or at least minimizing suffering. You can't keep him out of this forever, Nefret; I've seen the signs, and so have you. He's feeling guilty because he thinks he is not doing his part."

"He's done his part and more," Nefret cried. "It wasn't only that ghastly business two years ago, it was the same sort of thing again last winter; if he hadn't risked his life twice over, the War Office would have lost its favorite spy and a German agent would have got away. What more do they want from him?"

It did seem to me as if she were underestimating my contribution and that of Emerson, but I did not say so; where her husband was concerned, Nefret was passionately singleminded. Her eyes were bright with tears of anger. Emerson stopped by the chair in which she sat and put his hand on her shoulder.

"I know, my dear," he said gently. "But I cannot suppose they want us to go chasing spies again. The situation has changed. With the Turks driven out of the Sinai, the Canal is no longer in danger, and the Senussi are in full retreat. There is nothing going on that requires Ramses's unusual talents, or," he added with a grin, "mine."

"Unless," I said, "this has something to do with Sethos."

Emerson shot me a reproachful glance, but I had only voiced aloud what was in all our minds.

"There's been no further word from him?" Nefret asked. I shook my head.

"If Ramses gets in trouble because of him, I'll murder him," she muttered.

She did not go to the hospital that morning. She did not want to leave the hotel, though I pointed out that we could probably not expect Emerson and Ramses back before luncheon. Finally I managed to persuade her to go walking in the Ezbekieh Gardens with Sennia and me. I always say there is nothing like the beauties of nature to distract one from worrisome thoughts. The Gardens are planted with rare trees and shrubs and the air is harmonious with bird-song. Sennia was even more of a distraction; it required both of us to keep track of her as she ran up and down the graveled paths. It did Nefret good, I believe. When we started back, both of us holding tight to Sennia's hands, she said ruefully, "You think I'm behaving like a silly coward, don't you?"

"Perhaps just a bit. But I understand. One becomes accustomed to it, you see," I continued. "One never likes it, but one becomes resigned."

"I know I can't keep him out of trouble," Nefret said. "It's just this particular—"

"Little pitchers have big ears," I warned.

"If you are referring to me," said Sennia, with great dignity, "my ears are not at all large. Ramses says they are pretty ears. Is he in trouble?"

Nefret laughed and picked her up. We were about to cross

the street, which was crowded with traffic. "No, Little Bird. And we will make sure he doesn't get into it, won't we?"

We had been waiting for almost an hour before they returned. Sennia was reading aloud to us from a little book of Egyptian fairy tales, but the moment the door opened she dropped it and ran to meet them. Throwing her arms round Ramses's waist, she asked anxiously, "Are you in trouble?"

"Not unless you crack one of my ribs," Ramses said, with a theatrical gasp of pain. "Who told you that?"

"Let us go to luncheon," I said.

"Yes, I am starving," Sennia announced, rolling her eyes dramatically. "I didn't mean to hurt you, Ramses."

Emerson detached her from Ramses and swung her up onto his shoulder. "We will go down now."

I let them go ahead. "Well, Ramses?" I inquired.

"You shouldn't worry the child, Mother."

"It wasn't Mother, it was me." Nefret took his arm. "I'm sorry."

"It's all right." He offered me his other arm, and as we proceeded to the dining salon he explained.

"All he wanted was a consultation. He's new at the job, and apparently nobody bothered to put him in the picture about certain matters. The military and the civil administration have always been at odds. He'd heard of some of our activities, and wanted to know the facts."

"That's all?" Nefret demanded. "Nothing about . . ."

"He wasn't mentioned." Ramses grinned. "Under any of his pseudonyms. Father agreed to stay on in Cairo for another day or two, and meet with Wingate again. That should please you; you'll have more time at the hospital."

From Manuscript H

The second meeting with Wingate was shorter than the first, and somewhat more acrimonious. Wingate wanted more details about a number of people Emerson was not anxious to discuss, and the roles they had played; when he asked about their dealings with "a certain gentleman named Smith," Emerson lost his temper. (He had been itching to do so for some time.)

"Good Gad, man, if you don't know who the bastard is and what he's up to, how should we? Come, Ramses; we have wasted enough time telling people things they ought to have known anyhow and going over and over facts that are either self-explanatory or irrelevant."

The new high commissioner took this rudeness better than Ramses had expected. Now in his sixties, he had had a long and illustrious career as governor of the Sudan, and Ramses got the impression that he was finding it harder to deal with his peers in Cairo than with rebellious Sudanese. As Emerson stalked out of the room, Wingate said mildly, "Thank you for your time, gentlemen," and returned to his papers.

"That's that," Emerson declared. "It's high time we got out of this bloody city. Is Nefret ready to leave?"

On the morning of their departure Nefret and Ramses breakfasted alone in their room, at what struck Ramses as an obscenely early hour.

"I need all the time I can get at the hospital," she declared. "Since Father is determined on leaving today."

"He'd have put it off again if you had asked him."

"I couldn't do that. He's on fire to get to Luxor and catch a few tomb robbers. There was no need for you to get up so early. You don't have to escort me."

"Would you rather I didn't?"

"You can if you like." Frowning slightly, she concentrated on the piece of toast she was cutting into strips. "It's boring for you, though. You hardly said a word the other night when we dined with Sophia and Beatrice."

"I'm sorry," he began.

"Don't apologize, damn it!" She put her knife down and

gave him a rueful smile. "There's no need for you to be so defensive, darling. I didn't mean it as a reproach. You couldn't have got a word in anyhow! It was rude of us not to include you in the conversation."

"That's all right." The pronouns jarred, though. Us and you. "I think I will come along, if you don't mind. There's someone I want to see, if I can find him."

"Who?"

He described his encounter with Musa as they walked through the ornate lobby and out the door of the hotel.

"You didn't tell me," Nefret said, and then laughed and took his arm. "You couldn't get a word in, could you? Sophia told me about el-Gharbi's being arrested. Did you know he had put the word out that we were not to be bothered?"

"I thought he might have done."

"I never supposed I would regret the arrest of the worst procurer in Cairo." Her face was troubled. "But Sophia says things have got worse. More injuries, and fewer of the women are coming to us."

"Musa wants me to intervene on behalf of el-Gharbi. Shall I try to get him out?"

"Could you?"

"Do you want him out?"

"Oh, I don't know," Nefret said despairingly. "How does one choose between two evils? Leave it alone, darling. I don't want you getting involved with the police again. Russell would try to recruit you for some rotten job, and I won't allow it."

"Russell's sticking to ordinary police work these days. There's a new military intelligence organization—or will be, if they ever get it right. They keep shuffling people around. Clayton and the Arab Bureau are now—"

"How did you find that out?" Her eyes narrowed and her voice was sharp.

"From Wingate, for the most part. Plus odds and ends of gossip here and there."

"Oh, very informative. Ramses, I don't care who is doing

what with whom, so long as 'whom' isn't you. Promise me
you'll stay away from them. All of them."

"Yes, ma'am."

Her tight lips relaxed into one of her most bewitching
smiles, complete with dimples, and as a further inducement
to good behavior, she told him she would be back in time for
luncheon. Ramses watched her run lightly up the steps and
in the door before he turned away.

Could he get el-Gharbi paroled? The answer was probably no. Unless . . . the idea hadn't occurred to him until Nefret asked. It had probably been Thomas Russell who reeled
him in. If he could persuade Russell that el-Gharbi had information that could be of use to him . . .

The answer was still no. Russell wouldn't make a deal
with someone he despised as much as he did the procurer.
Anyhow, there were only two questions Ramses would like
to have answered: the whereabouts of his infuriating uncle,
and the identity of the man who had sold the artifacts to
Aslimi. El-Gharbi had once had contacts with every illegal
activity in Cairo, but drugs and prostitution were his chief
interests; he dealt with illegal antiquities and espionage only
when they impinged on his primary business.

Musa was nowhere to be found, so Ramses spent a few
hours wandering through the green groves of the Ezbekieh
Gardens, to get the smells of el-Wasa out of his system. It
was a little after midday when he returned to the hotel. Nefret was not there, so he went to see what his parents were
doing. He found his mother alone in the sitting room,
placidly working at a piece of embroidery. Wondering what
had prompted this unusual exercise—she hated sewing and
did it very badly—he joined her on the sofa.

"Where is Father?" he asked.

"He took Sennia for a walk, in order to work off some of
her energy. Have you finished packing?"

"No," Ramses admitted. "Nefret told me I mustn't, she
says I always make a mess of it."

"Just like your father. His notion of packing is to dump

the entire contents of a drawer into a suitcase and then throw his boots on top."

"What's wrong with that?" Ramses asked, and got a smile in return.

"I'll ask Gargery to take care of it," she promised.

"That's all right, Nefret said she'd be back before luncheon. I suppose you are all ready?"

"Certainly." She looked searchingly at Ramses. "Is something wrong? You seem somewhat pensive."

"No, nothing is wrong. I'm sorry if I . . ." Her steely gray stare remained fixed on him, and he felt a sudden need to confess. His mother's stare often had that effect on people.

"I'm jealous—oh, not of another man, it's even worse. Jealous of the hospital and the time she spends there. Contemptible, isn't it, that I should resent Nefret's skills and interests?"

"Quite understandable," his mother said calmly. She poked her needle into the piece of fabric, muttered something, and wiped her finger on her skirt. Ramses noticed that the skirt and the embroidered fabric were spotted with blood. "Do you want her to give up her medical work?"

"Good God, no! I'd hate her to do that on my account. I'd hate myself if she did."

"She will have to make a choice, though. While we were working at Giza she could spend a certain amount of time at the hospital, but it appears we will be in Luxor for some time to come."

"Someone will have to make a choice."

His mother dropped her fancywork and stared at him. "You don't mean you would give up Egyptology!"

"Nothing so drastic. I can always get a position with Reisner, at Giza." She looked so horrified, he put his hand over hers. "I don't want to work with anyone but Father, you know that. But I have to be with her and I want her to be happy. Why should I expect her to give up her work when I'm not willing to make a reasonable compromise?"

"Honestly, Ramses." His mother gave him a look of exasperation. "I would expect any son of mine to appreciate the talents and aspirations of women, but you are carrying fairness to a ridiculous extreme. What makes you suppose Nefret wants to abandon archaeology? Have you asked her?"

"No. I didn't want—"

"To force the issue? Well, my dear, Nefret is not the woman to keep her opinions to herself. You are leaping to unwarranted conclusions and tormenting yourself about something that will never happen. It is a bad habit of yours."

"D'you really think so?"

"I am certain of it." She hesitated, but not for long. Indecision was not one of his mother's weaknesses. "She once told me something that perhaps you should know. 'I would leave the hospital forever, without a backward glance, if it would help to keep him safe.'"

"She said that?"

"I do not claim to remember the precise words, but that was unquestionably the gist of her remark. Goodness gracious, Ramses, don't look so stupefied. If you are really unaware of the strength of your wife's affection, you have not been paying her the proper attentions."

He didn't dare ask what she meant by that. Her prim circumlocutions always amused him, but he said humbly and without a smile, "You are right, Mother, as always. I haven't said anything to her, and I never shall. Please don't tell her."

"Why, Ramses, I would never betray another individual's confidence." She patted his hand. He flinched, and she let out an exclamation of distress. "Oh, dear. I forgot I was holding the needle. Suck it."

Ramses dutifully obeyed. "What is that you're making?" he asked. It was hard to tell the bloodstains from the pattern.

"It's just a little something to keep my hands occupied. Stop fretting, dear boy, I will talk to Nefret myself. Tactfully."

She stuck the needle into the fabric and folded her work. "It is past time for luncheon. Emerson is late as usual."

He turned up a few minutes later, with Sennia, and dropped rather heavily into a chair. Emerson could work under the hot Upper Egyptian sun from dawn until sunset without any sign of fatigue, but a few hours with Sennia left even him worn out. "Are we ready for lunch?" he asked.

"Nefret isn't back yet," his wife said.

Ramses had been watching the clock. It was after one. His father gave him a critical look. "Is she waiting for you to fetch her?"

"No," Ramses said, and went on, before his father could voice his opinion of a man who would allow his wife to walk the alleys of el-Wasa unattended. "I expect she's got involved and lost track of the time. The rest of you go down, I'll run over to the hospital."

He wasn't worried—not really—but she knew they were due to leave that evening, and she had said she'd be back before luncheon.

He took the most direct way to the hospital, the one they always followed, expecting at every turn of the street to see her hurrying toward him. The foul alleys were deserted; the denizens were indoors, resting during the heat of the day. Anger, born of concern, quickened his steps. She had no business worrying him like this, after he had done her the courtesy of leaving her free of his escort.

He had almost reached the hospital when a man stepped out into his path. "You must come with me, Brother of Demons."

"Get out of my way, Musa. I haven't time to listen to el-Gharbi's compliments."

"You must!" the other man repeated. He held out his hands. Stretched between his palms was the filmy scarf Nefret had worn round her neck that morning.

Seeing Ramses's expression, Musa jumped back a few feet and began to babble. "Do not strike me, Brother of Demons, she is not hurt, she is safe, I will take you to her."

"Damned right you will." Ramses's hand shot out, catching Musa's stringy arm in a bruising grip. "Where is she?"

"Come. Come with me, it is not far. She is unharmed, I tell you. Would any of us dare injure—"

"Shut up. Which way?"

Knowing he was no longer in imminent danger of violence, Musa said plaintively, "You are hurting my arm, Brother of Demons. I can walk faster if you do not hold on to me. I will not run away. I was ordered to bring you to her."

Ramses didn't bother to ask who had given the order. He released his grip and brushed at the enterprising fleas that had already found his hand. "Where?"

"This way, this way." Musa trotted ahead, around a corner and through a pile of discarded fruit rinds and peelings that squelched under his bare feet. "This way," he said again, and turned his head to nod reassuringly at Ramses. "Do you have a cigarette?"

"Don't push me too far, Musa."

He was no longer worried about Nefret, though. The man who must be responsible for this would not harm her. They ended up where Ramses had expected: in an outstandingly filthy alley behind the house el-Gharbi had once occupied. Musa went to the small inconspicuous door Ramses remembered from earlier visits. The police had barricaded it with heavy boards, but someone had removed most of the nails; Musa pulled the planks aside and climbed through the opening.

The house that had once been alive with music and the other colorful accompaniments of a contemptible trade was dark, deserted, and dusty. The windows had been boarded up, the rich furnishings removed or left to molder. There was a little light, streaking through cracks in the boards. When they reached the room in which el-Gharbi had held court, Ramses made out a massive shape squatting on the ruined cushions. Nefret sat next to him. A ray of sunlight sparked in her hair.

"Sorry," she said cheerfully. "I did it again."

Ramses got the words out through lips unsteady with relief. "Not your fault this time. Another black mark against you, el-Gharbi. What do you mean by this?"

"But, my dear young friend, what choice had I?" The voice was the well-remembered high-pitched whine, but as his eyes adjusted to the gloom, Ramses saw that the procurer was dressed in a ragged galabeeyah instead of his elegant white robes. He didn't appear to have lost any weight, though. Shifting uncomfortably, he went on, "You would not come to the camp. You would not have come to me here—so I invited your lovely wife. We have been having a most enjoyable conversation. Sit down, won't you? I regret I cannot offer you tea—"

"What do you want?" Ramses interrupted.

"Why, the pleasure of seeing you and your lovely—"

"I don't have *time* for this," Ramses said rather loudly. "You cannot keep us here against our will, you know."

"Alas, it is true." The procurer sighed. "I do not have the manpower I once had."

"What is your point, then?"

"You won't sit down? Oh, very well. It is the camp, you see. It is no place for a person of refinement like myself." A shudder of distaste ran through the huge body. "I want out."

"You are out," Ramses said, unwilling amusement replacing his annoyance. El-Gharbi was unconquerable.

"Only for a few hours. If I am not there tonight when they make the rounds, that rude person Harvey will turn out every police officer in Cairo to look for me. I do not intend to spend the rest of my life running away from the police, it is too uncomfortable."

"Yes, I suppose it would be. Can you give me one good reason why I should intercede on your behalf, even if I were able?"

"But my dear young friend, surely the many favors I have done for you—"

"And I have done several for you. If the score is not even, the debt is on your side."

"I was afraid you would see it that way. What of future favors, then? I am at your command."

"There is nothing I want from you. Nefret, let's go. The parents will be getting anxious."

"Yes, of course." She rose. "Good-bye, Mr. el-Gharbi."

She used the English words, possibly because the Arabic terms of farewell invoked a blessing or an expression of goodwill. El-Gharbi didn't miss the implications. He chuckled richly.

"Maassalameh, honored lady. And to you, my beautiful young friend. Remember what I have said. The time may come . . ."

"I hope to God it won't come," Ramses muttered, as they left the room. "Nefret, are you all right?"

"Musa was very polite. No damage, darling, except . . ." She scratched her arm. "Let's hurry. I expect Father is frantic by this time, and I'm being devoured by fleas."

"That makes two of us."

"My poor darling. What you suffer for me!"

The narrow back door was still unbarred. Ramses did not bother replacing the boards.

Taking the coward's way out, he sent a servant to the dining salon to announce their return, and they went straight to their room and the adjoining bath chamber. When he emerged, wearing only a towel, his father was sitting in an armchair, pipe in hand.

"Where is she?" he demanded.

"Still bathing. I'll tell her you're here."

"Oh," said Emerson, belatedly aware of his intrusion on their privacy. "Oh. Er—"

Ramses opened the door to the bath chamber and announced his father's presence. Water splashed and Nefret called out, "I'll be with you in a few minutes, Father."

It wasn't often that Ramses could embarrass his father and he was rather inclined to enjoy those moments. Emerson was blushing. "You've been the devil of a long time," he complained. "We are due to leave in a few hours, you know."

"It couldn't be helped." Ramses dressed as he told Emerson what had happened. He expected an outburst; Emerson had nothing but contempt for procurers in general and el-Gharbi in particular. Instead of shouting, Emerson looked thoughtful.

"I wonder if he knows anything about—um—Sethos."

"I didn't ask. I don't want to be in his debt, and I was in a hurry to get away. It's highly unlikely, Father. The illegal antiquities trade was only a sideline, and he's been shut up in Hilmiya for weeks."

"Hmm, yes." Emerson brooded.

The door of the bath chamber opened and Nefret appeared, wreathed in steam. She was wrapped in a long robe that covered her from chin to bare feet, but Emerson fled, mumbling apologies.

⋮

Getting my family onto the train—any train—is a task that tries even my well-known patience. Emerson had sent Selim and Daoud on to Luxor a few days earlier, to survey the site and determine what needed to be done. That left seven of us, not counting the cat, who was more trouble than anyone. The railroad station is always a scene of pure pandemonium; people and luggage and parcels and an occasional goat mill about, voices are raised, and arms wave wildly. What with Horus shrieking and thrashing around in his basket, and Sennia trying to get away from Gargery and Basima so she could dash up and down the platform looking for acquaintances, and Emerson darting suspicious glances at every man, woman, and child who came anywhere near him, my attention was fully engaged.

The train was late, of course. After I had got everyone on board and in the proper compartment, I was more than ready for a refreshing sip of whiskey and soda. Removing the bottle, the gasogene, and the glasses from the hamper, I invited Emerson to join me.

As I could have told him—and indeed, did tell him—it had been a waste of time to look for Sethos. He never did the same thing twice, and he had had ample time to communicate with us had he chosen to do so.

Emerson said, "Bah," and poured more whiskey.

I had dispatched telegrams to the Vandergelts and to Fatima, our housekeeper, informing them of the change in schedule, but being only too familiar with the leisurely habits of the telegraph office in Luxor, I was not surprised to find that no one was waiting to meet us at the station. No doubt the telegrams would be delivered later that day, after the unofficial telegraph, gossip, had already announced our arrival. It did not go unremarked. There were always people hanging about the station, meeting arrivals and bidding farewell to departing travelers, or simply wasting time. A great shout went up when the loungers recognized the unmistakable form of Emerson, who was—I believe I may say this without fear of contradiction—the most famous, feared, and respected archaeologist in Egypt. Some crowded round and others dashed off, hoping to be the first to spread the news. "The Father of Curses has returned! Yes, yes, I saw him with my own eyes, and the Sitt Hakim his wife, and his son the Brother of Demons, and Nur Misur, the Light of Egypt, and the Little Bird!"

It took some little time to unload our "traps," as Emerson called them, and get them from the station to the riverbank and onto the boats which would take us across. I managed to arrange matters so that Sennia was in one boat, with Basima and Gargery in close attendance—it required at least two people to hang on to her and keep her from falling overboard—and Emerson and I in another. On this occasion I wanted to be alone with my dear husband.

"Ah," I exclaimed. "How good it is to be back in Luxor."

"You always say that," Emerson grunted.

"I always feel it. And so do you, Emerson. Breathe in the clear clean air," I urged. "Observe the play of sunlight on the rippling water. Enjoy once again the vista before us— the ramparts of the Theban mountains enclosing the sepulchres of the long-dead monarchs of—"

"I suggest you write a travel book, Peabody, and get it out of your system." But his arm went round my waist and his broad breast expanded as he drew a long satisfied breath.

After all, there is no place like Thebes. I did not say this, since it would only have provoked another rude comment from Emerson, but I knew he shared my sentiments. The modern city of Luxor is on the east bank, together with the magnificent temples of Karnak and Luxor. On the west bank is the enormous city of the dead—the sepulchres of the long-dead monarchs of imperial Egypt (as I had been about to say when Emerson interrupted me), their funerary temples, and the tombs of nobles and commoners, in a setting unparalleled for its austere beauty. The stretch of land bordering the river, fertilized by the annual inundation and watered by irrigation, was green with growing crops. Beyond it lay the desert, extending to the foot of the Libyan mountains—a high, barren plateau cut by innumerable canyons or wadis. For many years we had lived and worked in western Thebes, and the house we had built was waiting for us. I moved closer to Emerson and his arm tightened around me. He was looking straight ahead, his clean-cut features softened by a smile, his black hair wildly windblown.

"Where is your hat, Emerson?" I asked.

"Don't know," said Emerson.

He never does know. By the time I had located it and persuaded him to put it on, we were landing.

Fatima had not received our telegram. Not that it mattered; she had been eagerly awaiting us for days, and the house was in its usual impeccable order. I must say that our relations with Fatima and the other members of Abdullah's family who worked for us was somewhat unusual; they were friends as well as servants, and that latter word carried no loss of dignity or implication of inferiority. Indeed, I believe Fatima thought of us as sadly lacking in common sense and of herself as in charge of the entire lot of us.

My first act, after we had exchanged affectionate greetings with Fatima, was to inspect our new quarters. The previous winter a remarkable archaeological discovery had necessitated our spending some months in Luxor. Our old house was then occupied by Yusuf, the head of the Luxor branch of Abdullah's family, but he had amiably agreed to move himself and his wives and children to an abode in Gurneh village. It had not taken me long to realize that the house was no longer commodious enough for all of us to live in comfort and amity. I had therefore ordered several subsidiary structures to be added. In spite of Emerson's indifference and total lack of cooperation, I had seen the work well under way before our departure, but I had been obliged to leave the final details to Fatima and Selim.

I invited Fatima to accompany me on my tour of inspection. Selim, who had been awaiting us, came along, not because he wanted to, but because I insisted. Like his father, he was never quite sure how I would respond to his efforts along domestic lines. Abdullah had been inclined to wax sarcastic about what he considered my unreasonable demands for cleanliness. "The men are sweeping the desert, Sitt," he had once remarked. "How far from the house must they go?"

Dear Abdullah. I missed him still. At least he had tried, which was more than Emerson ever did.

In fact, I found very little to disapprove, and Selim's wary expression turned to a smile as I piled compliment upon compliment. The new wing, which I intended for Sennia and her entourage—Basima, Gargery, and the cat—had a number of rooms surrounding a small courtyard, with a shaded arcade along one side and a charming little fountain in the center. The new furniture I had ordered had been delivered, and while we were there, one of the maids hurried in with an armful of linens and began to make up the beds.

"Excellent," I exclaimed. "All it needs is—er—um—well, nothing really, except for some plants in the courtyard."

"We thought we should leave that to you, Sitt," said Selim.

"Yes, quite. I enjoy my gardening."

I meant to make a few other changes as well, but they could wait.

The others were still in the sitting room, with several other members of the family who had turned up, including Kadija, Daoud's wife, all talking at once and doing absolutely nothing useful. I made a few pointed remarks about unpacking, to which no one listened, dismissed Selim, and asked Nefret to join me and Fatima for the rest of the tour.

She had seen only the unfinished shell of the second house, which was situated a few hundred yards away. The intervening space would be filled in with flowering plants, shrubs, and trees as soon as I could supervise their planting and cultivation. Just now it was desert-bare, but the structure itself looked very nice, I thought, its mud-brick walls plastered in a pretty shade of pale ocher. My orders had been carried out; the interior was as modern and comfortable as anyone could wish, including an elegant bath chamber and a small courtyard, enclosed for privacy. As we went from room to room I found myself chattering away with scarcely a pause for breath, pointing out the amenities and explaining at unnecessary length that any desired alterations could be accomplished quickly and easily. Nefret listened in silence, nodding from time to time, her face unsmiling. Finally she said quietly, "It's all right, Mother," and I got hold (figuratively speaking) of my wagging tongue.

"Dear me," I said somewhat sheepishly. "I sound like a tradesperson hoping to sell a house. I beg your pardon, my dear."

"Don't apologize. You mean this for us, don't you—for

Ramses and me. You didn't tell me last year that was what you intended."

"My intentions are not relevant, Nefret. It is entirely up to you. If you prefer to stay on the dahabeeyah, as you used to do, that is perfectly all right. But I thought . . . It is some distance from our house, you see, and once I have the plantings in place they will provide additional privacy, and we would not dream, any of us, of intruding without an invitation, and—"

"Can you imagine Father waiting for an invitation?" Nefret inquired seriously. "Or Sennia?"

"I will make certain they do," I said.

"It is a beautiful house. But a trifle large for two people, perhaps?"

"D'you really think so? In my opinion—"

"Oh, Mother!" Laughter transformed her face, from shining blue eyes to curving lips. She put her arm round me, and Fatima, who had listened anxiously to the exchange, broke into a broad smile. Nefret gave her a hug too.

"It is a beautiful house," she repeated. "Thank you—both of you—for working so hard to make it perfect."

From Manuscript H

The appearance of Sethos at the Cairo railroad station had worried Ramses more than he admitted. He would have been the first to agree that his feelings for his uncle were ambivalent. You couldn't help admiring the man's courage and cleverness; you couldn't help resenting the fact that he was always one or two steps ahead of you. Affection—yes, there was that, on both sides, he thought—a belated understanding of the tragedies that had turned Sethos to a life of crime, appreciation of the risks he had taken for them and for the country that had denied him his birthright . . . Ramses felt certain he was still taking those risks. Had he turned up to greet them because he was about to embark on another job, one from which he might not return? It was a far-fetched notion, perhaps, but Ramses had once been a player in "the Great Game," and he was only too familiar with that fatalistic state of mind.

He did not mention this, not even to his wife. It would worry her, and the others, including his father. Emerson's pretense of indifference didn't fool Ramses. "Bastard" was one of Emerson's favorite epithets. It was indicative that he never used it to refer to his illegitimate brother.

However, there had been no sign of Sethos since, and no indication that he was back in the antiquities business. Ramses was relieved when his father decided to leave Cairo. If Nefret had insisted on accompanying him on a tour of the coffeeshops he could not have denied her; she had demanded a role as equal partner in all his activities, and God knew she had earned it. He believed he had put up a fairly good show of willing acquiescence, but the idea of seeing her facing thieves and murderers still made his hair stand on end.

Anyhow, he preferred Luxor to Cairo and the Theban cemeteries to those of ancient Memphis. Emerson had managed to get official permission to excavate the ancient village at Deir el Medina and Ramses was looking forward to a long, peaceful period of purely archaeological work. They wouldn't find any buried treasure or long-lost tombs, which was fine with him. As for the recent discovery that had aroused Cyrus Vandergelt's interest, he hoped he could persuade his father to stay out of that matter. They had had enough trouble with tomb robbers the year before.

His mother's energetic renovations had altered the house almost beyond recognition. There were new structures all around. The shaded veranda was the same, however, and the sitting room still had its handsome antique rugs and familiar furniture. Nefret went at once to the pianoforte and ran her fingers over the keys.

"Is it not right?" Fatima asked anxiously. "I will find someone—"

"I can't imagine where," Nefret said with a smile. "Actually it's in remarkably good tune, considering."

"Sounds fine to me," declared Emerson, who was blissfully tone-deaf. He looked round with an air of great satisfaction. "Help me unpack these books, Nefret. First things first."

A brief and inconclusive argument with his wife, who wanted him to inspect the new wing, ended with her marching off with Fatima and Selim and Emerson happily wrenching the tops from cases of books, which he proceeded to put in piles all over the floor. He hadn't got very far before they were interrupted by visitors. News of their arrival had reached Gurneh before them. Abdullah's extended family numbered almost fifty people, and it seemed to Ramses that most of them had come hurrying to welcome them back. The maids served coffee and mint tea, and a cheerful pandemonium ensued. Sennia was in her element, running from one pair of welcoming arms to another, and Emerson was talking to several people at once.

Ramses looked round for Nefret, and saw she was deep in conversation with Daoud's wife, Kadija, a very large, very dignified woman of Nubian extraction. According to Nefret, Kadija had a lively sense of humor, but the rest of them had to take that on faith since she never told them any of her stories. She was obviously telling one now; Nefret's cheeks rounded with laughter. Ramses went to join them. He was disappointed but not surprised when Kadija ducked her head and slipped away.

"What was so funny?" he asked.

Nefret slipped her arm through his. "Never mind. It loses something in the translation."

"But I understand Arabic."

"Not that sort of translation." She laughed up at him and he thought again, as he did several dozen times a day, how beautiful she was and how much he loved her. That lost something in the translation, too.

"Yusuf isn't here," she said, a look of puzzlement replacing her smile. "That's rather odd. As the head of the family, courtesy would demand he welcome us back."

"Selim says he isn't well."

"Perhaps I ought to go to him and see if there is anything I can do."

"I don't think your medical skills would help, darling." Poor Yusuf's world had been overturned the past year when he had lost his two favorite children. Jamil, the handsome, spoiled youngest son, had fled after becoming involved with a gang of professional thieves. He had not been seen since. Jumana, his sister, had found a happier ending; fiercely ambitious and intelligent, her hopes of becoming an Egyptologist were being fostered by the Vandergelts and Ramses's parents.

Nefret understood. "I didn't realize it had hit the poor old chap so hard."

"Neither did I, but it isn't surprising. Having his daughter flout his authority, refuse the fine marriage he arranged for her, and go off to become a new woman—educated, independent, and Westernized—must have been almost as great a blow as discovering that his best-beloved son was in trouble with the law."

"Greater, perhaps, to a man of his traditional beliefs," Nefret said. "Is it true that he disowned her and refuses to see her?"

"Who told you that?"

"Kadija. She tried to reason with him, but he wouldn't listen."

"Selim said the same. It's a pity. Well, we'll send Mother round to talk to him. If she can't set him straight, no one can."

"What about Jamil?"

"According to Selim, there's been no sign of him. Don't

get any ideas about trying to track him down. There's a trite old proverb about sleeping dogs."

"All right; don't lose your temper."

"I thought you liked me to lose my temper."

"Only when we're alone and I can deal with you as you deserve."

Before he could respond to that, his mother came back and began organizing everyone. The women of the family carried Sennia and her luggage off to her new quarters. His father refused to budge; he was having too fine a time making plans for the season's work. He insisted that Ramses and Selim join him, but he lost Nefret to his wife. The two of them went off with Fatima.

"So, Selim," said Emerson. "Have you got a crew together? I hope you didn't let Vandergelt take our best men."

"He has hired my father's cousin's son Abu as his reis, but we will have a full crew, Emerson. There is not much work here now."

Emerson did not ask about Yusuf. He was too busy making plans for work to begin the following day.

A series of high-pitched shouts from the children who were playing on the veranda heralded a new arrival.

"I might have known you couldn't leave us in peace for a few hours," Emerson grumbled; but he went quickly to meet the newcomer with an outstretched hand.

Cyrus Vandergelt's leathery face creased into smiling wrinkles. The American was dressed with his usual elegance, in a white linen suit and polished boots. "Yes, you might," he said with a grin. "No use trying to sneak into town unnoticed—just got your telegram a while ago, but I'd already heard you were here. Good to see you. Here's somebody else who couldn't wait to say hello."

He had stood back for her to precede him through the door. Once inside, she put her back against the wall and watched them, wide-eyed and unsmiling, like a wary animal. Emerson, always the gentleman with women, took her small hand in his and gave it a hearty squeeze.

"Jumana! Good of you to come, my dear. Er—how you've grown the past few months!"

Not so you could notice, Ramses thought. She was a tiny creature, barely five feet tall, with the exotic coloring and wide dark eyes of a lady in a Persian miniature, but her clothing was defiantly English—neat little boots and a divided skirt, under a mannish shirt and tweed jacket. After spending the spring and summer with them in England, being tutored in various subjects and absorbing information as a dry sponge soaks up water, she had returned to Egypt in November with the Vandergelts.

What was wrong with her? Usually her small face was alive with excitement and she could outtalk everyone in the family—which was no small feat. Now she replied to Emerson's greeting with a wordless murmur and her dark eyes moved uneasily around the room.

"Where is Nefret?" she asked.

"She and Mrs. Emerson have gone off to look at the new house," Emerson said.

"I will go too. Please? Excuse me?"

She hurried out of the room without waiting for a reply. She's got something on her mind, all right, Ramses thought. Well, whatever it was, it was not his problem. His mother thought she could solve everything; let her deal with it.

She came bustling in a few minutes later and went straight to Cyrus, holding out her hands. "Jumana told me you were here. Didn't Katherine and Bertie come with you?"

"Bertie wanted to, but Katherine had some chore or other for him," Cyrus answered.

Ramses wasn't surprised to hear it. Katherine disapproved of her son's fascination with the pretty Egyptian girl.

"She was hoping you'd come to us for dinner tonight," Cyrus went on.

"Bah," said Emerson. Cyrus burst out laughing and stroked his goatee.

"I know, old pal, you don't have time for social engagements. This'll just be us, nothing formal, come as you are."

Emerson's jaws parted, but his wife got in first. "Certainly, Cyrus, we accept with pleasure. Ramses, Nefret wants you to join her. She is at the new house."

"Oh? Oh, right."

A sensation his mother would have described as a "hideous premonition" came over him. Why hadn't he realized? Of course—she had built the house for Nefret and him. It was just like her to do it without consulting them. And there was no way on earth they could refuse without sounding churlish and ungrateful and selfish. Nefret was too fond of his mother to tell her no to her face. She would want him to do it!

He expected to find his wife on the doorstep, vibrating with indignation. She wasn't there. He had to track her down, looking into room after room as he searched. The place was quite attractive, really—large, low-ceilinged rooms, with the carved mashrabiya screens he liked so much covering the windows, tiled floors, bookshelves on many of the walls. Otherwise the house was almost empty except for a few tables and chairs and couches. She'd had sense enough to leave the choice of furnishings and decorations to them. Not at all bad, on the whole. If it had been up to him . . .

If it had been up to him, he would rather live in a hole in the rock than tell his mother he didn't like it.

He found Nefret sitting on the shady porch that looked out on a small courtyard. Jumana was with her, their heads close together.

"I'm sorry, Nefret," he began.

"You apologize too often." It was an old joke between them, but when she looked up he saw that her face was grave.

"It's not so bad, is it?" he asked. "She meant well, and it is some distance from the main house, and—"

"It's fine," Nefret said impatiently. "Never mind the house, Ramses. Jumana has something to tell you."

There were wicker chairs and a table or two. He sat down. "Well?"

She had obviously been talking freely with Nefret, but the sight of him froze her tongue. She twisted her hands together.

"What is it?" Ramses asked. "Something about Bertie? Don't worry about him, Jumana, you'll be staying with us from now on. That was the agreement."

"Bertie?" She dismissed him with a shrug. "He is not a worry. No. I must tell you, but . . ." She swallowed, hard. "I have seen Jamil."

"My God." Ramses breathed. "Where? When?"

"Two weeks ago." Now that she had got the worst of it out, the words flowed freely. "I went to Luxor Temple, while Mrs. Vandergelt was shopping at the suk and Mr. Vandergelt was at Mohassib's. Bertie wanted to go with me, but Mrs. Vandergelt said—"

"I understand," Ramses said. "Jamil was at the temple?"

She nodded. "He had been waiting for days to find me alone. He wanted money. He said that he had discovered a rich tomb, but the others had cheated him and he cursed them all and said he would get even, but he needed money . . . I gave him all I had."

"You shouldn't have done that," Nefret said. "The best thing for Jamil would be to turn himself in."

Her mouth drooped like that of a child on the verge of tears. "He is my brother. How could I refuse to help him? But he said . . . Oh, I have been so afraid! I didn't know what to do. But now you are here, you will tell the Father of Curses, and he will not let Jamil—" Her voice broke.

"It's all right," Ramses said gently. He took her small shaking hands in his. "He won't let Jamil hurt you. Is that what he threatened? That he would harm you if you told anyone you had seen him?"

"No, oh, no!" She clung tightly to his hands and looked up into his face. "It is you the Father of Curses must guard. It is you Jamil hates most. He said if I told anyone he would kill you."

⋮

. .

Three

. .

"**B**ah," said Emerson.

We were seated on the veranda drinking tea. The rays of the sun, low in the west, cast golden gleams through the roses that twined around the open arcades. It was like the old days, when we had so often gathered in that shaded spot; the wicker chairs and settees and tables were not much the worse for wear, and Ramses had taken up his old position, perched on the ledge with his back against a pillar. Now Nefret sat beside him, and her hand was in his. Fatima had insisted upon serving sandwiches and tea cakes, despite the fact that we were to leave shortly to dine with the Vandergelts. Rather than disappoint the dear woman, I nibbled on a cucumber sandwich or two.

After learning of the reappearance of Jamil, I had decided a private council of war was imperative. Sennia, who had expected to take tea with us, strongly objected to being sent away and was only mollified when—before I could stop him—Emerson handed her the entire plate of cakes to take with her. As soon as she was out of earshot Nefret repeated what Jumana had said, and Emerson responded in characteristic fashion.

"That is not much help, Emerson," I said. "A threat cannot be dismissed so cavalierly."

"It was an idle threat," Emerson declared. "How can that

miserable little coward constitute a danger to Ramses?" He gave his tall son an approving look, and Ramses replied to the implied compliment with an exaggerated lift of his eyebrows.

"Come to that, why Ramses?" Emerson went on. "I take it as an affront that he didn't threaten *me*. Are you going to eat all the cucumber sandwiches, Peabody?"

"I think," said Nefret, passing Emerson the plate, "that in Jamil's eyes Ramses was the hero of last year's affair. Or villain, from Jamil's viewpoint! Not to take anything away from you, Father—or you, Mother—"

"You are quite right, my dear," I said graciously. "We did our part, but if it had not been for Ramses—"

"You ought to take it as a compliment, Father," Ramses said. He does not often interrupt me, but he does not like to hear himself praised. "Jamil would consider it below his dignity to threaten a woman, and he obviously feels I am less dangerous than you. 'No man dares threaten the Father of Curses!' "

"What an annoying development!" I mused. "I had hoped the wretched boy had taken himself off to distant parts, or that he had met with a fatal accident."

"That is rather cold-blooded, Mother," my son said.

"Your mother is a practical woman," Emerson declared. "I suppose now we'll have to find him and turn him over to the police, which will be cursed embarrassing for everyone concerned, especially his father. We've left him alone, and instead of taking to his heels he has the effrontery to challenge us! He must be mad."

"Or mad for revenge," Nefret said, her brows furrowing.

"No," I said judiciously. "He's too much of a coward. However, his true motive is not difficult to discover. One of his most notable traits is greed. He also has an uncanny instinct for locating lost tombs. Depend on it, that is why he hasn't left Luxor. He hopes to find another; good Gad, perhaps he has already done so!"

An all-too-familiar glint brightened Emerson's sapphirine

orbs, but after a moment's thought he shook his head regretfully. "Pure conjecture, Peabody, born of your rampageous
imagination. It's more likely that he hasn't the courage to
leave familiar surroundings and strike out on his own. He
made enough from his share of the princesses' treasure to
live comfortably for a while; I would guess that the money
has been squandered, and that he approached Jumana as a
last resort. He won't try it again. As for attacking Ramses—
stuff and nonsense!"

"Yes, but he might try and get back at Jumana," I said.
"Especially if he learns she told us he is still in Luxor. She
probably won't believe that she could be in danger from
him, so we must make certain she is not allowed to go off
alone. Katherine and I had agreed she would come to us; we
will bring her back with us tonight. I will ask Fatima to get a
room ready for her. David's old room, I think; it is next to
ours, Emerson, with windows that open only onto the courtyard. It will not be easy for anyone to get at her there—or for
her to creep out unobserved."

"Are you going to tell Cyrus and Katherine about Jamil?"
Nefret asked.

"I am glad you raised that point, Nefret. I will explain the
situation to them eventually, but I do not believe it would be
advisable to mention it this evening. The walls have ears and
the tongues of Luxor wag at both ends. We certainly don't
want Jamil to find out that his sister has informed on him."

"There you go, trying to make a mountain out of a mole-
hill," Emerson declared. "In my humble opinion, the sooner
Jamil learns that we are aware of his pathetic threats, the better. He won't dare show his face again."

"In your opinion?" I repeated. "Humble? I trust that you
agree that Selim and Daoud must be informed. Harmless
the wretched boy may be, but he is their cousin—of some
degree—and—"

"Here is Cyrus's carriage, come for us," Nefret said
quickly. "Are we ready? Mother, where is your hat?"

Cyrus's carriage was a handsome open barouche, drawn

by a splendid pair of grays. A brilliant sunset washed the western sky, and across the river the lights of Luxor began to shine. When the carriage turned into the narrow way that led to the Valley of the Kings, the hills rose up around us, cutting off the last of the sunset light. Few spots on earth are as magical as the Valley; it is not only the grandeur of the scenery, but the romance of its history. In the gray twilight one could easily imagine that the shadows cast by the carriage lamps were the ghostly forms of the royal dead, and that the howling in the hills came from the throat of the divine jackal Anubis, god of cemeteries.

"Now that we are settled here for a long time, we must think seriously of getting our own carriage," I remarked. "I don't like depending on Cyrus or on the rattletraps for hire at the dock."

Emerson said something under his breath, and I said, "I beg your pardon?" and Emerson said, "Motorcar."

That subject caught everyone's attention and we had a nice little argument that lasted all the way to the Castle. I pointed out that the utility of such vehicles was limited by the condition of the roads and Emerson retorted that the military was using them, and that the new Ford cars had proved to perform admirably in desert terrain. Nefret and Ramses contributed very little. To be fair, they didn't get a chance to say much.

Cyrus's Theban residence was called the Castle, and it well deserved the name. From certain angles it reminded me of the Mena House hotel; it was almost as large as that excellent hostelry and had the same screened balconies attractively arranged at various levels. There was a stout wall around the entire estate; that night the heavy gates stood hospitably open, and flaming torches lined the drive leading to the house, where Cyrus stood waiting to greet us.

He had, as promised, invited no other guests. I asked after William Amherst, who had worked for Cyrus the previous year, and was told that he had left.

"Finally wangled his way into the army," Cyrus said

rather enviously. "Some kind of office job. Leaves me confounded shorthanded," he added. "But Abu is a good reis, and Bertie's filling in real well."

Katherine gave her son a fond look. She had grown a touch stouter, but the additional weight was, in my opinion, quite becoming. She wore a long loose gown in the Egyptian style and an emerald necklace that matched her eyes. Now that she was freed from worry about her son, who had been severely wounded in action the past year, her face had lost its haggard look and once again she resembled the pleasant, plump-cheeked tabby cat of which she had reminded me at our first meeting.

Bertie was looking well too. He had taken up the study of Egyptology, partly to please his stepfather, but primarily to win favor with Jumana, and there is nothing like the vigorous pursuit of archaeology to give an individual healthy color and a sturdy frame. I did notice, when he advanced to greet me, that one leg still dragged a little. I had hoped that time would bring about a complete cure. Evidently it had not. Ah well, I thought, it will keep him from going back into the military.

The only other person present was Jumana, who sat as still as a little mouse until Emerson went to her. Everyone was talking and laughing; I believe I was the only one who heard what he said to her.

"You did the right thing, child. The matter is in my hands now, and there is nothing to worry about."

I could only hope he was right.

It wasn't long before Cyrus turned the conversation to the subject that had obviously become an idée fixe. "I want a crack at that treasure," he declared. "Emerson, you're gonna have to help me with Mohassib."

Ramses glanced at me. His dark brows tilted in an expression of amused skepticism, and I intervened before Emerson could answer.

"Now, Cyrus, you know perfectly well that Emerson is the last person in whom Mohassib would confide. Emerson has told him only too often and only too profanely what he thinks of dealers in antiquities. I would like to hear more about the business. How was the tomb found, has it been investigated, why hasn't the Service des Antiquités taken steps?"

That ought to keep Emerson quiet for a while, I thought complacently.

Nothing loath, Cyrus launched into a tale that was even more bizarre than the usual stories of such discoveries—and that, I assure you, Reader, is saying a good deal.

It does not often rain in Luxor, but when it does, the storms are severe. One such storm had struck the previous summer, washing away houses and cutting deep channels through the land. The canny thieves of Luxor knew that such downpours were more effective than excavation in removing accumulated debris and, perhaps, exposing tomb entrances. Scrambling around the cliffs, they had found a place where a stream of falling water disappeared into a crevice and then came out again, forty feet away.

What they saw when they squirmed through the choked passageway into the tomb chamber must have left even those hardened thieves speechless. Unrobbed tombs aren't found every day, and this one was spectacularly rich. Astonishment did not render them less efficient; within a few hours the treasure had been removed and deposited with Mohassib, who paid them in gold coins. The money was divided among the miscreants, who immediately began to spend it.

"That old fool Mohammed Hammad bought himself a young wife," Cyrus said. "It turned out to be a mistake. The news of the tomb got around, as it always does, and a few weeks later the local mamur and his lads descended on the village. Mohammed had time to hide the rest of his money in a basket of grain, and sent the girl off with it, but she hung around flirting with the guards, and one of them knocked the basket off her head. Well, folks, you can imagine what happened after that. There was a free-for-all, villagers and police rolling around the ground fighting each other for the gold pieces. Mohammed ended up with nothing, not even the girl. She went off with the mamur."

"Disgusting," Katherine murmured.

"Poetic justice," said Emerson with an evil grin. "Mohammed must be feeling hard done by. He may be persuaded to show me the location of the tomb. They can't have done a complete clearance."

"Oh, it's been located," Cyrus said. "In the Wadi Gabbanat el-Qirud—the Cemetery of the Monkeys. I've been thinking I might spend a little time out there looking for more tombs."

"You are supposed to be working at Medinet Habu," Emerson said with a severe look at his friend. "Not going off on wild-goose chases."

"It's all very well for you to talk," Cyrus said indignantly. "You've had your big finds, but how about me? All those years in the Valley of the Kings and not a durned tomb for my trouble! There's got to be more of them in the southwest wadis. With Carter's find that makes two tombs of royal females in those wadis. What I figure is that that area could have been a kind of early queens' cemetery."

"It is a strong possibility," Ramses agreed.

Cyrus's eye brightened, but Emerson said firmly, "You'd be wasting your time, Vandergelt. Carter didn't find that tomb of Hatshepsut's, he trailed a group of the locals who had discovered it. You had better stop chasing rainbows and get to work, as I intend to do. You have the firman for Medinet Habu, and you were damned lucky to get it. It is one of the best-preserved temples on the West Bank."

"At least there are some tombs at Deir el Medina," Cyrus muttered.

"Private tombs," Emerson pointed out. "And I will not be searching for more. I mean to finish excavating that settlement in its entirety. In archaeological terms it is far more important than any cursed royal tomb. Town sites are rare, and we will gain valuable information about the daily life, occupations, and amusements of the working classes . . ."

There are few aspects of Egyptology that do not interest Emerson, but in this case he was bravely disguising a certain degree of disappointment and envy. He had always wanted to work at one of the great temples like Medinet Habu. To be honest, I was not especially excited about the village either, but we would not have got even that site if the individual who had held the firman the previous year had not been taken into police custody. According to Emerson, his excavation methods had been careless in the extreme, so there was a good chance we might come upon artifacts he had overlooked or discarded as worthless.

And I just might have a look round for more of the private tombs. Some of them were beautifully decorated, and two had contained their original grave goods—not as rich as those of the princesses, but full of interest.

Emerson concluded his speech by remarking, "I trust, Vandergelt, that you will concentrate on Medinet Habu. You cannot expect the Department of Antiquities to think well of you if you keep wandering off on fanciful quests."

When we took our departure, we were loaded down. There was room for Jumana on the seat with Ramses and Nefret, but her boxes and bundles took up quite a lot of space. Upon our arrival I showed the girl her room. I had the distinct impression that she was not impressed by its amenities. They were certainly inferior to the ones she had enjoyed as Cyrus's guest.

However, she expressed her appreciation very prettily. I then informed her that Emerson wanted a word with her.

"What about?" she asked.

"I think you know what about, Jumana. For goodness' sake, child, you look like a cornered rabbit. You aren't afraid of him, surely."

"Not of him," Jumana murmured. "I have done nothing to be ashamed of, Sitt Hakim."

"I didn't say you had. Come along."

We had agreed in advance that Emerson and I would have a private chat with Jumana, so I was somewhat surprised to find the children with him in the sitting room.

"We only waited to say good night," Nefret said, coming to give me a kiss.

"I hope the house is satisfactory," I said, addressing Ramses, who had not yet given me his opinion. "And that you have everything you need for tonight."

"So long as there is a bed," said my son, and broke off with a grunt as Nefret elbowed him in the ribs.

"I want to leave at daybreak," Emerson said self-consciously.

"Yes, sir," said Ramses.

"Breakfast here at six," I said.

"Yes, Mother," said Nefret.

Jumana's wide eyes followed them as they went off, arm in arm, their heads close together. Or was it Ramses she watched with such wistful attention? She was of an age where girls fancy themselves in love with unsuitable persons, and Ramses had every quality she could want in a prospective husband (aside from the inconvenient fact that he was already married). If Jamil knew or suspected her attachment it would explain why he had selected Ramses as the object of his ire.

"By the by," said I to Emerson, "you didn't tell Cyrus about the artifacts I bought in Cairo. I had expected you would want to show them off."

"Quite the contrary," said Emerson to me. "He'd go haring off to Cairo looking for more of the cursed things. He should be thinking of his excavations."

He fell silent, concentrating on his pipe. Now that the moment had come, he was regretting having offered to question Jumana; he was afraid she would cry. Emerson is a hopeless coward with women.

He did not know this one. Before either of us could speak, Jumana sat up straight and raised her chin defiantly.

"I was very silly," she declared. "Jamil can't do anything . . . can he?"

"No," said Emerson. "Except, perhaps, to you."

"He wouldn't hurt me."

I was pleased to see she had recovered her nerve—timid women are a confounded nuisance—but her confidence was somewhat alarming.

"He won't get the chance," I said. "Listen to me, Jumana. You were right to warn Ramses about Jamil, but you are wrong if you believe he is harmless. I want your word that you will go nowhere alone and that if Jamil attempts to communicate with you, you will inform us immediately."

"What will you do to him if you find him?"

For once, Emerson was too quick for me. "Lock him up. You must see that we cannot allow him to hang about threatening people and . . . Why are you glaring at me, Peabody?"

"I am not glaring, Emerson," I said, forcing my features into a smile. "It is just that I believe I can explain our intentions more accurately than you. Jumana, if Jamil would come to us and express repentance, we will do all we can to help him."

"You would?"

"Yes," I said firmly. She still loved the wretched boy and probably believed she could redeem him. This is a common delusion of women.

After all, I had not been specific. In my opinion the best way to help Jamil would be to put him in a cell—a nice, clean, comfortable cell, naturally—and let him consider the advantages of an honest life.

I had expected Emerson would want to go straight to the site next morning. I had no objection to his doing so; there was a great deal to do round the house, and Emerson was more of a hindrance than a help, always grumbling and complaining. However, when we sat down to breakfast I saw that he and Ramses were dressed for rough terrain, in old tweeds and stout boots. It did not require much thought to deduce where they meant to go. I ought to have known! My hypocritical husband's lecture to Cyrus had been meant to deter the latter from doing precisely what Emerson intended to do that day. The southwest wadis are remote and difficult of access.

I attempted to catch Emerson's eyes but failed; he was looking at the sugar bowl, the coffeepot, the salt cellar—anything but me. "Emerson," I said loudly, "I trust you had the courtesy to inform Fatima last night that we would want a packed luncheon?"

"Luncheon? We?" Emerson's heavy black brows drew together. "See here, Peabody—"

"I will tell her now," I said with a sigh. "Fortunately she always has a full larder. Are we taking Selim and Daoud with us?"

"Yes. No. Oh, curse it," said Emerson.

"What about Jumana?" I persisted.

"No," said Emerson firmly.

"I don't believe we ought to leave her alone."

"She won't be alone. There are a dozen people . . . Damnation. You don't think she would creep out to meet that young swine? She gave me her word—"

"No, she did not. I don't trust her out of my sight. She's been climbing over those hills since she was a child, she can keep up as well as the rest of us."

"If you are going to make a full-scale expedition of this—"

"You would have gone off without so much as a water bottle," I retorted. "I will change my boots and get my parasol, and have a few words with Fatima."

Emerson made one last, and as he ought to have known, futile attempt to head me off. "But, Peabody, I thought you meant to spend the day here. There is a great deal to do, unpacking and—"

"Yes, my dear, there is. Obviously it will have to wait. I won't be long."

I had my few words with Fatima and sent one of the maids to tell Jumana she was wanted in the sitting room. It took me

a while to find my boots, which were buried under a heap of
Emerson's clothes. The most important part of my costume
was ready at hand. Though my working attire of trousers and
tweed coat is well equipped with pockets, I have never abandoned my invaluable belt of tools. Over the years I had refined and added to these accoutrements: a pistol and knife, a
coil of rope, a small flask of brandy, candles and matches in
a waterproof box, and other useful items. On an expedition
such as this, one could not take too many precautions. I hung
a small first-aid kit and a brush from two of the empty
hooks, and returned to the breakfast room, where I found
that Jumana had joined the others.

Emerson, who objects to my being hung all round with
sharp-edged or blunt objects, gave me a sour look but re-
frained from comment. I turned to Nefret.

"Are you coming, my dear, or would you prefer to stay
here and get your new quarters in order? I purchased goods
for draperies—a very pretty blue, shot with silver—but I
haven't done anything about servants, since I assumed you
would wish to select them yourself. One of Yusuf's brother's
cousins has already come round asking—"

"Yes, Mother, you mentioned that. I am coming, of
course. Do you suppose I would allow my poor helpless
husband to go off without me to protect him?"

Jumana gave her a startled look, and Ramses's lips parted
in a grin. He must have told Nefret of the plan the night before. She certainly had him well in hand—better than I had
Emerson!

Fatima bustled in with two heavily laden baskets, and we
went to the stable, where we found Daoud chatting with the
stableman and Selim chatting with the horses. He was a fine
rider, and he had been in charge of the splendid Arabians
while we were away. Risha and Asfur had been gifts to Ramses and David from a Bedouin friend. Their progeny, which
included Nefret's mare Moonlight, had increased over the
years.

"Are we taking the horses?" I inquired. I knew the answer

even before Emerson shook his head. He had told Selim and
Daoud to meet him in the stable so I wouldn't see them!
Neither appeared surprised to see me, however. Selim
greeted me with a knowing smile. He and Daoud both carried coils of rope. I had a feeling we would need ropes before the day was over, if the paths Emerson meant to take
were too rough for the horses.

I have clambered over the Theban mountains many a
time, by day and by night. The exercise is delightful during
the time of full moon, when the rugged surface is a sym-
phony of silver and shadow. The first part of the trek was familiar to me, and not difficult—up the slope behind Deir el
Bahri to the top of the plateau and the path that led from the
workmen's village to the Valley of the Kings. How often had
I stood there gazing out upon the panorama of temples and
villages, desert and sown, with the waters of the Nile
sparkling in the sunlight! It was a hallowed spot; for as our
dear departed reis Abdullah grew older, I would often pretend fatigue after the climb so that he could stop and catch
his breath. I dreamed of him from time to time, and it was always in this setting that I saw him.

Difficult as it is to believe of such a barren, rocky region,
the wadis of the Western Desert were cut by water pouring
down the cliffs of the high plateau to the plain below. I believe I can best make the Reader come to an understanding
of this particular terrain, which is nothing at all like the sand
deserts of the Sahara, by comparing the plateau to a plum
cake which has been set down on a flattish platter (the Nile
Valley). Imagine that some monstrous being has thrust
taloned claws into the soft top and sides of this confection
and withdrawn them, leaving ragged fissures and tumbled
lumps.

(When Emerson happened to read this particular section
of my narrative, he remarked that in his opinion no rational
person could make such an absurd comparison. In my opinion, it is a valid figure of speech, and very descriptive.)

Paths wind to and fro across the slopes and over the gebel;

some are fairly easy, others are more suitable for goats. These latter were the ones we followed, for whenever there was a choice between an easier, roundabout route, or a steeper, direct path, Emerson chose the second. I had to trust to his leadership, since I had never come this way, but various landmarks gave me a general sense of where we were. Above rose the great pyramid-shaped peak known as the Qurn; beyond, below, and behind it were ravines of all sizes, including the great Valleys of the Kings and the Queens. As we went on, scrambling up stony slopes and over projecting ridges, the scenery became wilder and more spectacular, but even in that remote region there were signs of the presence of man, both ancient and modern: a scrap of newspaper that might have wrapped someone's lunch, the tumbled stones of crude huts, scraps of broken pottery and animal bones.

After an hour of strenuous walking I persuaded Emerson to stop for a brief rest and a sip of water. The view was breathtaking but monotonous—tumbled stone and bare ground, with the blue of the sky above the only color.

"Emerson, are you sure you know where you are going?" I inquired, mopping my perspiring face.

"Certainly," said Emerson, looking surprised. He pointed. "We are only eight thousand feet from Medinet Habu. Cheer up, Peabody, we'll be going down from here; there is a perfectly good path to the next wadi and from there it's only a hop, skip, and a jump to the Cemetery of the Monkeys."

By the time we reached the end of his "perfectly good path," which was nothing of the sort, the sun was high overhead. A long, relatively low ridge of rock separated the first wadi from the second, though I certainly would not have described its traverse as a hop, skip, and a jump. A scramble, a slip, and a stretch would be more like it. Once over the ridge we saw a narrow, irregular canyon, stretching out to the north. The ground was extremely uneven, littered with fallen rock and archaeological debris—fragments of red pottery, flints, and so on.

Hot, out of breath, and faced with this unpromising view,

I allowed myself to speak candidly. "That, I take it, is the wadi where the princesses' tomb is located. Would you now care to explain what the devil we are doing here? You told Cyrus he would be wasting his time looking for tombs here."

"Hmph," said Emerson. "Modesty forbids me to mention that I am perhaps a trifle more qualified than Vandergelt. However, that is not my primary aim. I just—er—want to have a look at the princesses' tomb. The bastards can't have made a complete clearance."

"Oh, yes, they could have. I tell you, Emerson, you won't find anything of interest—and how are we to locate the exact spot? The tomb was well hidden, and there are dozens of clefts and rifts in those walls."

"There may be signs," Emerson insisted. "Watermarks, fresh stone chips, possibly even scraps of the burial equipment. Do you see anything, Ramses?"

"No, sir." Ramses bent and picked up a piece of worked stone, covered with a thick patina. He tossed it away. "Paleolithic."

We made our way slowly along the uneven floor of the wadi, scanning the rocky walls on either side. There was a good deal more debris, in the form of pottery shards and scraps of stone. I came to a halt next to a gaping hole and let out a cry of excitement. "Emerson! A pit tomb, is it not? And here—" I reached for an object half hidden in dusty chips— something that was surely metallic, for a glint of sunlight had shone off it. "Here is—oh."

It was a crumpled cigarette tin.

"Carter," said Emerson, making the name sound like an expletive.

"How do you know?"

"None of the local men can afford European cigarettes," Emerson said. "It's the brand he smokes, isn't it?"

As we went on, the ground underfoot became even more uneven; it appeared as if someone had conducted a random but extensive excavation. Emerson growled. "Either Carter has lost all remnants of archaeological conscience, or the locals have been digging, looking for tombs."

"The latter, surely," said Ramses. "Carter had every right to be here, Father; he has done nothing wrong."

"Hmph," said Emerson, who could not deny this, but who, in his heart of hearts, regarded the entire country of Egypt as his personal property, archaeologically speaking.

We had almost reached the end of the canyon when I became aware of a faint, unpleasant smell. I looked up, expecting to see floating overhead the winged predators that feed on carrion; but the sky was empty of all but light.

Jumana was the first to see the signs for which we had been searching. She ran on ahead, quick and sure-footed over the uneven ground, and came to a stop. "See!"

The object she held up was a small gold bead.

"Ha," said Emerson. "Well done, Jumana. Yes, just as I expected. The tomb must have been partially filled with rock fallen from the walls and ceiling. The villains were careful not to remove any more of it than they had to, but they were bound to lose a few items. By Gad, that looks like a bone."

It fell to pieces in a shower of dust when he picked it up. "Water-rotted," Emerson muttered, and began rooting around in the debris.

"The tomb must be up there," Ramses said, shading his eyes with his hand. "Directly above, in that rift."

Emerson got to his feet. Only then did something odd seem to strike him. He threw his shoulders back, raised his head, and sniffed. "Have the local lads been up to their old tricks—throwing the carcass of a dead animal into the shaft to deter other explorers? You remember the Abd er Rassuls, and the Royal Cache."

"Why would they bother to do that, if there is nothing left in the tomb?" I asked. I pinched my nose with my fingers.

"Precisely," said Emerson, looking pleased. "I will just have a look."

We were at the far end of the valley, facing a steep cliff

that I judged to be over a hundred feet high. Some thirty feet above us I made out a cleft running deep into the rock.

"Emerson," I said, choosing my words with care, "it is a sheer drop from the cleft down to the base of the cliff. If you are bent on breaking your arm or your leg or your neck or all three, find a place closer to home so we won't have to carry you such a distance."

Emerson grinned at me. "You do enjoy your little touches of sarcasm, Peabody. I can make it."

"No, sir, I don't believe you can," Ramses said, quietly but firmly. "I wouldn't care to try it either. I'll go round and up, with the rope, and lower myself from the top as the thieves did."

I let out a sigh of relief. Ramses seldom contradicted his father, but when he did, Emerson heeded his advice—a compliment he paid few people, including me.

"Oh," he said, stroking his chin. "Hmph. Very well, my boy. Be careful."

"Yes, sir."

"I will go too," Daoud volunteered. "To hold the rope."

He slung a coil of rope over his shoulder and the two of them set out toward the mouth of the wadi, where the enclosing cliffs were lower and easier to climb. They would have quite a scramble to get to the top, but I was not concerned about them; Ramses was the best rock climber in the family and Daoud had been up and down cliffs like these since childhood. He would make certain Ramses took sensible precautions.

I occupied the time by writing up a few notes about the appearance and location of the tomb, while Emerson dug in the rubble as happily as a dog looking for buried bones, and Nefret paced restlessly back and forth, glancing from time to time at the top of the cliff. The sun was almost directly overhead and it was very warm. I removed my coat, folded it neatly, placed it on the ground beside me, and went on with my journal. The smell did not seem so strong now. The olfactory sense is quick to adjust.

Despite Nefret's frequent glances upward, Jumana was the first to see them. She began jumping up and down and waving her arms. The two figures, diminished by distance, made me realize how high the cliff was, and how precipitous the drop. I wondered if the rope would be long enough, and if they could find some stout object to which it could be fastened, and if Ramses would have sense enough not to rely solely on Daoud to hold it. Our friend's strength was legendary, but if a slip or a snakebite caused him to lose his grip, even for a second . . .

The rope came tumbling down, and one of the small figures began to descend—rather too rapidly, in my opinion. It was Ramses, as I had known it would be. It was hard to make out the outlines of his form, even with the sunlight full upon him, since his dusty clothing blended with the color of the stone, but his bare black head was clearly discernible. When he reached a point some forty-five feet above us he stopped, feet braced against the cliff, and waved.

"Keep hold of the damned rope!" I shouted.

He heard me. A faint and unquestionably mocking "Yes, Mother" floated down to us. Then he disappeared.

"Into the cleft," Emerson muttered. "How long . . ."

It was only a few minutes before Ramses reappeared. Instead of reascending he looked up and shouted something at Daoud. Apparently the rope was not long enough to reach all the way to the ground; after Daoud had untied it, Ramses pulled it down and busied himself doing something I could not see—fastening it again, I assumed, since in a short while it uncoiled, the lower end touching the ground not far from where we stood. It had been knotted at regular intervals—a primitive but effective method of preventing the climber from losing his grip.

Ramses swung himself out of the cleft and descended. Even before he turned to face us I knew something was amiss.

"It isn't an animal," he said. "It's a man. Was a man."

Nefret reached for the rope. Ramses pulled her back and turned her to face him, holding her by the shoulders.

"He's dead, Nefret. You can't do anything for him."

"I can tell how he died." She tried to twist away from him but he tightened his grasp.

"Nefret, will you listen to me? I'm not talking about a nice dry mummy. There's still water in the chamber, and he's been there for days, possibly weeks."

Her face was flushed with heat and rising temper. "Damnation, Ramses, I've examined more cadavers than you have!"

"You aren't going to examine this one."

"Who's going to stop me?"

"Er," said Emerson.

I poked him with my parasol. "Not you, Emerson. Nefret, stop and think. I am in full sympathy with your interest in corpses, but I do not see that anything is to be gained by your inspecting this one at this time."

The smell seemed to have intensified since Ramses's announcement. I pressed my handkerchief to my nose, and Emerson gaped at me.

"You mean you don't insist on inspecting it, and the tomb, too? Good Gad, Peabody, do you feel well?"

"Quite well, my dear, thank you, and I intend to remain so."

The children, still facing each other in somewhat belligerent attitudes, turned their heads to look at us. I was happy to observe that my reasonable remarks had lowered the emotional temperature. The corners of Nefret's mouth quivered, and the angry color faded from Ramses's face. His hands moved from her shoulders down her arms in a quick, caressing gesture. "Please," he said.

Nefret tilted her head back and looked up into his eyes. "Since you put it that way . . ."

Emerson let out a gusty breath. "Very good. We'll have to have him out, though, if we want to examine the tomb."

"Common decency requires that we have him out," I said.

"And give him a proper burial. I suppose he met with an accident while looking for another tomb to rob."

"It was no accident. He'd been arranged, propped up in a sitting position against the side of the passage, and held upright by . . ." Ramses hesitated for a moment before he went on. ". . . By a metal spike driven through his throat and into a crack in the rock."

Four

We retreated some distance down the wadi before opening the baskets of food. There was not a breath of air stirring
and very little shade; we all removed as many garments as
propriety allowed. I looked enviously from Ramses and
Emerson, shirtless as well as coatless, to Selim and Daoud,
who appeared perfectly comfortable in their enveloping but
loose garments.

I knew I was going to have another argument with Emerson about how to proceed. He was bound and determined to
get into the confounded tomb.

"We have not the proper equipment for dealing with a de-
composing corpse," I declared, peeling an orange. "And how
would we get it back? You aren't proposing we take it in turn
to carry it over those hills, I hope?"

Emerson is the most stubborn individual of my acquaintance, but even he was temporarily silenced. He bit into a
chicken leg and masticated vigorously. His blue eyes took
on a dreamy, pensive look, and his noble brow was untrou-
bled; but I knew he was only biding his time till he could
think of a way of getting round the logic of my statement.

"Decidedly unpleasant, if not actually impossible," said
Ramses, who knew his father as well as I did. "I propose we
go to Gurneh and try to locate his friends or his family.
Someone may have reported him missing."

"To the police?" Emerson snorted. "Not likely, with that lot."

"They will admit the truth to us, or to Selim," Ramses argued. "We will have to come back in any case. Mother is right about that."

"Oh, very well." Emerson finished his chicken leg and jumped up. "I will just have a quick look before—"

"No, you will not! You see what comes of your schemes, Emerson. We ought to have made inquiries before ever we came here. If you would listen to me—"

"Bah," said Emerson.

Selim had tried several times to get a word in. Now he said, "I think I know who the man might be, Father of Curses. If you had asked me—"

"Not you too, Selim," Emerson shouted. "I will not be criticized by my wife *and* my reis. One of you at a time, but not simultaneously."

However, the combined arguments of Ramses, Selim, and myself carried the day. Emerson is stubborn, but he is not completely unreasonable—and he counted on getting into the wretched tomb another time.

Emerson chose another path this time, straight down to the end of the wadi and through another, narrower canyon, descending all the while. It was certainly easier than the way we had come, but it was necessary to watch where one stepped for fear of twisting an ankle, and Emerson set such a rapid pace that conversation was impossible. Neither of these considerations prevented me from ratiocination.

There was no doubt in my mind that the unfortunate individual whose remains Ramses had found had been murdered. Was it only a coincidence that Jamil was still in the vicinity, resentful of the men who had, as he claimed, robbed him of his fair share? Remembering the lazy, surly youth I had known, I found it hard to believe that Jamil was a killer. Someone was certainly guilty of something, however, and it behooved us to take all possible precautions.

The last of the foothills dwindled and I saw before me the

Theban plain, stretching out across desert and cultivation to the river. I made Emerson stop while we drank thirstily, finishing the last of the water. He gave us no time to rest or converse, however.

"If you want to reach home before dark, we had best be getting on," he said.

I patted my damp face daintily with my handkerchief. "There are still several hours of daylight left. Where are we?"

"A mile or so from Medinet Habu." He gestured. "I thought we might go home by way of Deir el Medina, have a look round, see what—"

"Not today, Emerson." I knew Emerson's little "look round" and "mile or so." The first could take up to three hours, the second might be two miles or more. I continued somewhat acrimoniously, "Why didn't we take this path when we went out? We could have brought the horses as far as Medinet Habu at least."

"Faster the other way." Emerson rubbed his chin and gave me a puzzled look. "You aren't tired, are you?"

"Good gracious, no," I said, with a hollow laugh.

I must give Emerson credit; his mile or so was in fact only a little more than a mile. The path soon widened into a fairly well trafficked road and before long I saw the towering pylons of the temple of Ramses III. We were passing the gateway when a man emerged. He gave a start of surprise and came toward us.

"Stop, Emerson," I ordered. "There is Cyrus."

Emerson had seen him, of course. He had hoped he would not, but he was fairly caught. As Cyrus came hurrying up, Emerson burst into speech.

"Still here? I was under the impression you left off at midday. I commend your ambition. I—er—"

"I took your little lecture to heart," Cyrus said. His voice had its usual soft drawl, but his expression was neither soft nor welcoming. "Gol-durn you, Emerson, where've you been? Not at Deir el Medina, where you're supposed to be;

you're coming from the wrong direction. Did you have the consarned audacity to warn me away from those queens' tombs and then go looking for them yourself, behind my back?"

The rest of the men had come straggling out of the temple, followed by Abu and Bertie. The latter immediately hastened toward us. Abu took one look at the flushed countenance of Emerson and the scowling countenance of his employer, and discreetly vanished.

"Good evening," Bertie said, removing his pith helmet. In the heat of exasperation Cyrus had, for once, neglected to do this. He remedied the omission at once and gave me a rather sheepish look.

"I beg your pardon, Amelia, and yours, Nefret. Guess I shouldn't have got so riled up."

"Riled up?" Bertie repeated. The Americanism sounded odd in his diffident, educated English voice. "What about? Is something the matter?"

"No," Ramses said, as Nefret acknowledged Cyrus's apology with a smile. "Two such old friends as Cyrus and my father would never have a serious falling-out about a trivial matter."

Emerson grinned and fumbled in his pockets. Any other man would have been searching for a handkerchief, to wipe the perspiration from his face, but Emerson never feels the heat and he can never find his handkerchief anyhow. Taking out his pipe, he studied it with great satisfaction and began another search for his tobacco pouch.

"Don't do that now, Emerson," I ordered. "We must be getting home."

"May as well have the matter out," Emerson said. "Vandergelt has some justice on his side. Perhaps I should explain that we were not looking for new tombs, only investigating that of the princesses."

It wasn't much of an apology, but, as Cyrus knew, it was a considerable concession for Emerson.

"So what did you find?" he demanded.

"You'll never guess," said Emerson, his keen blue eyes twinkling.

"Now stop it this minute, Emerson," I exclaimed. "We will tell you all about it, Cyrus, but can't we converse as we walk—or, even better, wait until we get home, where we can be comfortable?"

Cyrus insisted I ride his mare, Queenie, and Bertie offered his mount to Nefret. She declined, but Jumana, who had had very little to say since the discovery of the body, was persuaded to accept. Cyrus and Emerson walked along beside me, and Emerson gave Cyrus a condensed version of our activities. I regret to say that Cyrus's first reaction was one of amusement.

"Every year another dead body, as Abdullah used to say," he remarked with a chuckle.

"Your frivolous attitude does not become you, Cyrus," I chided. "A man is dead—horribly murdered."

"You don't know that," Emerson growled. "And even if he was, he probably had it coming to him. Let us have no more of your imaginative speculations, Amelia. Wait until the others can join in before we discuss the matter further."

Since I had been forbidden to talk, I proceeded to speculate.

By the time we reached the house, I had my conclusions well organized and was ready to express them; but Sennia was on the veranda, vocally annoyed because she had been left "alone" all day with "nothing to do." Clearly we could not discuss a grisly corpse, or the unpleasant speculations it aroused, in her presence.

"Why don't you wash your face and hands and put on one of your good frocks?" I suggested. "You see Bertie and Mr. Vandergelt are here; we will have a little party. Jumana, please tell Fatima we have guests and—er—tidy yourself a bit."

I knew it would take Sennia at least a quarter of an hour to primp; she was a vain little creature and loved parties. My excuse for dismissing Jumana was less convincing. The rest of us were as much in need of tidying as she, but my inventiveness had given out, and I did not want her present when we discussed the possibility of her brother's being a murderer.

Selim was no fool. His eyes followed the girl's slim form as she retreated into the house. Then he looked at me. "Why did you send her away?"

"Her brother is in Luxor," I said. "Jamil."

"Is it so?" Selim's eyes widened.

I repeated what Jumana had told us. "We intended to inform you—all of you—in due course, but in my opinion there was no reason to take his threats seriously. Our discovery today casts a different light on the matter. Selim, you said you know who the corpse might be—er—might have been?"

Selim was slow to answer. He appeared to be brooding about something. "The wife of Abdul Hassan has been looking for him. He was one of the men who found the princesses' tomb." Then he burst out, "Why did you not tell me that Jumana had seen Jamil and spoken with him?"

"We didn't find out until yesterday." Emerson does not like to be put on the defensive. He came back with a question of his own. "How is it that you had not heard of his return, you, who are respected by all in Gurneh?"

"Not by tomb robbers and thieves. There were rumors . . ." Selim looked up, his jaw set. "I thought they were lies, or not important. I was wrong. I ask your pardon."

"Now, now, Selim, no one is blaming you," I said soothingly. "Let us return to the point. I sent Jumana away because in my opinion she is not yet ready to accept the possibility that her brother is a thoroughgoing villain and possibly a murderer. If he were directly accused by one of us, she might try to steal out of the house in order to warn him."

"I say," Bertie interrupted. "Here, I say . . ." But he didn't; indignation had rendered him incapable of reasoned speech.

"No one is accusing her of anything except misplaced loyalty," I informed him. "Our principal concern is for her, Bertie, but we cannot dismiss the possibility that Jamil is capable of violence against others—including us."

"That's right." Cyrus, who had listened interestedly, lit one of his cheroots. "But, Amelia, I think you've gone a little overboard. Jamil never amounted to much. I feel sorry for him if he's fool enough to face the whole lot of us, not to mention Daoud."

We were indeed an impressive group. My eyes followed those of Cyrus, from Emerson's stalwart form to that of Ramses, who was leaning on the back of Nefret's chair, lean and lithe as a panther. Either of them would have been more than a match for Jamil. And so would I.

"I believe we have covered the main points," I said. "Selim, you will speak with your kin and your friends in Gurneh; perhaps some of them will respond to direct threats—questions, I mean to say. It only remains to inform Gargery of what is going on."

"Good Gad," said Emerson, his brow furrowing. "You don't suppose there is any danger to Sennia, do you?"

"I don't know, Emerson, but I propose to take no chances. Fatima and Basima must be warned as well."

It was agreed that we would return to the Valley of the Monkeys next day, after stopping at Gurneh to interrogate the family of the missing man and the other thieves. There was no time for further discussion; Sennia bounced in and took command of the proceedings. She directed Ramses to take a seat on the settee so that she could sit beside him. Horus, who had followed close on her heels, proceeded to spread his considerable bulk across the rest of the space, and Nefret had to find another chair, which she did without resentment. As she had once said to me, "She had planned to marry him herself when she was older. A less amiable child wouldn't tolerate me at all."

Cyrus and Bertie did not linger long. Selim soon followed

them; his grim expression indicated that he meant to make up for his failure, as he considered it, as soon as possible.

The sight of Sennia had reminded me that arrangements for her continuing education should not be long delayed. There was in Luxor an excellent girls' school run by the American mission, but to send her there presented insurmountable difficulties, in the shape of Emerson. The American ladies were worthy individuals, he did not deny that; however, religious instruction was part of the curriculum, and Emerson does not hold with religion in any form. At my request he attempted to keep his heretical opinions to himself when Sennia was present, but if Sennia came home quoting the Bible at us, sooner or later Emerson would crack under the strain.

There was now an additional reason for keeping her closer to home. Jamil's threat had been directed against Ramses; but who could tell what form his malice would take?

So I interrupted Miss Sennia in the middle of a long peroration with the announcement that she would begin her schooling next day. She turned an indignant look on me and tossed her black curls. "But, Aunt Amelia, I have a great deal to do!"

"You just now complained that you hadn't enough to do," I retorted. "I have it all worked out. Mrs. Vandergelt has kindly offered to tutor you in the basic subjects—history (of England, that is), English grammar and composition, mathematics, and botany."

"Flowers?" Sennia's pretty little mouth drew up in a good imitation of Emerson's sneer. "I don't want to learn about boring flowers, Aunt Amelia, I want to learn about animals and mummies and bones."

"Biology," I said. "Hmmm. Well, that will have to wait. Mrs. Vandergelt prefers not to discuss mummies and bones."

"What about Aunt Nefret? She knows all about them." She fluttered her long lashes at Nefret, who grinned at this transparent flattery.

"I don't know how good a teacher I might be, Sennia, but I could try. Two or three lessons a week, perhaps."

"And when shall I take my lessons in hieroglyphs with Ramses?" was the next question. The little witch had the entire curriculum worked out in her head and knew exactly how to get her way. Emerson cravenly agreed to tutor her in ancient Egyptian history, and having settled the essentials to her satisfaction, Sennia kindly agreed to go to Katherine three days a week for the less important subjects. She then settled down to make serious inroads on the tea cakes.

Jumana did not return. After Fatima announced that dinner was ready, I went looking for the girl. I found her in her room, her sleek black head bent over a book.

"I am glad to see you applying yourself to your studies," I said, for I had observed that the book was the fourth volume of Emerson's *History of Egypt*. "But you must not be late to meals. Dinner will be served in a few minutes."

Her long lashes veiled her eyes. "If you don't mind, I would rather eat with Fatima and the others."

"I do mind, though," I said pleasantly but firmly. "You are a member of our archaeological staff. Do you wish to resign from that position?"

"No. It is a privilege, an honor, to work with Ramses and the Father of Curses . . . and you," she added hastily.

"Come along, then."

"Yes, Sitt Hakim. I will come at once."

Naturally we did not discuss the body at dinner. Deteriorating corpses are not a suitable subject for conversation at the dinner table in any case, and Jumana's behavior reinforced my doubts about her. She spoke only when she was spoken to, and she kept her eyes fixed on her plate. Even if she had not eavesdropped on our discussion—and I wouldn't have put it past her—she was too intelligent to miss the implications of our discovery. Jamil had more or less admitted to her that he had been involved with the looting of the princesses' tomb, and he had accused the others of cheating him. I considered asking her directly whether she and Jamil had arranged to meet again, but decided to wait and give her an opportunity to confess. Assuming, that is, that she had anything to confess.

And, with any luck, Jamil would do something that would open her eyes—another murder, perhaps, or an attack on one of us.

The children excused themselves immediately after dinner, and I said I would go with them, since there were a few domestic matters with regard to the new house that I wanted to discuss with them.

"You haven't had time to settle in or decide what additional furnishings you need," I pointed out. "And if I know Emerson, he won't give you a chance. If I can help in any way—"

"That is very kind of you, Mother," Nefret said.

Ramses said, "Thank you, Mother."

We went through the house room by room. I took copious notes and made a few little suggestions. I had not expected Ramses would be of much assistance, nor was he.

"Now then," I said, referring to my list. "What about household help? Fatima's girls have been doing the cleaning, but in my opinion it would be advisable for you to select two of them to work for you on a regular basis. If you prefer to take certain of your meals alone, a cook—"

"We'll worry about a cook later, shall we?" Nefret glanced at her husband, who was staring off into space. "As for the maids, I will leave that to Fatima. One of the girls who's been working here asked me yesterday if she could continue doing so; she is very hardworking, if a little shy, so I told her that would be fine. Her name is Najia."

"Ah, yes, Mohammed Hammad's niece. Or is he his stepdaughter? Never mind. The poor girl is somewhat self-conscious; it is that liver birthmark, I suppose."

"It won't bother us," Nefret said.

"Of course not. Now, concerning the garden . . ."

Finally Nefret said, "I think that's everything, Mother. We

will probably have to run up to Cairo to find some things, but I will talk with Abdul Hadi about making a few chairs and tables. He is the best woodworker in Luxor."

"And the slowest," I said.

Nefret smiled. "I can hurry him up."

I observed that Ramses was yawning, and took the hint. He insisted on walking back with me, despite my objections.

"Nothing can possibly happen to me between your door and mine," I declared.

"Ah, but you don't have your parasol," Ramses said.

I took Gargery into our confidence next morning at breakfast, while Sennia was dawdling over her preparations for departure. He and Fatima took it in turn to serve meals; it had been a compromise proposed by me, to prevent them from quarreling over which of them had that right. It was his turn that morning, and he followed my well-organized account with such interest that I was forced several times to remind him to serve the food. He then straightened to his full height—five feet six inches or thereabouts—and stood at attention. It would have required more than that to make him appear impressive; his frame was meager, his face lined, and he had taken to combing his hair across his forehead in an unconvincing attempt to conceal a receding hairline. He looked like a butler, which is what he was, but he possessed a number of qualities that are not often found in persons of that position. At the moment he was a very happy butler. As he had once observed to me, "If there's got to be a murder, madam, it might as well be us that gets the use of it."

"I depend on you, Gargery, to keep a close eye out when you take Miss Sennia to the Castle for her lessons with Mrs. Vandergelt. I doubt there is any reason for concern, but it would be foolish to take chances."

"I agree, madam," said Gargery, standing stiff as a wooden soldier and smiling broadly.

"How good of you to say so, Gargery. Where the devil is

that girl? Gargery, please go and . . . Ah, there you are, Jumana. Sit down and eat something and be quick about it."

We were to meet Daoud and Selim at Gurneh and go on from there to the Cemetery of the Monkeys, taking with us the necessary equipment for the ghoulish task that lay ahead. Since no one was keen on carrying the dreadful burden any farther than they had to, we planned to go the long way round, by way of the road which would enable us to bring a donkey-drawn cart part of the distance.

The cart was ready when we arrived at Selim's house, to find him and Daoud and Hassan, another of our fellows, waiting. I could see by their faces that they had been warned of what they were supposed to do, and I didn't blame them for looking gloomy.

"I have everything we will need," Selim announced. "But before we go, I think you will wish to talk with Mohammed Hammad. He is here."

"Ah," said Emerson. "The disappointed bridegroom. Have you told him of our discovery yesterday?"

"No, Father of Curses," said Selim, looking as demure as a husky young man with a large black beard can look.

Emerson laughed aloud and clapped him on the back. "Good. It will be an even greater shock coming from me."

Mohammed Hammad was a wiry little man with a face as wrinkled as a raisin and a graying beard. Like most Egyptians of the fellahin class, he was probably younger than he looked. Inadequate diet, insanitary living conditions, and an absence of proper medical care can age an individual rapidly. Now there, I thought, is a cause that might attract Nefret, and allow her to use her medical skills in the place where I intended she should be—a clinic on the West Bank, to treat common ailments such as parasites and infections. Not a stimulating practice, perhaps, for a trained surgeon, but one thing might lead to another . . .

I put the matter aside for the moment, so that I could concentrate on our suspect. Expecting to be lectured by Emerson about the tomb, and prepared to deny everything, he greeted us with a certain reserve. Emerson did not beat around the bush.

"We found one of your friends yesterday, in the tomb you robbed. Dead. Murdered."

It was an effective, if somewhat brutal, method of shocking Mohammed into an admission. I thought for a moment the poor man would have a stroke or a heart attack. He finally managed to gasp out a word. "Who . . ."

"You would know better than we," Emerson said. "Selim tells me that Abdul Hassan has not been seen for a week. He was one of your . . . Damnation," he went on, in English. "He's about to have a fit. Give him some brandy, Peabody."

Mohammed accepted the brandy (one of the little items I always carry attached to my belt) with an eagerness unbecoming a good Moslem (which I had never thought he was). He was ready to talk; the words poured out of him, and a disturbing story it was.

Of the original thieves, two were now dead. The other death had been attributed to accident; the body had been found at the base of the cliffs and it was assumed he had fallen.

"The curse of the pharaohs," said Emerson, unable to resist. "Death to those who defile the tombs."

The brandy had restored Mohammed's nerve. He gave Emerson a cynical look. "It took the pharaohs a long time to act, Father of Curses. Abdul has been robbing tombs since he was a boy."

"He won't rob any more," Emerson pointed out. "Who were the others?"

Mohammed rattled the names off without hesitating. Everyone in the village knew, including his rivals in the business, so there was no profit in reticence. He demanded extralarge baksheesh for his candor, of course. "That is all I can tell you, Father of Curses. Can I go now?"

"You have not told me everything," Emerson said. "You gave me six names. There was a seventh man, wasn't there?"

"He was not one of us," Mohammed muttered.

"I know who he was."

"The Father of Curses knows all," Daoud intoned.

Emerson acknowledged this tribute with a gracious nod, and went on, "Was it Jamil who found the tomb?"

"We all found it! We shared with him—we were generous."

Mohammed's voice was shrill with unconvincing indignation. The falsity of his claim was obvious. Jamil was not a regular member of their little gang; they would never have shared the treasure with him unless he had been the one responsible for discovering it.

"Have you seen or heard from him since you divided the money?" Emerson persisted.

A look of calculation, not unmixed with fear, sharpened Mohammed's features. "No, Father of Curses." He clutched his chest and rolled his eyes. "Ah! The pain!"

He was not too feeble to hold out his hand. Emerson dropped a few coins into it. "There will be more for you, Mohammed, if you bring us news of Jamil. Tell the others the same—and warn them to watch out for accidents."

"Hmmmm." Mohammed scratched his neck. "Accidents."

"You should have asked him to break the news to Abdul's family, Emerson," I said, after Mohammed had scuttled off.

"He will anyhow," said Emerson. "Let's go before the bereaved relatives descend on us."

After all, there is nothing like an early-morning ride in the brisk desert air to raise the spirits. We were taking the horses as far as they could safely go, and even the thought of the nasty job ahead of us faded as we went on. Admittedly, the worst part of the business was not something I had to tackle. I wondered what Abdullah would have thought of it. He would probably have remarked that it served the fellow right, and that we should leave it to his family to have the body out; but if he had been asked to take the responsibility he would have carried it out with his usual efficiency.

I had not dreamed of him for a long time. They were

strange dreams, unlike most others—as vivid and consistent as a real-life encounter would have been. I am not at all superstitious, but I had come to believe that in some way the profound affection Abdullah and I had felt for one another transcended the barrier of death, and I looked forward to those dreams as I would have anticipated another meeting with a distant friend. Perhaps now that I was back in Luxor, where we had shared so many unforgettable experiences, Abdullah would come to me again.

After we passed Medinet Habu the road narrowed to a path and then to a track as it turned toward the hills. It was Ramses who halted our caravan and Ramses who was the first to dismount, swinging himself off Risha's back in a single smooth movement. The rest of us followed his lead.

It was over a mile to the end of the wadi. Leaving the cart and the horses there, we proceeded on foot for a few hundred yards, to the place where the wide mouth of the canyon narrowed and the hills began to rise, dividing the southern branch of the wadi from another tongue that ran off to the north. Ramses stripped off his coat and took one of the coils of knotted rope.

We had discussed the best method of proceeding the night before, and had agreed, or so I believed; Emerson had not liked it then and he did not like it now.

"My turn," he insisted. "You've been in the stinking place already. Once was enough."

Ramses's mouth tightened with annoyance. I knew how he felt; when there is a dirty job to be done, one wishes to get it over. He wanted to spare his father, who wanted to spare him, and neither of them would give in without a struggle. Then Bertie, who stood a little to one side, said suddenly, "I'll go."

Taken by surprise, all of us turned to stare at him. Meeting my doubtful eye, he smiled. "I've almost certainly seen worse, you know."

It was almost certainly true. He had been in the trenches in France for almost two years before he suffered the wounds that sent him home, ill and embittered. I had heard stories . . .

"You are not a good climber," said Jumana, arms folded. "Ramses is much better."

I could have shaken the girl. Bertie flushed painfully, and I believe Cyrus was about to express his fatherly concern when Ramses cut him off.

"Right, then. Here you go." He handed Bertie the rope and gave Daoud an almost imperceptible nod. They started off, Daoud sticking close to Bertie, Hassan trailing at a slight distance.

"Ramses," I said. "Was that wise?"

"He'll be all right, Mother." Hands on hips, he watched the men climb up out of sight.

"He's got that bad leg," Cyrus said anxiously.

"What's needed for this job is strength in the arms and shoulders," Ramses said. "And nerve. He's got them. Daoud knows what to do."

We went on to the end of the valley and the cliff in which the tomb lay hidden. The rope Ramses had descended the previous day was still there, but we had concluded it would be safer for the men to approach from above rather than climb the sheer face. They would then lower the remains down, and descend themselves.

The first part of the procedure went as planned. His white handkerchief pressed to his face, Cyrus watched every move made by the small forms atop the cliff with a concern he was not unwilling to express. He had taken Katherine's children for his own, and Bertie had repaid his affection, even adopting Cyrus's name. "Have they got something to cover their faces?" he demanded, his voice muffled by the linen. "And gloves? And—"

"Daoud knows what to do," Ramses said again. He was watching, too, his brow furrowed. Jumana was the least concerned; having found a rock on which to sit, she was refreshing herself from a water bottle and humming under her breath.

Bertie was the first to descend, and I was relieved to observe that he was being lowered by Daoud instead of going down hand over hand as Ramses had done. He disappeared into the cleft and was followed by Hassan, who was carrying a folded piece of canvas and a length of rope.

I suppose it did not take more than ten minutes for them to finish what they had come to do, but it seemed longer. The first thing I saw was the neat white turban of Hassan. Emerging with some haste, he caught hold of the rope and slid to the ground.

"Hell and damnation," Emerson remarked, in a voice that echoed between the cliffs. "Did you leave him alone up there?"

"It's all right," Bertie called. "Look out below."

The canvas-wrapped bundle swung as he lowered it, and kept banging against the rock face in a grisly fashion. The stench was really quite horrid, but not even Cyrus backed away. He was watching Bertie, who stood with feet braced, paying out the rope. Ramses's assessment had been correct; he had strength enough for this. The bundle was not very large.

It settled onto the rock-strewn ground with a flexibility I prefer not to describe, and Bertie immediately began to descend. Drawing his knife, Ramses cut the rope and would have lifted the body out of Bertie's way had not Selim intervened. Hassan hastened to help him lift it onto a rough litter and carry it away.

"Well!" I said, drawing the first deep breath I had taken for several minutes. "Thank goodness that is safely accomplished. Now let us . . . Nefret? Nefret, where are you going?"

She had followed after Selim and Hassan and stopped them, far enough away so that the horrible smell did not reach us.

"Hell and damnation," Emerson ejaculated. "She isn't . . . She surely won't . . ."

The men lowered the litter to the ground. Emerson emitted an even more blistering oath and started toward them.

"No, Father," Ramses said.

"But—did she tell you she—aren't you going to stop her?"

Ramses shook his head. "She didn't tell me, but I suspected she would, and no, I am not going to stop her. I played the masterful husband before. I ought not have done so. It is her decision and her right. Please don't interfere."

He went to join Nefret and stood watching, his hands in his pockets. She looked up at him and spoke, briefly, before returning to her grisly task. "What is he doing?" Emerson demanded.

"Just being with her," I said. "Sharing the unpleasantness in the only way he can. It is really very sweet, Emerson."

"A sweet experience to share," Emerson growled. "Well, curse it, I can do no less. I will just go and—"

"No, Emerson. What about a spot of lunch while we are waiting? Bertie, I neglected to commend you on a task well done. Would you care for a cheese sandwich?"

Bertie had removed the cloth that had covered his mouth and nose. "Good Lord, Mrs. Emerson, I . . . Well, yes, thank you, if it isn't too much trouble, but she—Nefret—it is quite a horrible object, you know, and the sight of food—"

"Don't worry about her," I said.

Cyrus only shook his head. He had known Nefret longer than Bertie had.

Though I am accustomed to corpses in all stages, from newly slain to long mummified, I was not particularly anxious to examine this one, or even to watch from a distance. I kept my eyes averted until Selim and Hassan rewrapped the bundle and replaced it on the litter. When Nefret and Ramses came back I observed that her hands and forearms were red, not with blood, but from the gritty sand with which she had cleaned them. She was perfectly composed—more so than Ramses, whose features were not so controlled as they usually were. At my suggestion he got out the bottle of alcohol and poured it over her hands. She then seated herself and asked for a sandwich.

The others watched her with varying degrees of admiration and consternation. Jumana's eyes were enormous in a face that had lost its healthy color. "How could you?" she quavered.

"It's my profession," Nefret said calmly. "Not an enjoyable profession at times like this one, but I'm used to it. I knew the family wouldn't allow a proper autopsy, so this was my only chance to determine how the poor man died."

"Well?" Emerson demanded. "Did you?"

Nefret drank deeply from the water bottle before replying. "Fractured skull. The back of his head was . . . I won't go into detail."

"Thank you," Cyrus muttered, eyeing his sandwich with distaste.

"There were a number of broken bones," Nefret went on. "I looked for a bullet or knife wound, but it wasn't easy to . . . Well, I won't go into that either. The head injury was enough to have killed him."

"Fall or blunt instrument?" I inquired.

Nefret shrugged. "Impossible to determine. I did the best I could, but without the proper instruments—"

"Yes, quite," said Emerson.

Selim returned to announce that Hassan had gone on with the cart and its burden, and we continued with our lunch. Daoud soon joined us. He had come round the long way, since he was not fond of climbing ropes, up or down.

"Are there more tombs in these cliffs?" Bertie asked, accepting another sandwich.

"Unquestionably," Ramses replied. "If this area was used for the burials of royal females during the Eighteenth Dynasty, which seems likely, there are a number of known queens whose mummies have never been found, and Heaven knows how many unknown princesses and kings' lesser wives."

"Not to mention princes," Nefret added, her eyes shining with archaeological fervor. "And royal mothers and sisters and—"

"Cousins and aunts," I said, with a chuckle, reminded of one of my favorite Gilbert and Sullivan arias.

The others acknowledged my little joke with smiles and nods, except for Emerson, who sat like a boulder, staring off into space, and Selim, who was growing restless.

"The horses will not run away," he said. "Not our horses. But we should not leave them there too long."

Emerson jumped up. "Quite right, quite right. I will—er—this will only take a minute."

I had expected Emerson would want to get into the cursed tomb. I was not the only one who attempted to make him see reason, but he waved all objections aside. "I only want to have a look."

"Put on your pith helmet, Emerson," I called after him.

"Yes, yes," said Emerson, not doing so.

He started to climb the rope, moving with an agility remarkable in so heavy a man. He had not got very far when the quiet air was rent by a prolonged, high-pitched scream. It was not an animal. No creature in Egypt made a sound like that. Emerson lost his grip on the rope and dropped down, staggering a bit before he got his balance.

"What the devil—" he began.

"He's up there." Ramses handed his father the binoculars he had snatched up. I saw the figure now, atop the cliff. It was too far away for me to make out details, but it was capering and prancing, waving its arms and kicking up its heels, as if in a grotesque dance. Small bits of rock rattled down the sheer face.

I took the binoculars from Emerson and when I raised them to my eyes the bizarre figure took on form and substance. Its only garment was a short skirt or kilt. The body was human. The head was not. Pricked ears and protruding muzzle were covered with coarse brown hair, and fanged teeth fringed the jaws.

Ramses ran toward the cliff. I knew what he intended, and I felt reasonably certain that Emerson would follow after him. Handing Nefret the binoculars, I drew my little pistol from its holster, aimed, and fired.

I did not expect I would hit the creature. Obviously I did not, for a long mocking laugh, almost as unpleasant as the animal scream, followed, and the monstrous figure vanished from sight.

"Come back here this instant, Ramses," I shouted. "Emerson, if you attempt to climb that rope I will—I will shoot you in the leg."

"Don't fire that damned pistol again," Emerson exclaimed, hurrying toward me. "Give it to me."

"I wouldn't really have shot you," I said, as he carefully removed the weapon from my hand. "But really, Emerson, haven't you better sense than to climb a cliff when there is someone up above who could knock you off the rope with a few well-placed rocks?"

"That's reasonable," Emerson conceded.

"Right," said Ramses, who had obviously had second thoughts. "We'll go up and around. No, not you, Bertie, you've done your bit for today."

"Nor you, Peabody," my husband added. "Stay here and—and head him off if he comes down."

"Give me back my pistol, then," I shouted, as he and Ramses went trotting off, accompanied by Selim. Emerson did not pause but his reply was clearly audible. "Hit him with your parasol."

I patted Nefret on the shoulder. "Don't be concerned, my dear. He will have taken himself off by the time they get to the top."

"Then what is the point of their going?" Nefret demanded. "Oh, I know; it's Father, of course. He is determined to get into that bloody damned tomb one way or another."

"Well now, you can't blame him," Cyrus said. "There must be something in there the fellow doesn't want us to find or he wouldn't have tried to scare us off."

"It was an afrit, a demon," Jumana muttered, twisting her slim brown hands together.

It was not one of her better performances, but Daoud, utterly without guile himself, patted her reassuringly. "Where the Father of Curses walks, no afrit dares approach."

"That was no afrit, it was a man, wearing some sort of mask," Bertie said coolly. "How could he have supposed such a silly stunt would frighten us away?"

I had wondered myself.

Knowing it would be some time before Emerson finished rooting around in the disgusting tomb, I found a (comparatively) comfortable seat and invited the others to do the same. We were able to observe some of their activities, rather like spectators in the pit of a theater or opera house, but after they had descended into the cleft, all three were out of sight. We saw no one else. I had not expected we would.

When they finally rejoined us, descending by means of the rope, they were all three in an appalling state of filth. Emerson, naturally, was the worst. He had removed his coat early in the day; he was now without his shirt. I recognized this garment in the bundle he carried under one arm. The bronzed skin of his chest and back was smeared with a disgusting paste compounded of dust, perspiration, bat guano, and blood from a network of scratches and scrapes, and his hands were even nastier. He did not smell very nice.

"Good Gad, Peabody, you won't believe what a mess they made of the place," he exclaimed. "The floor of the burial chamber looks like a rubbish heap, with chunks of rotted wood and soggy bones mixed with bits of stone."

He squatted and began unwrapping his bundle. Selim, who was far more fastidious in his habits than my husband, set about scrubbing his hands and arms with sand.

"If there was nothing left, what were you doing all that time?" Nefret asked, handing Ramses a dampened handkerchief.

"Taking measurements and notes." He wiped his mouth

before he went on. "Father managed to salvage a few odds and ends."

Still squatting, Emerson studied the motley objects he had collected. They included a rim fragment from a stone vessel, scraps of gold foil, and a number of jewelry elements, beads and inlays and spacers. Rapt in contemplation of these uninspiring artifacts, he did not so much as twitch when I uncorked my bottle of alcohol and trickled the liquid down his scraped back. I honestly believe I could amputate one of Emerson's limbs without his taking notice if he had found something of archaeological interest.

"We had some trouble getting into the descending passage," Ramses explained. "It had been blocked with stones, and the thieves removed only enough for them to wriggle through. It was rather a tight squeeze for Father."

"And you," said Nefret. "At least you had sense enough to wear your coat."

"I had writing materials and a torch in my pockets," Ramses said. He fished a wad of crumpled paper from inside his coat.

"You can work up your notes into a detailed plan tonight," said Emerson, without looking up. "Curse it, Peabody, what are you doing?"

"You have scratches all over your chest too," I said. "Lean back."

"Not a scrap of organic material survived," Emerson grumbled. "Wood, mummy wrappings, bones— Ouch."

"I doubt that even we could have preserved the coffins or the mummies," Ramses said.

"We could have tried," Emerson muttered. "Damn the bastards! Who knows how much historical data was lost through their carelessness?"

"The damage is done, and regret is the most futile of all emotions," I said.

"No, it damned well is not," Emerson snarled. "Don't quote aphorisms at me."

"What, in your opinion—"

"Mother," said Nefret, gently but firmly, "you and Father can argue about aphorisms all the way home if you like. I think we should start back."

"A very sensible suggestion, my dear," I replied. I could see she was itching to get Ramses home so she could clean him up and disinfect the abrasions that marked his hands and face. "Emerson, give me my pistol back."

"Not on your life, Peabody. If any shooting is required, I will do it."

None was required, though we kept a sharp lookout along the way. As the sun sank lower, the shadows lengthened, affording some relief from the heat but, as I was uneasily aware, offering greater possibilities of concealment for a following foe. We reached the place where the horses were waiting without incident, however, and started on the homeward path. Daoud walked beside Jumana, talking nonstop in an effort to cheer her up. Like the rest of us, Selim was not so charitably inclined toward the girl.

"She knows where he is," he muttered. "She must be made to tell us."

"Give her a little time," Emerson said.

Selim's eyes were as hard as obsidian. "Jamil has disgraced the family. It is a matter of honor."

Oh dear, oh dear, I thought—more trouble! Men have very odd definitions of honor, and even odder notions of what to do about it. To all intents and purposes Selim was the head of the family, as his father had been. Yusuf was too old and vacillating to play the role that was nominally his. If Selim spoke for the family and they were of the same mind . . . They would be, of course. The men, at any rate.

"Selim, we don't know that that was Jamil," I said. "In fact, we don't know that he has committed any criminal act except rob a few tombs. I doubt any court would bother prosecuting him for that. Everybody in Gurneh does it."

"Not our family," said Selim, displaying his teeth. "My father—"

"I know what Abdullah would have done," Emerson

broke in. "I promise you, family honor will be satisfied. If Jamil has a scrap of sense he will come to me and I will give him a chance to redeem himself. The Father of Curses does not break his word!"

"You needn't shout, Emerson," I exclaimed.

"Hmph," said Emerson. "Confound it," he added petulantly, "I have wasted too much time on this foolery. We will start work at Deir el Medina tomorrow."

Dinner was a trifle late that evening, since Emerson was determined to stow his bits and pieces away before he bathed. They looked rather pitiful on the shelves of our storage room—the only artifacts we had discovered thus far. Emerson was pleased with them, however, and could talk of nothing else all through dinner. The meal was excellent. We had a new chef, Maaman, one of Fatima's cousins; our old cook, Mahmud, had been persuaded to retire. For years he had punished us for coming late to meals by scorching the soup and letting the beef dry out.

After dinner, when we had retired to the parlor, and Jumana had gone to her room to study, I managed to get Emerson off the subject of archaeology. "I hope you convinced Selim that he must leave Jamil to us. If he and the other men injured the boy, it would split the family apart. Not all of them take the matter as seriously as Selim does; some may even sympathize with Jamil."

"Why do you suppose I was talking so loudly to Selim? I wanted the others, especially Jumana, to overhear. The boy has done nothing except bully his sister and play the fool— if it was he we saw. We don't know that. We don't know that he killed that fellow, or even that murder was committed! It may have been an accident, or self-defense. These beggars squabble constantly amongst themselves. All we know for certain is that some person unknown placed the body in position, possibly as a warning or a threat, possibly only to hide it."

"That is all very well, Emerson, but two of the original

thieves have met a violent death. In criminal investigation—"

"This is not a criminal investigation," said Emerson, with a snap of his teeth. "We have no proof of murder."

Undeterred, I proceeded. "Then how do you explain the position of the body? It is a most inconvenient hiding place. How did Jamil—oh, very well, whoever it was—how did he get the body there?"

Emerson replied with a rhetorical question. "How did the ancient workmen get that damned sarcophagus of Hatshepsut's into her tomb in the cliff? That tomb is even less accessible than this one, and a stone sarcophagus is considerably heavier than a man."

"Perhaps it was meant to warn us, and others, away from the place."

"There was nothing of value left in the tomb," Emerson said. "Anyhow, Jamil knows better than to threaten *me*."

The shrubbery outside rustled, and Horus came in through the open window. He was carrying something in his mouth.

"Oh, my goodness," I exclaimed. "It's not a mouse—it's too big. A rat. Disgusting. Emerson—"

Emerson was too slow. Horus darted past him and laid the object at Nefret's feet. He then sat down and stared fixedly at her.

"It's not a rat," Ramses said. He reached down and scooped the motionless form into his hands. "It's a cat—a kitten. I'm afraid it's . . ."

A faint but unmistakable purr contradicted his assumption. The small creature was so dirty I could not make out its markings.

Nefret said gently, "Cats sometimes purr when they are frightened or in pain. If it is beyond help, we had better put it out of its misery."

The parlor door opened. Sennia stood on the threshold, rubbing her eyes. "Horus woke me up. He had . . . Oh!"

Emerson caught hold of her. "Now, child, don't touch it. It is sick, or hurt, or . . ."

Sennia leaned against Emerson. She looked charming, her hair ruffled with sleep and the hem of her white nightdress baring slim brown feet and ankles. "If it is sick, Aunt Nefret will make it well."

"Oh, Sennia . . ." Nefret glanced at the motionless body Ramses cradled in his cupped hands. "I'll try. I'll do my best. Go back to bed, darling."

"Yes, Aunt Nefret. Horus, you are a good boy. Come to bed now, Aunt Nefret will take care of the kitty."

Horus considered the suggestion. With what looked alarmingly like a nod of acquiescence, he got up and followed Sennia out.

"Oh, dear," I said. "Nefret, do you think you can . . . What is wrong with it?"

"I don't know yet." Nefret shrugged helplessly. "But I'll have to find out, won't I? Bring it along, Ramses."

As I might have expected, Sennia was the first one down next morning. Gargery was trying to get her to eat her porridge—never an easy task—when we entered the dining room. She bounced up from her chair and ran to me. "How is the kitty? When can I see it?"

"I don't know, Sennia. Ramses and Nefret have not come yet. Sit down and eat your breakfast. Where is Horus?"

"Under her chair," said Gargery grimly. "As usual. Madam, what is all this about another cat? We don't need one. We don't need *that* one," he added, with a baleful look at Horus.

"It is only a little cat," said Sennia. "It is sick, but Aunt Nefret is going to make it well."

Her bright, confident face made my heart sink. What she expected, in her innocent fashion, might be impossible, even for Nefret. Emerson cleared his throat. "Er—Sennia, the cat was—er—very sick. It may not . . ."

"There they are!" Sennia was out of her chair again, running to them. She threw her arms round Nefret's waist. "Why didn't you bring the kitty, Aunt Nefret?"

"It needs to rest," Nefret said, after the obligatory grunt of expelled breath. "But it is better. Much better."

Emerson's face displayed his relief. He is such a sentimentalist about children, he could not bear to see Sennia disappointed. He did not even object when the entire conversation centered on the cat, for Sennia would talk of nothing else. She demanded a detailed diagnosis.

"Malnutrition and dehydration," Nefret said. "With the attendant infections. The little creature has quite a will to live, though. The first thing it did was stagger to the food we put out for it and gulp it down. Then it tried to climb up Ramses's leg."

Sennia laughed. "Did it scratch, Ramses?"

"Not really. Its claws aren't any longer than your eyelashes."

"It thinks Ramses is its mother," Nefret said. Sennia chortled, and Nefret added, "He sat up most of the night holding it."

"It needed to be kept warm," Ramses mumbled, looking embarrassed. "And it wouldn't stay in its basket."

"I am going to see it now," Sennia announced. "You want to see it, too, don't you, Gargery?"

Gargery tried to think of something that would express his feelings to the rest of us without betraying them to Sennia. He failed. "Yes," he said resignedly.

The kitten served one useful purpose. I did not want to take Sennia with us on our first day at the dig, and she would have insisted on coming but for the distraction. Nefret offered to give her her first lesson in bones after the patient had been inspected, and Sennia promised to leave it alone the rest of the day. A convalescent does not fare well with an enthusiastic child poking at it, however good the child's motives, and I took it for granted that the creature was not housebroken.

Naturally Ramses stayed with them, and Sennia kindly agreed to let Jumana join her biology lesson. They were to

bring the horses and meet us later at Deir el Medina, where
Selim and Daoud were waiting for us with the men they had
hired.

Few tourists visit the site, which is tucked into a little valley in the hills of the West Bank. The only attraction for
them is the Ptolemaic temple at the north end of the valley. It
is a nice enough temple in its way, but it is too late in date to
interest us. The people who do go there follow the route that
includes more popular tourist attractions, from Deir el Bahri
to Medinet Habu.

There is another path, however, that ascends one of the
hills enclosing the settlement and continues at a considerable elevation, passing above the temples of Deir el Bahri on
its way to the Place of Truth, as the Valley of the Kings was
called in ancient times. We had often followed part of this
route, climbing the slope behind the temple and going on to
the Valley—or, as we had done two days earlier, striking off
on that hair-raising climb over the plateau.

It was not the easiest way of getting to Deir el Medina, but
Emerson proposed we follow it that first morning. He
wanted to see what condition the southern section of the
path was in, he explained. I was reasonably sure it was in exactly the same condition it had been the previous year and
for countless years before, but I did not demur. When we
reached the top of the hill above Deir el Bahri we stopped
for a moment, as Abdullah and I had so often done.

I knew that Emerson was also thinking of Abdullah as we
stood looking out across the desert and the cultivation. The
air was clear that morning; we could see the miniature
shapes of the temples on the East Bank, with the eastern
cliffs behind them. However, his only audible expression of
emotion was a loud clearing of his throat.

Instead of turning south toward Deir el Medina, Emerson
set off along the trail that led to the Valley. He had not gone
far before he stopped with a grunt of satisfaction. I could not
see what had occasioned the satisfaction; he was looking at

what appeared to be a row of tumbled stones, half-buried in sand.

"Emerson, what are you doing?" I demanded, as he knelt and began scraping away sand. "Stop that at once. You aren't even wearing gloves."

Emerson rose, not because I had told him to, but because he had had second thoughts. "They will have to be properly excavated."

"Those rocks? Why?"

"Good Gad, Peabody, what has become of your trained excavator's eye? That's a wall, or what is left of one, and there are others hereabouts. I noticed them some time ago, but saw no reason to investigate them."

"I don't see any reason to do it now."

"Think about it. It's quite a distance from the Valley to Deir el Medina. Wouldn't it be logical for a gang of workmen to camp here, close to the job, part of the time? A few smallish huts, such as these appear to be, would not be difficult to construct."

His eyes sparkled. Emerson is one of the few excavators in the business who derives as much pleasure from the humble minutiae of archaeology as from impressive temples and rich tombs. If he was correct, a small bit of the puzzle of the past would be filled in—and he usually was correct about such things.

"Well, my dear, that is very interesting," I said. "But hadn't we better be getting on? Nobody is going to bother your—er—huts."

Emerson tore himself away. The path was well traveled; we met goats and a few Egyptians afoot or on donkey-back. Emerson greeted them by name (except for the goats) but did not stop, though it was clear to me that one or two of the men would have liked to have gossiped a bit. The news of what had happened the day before must be all over the West Bank by now. We had not gone far, however, before we came upon persons of quite a different sort. There were nine

of them, six donkey drivers and three people in European
dress, and when they hailed us it was impossible to push on
past. I recognized the American party we had encountered
on board ship and later in Cairo.

Mrs. Albion's tall, spare frame was clad in garments that
were, I supposed, the latest in American notions of sporting
attire for ladies. Her linen coat had the fashionable military
cut and her skirts were calf-length. Her head was so
wrapped in veiling that her features were only a blur. She
was sitting sideways on the donkey, her neat boots dangling.
A true lady, of course, would rather fall off than ride astride.
It probably required two drivers to keep her in the saddle,
and the same was true of Mr. Albion, who rolled first from
one side and then to the other, with his drivers shoving him
back and forth. The process seemed to entertain him quite a
lot; he was red-faced with heat and laughter when the little
cavalcade halted. The younger man was red, too, but with
sunburn, not amusement. He removed his hat and inspected
me with cool curiosity.

Emerson, being Emerson, greeted the Egyptians first.
"Salaam aleikhum, Ali, Mahmud, Hassan . . . Good morning, er—um—"

"Albion," the gentleman in question supplied, while his
son stared curiously at us. "We met on the boat."

"No, we didn't," said Emerson.

Albion chortled. His face turned even redder. "Not for
want of effort on my part. Tried to track you down in Cairo,
too, but didn't succeed. Figured we'd run into you sooner or
later. How's the rest of the family?"

"Very well," I said. "Thank you. Where are you on your
way to this morning?"

"Just out for a little ride," said Mr. Albion. He took out a
large white handkerchief and mopped his face. "Say, you
folks couldn't introduce me to a few tomb robbers, could
you?"

Emerson had begun backing away. This remarkable request stopped him dead. "What did you say?"

"Well, we're collectors," Albion said calmly. "Especially Sebastian here. He's just crazy about ancient Egypt."

If I understood the meaning of that slang word, it did not suit young Mr. Albion. He did not look like a man who would go "crazy" over anything. His eyes were wide-set and somewhat protuberant, and as cool as ice-clouded water, whose color they matched.

"Yessir," his father went on cheerfully. "We've been collecting for quite a while. That's why we came out this winter, looking for more good stuff."

Emerson was staring, his astonishment now mitigated by amusement. I feared annoyance would soon mitigate the amusement, when he realized, as had I, that Albion was absolutely serious.

"The usual method of collecting antiquities," I said somewhat sarcastically, "is to buy from dealers. Mohassib in Luxor—"

"Been to see him already," said Albion. "'Scuse me for interrupting, ma'am, but I didn't want to waste your time."

"Thank you," I said, taken aback.

"You're welcome, ma'am. Now Mohassib has some fine things, but he's playing the dealer on me, trying to raise the price. I figure the best way is to go straight to the people he gets his stuff from. Cut out the middleman, eh?"

I looked at Mrs. Albion, wondering if she would display embarrassment at her husband's outrageous speech. She had loosened her veils. There was no doubt which side of the family her son favored. She had the same long face and thin lips and pale gray eyes. They were fixed on Mr. Albion with a look of fatuous admiration.

"Well?" said Mr. Albion hopefully. "You'd get your cut, of course."

"We are not dealers," Emerson said. "And I must warn you, Mr. Albion, that what you have proposed—in all innocence, I trust—is not only illegal but dangerous."

"Dangerous?" Mrs. Albion transferred her stare to Emerson. Her lips straightened out and her eyes lost their warmth.

"What possible danger could there be for us? We are American citizens."

"The danger," said Emerson, "is me. If you have not heard enough about me to understand my meaning, ask your guides. Let us go, Peabody."

I thought it best to take his advice. Emerson had kept his temper remarkably well—though I was unable to say the same about his grammar—but he was bound to lose it if the Albions went on in the same way. We went on, leaving three people gaping at us and six others concealing their grins behind rather dirty hands.

"Very good, Emerson!" I exclaimed. "You did not use bad language—and under considerable provocation, too."

"Don't talk to me as if I were Sennia," Emerson grumbled. His well-shaped lips twitched, and after a moment he began to laugh. "One can't become angry with people like that. Introduce him to a few tomb robbers! I would be tempted to cultivate him for comic relief, if we didn't already have enough of it in this family."

"The boy didn't utter a word," I said.

Emerson was still in an amazingly good humor. "He isn't a boy. He appears to be about the same age as Ramses. I suppose you find his reticence suspicious?"

He began to chuckle again, and I joined in; not for worlds would I have taken umbrage at his little joke. I did find the younger Mr. Albion suspicious, however. Either he was completely cowed by his father or he did not deign to express his own ideas, whatever they might be. And what had brought that oddly assorted trio to the difficult path? Where had they come from, and why? It was possible, if nerve-racking, to ride a donkey up the steep path from the Valley of the Kings, but I would not have supposed that Mr. Albion or his elegant wife would be up to it. The downward path was even more hazardous on donkey-back, and so was the descent behind Deir el Bahri.

Our path was relatively level until we reached the hill overlooking the little valley of Deir el Medina. We paused there, not to rest, for it had been an easy stroll, but to get a bird's-eye view of the site.

The tombs of Deir el Medina had been known and looted for many years. They were relatively unpretentious, the shaft leading down to the burial chamber surmounted by small chapels crowned with miniature brick pyramids. Many of the latter had crumbled and fallen and the remaining chapels were in very poor condition. However, the underground chambers were often beautifully decorated. They were the tombs of the people who had lived in the village below. It was still largely unexcavated. Studying the rough, partially exposed walls, Emerson burst out, "Confound the lazy, incompetent scoundrel! Only look what he has done to the place!"

He was referring to Mr. Kuentz, our predecessor, who had been arrested (thanks to us) the previous year. "He hasn't done much," I said, hoping to calm my grumbling spouse. "I expect he was too busy with his other activities—spying and tomb robbing. They do take time."

"He has put his damned rubbish dump smack in the middle of the site," Emerson exclaimed. "I will have to do it all over again."

He always said that.

We scrambled down the hillside. Selim joined us, and Emerson began rapping out orders. The men scattered. Emerson stripped off his coat and rolled up his sleeves. "Where is Ramses?" he demanded.

"They will be coming shortly, I am sure. If you want to start the surveying, I am perfectly capable—"

"Very good of you, Peabody, but I believe I will just wait for Ramses. Why don't you arrange one of your—er—your little rest places?"

I had intended to do it anyhow. In my opinion, periods of rest and refreshment increase efficiency. Shade is hard to come by when the sun is directly overhead, and it was at that time of day we—and the dear devoted horses—would need it most. I prefer tombs to all other forms of shelter, naturally, but there was not much left of the superstructures of the small tombs on the hillside. I concluded that the temple at the far end of the village would serve me best.

A number of deities had shrines there, but the principal dedicatee was Hathor, one of the great goddesses of the Egyptians. Since these broad-minded ancients were not especially concerned with consistency, Hathor played a number of different roles over the long centuries and was identified at various times with other goddesses, but her primary function was that of nurturer and protector, of the living and the dead. The lover called upon her for help in winning his beloved; the barren woman prayed to her for a child. She was worshiped with music and dancing, and her epithets included some of the loveliest phrases in the liturgy—Mistress of All That Exists, Lady of the Sycamore, Golden One.

I wandered about for a time, examining some of the reliefs. One of our fellow Egyptologists had partially restored the temple a few years earlier, and there was a nice little corner in the vestibule which suited my purposes admirably. With the efficiency I had come to expect of him, Selim had brought all the equipment I would need, including a large piece of canvas. He was too busy chasing after Emerson to assist me, so I got one of the other men to help me arrange rugs and campstools and tables, and make a temporary roof of the canvas next to the enclosure wall to provide shade for the horses. I was just finishing this essential task when the others arrived. Emerson, whose eye is everywhere, immediately bellowed "Ramses!" and after a nod at me, Ramses trotted off.

I ended up, as I usually did, with the rubbish heap.

I do not mean to minimize the importance of this task, for it is the aim of a good excavator to find every scrap, however uninteresting it may appear to be. Our men were very well trained, but when one is scooping up sand and rubble it is easy to overlook something. It was my task, therefore, to put the contents of the baskets brought me by the men through a sifter. It turned out to be a more interesting task than was often the case, since the previous excavator had been careless. I found quite a few interesting ostraca, scraps of limestone all scribbled over with hieratic. I puzzled over a few, while no one was looking, but could make out only a few signs. When we stopped for luncheon I handed them over to Ramses.

The ancient language was his specialty, as excavation was Emerson's, and he reacted with as much enthusiasm as Emerson had done over his wretched huts. We got not a word out of him during luncheon. Nefret had to keep jogging his elbow to remind him to eat.

"What does it say?" I asked.

"Hmmm?" was the only response.

Nefret brushed a lock of curling hair away from his forehead, and he gave her an abstracted smile before returning his attention to the scrap he held. I understood why she had been moved to that tender gesture. Absorbed in a task that challenged and delighted him like no other, he looked as happy as a child over a new toy. This was what he was meant to do. This was what he ought to be doing for the rest of his life, undisturbed by crime and war.

Knowing Ramses as I did, I realized there was not much chance of that, and I consoled myself with the thought that it was not my fault that he got in so much trouble—not entirely. According to the latest psychological theories, he must enjoy a certain amount of danger, or he wouldn't go out of his way to invite it. It made a change from hieratic, at any rate.

We put in a long hard day, removing Kuentz's rubbish dump, and Emerson began the survey of the site. This was an onerous and time-consuming procedure, which some archaeologists neglected, but which Emerson considered absolutely necessary. If Kuentz had done such a survey, he had left no record of it. (Emerson would have done it again anyhow.)

Jumana was back to her normal self, cheerful, interested,

and willing, and even Ramses admitted she was of considerable help. All she had to do, really, was hold a stick level while the measurements were made, but it was a rather tedious task and she followed orders meticulously.

Naturally I kept a close eye on her. There were two possible explanations for her recovered good spirits: either she was not as attached to her brother as I had believed, and had dismissed him from her thoughts—or she was more devious than I had believed, and expected to hear from him again.

When we returned home I had several more nice ostraca for Ramses.

From Manuscript H

The windows of their bedroom faced the stables, but that building was some distance away and they would not have heard the soft noises if they had not been awake. They had been late getting to bed, since Ramses had to be pried away from his "nice ostraca." Once Nefret had got his attention she had no difficulty holding it, but it was he who heard the sounds, not she. Responding to the slow movements of his lips and hands, she was jarred out of her state of drowsy pleasure when he suddenly jumped up and went to the window.

"Hell and damnation," she began.

"Sssh. It's Jumana. She's leading one of the horses."

He started to climb out the window. "Put on some clothes," Nefret said, rising in her turn and fumbling in the dark for various discarded garments.

"Well, then, damn it, find—I don't care what—something. I can't let her get too far ahead."

He snatched the trousers from her hand and put them on, and then he was gone, over the sill and into the darkness. Nefret pulled a caftan over her head and found a pair of boots that turned out to be hers. She would need them; her feet were not as hardened as his. She caught him up as he was leading Risha, unsaddled and unbridled, out of the stable.

"Wait for me," she gasped.

"No time." He vaulted onto Risha's back, and in spite of her excitement and worry, the sheer beauty of the movement stopped her breath. She could do it sometimes, but never like that, never in a single seemingly effortless flow of muscle and sinew. He turned Risha with a touch of his knee and the stallion responded instantly, breaking into a canter. They looked like figures from the Parthenon frieze, the slender strength of the rider at one with his mount.

"Damn," said Nefret under her breath. She'd lost an additional few seconds gaping after him like a lovestruck girl. It was his fault for being so bloody beautiful on horseback.

And if she couldn't catch him up she wouldn't be there to help if, as seemed likely, Jumana was on her way to meet Jamil. What other reason could she have for stealing out at this hour of the night?

Moonlight stretched an inquiring head over the door of her stall; she was accustomed to go where Risha went, and wondered what was happening at this strange hour. Nefret led her out of the stall.

No acrobatics for her tonight, not in a long robe with nothing under it. She used the mounting block, grimacing as her bare thighs gripped Moonlight's hide, and tucking part of the robe under her.

Moonlight was too adult and well-behaved to prance with anticipation, but as soon as Nefret gave her the word she was off. Hands twisted in the mare's mane, Nefret let her have her head, knowing she would follow her sire.

The road was in fair enough condition the first part of the way, rising and falling and curving round the hills that rose out of the plain. She was nearing the edge of the cultivation, and the ruined temples that fringed it, before she saw Risha. Ramses had dismounted and was waiting for her. He greeted her with a grin.

"I hate to think what Mother would say about that ensemble, but I rather like the effect of the boots and the bare—"

"Where is Jumana?"

"Gone ahead, on foot." He gestured, and she saw another horse, the mare that had been assigned to Jumana. "We'd better leave the horses here, too."

"Thank you for waiting for me."

"If I hadn't, you'd have gone thundering by in hot pursuit," said her husband, lifting her off Moonlight and politely adjusting her skirts. "She doesn't seem to be aware that she is being followed, and I'd like to keep it that way."

"What are you going to do?"

"Catch him and put an end to this nonsense once and for all so we can get on with our work. Let's see if we can get close enough to overhear their conversation."

The walls of the Ramesseum raised shadowy outlines ahead and to their right. The temple was half ruined, but it was in better condition than the tumbled piles of stone and mud brick stretching off to the north—all that remained of the once-proud mortuary temples of other pharaohs. West of Ramses's temple the ground was broken by extensive brickwork, probably the former storage areas of the temple.

"How are we going to find them in this maze?" Nefret breathed, trying to step lightly.

"Sssh." Ramses stopped and listened, his head raised. He must have heard something, for he took her arm and led her on, toward one of the piles of rubble. They had almost reached it before Nefret heard the voices.

"You're late," Jumana whispered. "Are you well?"

"Did you bring the money?"

"All I could. It isn't much."

"It is not enough. I need more. Get it from the Inglizi and bring it to me tomorrow night."

"Steal from them? No, I will not do that. Jamil, the Father of Curses has said he will help you. Go to him, tell him you—"

"What will the Father of Curses do for me—make me a basket carrier? Why are they at Deir el Medina?"

"Excavating—what do you suppose? They trust me. They are teaching me what I want to know."

"But they were in the Cemetery of the Monkeys. I thought they meant to work there."

"You have been spying on them!"

"Watching them," Jamil corrected. "What is wrong with that?"

"Nothing . . ." Her voice trailed off. "Jamil, they found the body of Abdul Hassan in the tomb. Did you . . . It was not you who killed him, was it?"

"It was an accident. He fell." Jumana's gasp was loud enough to reach Nefret's ears, and Jamil realized he had made a mistake. His voice became soft and caressing. "Jumana, I didn't mean it when I threatened to kill the Brother of Demons. I was frightened and hungry and lonely. I mean no harm to anyone! Dear sister—I know where there is another tomb. It is in the Gabbanat el-Qirud. Do you see how I trust you? All I need is enough money to keep me for a while, until I can sell some of the small objects from the tomb. There is no crime in that. The tombs do not belong to the Inglizi, they belong to us."

Ramses put his mouth to Nefret's ear. "I'm going round the back. I doubt he's armed, but if he is, don't get in his way."

He squeezed her shoulder and slid away. A jackal howled in the hills, and the village dogs answered it. Cautiously Nefret shifted one foot and then the other. She could see them now, dark shapes near one of the standing sections of wall. Jamil skulked in the shadow; he was wearing a robe of some muted color, dark blue or brown, but his headcloth showed palely against the mud brick. Jumana's small form was faintly lit by starlight. She was still arguing with him, trying to convince him to turn himself in, but she was wavering. Jamil no longer made demands, he pleaded and wheedled. He put his arm round her, and she embraced him.

The ground was a bewildering jumble of stone and masonry, of shadow and pallid light, but Nefret could see a path of sorts, winding its narrow and tortuous way from the opening where she stood toward the wall. It was the quickest and easiest way out of the area, but surely not the only one.

"Come again tomorrow night," Jamil begged. "Even if you cannot bring the money, just so I can see you again. I have missed you."

"I'll try," Jumana whispered. "I have missed you, too, and worried about you. Jamil, please, won't you—"

"We will talk about it tomorrow." He freed himself from her clinging arms and moved away, along the path Nefret had seen, toward her.

"Jamil!" Ramses had waited until Jamil was some distance away from his sister. Now he rose into view from behind one of the fallen sections of wall. Even though Nefret had known he was somewhere about, his sudden appearance and clear hail startled her into an involuntary cry. Jamil stopped as if he had been struck, spun round, and let out a much louder cry when he saw Ramses poised atop the rubble, looking—Nefret could not help thinking—like one of the more attractive djinn.

"Don't move," Ramses ordered. "We only want to talk to you."

The boy's paralysis lasted no more than a second or two. He bolted, with Ramses after him; but he had a clear run, and Ramses had to scramble over the debris that separated him from the path. Nefret stepped out into the open.

"Jamil, stop!" she called. "We won't hurt you."

He was ten feet away, close enough for her to see the scarf he had drawn over the lower part of his face. He dropped down, as if he were kneeling, and she thought exultantly, we've got him now.

She had no warning. Jamil straightened, and the missile came hurtling toward her. There was only time enough to turn, her arms clasped protectively around her body, so that the stone struck her shoulder instead of her breast. She fell sideways, her other shoulder and hip smashing against the hard unevenness of the ground. The fall knocked the breath out of her and she curled herself up like a hedgehog as Jamil ran past. Ramses must have been hot on his heels; a moment later she felt a touch she could never have mistaken for that of anyone else. She rolled over, into the curve of his arm.

"Go after him," she panted.

"The hell with him. Lie still. Where does it hurt?"

"Everywhere." She managed a smile. "It's all right, darling, nothing is broken."

His answering smile was forced. "You wouldn't lie to me, would you?"

"Not about a broken leg." She let out a yelp of pain as his hand explored her arms and shoulders. "Ow! I'll have some spectacular bruises, but that's all."

She realized then that his were not the only hands she felt. Kneeling, her eyes like dark holes in the small oval of her face, Jumana was straightening her skirt, smoothing it carefully over her calves. It was a useless gesture, but the girl seemed to be in a state of shock.

Not so shocked she couldn't speak, though. "It was my fault. You might have been struck in the face. He didn't care if you were hurt. I will go back to my father's house."

"No, you won't." Ramses lifted Nefret and stood up. "You will follow us, leading Moonlight. You"—he looked down at his wife—"are coming with me, on Risha."

"All right," Nefret said meekly.

His heavy black brows drew together. "You *are* hurt!"

"Mostly in places I wouldn't care to mention." She raised one hand to his cheek. "Riding astride, sans trousers, is something I won't try again for a while."

Five

Emerson and I and Sennia were halfway through breakfast when the children made their appearance, followed by the kitten. I observed immediately that Nefret was walking without her usual grace—not limping, but trying not to. Sennia bounced up out of her chair and ran to them; before she could give Nefret one of her fierce hugs, Ramses snatched her up and swung her round and round until she squealed with pleasure.

"Has something happened?" I asked.

Nefret subsided, very carefully, into the chair Emerson held for her, and gave me a warning look. "Just a fall. Good morning, Little Bird. You had better hurry and finish breakfast, or you will be late for your lessons."

"I think I will not go to them today," Sennia announced. "I think I will stay and take care of Aunt Nefret." She sat down on the floor and began stroking the kitten.

"I think you will not," I said. "Don't dawdle. You must not keep Mrs. Vandergelt waiting."

We got Sennia off after the usual argument; it was not so much the lessons, which she had proclaimed "only somewhat boring," as her desire to be with us. Emerson caved in, as she had known he would, and promised she could come with us to Deir el Medina next day.

"We must go," he declared. "Where is Jumana? Good Gad, the girl is always late."

"I told her not to join us until after Sennia had left," Ramses said. "That must be she now."

When she crept in I understood why Ramses had not wanted Sennia to see her. The girl had no self-control; every emotion she felt showed on her face and in her movements. Just now she looked like a little old woman, her head bowed and her movements slow.

"Did she suffer a fall too?" I inquired.

"No!" Jumana raised her head. Her brown eyes were pools of tragedy. "I have done wrong. Very wrong. I wanted to run away, but I did not, because I knew I should be punished. Do to me whatever you—"

"Stop carrying on and sit down," I said impatiently. "Something to do with Jamil, I suppose. No, Jumana, I do not want any more theatrics. Emerson, be quiet. Ramses?"

He gave us a bare outline of what had transpired; and the sympathy for Jumana that had softened Emerson's keen blue eyes turned to wrath.

"Good God," he shouted. "He might have killed you! Nefret—Ramses—why didn't you wake me?"

"There wasn't time, Father," Ramses said. He was certainly correct about that; it takes Emerson at least ten minutes to get his wits together when he has been suddenly aroused. Ramses went on in the same quiet voice, "I miscalculated. I ought to have sent Nefret round to flush him out instead of leaving her there alone."

"Let us not have any further beating of breasts," I said, for I knew his tendency to blame himself for anything that went wrong, whether it was his fault or not. To be sure, it often was his fault, but in this case anyone might have done the same.

Emerson had gone to stand by Nefret. He put out his hand, and then drew it back. "The stone struck your shoulder?"

"Yes." She turned her head to look up at him and winced

even as she smiled. "I have a few bruises, but that's all the damage."

I cleared my throat. "Your medical expertise is far beyond mine, of course, but if you would like me—"

"Thank you, Mother, but there is no need. It's all right. Everything is all right," she added softly.

"Ah," I said. "Good. Well. What are we going to do about Jamil?"

That produced another outburst from Jumana, in the course of which she swore she would never trust Jamil again, and proposed that we beat her and lock her up on bread and water, or marry her off to disgusting old Nuri Said, who had often asked her father for her. She deserved nothing better. She deserved any fate we might decree, and would accept it.

I was tempted to shake her, but forbore, deciding I might as well allow her the privilege of self-expression. When she finally broke off for want of breath, her eyes were swimming with tears. I did not doubt she was utterly sincere, nor did I doubt that at the same time she was enjoying herself immensely.

"Now, now," said Emerson feebly, "it's all right. Curse it, don't cry."

"How can you forgive me?" she demanded in tragic accents.

"We offered Jamil a second chance. Can we do less for you, who are guilty of nothing except misplaced love and loyalty?"

"Quite right," I said, before the melodrama could continue. "What is wanted now, Jumana, is for you to behave like—well, like Nefret and me. Tears and self-reproach are tricks some females employ in order to evade responsibility. I do not permit them here. You are—potentially—the equal of any man, and you must—"

"Peabody," Emerson said. His accents were severe, but there was a twinkle in his handsome blue eyes.

"Yes, quite. I believe I have made my point, Jumana. You

did a foolish thing, and I trust you have learned a valuable lesson. The question I asked has not been answered. Have you another appointment with Jamil?"

Ramses answered for her. "I doubt he will keep it now. It was for tonight. The same place, Jumana?"

"Yes. We played in the ruins there, when we were children. But Ramses is right; he will not come now, he will believe I betrayed him. He has found another tomb. It is in the Cemetery of the Monkeys. But—" She was watching Nefret. "But you know. You were listening!"

Her voice held a note of accusation. Ramses, who in my opinion suffers from an overly sensitive conscience, was not moved on this occasion to apologize.

"You should be glad we did," he said. "You have nothing to be ashamed of, Jumana. You told him you would not steal for him, and you tried to persuade him to give himself up, and now you have confessed, of your own accord."

"So long as you have confessed all," I added, for Jumana had responded to his praise with a complacent smile. The young are resilient, and a good thing, too, for brooding over past mistakes is a waste of time; but it wouldn't do to let the girl off too lightly. "We are willing to give you a second chance, Jumana, but if I learn that you have held something back—"

"No. No, I swear!"

"So he's found another tomb, has he?" Emerson mused. "Talented young rascal."

I frowned at Emerson, who is too easily distracted by archaeological speculation, and continued my questioning of the girl.

"How did he communicate with you before?"

"I was given a message—just a scrap of paper, with a few words scribbled on it—yesterday, when we were at Gurneh. By Mohammed Hammad."

Swearing inventively, Emerson agreed we must stop at Gurneh on our way to the site and question Mohammed

Hammad. The village was up and about its daily business and we were greeted politely. However, when we called on Mohammed Hammad, we discovered that the bird had flown. His wife—his elderly wife—said he had business in Coptos. His son said he had gone to Cairo. One of his acquaintances was more forthcoming. "He ran away, Father of Curses, when he found out about the death of Abdul Hassan. I would have done the same." He added with a certain air of regret, "I was not one of those who robbed the tomb."

"You should thank Allah for that," Emerson said. "And pay more heed to his laws. You see how he punishes evildoers."

"There is nothing in the Koran about robbing tombs, Father of Curses."

Emerson's forbidding frown was replaced by a look of interest. He does so enjoy arguing theology. Before he could get off onto this sidetrack, I intervened. "Did Mohammed say who it was he feared?" I inquired.

The fellow hesitated, his eyes on Emerson's hand, which had gone into his pocket. He knew he would get more baksheesh if he came up with a name; he also knew that if he was caught in a lie, he would arouse the wrath of the Father of Curses.

"He did not have to say. One death may be an accident, but two is a warning. Jamil had threatened them. They laughed." He shrugged, spreading his hands wide. "They are not laughing now."

"Ah," said Emerson. "There would be a reward for the man who told us where the boy is hiding."

"A large reward?" The fellow thought it over and shrugged again. "Money is of no use to a dead man, Father of Curses."

"Quite a philosopher, isn't he?" Emerson remarked in English. He dropped a few more coins into the leathery brown palm and turned away.

The interview had taken place on the street, if it could be called that; in contrast to the ancient workmen's village, with its gridlike plan, the houses of Sheikh el Gurneh had been fitted into whatever space was available—along the slopes of the hill, around the tombs of the nobles of the Empire. Some of the less important, uninscribed tombs were occupied; the forecourt, where offerings had been made to the honored dead, now served the ignominious role of stables for the beasts of the tomb dwellers. In front of many of these tomb-caves stood cylindrical mud-brick structures like giant mushrooms with their edges turned up. They served the double purpose of granaries and sleeping quarters. The hollow on top is safe from scorpions, and there are even egg-cup-shaped projections along the rim to hold water jars—an interesting and unusual adaptation to local conditions, which I mention for the edification of the Reader.

After he had gone a few feet, Emerson stopped. "Mohammed can't have got the note directly from Jamil."

I might have accused him, as he often accuses me, of jumping to conclusions, but in this case I had to agree. "I hadn't thought of that," I admitted handsomely. "It does seem unlikely that Jamil would show his face openly in the village or risk betrayal by a man he had threatened."

"But he might have come secretly, by night, to a house where at least one person was likely to welcome him," Emerson said.

A brief, rather awkward silence followed. Jumana had stuck close by me; she was obviously uncomfortable in the village of her birth. How could she be otherwise, dressed as she was, the object of curious and hostile glances, especially from the older women?

"Is it my father you mean?" she asked.

"Yes," Emerson admitted. "How does he feel about Jamil?"

"I have not spoken to my father since he told me to leave his house and never come back."

There was not much anyone could say to that. Her hard, cold voice told me that even an expression of regret would be unwelcome.

"I meant to call on Yusuf before this," I said. "Shall we go round to see him now?"

Emerson took out his watch, looked at it, groaned, and said, "We are already late."

"Supposing you go on, then," I said. "You and Jumana. Nefret and I will inquire after his health and offer our medical skills. Ramses will go with us. No, Emerson, I really believe that is the best course. You would go thundering into the house and bully the old man until he confessed to anything and everything. My methods of interrogation—"

"I know what they are like," said Emerson, eyeing my parasol, which I had been using as a walking stick. "Oh, very well."

He stalked off. Jumana shot me a grateful look and trotted after Emerson. The rest of us went on up the hillside toward Yusuf's house, which was one of the finest in the village, and as we wended a tortuous path round granaries, walls, and rubbish heaps, I could not help thinking what an admirable place this would be for hide-and-go-seek—or for a fugitive who knew every turn of the path and every concealed tomb entrance.

Our arrival was not unheralded; we were trailed by a number of the curious, some of whom ran on ahead to announce we were coming, so that when we reached the courtyard in front of the house the entire household was waiting to greet us. Most of them were women and children; the men, skilled workers like the majority of Abdullah's kinsmen, had been employed by us or by Cyrus.

Courtesy demanded that we accept refreshments, and it was necessary to go through the formal rituals of greeting before I could get round to my inquiries. When I asked after Yusuf, there was no reply at first. Then Yusuf's chief wife, Mahira—a wrinkled little old lady who looked as if a strong wind would blow her over, but whom I had seen carrying loads that would have strained my back—replied, "He is at the mosque, Sitt Hakim. He will be sorry to have missed you."

"It is not the hour for prayer," said Ramses.

"He is always at prayer" was the reply. "At the mosque, here, or elsewhere. Will you have more tea, Sitt?"

I made our excuses and we took our departure.

"I thought you were going to question them about Jamil," Nefret said, as we made our way down the hill.

"It is unlikely that they know any more than we do," I replied. "Jamil's mother is long dead, and I fancy that the mothers of Yusuf's other sons were secretly delighted at seeing the old man's favorite fall from grace. He wouldn't ask any of them for help."

"I wonder what Yusuf is praying for," Nefret mused.

"One could hazard a guess," Ramses said dryly. "We may be on the wrong track here, Mother. Has it struck you that neither Jamil nor Yusuf can read or write?"

"Are you sure?"

"I'm sure about Yusuf. Jamil gave no evidence of literacy when he was working for us. But," Ramses admitted, "he might have had limited skills, which he was embarrassed to display because they *were* limited, or acquired them since."

He cupped his hands and helped me into my saddle.

"Ah well," I said, "we have done all we can for the moment, and speculation can get us no further. Perhaps this latest incident has finally convinced Jamil to leave Luxor."

The more I thought about it, the less likely it seemed that Jamil was capable of cold-blooded murder. The attack on Nefret had not been deliberate; he had responded in sheer panic, like a cornered animal. As for the body in the tomb, there was no evidence that Jamil had been responsible, nor did we know precisely how the man had died. He might have been struck on the head or pushed over a precipice, or fallen by accident. (Though that last possibility was, in my opinion, the least likely.)

The most worrisome part of the business was Jamil's claim that he had found another tomb—not because I believed he had, but because I feared Emerson did believe it. Jamil was a braggart and a liar, and I could think of several reasons why he might have wished to mislead us and his sister. In my opinion it would be the better part of wisdom to ignore his capering about the cliffs of the western wadis. He might be stupid enough to suppose he could frighten us off, but it was more likely that he was trying to entice us to follow him. But if he'd got in the habit of pushing people off cliffs . . .

As soon as we reached Deir el Medina I took Emerson aside and explained my conclusions. He listened in frowning silence, and when I went on to inform him of our failure to speak with Yusuf, he cut me off with a wave of his hand. "I didn't suppose you would learn anything from him anyhow, Peabody. The devil with him and Jamil."

By the end of the week we had surveyed the site and laid it out in regular grids. Emerson had of course decided to reexcavate the area our predecessor had examined, and the wisdom of his decision soon became evident. We found a number of interesting objects, including a basket of papyri. They were in wretched condition, but Ramses's eyes lit up at the sight of them, and for several evenings he worked late in the little laboratory he had set up at the house, carefully repairing and restoring them.

Sennia had been out with us twice, and had enjoyed herself a great deal running from one person to another and "helping" them. Gargery took to his bed as soon as we returned from these excursions. I pointed out to him that there was no need for him to follow so close on her heels; the site was enclosed, dozens of people were there, and I had strictly forbidden her to climb the hills on either side.

He shook his head. "You know how she is, madam, she can disappear in a twinkling when she wants, and she is all over the place, here one minute and there the next. What if that young villain Jamil lured her away, or she fell into one of those holes the men are digging?"

I thought it much more likely that Gargery would fall in, but he could not be dissuaded. His self-appointed duties were complicated even more by his suspicion of Jumana; he considered us hopelessly naive for believing in her reformation, and tried to keep an eye on her as well as on Sennia. The days Sennia spent with us were extremely lively, what with one thing and another. Horus was one of the things. We could not leave him at the house, since he bullied the maids and went raging about, breaking bric-a-brac and furniture. His determination to follow Sennia wherever she went led to several unpleasant scenes between him and Gargery.

The other cat was far less trouble. It had made a remarkable recovery, and once we had got it cleaned up it turned out to be quite a pretty creature, with an interesting pattern of black spots and a ringed tail; but it didn't want to stay at the house either. It trotted after Ramses, shrieking pitifully when he tried to leave for the dig, and it managed to escape from any confinement we arranged. Ramses would not allow it to be caged, and closed doors and shutters proved no impediment. I could not imagine how it got out, but Sennia felt certain she knew. "It is the Great Cat of Re," she announced. "It has magical powers."

Ramses's eyebrows tilted up in silent skepticism as he looked at the miniature creature sitting on his knee, and Sennia elaborated. "I know it is not very large just now, but it will grow."

Nefret had planned to name the creature Osiris, since it had virtually come back from the dead, but from then on it was the Great Cat of Re, and soon learned to answer to its name. Emerson, who is fond of cats and whose sense of humor is somewhat childish, found it very amusing to bellow out those sonorous syllables and have his summons promptly answered by a very small, very fuzzy kitten. At first Horus was fascinated by the creature. Seized by what appeared to be a misplaced maternal instinct, he would wash it till it squealed and carry it around in his mouth. He became bored with this eventually. Such is often the case, even with human parents.

Toward the end of the week Emerson proposed that we stop work early and go to Medinet Habu to see how Cyrus was getting on. We took the cat with us, since it would not be left behind. It was still small enough to fit into one of Ramses's pockets, and I must say it looked very peculiar with its paws hooked over the flap and its small head peering interestedly out at the world. Our cats had a considerable reputation in Egypt, being regarded as possessing supernatural powers. I suspected this one would prove to be no exception.

During the Pyramid Age, the temples serving the dead monarch's funerary cult were built close by the monuments. When the pharaohs of the Eighteenth Dynasty decided to hide their tombs in the depths of the western mountains, the temples had to be located elsewhere. At one time a long row of them ran along the edge of the cultivation. Most were now in a sad state of ruination, but Medinet Habu, the temple of Ramses III (not to be confused with Ramses II), was still well preserved, and full of interest. The fortified towers through which one entered the area were decorated in the conventional style, with reliefs of the king smiting various enemies; but the interior contained some charming scenes of his majesty dallying with ladies of the court. (Let me hasten to add that there were no vulgarities depicted.) The first great pylon stood almost intact, its walls and the walls of the courts and colonnades covered with reliefs and inscriptions. The place had been a residence as well as a religious edifice; a tumble of mud-brick walls indicated the site of what had once been a palace. In addition to the monuments of Ramses III, there were two other structures, one of which, begun in the early Eighteenth Dynasty, had been added on to by successive rulers clear down to the Roman period. Another, smaller, complex belonged to the God's Wives of Amon, who had held almost royal status in Thebes during the late dynasties. It was this area Cyrus was excavating.

We passed through the towers of the gateway into the great open court. Emerson's keen gaze swept the surroundings, from the smaller temple on our right, past the great pylons of Ramses III, and on to the left, where the chapels of the God's Wives stood. His handsome countenance proclaimed his emotion: greed, pure and simple. If Emerson has a particular Egyptological passion, it is for temples, as mine is for pyramids, and he had wanted for years to tackle Medinet Habu. However, as he had admitted to me only this past year, it would be the work of a lifetime. He said it again as he stared wistfully about—a man trying to convince himself of something he knows is true and does not want to believe.

"We haven't a large-enough staff," I said, as I had said before. "And there is no hope of hiring skilled persons at the present time. Many of our younger colleagues are in the army."

"Damned war," Emerson muttered. "But with Lia and David, and Walter and Evelyn—"

"Yes, my dear, that would be very nice, and I hope with all my heart that one day they will join us. Until then we must make the best of what fate has to offer, and accept the good with gratitude and the bad with fortitude."

"Good Gad," said Emerson, and went stamping off toward the rope-enclosed area where Cyrus's men were working.

Cyrus hailed us with pleasure and offered tea, which Emerson refused, without consulting anyone else. "I want to have a look round first, Vandergelt."

"You wasted your time coming here if you expected I'd have anything new to show you," Cyrus said grumpily, but he led the way toward the small building. On the lintel of the doorway were several rows of hieroglyphs, which Ramses scanned with an expert eye. The cat, which had climbed up onto his shoulder, leaned forward and stared as intently as he. I caught myself on the verge of asking it for a translation.

"What does it say?" I inquired, addressing Ramses.

"It's an invocation to visitors, asking them to pray for the Adorer of the God Amenirdis and her successor, who built the chapel for her. 'O you living ones who are on earth . . . if you love your children and would leave to them your positions, your hopes, your lakes, and your canals . . . please say . . . ' The usual prayer, asking for bread and beer and every good thing for the lady's spirit."

"How sweet!" I exclaimed.

Ramses gave me an amused look. "Not really. The lady asks very nicely, but the inscription ends with what can only be described as a threat. If a visitor doesn't speak the proper words, he and his wife will be afflicted with illness."

The open forecourt, with columns on either side, led to an enclosed sanctuary. On the right of this building, which was both tomb and mortuary temple, were three smaller chapels, dedicated to a queen and two more of the God's Wives. I had always been intrigued by these ladies, for their status was unusual. Kings' daughters all, they were not kings' wives, but wives of the god Amon, who had apparently lost the ability to procreate as he had done in the Eighteenth Dynasty, when he visited the queen in the shape of her husband and fathered the royal heir. These God's Wives, who also held the title of Adorer of the God, did not bear children but adopted their successors. There were practical political reasons for this policy; the Late Period was a time of turmoil, with the throne of Egypt passing from pharaoh to usurper to conqueror and back; many of these men, residing in the north, sent royal daughters to Thebes to succeed the reigning God's Wife, achieving thereby continuity and a certain legitimacy.

The position was one of high honor, the occupant surrounded by luxury and prestige; but I had often wondered about the women themselves. Doomed to lifelong celibacy, forbidden the joys of motherhood, they had not even the pleasures of power to compensate, for it is more than likely—men being what they are—that the ladies were mere figureheads, controlled by the king and the powerful nobles of Thebes.

However, I would be the last to deny that celibacy has its advantages, when the alternative is a state marriage to a man unloving and unloved. As for the joys of motherhood . . . I glanced at Ramses, who was wandering about reading the inscriptions. We were using torches, since the inner chamber was enclosed and unlighted. Shadows outlined his well-cut features and the little half smile that betokened his total absorption. Yes, it had been worth it, though there had been times when I had serious doubts. However, not all children turned out as well as he had done.

We inspected the other chapels, which were not so well preserved. In the floor of one an irregular hole gaped, where the stone flooring blocks had been taken up.

"Not a durned thing down there," Cyrus complained.

Emerson glared at him. "Curse it, Vandergelt, I told you the burial chambers were empty. You had better replace the flooring before some damned fool tourist falls in."

"I thought maybe there might be another burial," Cyrus said defensively. "There are four chapels and five God's Wives."

"More than five," Ramses said. He proceeded to reel off the names. They had an exotic, almost poetic cadence. "Karomama, Tashakheper, Shepenwepet, Amenirdis, Nitocris, Ankhnesneferibre."

"So where are the rest of 'em?" Cyrus demanded. "And the coffins and mummies of the ones who were buried here?"

"Jumana asked me that once," Ramses said. "She had a romantic notion that they might have been hidden away to protect them from tomb robbers."

"Nonsense," grunted Emerson.

"We know where two of the sarcophagi are, or were," I explained. "At Deir el Medina, in tomb shafts high on the hillside. They were dragged there by individuals who meant to usurp them for their own burials. One had actually been reinscribed with the name and titles of—er—"

"Pamontu," Ramses said. "A priest of the Ptolemaic or early Roman period, approximately five hundred years after the last God's Wife died and was buried."

"Just what I was about to say, Ramses."

"I beg your pardon, Mother."

"It seems likely, therefore," I continued, acknowledging his apology with a nod, "that by the first century A.D. the original burial chambers here at Medinet Habu were empty except for the sarcophagi. They were too heavy and of no value to ordinary—"

"Yes, yes, Peabody," said Emerson. "Vandergelt, you're as bad as Jumana. There is some excuse for her, but you ought to know better. The brickwork west of here may be the remains of a fifth chapel."

"Abu and Bertie are working there now," Cyrus said, with a vague gesture toward the west. "So far, no luck. I'm getting tired of this, Emerson."

"Of what, the Saite chapels? I hope you aren't thinking of shifting to another area. You haven't the manpower to tackle the larger temples."

"Well, I know that!" He glanced at Ramses, who was talking to Nefret, and lowered his voice. "The truth is, Emerson, none of us has got the skill for this job. Oh, sure, we can clean the place up and make proper plans, but what's needed here is somebody to record the inscriptions and reliefs."

"You can't have Ramses," said Emerson.

"Emerson," I murmured.

"Well, he can't! I know, I said the boy could do anything he liked and work for anyone he chooses, but—er—confound it, Vandergelt, stealing another man's staff away is one of the lowest, most contemptible—"

"Gol-durn it, Emerson, I wouldn't do a thing like that!"

Their raised voices had caught Ramses's attention. "What seems to be the trouble?" he asked.

"No trouble," Cyrus declared. "Um—see here, Emerson, I just got to thinking . . . How about if we trade places? You take Medinet Habu and I'll take Deir el Medina."

Emerson opened his mouth, preparatory to delivering a cry of protest. Then his scowl smoothed out. He stroked his chin. "Hmmm," he said.

"Cyrus, that is an outrageous suggestion," I exclaimed. "You can't go trading archaeological sites as if they were kitchen utensils!"

"I don't see who's gonna stop us," Cyrus said stubbornly.

"The Service des Antiquités has got too much on its plate to bother with two respectable excavators like us. What do you say, Emerson, old pal?"

Emerson's face widened in a grin. "You want to get at those tombs at Deir el Medina."

"Any tomb's better than none," Cyrus retorted. "There's none here. What I'd really like to do is mount an expedition to the Cemetery of the Monkeys, but—"

"You'd break your neck climbing round those wadis," Emerson declared forcibly. "And waste your time. The most practical method of locating tombs in that area is to follow the Gurnawis—or go out after a heavy rainstorm, as they do."

"Well, it doesn't look like rain. Come on, Emerson, this job is right up Ramses's alley. Look at him."

He did appear to be enjoying himself. He and Nefret were absorbed with the reliefs—and each other. They were holding hands and talking in low voices as they moved slowly along the wall. With my customary rapidity of thought, I considered the pros and cons of Cyrus's suggestion. There were a good many things in its favor. The reliefs needed to be recorded before time and vandals destroyed them. This was a perfect place for the photographic technique of copying Ramses had developed, and Nefret would work at his side—close by him, in a nice, safe, enclosed area. And while they were doing that, Emerson could root around the ruins to his heart's content. However . . .

"Are we agreed?" Cyrus asked hopefully.

"Agreed on what?" Nefret asked, turning.

"Come and have some tea with Bertie and me, and we'll tell you all about it," Cyrus said.

As we left the chapel I lingered, looking up at the carved lintel. "An offering which the King gives, a thousand of bread and beer and every good thing . . ."

"Did you say something, Mother?" Ramses inquired.

"Just—er—humming a little tune, Ramses."

"What is Father up to now?"

"I will leave it to him to tell you, my dear."

And tell us he did, without asking anyone else's opinion or voicing a single reservation. Having had time to reconsider the matter, I had thought of several. M. Lacau, who had replaced Maspero as head of the Antiquities Department, might not find out about our violation of the rules for some time; he had returned to France for war work, leaving his second-in-command, Georges Daressy, to carry on. Daressy was a genial soul, whom we had known for years, but even he might be offended by our proceeding without his permission.

Considerations of this sort did not enter Emerson's mind. He had always done precisely as he liked, and had taken the consequences (though not without a great deal of grumbling). Realizing that Ramses had fixed me with a pointed stare, brows tilted, I was reminded of certain of those consequences, such as the time we had been barred forever from the Valley of the Kings after Emerson had insulted M. Maspero and everybody else in the vicinity.

I cleared my throat. "Perhaps we ought to give the matter a little more thought before we decide, Emerson."

"Why?" Emerson demanded. "It is an excellent idea. Ramses will enjoy copying the inscriptions—"

"I would prefer to go on at Deir el Medina, Father," Ramses said, politely but firmly. Emerson looked at him in surprise, and I gave Ramses an encouraging nod. It had taken him a long time to get courage enough to disagree with his father. "The site is unique," Ramses went on. "Do you realize what we might learn from it? We've already come across a cache of papyri and a number of inscribed ostraca; they confirm my belief that the people who lived in the village were craftsmen and artists who worked on the royal tombs in the Valley of the Kings."

"They were servants in the Place of Truth," Emerson interrupted. "Some scholars believe they were priests."

"Their additional titles indicate otherwise. Draftsman, architect, foreman—"

"Well, well, most interesting," said Emerson, who had

lost interest almost at once. "Your opinion is of course important to me, my boy. We will discuss it later, eh?"

He was set on his plan and had no intention of reconsidering it. When Cyrus reminded him that we had agreed to attend one of his popular soirees that evening, he did not even swear.

I turned to Bertie, who appeared to be in a pensive mood, for he had not spoken after his initial greeting.

"What do you think, Bertie?"

His brown hair had become sun-bleached and his face was tanned, so that he was a pale shade of brown all over. One could not call him handsome, but his pleasant, guileless smile was very attractive. "Whatever you decide is fine with me, Mrs. Emerson. I'm just a hired hand, as Cyrus would say."

"You appear to be in a pensive mood," I persisted. "You are feeling well?"

"Oh, yes, ma'am. Thank you."

"You took up archaeology to please Cyrus," I said, and patted his hand. "It was kind of you, Bertie, but he wouldn't want you to go on with it if you find it distasteful."

"I'd do more than that for him." Bertie blushed slightly, as Englishmen tend to do when they give vent to their emotions. "He's been jolly good to me, you know. I only wish . . ."

"What, Bertie?"

"Oh—that I could find something really first-rate for Cyrus. Not that I'm likely to," he added diffidently. "I really am keen, Mrs. Emerson, but I'll never be as good as Ramses. Or you, ma'am."

"One never knows," I said. "Many great discoveries are serendipitous. There is no reason why you should not succeed as well as another."

After finishing our tea we returned to Deir el Medina to consult Selim and Daoud. Daoud had no opinion on the subject; anything Emerson chose to do was acceptable to him. Selim folded his arms and looked severely at Emerson.

"We have made a good beginning here, Emerson."

"Cyrus and Bertie can carry on," Emerson replied blithely. "The boy is turning into a pretty fair excavator."

Selim glanced at Jumana, who was helping Ramses collect the ostraca that had been found that morning. "Will you leave her here with Vandergelt Effendi?"

Emerson grinned. "Does she annoy you?"

"She talks very loudly all the time. And I do not trust her."

"You are becoming as cynical as your father," I said. "I feel certain Jumana will tell us if Jamil attempts to reach her. Your inquiries in Gurneh have not produced any new information, have they?"

"No," Selim admitted.

"Then if you have no further objections, Selim, we will proceed with our plan," Emerson said. "You and Daoud with us at Medinet Habu, of course, and Jumana as well."

"Vandergelt Effendi will want to look for tombs here," Selim said dourly.

"No doubt." Emerson chuckled. "What's the harm in that?"

Cyrus's soiree was like all his parties—elegant and genteel. Since he was the most hospitable of men, he always invited everyone he could get hold of, so the company was mixed: friends who lived year-round in Luxor, tourists, a few professional associates—too few, alas, in these terrible times—and members of the military. I had got to the point where the very sight of a uniform depressed me, and I prayed that the day would soon come when the men who wore them could take them off and go back to their normal lives.

Those that survived.

I took a sip of the champagne Cyrus handed me and told myself to cheer up! No cloud shadowed Cyrus's lined countenance, and indeed he was one of the most fortunate of men. Wealthy and respected, happily married, absorbed in work he loved, he had required only one thing to fill his cup, and Bertie had given him that—the devoted affection of a son, and a companion in his work.

"What's on your mind, Amelia?" Cyrus asked. "You look kinda gloomy. Has that young villain Jamil turned up again?"

"No, we have heard nothing of him. I am sorry if I gave the impression I am not thoroughly enjoying myself, and I am ready to do my duty in entertaining your guests. Is there anyone you would like to be soothed, amused, or stirred up?"

Cyrus chuckled. "Especially the last. Anything you like, Amelia; but if you want to pick on someone, have a go at Joe Albion. He was a business rival of mine some years back, and he's got one of the best private collections of antiquities in the world. I wouldn't like to guess how he acquired some of them."

"I didn't know he was an acquaintance of yours," I said, recognizing the rotund shape and round red face of Mr. Albion. "He and his family were on the boat coming over, and we ran into them the other day near Deir el Bahri. What an odd family they are, to be sure. Mr. Albion asked us to introduce him to some tomb robbers."

Cyrus let out an emphatic American ejaculation. "Goldurn it! Sounds like Joe, all right."

"I thought he was joking. He is such a jolly little man."

"Jolly Joe." Cyrus grinned, but he began tugging at his goatee—a sure sign of perturbation. "Don't let that fool you, Amelia. He's got a reputation for going straight for the jugular."

"His wife appears quite devoted to him."

"It is an odd marriage," Cyrus admitted. "She's from one of the best families in Boston and Joe is common as dirt. Nobody could figure out why she married him; but she's living like a queen now—and the boy was raised like a prince."

I had no particular interest in talking with any of the Albions, so I moved about from one group to another, paying particular attention to those who were strangers or seemed ill at ease. It was my duty, but I cannot say I enjoyed it; most of the gentlemen would talk of nothing but the war. Emerson had been correct; the Germans had announced they would begin unrestricted submarine warfare, on all vessels of Allied and neutral nations. This put the tourists present in a somewhat awkward position. One of them, a tall, distinguished American named Lubancic, took the matter philosophically.

"They can't keep it up for long. This is going to get the American government riled up, and I wouldn't be surprised to see us get into this business pretty soon. Anyhow," he added with a smile, "Egypt's not such a bad place to be stuck for the duration. There's plenty to see and do, and prices are cheap, with the tourist trade down. Do you suppose there's any chance of my doing a little digging, Mrs. Emerson? Plenty of local men for hire, I believe."

It was a common enough question; few visitors understood the regulations that governed excavation and many of them naively believed that all they had to do was dig to find a rich tomb. I was sorry to disillusion Mr. Lukancic, for he seemed a very pleasant fellow, but I felt obliged to explain.

"One must have permission from the Department of Antiquities, and all excavations must be supervised by a trained archaeologist. At this particular time there aren't many such persons available."

"The Brits and French have got something else on their minds besides archaeology," said another gentleman. "The war on this front seems to be going well, though. The Senussi are in retreat and the Turks have been driven out of the Sinai."

"But the British advance has stalled outside Gaza," Mr. Lukancic objected.

"It's only a matter of time before we take Gaza," said a military officer, stroking his large mustache. "Johnny Turk isn't much of a threat."

His insignia identified him as a member of the staff, and his portly frame and flushed face suggested that he had fought the war from behind a desk in Cairo. Another, younger, officer gave him a look of thinly veiled contempt. "Johnny Turk was a considerable threat at Rafah, and Gaza won't be easy to take. The city is ringed round with trenches and they've got fortifications along the ridges all the way from Gaza to Beersheba."

The conversation turned to a discussion of strategy and I excused myself. The remote city of Gaza held no interest for me.

From Manuscript H

Cyrus's soiree was like all his other parties—elegant, genteel, and full of boring people. Ramses always found Cyrus congenial company when there were no strangers present; he couldn't understand why a man would willingly endure, much less invite, such a motley mob. There was no one he wanted to talk to. His family had deserted him; his mother was chatting with Katherine, Nefret was "mingling," and his father, whose social graces were the despair of his wife, had ignored everyone else and gone straight to Bertie. From his animated gestures and Bertie's deferential pose, Ramses felt certain Emerson was telling him what they had done at Deir el Medina, and what he should do from here on in.

Jumana was with them, looking very pretty in a pale yellow frock that set off her brown skin and sleek black hair. Ramses wondered how she felt about gatherings like this one. Even her superb self-confidence must be slightly daunted by so many strangers, many of whom, uncertain about her precise status, ignored or snubbed her. They wouldn't dare be rude to another of Cyrus's guests, but she was obviously Egyptian and they were not accustomed to mingling socially with "natives."

His eyes returned, as they had a habit of doing, to his wife. She saw him; one eyelid lowered in a discreet but unmistakable wink before she returned her attention to the woman with whom she was conversing. She was tall and stately and glittering with jewels; when she turned her head, pointing out something or someone to Nefret, he knew he'd seen her somewhere, but couldn't remember where.

He was rather enjoying his role as detached observer when someone touched him on the shoulder and he turned. The face beaming up at him looked vaguely familiar, but he was unable to identify it until the fellow spoke.

"Albion. Joe Albion. We met on the boat coming over."

Ramses did not contradict him. "I remember you, sir, of course," he said politely.

The little man burst out laughing. "No, you don't, young fella. Tried to meet you folks, but you managed to avoid us. Did your ma and pa tell you we met the other day on the path to the Valley of the Kings?"

"Er—no, sir."

"I asked your pa if he'd introduce me to a few tomb robbers," Albion went on. "He said no. Seemed a little put out."

"Ma" and "Pa" had been bad enough; this bland statement made Ramses choke on his champagne. Albion smacked him on the back.

"Shouldn't try to talk and drink at the same time, young fella. Don't need your advice anyhow; there's plenty of the rascals hereabouts, especially in that village—Gurneh. Talked to a couple of them the other day."

"Who?" Ramses demanded.

"Fella named Mohammed." Albion chortled. "Seems like everybody's named Mohammed."

Ramses had recovered himself, though he still couldn't believe the man was serious. "I think I know which Mohammed you mean. You can get in serious trouble dealing with him and his friends, Mr. Albion."

"Just let me worry about that." The smile was as broad, but for an instant there was a look in the deep-set eyes that made Ramses wonder if Albion was as naive and harmless as he seemed.

"Come meet my son," the little man went on. His pudgy hand gripped Ramses's arm with unexpected strength, and Ramses allowed himself to be towed toward a young man who stood apart from the rest, slouching a little, a glass of champagne in his hand and an aloof expression on his face. Probably the same expression that is on my face, Ramses thought. Either young Mr. Albion found the other people present not worth his notice, or he was shy.

He straightened to his full height, a little under six feet, when his father came up with Ramses. His thin reserved face and eyeglasses were those of a scholar, but he looked to be in good physical trim, except for being a bit thick around the middle. His sharply chiseled features warmed a trifle when his father introduced Ramses.

"Figure you two young fellas have a lot in common," the older man went on breezily. "Get to know each other, right? Don't stand on ceremony. Folks call you Ramses, don't they? Some sort of private joke, I guess. Ramses—Sebastian. Sebastian—Ramses." He chortled. "Never could understand the British sense of humor."

He trotted off, and Sebastian said, "Glad to meet you. I glanced at your book on Egyptian grammar; seemed quite adequate, but I don't pretend to be an expert on the language. Egyptian art is my specialty."

Not shy. "Where did you study?" Ramses asked.

"Harvard."

Of course, Ramses thought. The accent was unmistakable, and completely different from his father's. Albion was what his mother would call a "common little man." Ramses rather liked "common" people, but he wondered how the jolly, uninhibited Albion had produced such a supercilious, self-consciously intellectual prig. Sebastian didn't seem to be embarrassed by his father's manners, which was one point in his favor.

Just about the only one. Young Albion went on. And on. He was not inclined to give America's oldest university any credit for his present state of admitted erudition. "There's not much being done with Egyptian art qua art," he stated. "I had to work it out myself. I've pretty well exhausted what the Metropolitan Museum and the Boston Museum of Fine Arts have to offer. A winter in Egypt seemed the logical next step."

"And a spot of tomb robbing?" Ramses finally managed to get a word in. "I trust your father was joking about that. A number of people, including *my* father, wouldn't be amused."

"It goes on all the time, doesn't it?"

"To some extent; but—"

"Yes, yes," Sebastian said condescendingly. "I understand how people like you feel about it. Now my book—"

Ramses caught Nefret's eye again and grimaced. It was a distress signal, and she responded with a grin and a slight nod.

Sebastian rambled on. He would be writing a book, Ramses thought. One of those books—the kind that will never be finished, because the author keeps finding additional material. Ramses had known a few scholars like that; he had always suspected their real reason for procrastinating was a reluctance to risk criticism. Sebastian declared that it was his intention to view every piece of Egyptian art in the world. It would be the definitive book on Egyptian art—when he finished it.

"What are you doing in Luxor, then?" Ramses asked. "The Cairo Museum—"

"Yes, yes, I know. I will get to the Museum in due course, but I wanted to see the tomb painting in situ, as it were—take photographs, make sketches, and so on. I'm a collector in a small way, and hoped to pick up a few good pieces here."

Ramses realized that if he went on talking to Sebastian he would say something rude. "If you'll excuse me," he began. "My wife—"

"That's she, isn't it?" Sebastian's head turned. "Lovely woman. Hope you don't mind my saying so."

Ramses did mind, but though Sebastian's tone was mildly

offensive, he could not take exception to the words themselves. Sebastian went on, "There's a delicious little creature. Is she available to anyone, or is Vandergelt keeping her for himself and Bertie?"

For one incredulous moment, Ramses thought the fellow was referring to Nefret. Then he realized that Sebastian was looking at Jumana.

Nefret had been on her way to join them when she saw Ramses's face freeze. It wasn't the old "stone pharaoh" face that concealed his thoughts, but a sign of fury so consuming it canceled thought and reason and everything else except a primitive need to act. She crossed the remaining distance in two long steps, slipped her arm through that of her husband, and caught hold of his hand. Under the pressure of her fingers his own fingers slowly uncurled. "You must be Mr. Sebastian Albion," she said lightly. "I've just been talking with your mother. I'm Nefret Emerson."

"How do you do." Albion hadn't missed Ramses's reaction. He took a step back.

"Katherine wants to ask you something, Ramses," Nefret went on. "Will you excuse us, Mr. Albion?"

"Just a minute," Ramses said. "We need to get something straight, Albion. The lady to whom you referred is a protégée of Mrs. Vandergelt's and a member of our family."

"Your family? But surely she is—"

"A member of our family," Ramses repeated. "And a young, respectable girl. Where the hell did you get the idea that an Egyptian woman is free to any man who wants her? In the Cairo brothels?"

"Ramses," Nefret murmured.

Albion had gone white. He mumbled something that might have been an apology, nodded at Nefret, and walked off.

"What on earth did he say?" Nefret asked. "You were going to hit him!"

"I was, wasn't I?" His fingers twined with hers. "In a way I'm sorry you stopped me."

"It would have ruined Cyrus's party," Nefret said practically. "I was watching you, and I could see it building up. Something about Jumana?"

"You can probably guess what."

"Yes. Bastard," she added.

"What were you talking about with his mother?"

"Him. And his father. That's all she can talk about! She refers to the old boy as 'my husband, Mr. Albion.' I thought women stopped doing that fifty years ago."

Her amusement reduced the Albions to the eccentric nuisances they were and made Ramses ashamed he had let Sebastian rouse his temper. "What does she call the bastard?"

Nefret chuckled. "Well, I don't think he is, literally. He is always 'my son Sebastian.' The way she pronounces the words, they sound like a royal title."

"When can we go home?"

Nefret squeezed his hand. "Anytime, poor darling. You've been a very good boy and deserve a reward."

He smiled and her heart skipped a beat, as it always did when he looked at her in a certain way. I'm hopeless, she thought. Hopeless, and glad of it.

Emerson wasn't ready to leave. He still had a few things to explain to Bertie, and then he had to go over the whole thing again with Cyrus, who had joined the group.

"Go on, if you like," he said amiably.

"May I come with you?" Jumana asked.

"Of course," Nefret said, reproaching herself for having neglected the girl. In company like this she needed all the support she could get.

Ramses gallantly offered Jumana his arm, and didn't even wince when she giggled and hung on to it. He was making it up to her for an insult she didn't know she had received, and his infatuated wife was reminded again of how utterly she adored him.

She took his other arm, and they made their way to the door. Then she felt the muscles under her hand harden. He would have hurried them on if Sebastian had not intercepted them.

"I misunderstood," he mumbled. "I beg your pardon."

Whose pardon? Nefret wondered. He had addressed Ramses, hadn't even looked at her or Jumana.

Ramses nodded brusquely and led his ladies to the waiting carriage.

"Who was that?" Jumana asked curiously. "He was very polite."

"A tourist," Ramses answered. "Very boring, as Sennia would say."

Jumana laughed, and began to chatter, repeating what Emerson had said about Deir el Medina. She had an excellent memory.

Nefret leaned back and let her talk. Young Albion had had to nerve himself for that encounter. Why had he taken the trouble? To ingratiate himself and his family with the Emersons? Ignoring Jumana was probably the most sensible thing he could have done. He certainly couldn't request an introduction to a girl he hoped to seduce from the man who had warned him off.

⁝

At breakfast Emerson droned on and on about his plans. He had arranged to meet Cyrus and Bertie at Deir el Medina so he could go over the whole thing again with them. Nothing Ramses and I had said had had the slightest effect on the stubborn man, and when I realized he meant to go ahead with his ridiculous scheme, I had to take a firm grip on my temper. I had no intention of allowing him to do any such thing, but a loud argument at the breakfast table would have been ill-bred, especially with Sennia present.

"If that is what you plan to do, you won't need me," I announced. "I am going to Luxor. Nefret, you had better come with me. Thanks to the selfish demands of certain persons, you haven't had a chance to purchase anything you need for the house."

Instead of objecting to the oblique reference to him, Emerson looked relieved. He didn't want to listen to a lecture from me any more than I wanted to listen to one from him. I had a brief discussion with Miss Sennia, who wanted to join the shopping expedition, but I finally got them all off. Nefret and I then went to her house so that I could make a few useful suggestions about necessities.

Everything appeared to be in order. I knew it would be, since Fatima was in charge, but there was no harm in seeing for myself. Najia was already busy in the parlor, sweeping and dusting. The birthmark was not really disfiguring—only a reddish stain that covered most of one cheek—but she kept her face averted while we conversed. She had tried, clumsily, to conceal it with a layer of whitish paste, which in my opinion was more conspicuous than the birthmark. I reminded myself to ask Nefret if there was not some cosmetic that would do a better job.

The other girl, Ghazela, was her cousin; they were all cousins to some degree. The name was not especially appropriate; she was no slender-limbed gazelle, but a round-cheeked sturdy young person of perhaps fourteen. She was delighted to have been chosen to work for Nefret and told me so at some length. Like most of the younger generation, even the girls, she had had some schooling. We were chatting about her plans and aspirations—and I was making a few small, tactful suggestions about cleaning the stove—when Nefret, who had gone to get her handbag and a more suitable hat, came in.

"I thought I'd find you here, Mother. Is everything satisfactory?"

"I see you have used the stove."

"Only for morning coffee. Najia makes it perfectly."

"So the girls suit, do they?" I inquired, after we had left the house.

"Oh, yes. What are we looking for today?"

"Don't you have a list?" I whipped mine out.

"It's in my head," Nefret said cheerfully. "Anyhow, half of the fun of shopping is to find something one didn't know one wanted."

We went first to the shop of Abdul Hadi, since the sooner we got him started, the better. Nefret did have a list in her head; she ordered a number of things, chairs and tables and chests, and made rough sketches of each, including the dimensions. Abdul Hadi kept bobbing up and down, his knees creaking every time he bent them, and assured her that the honor of her patronage would spur him on to work day and night. We left him creaking and bowing, and Nefret said, "Two weeks."

"He said one week."

"That was just his usual habit. But I think I can get some of them in a fortnight, if I keep after him."

The merchants all knew us, and they brought out their best, including some lengths of beautifully handwoven fabric that Nefret intended to have made into cushions for the parlor. I consider myself an efficient buyer, but never had I been whisked in and out of shop and suk as quickly as I was that day. We ended up at a potter's, where Nefret purchased a quantity of vessels of all shapes and sizes.

"Some of them will do for the courtyard," she declared. "I want hibiscus and lemon trees and roses, and bougainvillea."

"Then," I said, and stopped to clear my throat. "Then . . . you do like the house? It is satisfactory?"

"Yes, Mother, of course. Did you doubt it?"

I hadn't—not really—I had not given them much choice! But with two such strong-willed individuals one can never be certain. I knew now that I had them. A woman does not purchase new furnishings for a house unless she means to stay.

We treated ourselves to luncheon at the Winter Palace, where we had a merry time. No one is a better companion than Emerson—when he is in a friendly state of mind—but it is impossible to discuss household arrangements when men are present. After we finished, I suggested we call on Mohassib.

"Was that your real purpose in coming to Luxor?" Nefret asked, frowning slightly.

"Not at all, my dear. It only just occurred to me. We have plenty of time, and Heaven knows when we will get to Luxor again, and I promised Cyrus I would have a chat with Mohassib about—"

"Did you really?"

"Promise him? Implicitly."

"I see. All right, Mother. But you aren't fooling me. You are trying to track Jamil down."

"Someone must," I declared. "Emerson has lost interest— I knew he would, as soon as he became involved with his work—and no one else takes the wretched boy seriously."

The clot of dragomen and guides that infested the steps of the hotel parted before us like the Red Sea. We strolled on, past the Temple of Luxor. I could never pass those magnificent columns without a sidelong glance, but for once Nefret did not appear to notice them. Striding along with her hands clasped behind her back and her head bowed, she said, "Has it occurred to you that it might have been Jamil from whom Aslimi got those artifacts you bought in Cairo?"

"Certainly it occurred to me. The description fits. He secreted those particular items when they were clearing the tomb—they all do it, you know, cheating one another if they can—and used his share of the money to travel to Cairo. Jamil isn't especially intelligent, but he has sense enough to know he could get better prices from Cairo dealers than from Mohassib."

"Yes, of course," Nefret murmured. "You are terrifyingly single-minded when you go after something or someone, Mother."

"Not at all, my dear. I have no difficulty in thinking of several things at once."

Her brow cleared and the corners of her mouth turned up.

"So long as you aren't having one of your famous premonitions about Jamil."

To call the feeling a premonition or foreboding would not have been entirely accurate. It was, rather, based on expert knowledge of the criminal mind and a certain degree of informed cynicism. Criminals, in my experience, do not suddenly turn into honest men. Jamil was still in need of money and he was still resentful of us. Nothing had changed there, and the more often we frustrated his attempts to get what he wanted, the more resentful he would be.

Mohassib was the best-known and most highly respected (by everyone except Emerson) antiquities dealer in Luxor. He had been dying for at least ten years, and was dying at that very moment, so the doorkeeper informed me.

"Then he will wish to see me before he passes on," I replied, handing over the expected baksheesh.

He was in bed, propped up on pillows and looking like a biblical patriarch with his snowy beard and mustache; but he was not alone. I stopped short when I recognized the Albions.

"I beg your pardon," I said. "The doorkeeper did not tell me you had other visitors."

"That's okay," said Mr. Albion, who seemed to make a habit of answering remarks addressed to other persons. "We were about to leave anyhow. Good to see you, Mrs. Emerson—and Mrs. Emerson. Hope you didn't come here to bid on any of Mohassib's treasures. I've already made him an offer."

"Indeed?" I took a chair, indicating my intention of remaining. "I was under the impression that you meant to find yourself a tomb robber instead of buying from dealers."

Mrs. Albion's lips parted, like a crack in a block of ice. "Mr. Albion was teasing, Mrs. Emerson. He has a marvelous sense of humor."

"That's right," said her husband merrily. "I'm quite a tease, Mrs. Emerson. Well, see you folks later."

The younger Mr. Albion, mute as usual, followed his parents out.

After we had exchanged compliments and inquired after one another's health, and Mohassib had ordered tea for us, he said, "Are they friends of yours, Sitt?"

"Mere acquaintances."

"Good."

"Why do you say that?" I asked curiously.

"They are strange people. I am a good judge of strange people, Sitt Hakim, and I would not trust that happy little man. He wants too much for too little."

"What did he want?" Nefret inquired. "Part of the princesses' treasure? Or all of it?"

"Treasure?" Mohassib repeated, widening his eyes. No saint could have looked more innocent. "Ah—you are referring to the rumors about a rich find in the Gabbanat el-Qirud. The men of Luxor are great liars, Nur Misur. Perhaps there was no treasure."

"Come now, Mohammed," I said. "You know there was such a find and I know the thieves sold it to you, and you know I cannot prove that, and I know that even if I could there is little likelihood of your being charged with a crime. Why not speak freely to me, your old friend? Vandergelt Effendi would pay well for such objects, if they are as described."

We settled down, with mutual enjoyment, to the customary exchange of hints and innuendos, winks and nods and pursed lips and raised eyebrows. I rather prided myself on my ability to carry on this form of communication, which Emerson could not or would not do. Mohassib eventually remarked pensively that if he should hear of such objects he would be happy to do his friends a service.

"Excellent," I said, knowing that was as much as I could expect. Mohassib always played his little game of innocence and ignorance, but in this case the business had caused quite a stir, and I suspected he would not make any move to market the objects until things had died down.

We parted in the friendliest manner. Eyes twinkling, Mohassib sent his respectful regards to Emerson, whose opinion of him he knew quite well. At the door, I stopped and turned, as if a new idea had struck me. In fact, the question I asked was the one I had had in mind all along.

"Has Jamil been here?"

Caught off-guard, believing the interview to be over, Mohassib burst into a fit of violent coughing. I knew the paroxysm was only a device to give him time to think, so I pressed on.

"Don't pretend you don't know who I mean. Jamil, Yusuf's youngest son. Did he try to sell you artifacts from the princesses' tomb?"

Mohassib shook his head vigorously. "No," he gasped. "No, Sitt Hakim. I thought he had left Luxor."

"I hope you are telling the truth, Mohassib. Two of the other men who robbed the tomb are dead, under suspicious circumstances, and Jamil holds a grudge against everyone involved in that business."

Mohassib abruptly stopped coughing. "Are you saying that Jamil killed them?"

"I only repeat the latest gossip, old friend," I replied. "Since you had nothing to do with the disposal of the artifacts, there is no reason for you to be alarmed, is there?"

Mohassib grunted. He thought for a minute, and then he said, "Jamil brought me nothing from the tomb of the princesses. That is true, Sitt Hakim."

His lips closed so tightly they almost disappeared in the beard and mustache. Knowing that was all I was going to get out of the wily old fellow, I repeated my assurances of goodwill, and we left the house.

"Do you think he was telling the truth?" Nefret asked, waving aside a carriage that had stopped.

"About Jamil? The literal truth, yes. He did not deny he had seen the boy. My warning—for so it was meant, and so Mohassib took it—caught him by surprise, but it did not, as I had hoped, startle him into an indiscretion or worry him much. He is safe in his house, behind those stout walls, and well guarded. Ah, well, it was worth a try." We strolled on, acknowledging the greetings of passersby, and I continued, "What I found interesting was his opinion of Mr. Albion. We keep running into them, don't we? Do you think they are following us because they are up to no good?"

Nefret laughed and slipped her arm through mine. "Don't sound so hopeful, Mother. They are an oddly matched couple, though."

"What do you think of young Mr. Albion?"

She answered with another question. "Did Ramses tell you what he said at Cyrus's soiree—about Jumana?"

"No."

She repeated the young man's remark. I shook my head. "Disgusting, but not surprising. I trust Ramses put the young man in his place?"

"Ramses almost put him on the carpet," Nefret said. "You know that look of his—white around the mouth, and eyes almost closed? I made a leap for him and grabbed his arm, in time to stop him; but he uttered a few well-chosen words. Let's take a felucca, shall we? It's such a nice day."

"It has been a very pleasant day, my dear. I hope the others have had as nice a time as we."

From Manuscript H

"That's got rid of her," said Emerson in a satisfied voice, watching his wife and daughter-in-law walk away from the house. He and Ramses had been skulking—there was no other word for it—in a secluded corner of the garden. "We can get our gear together now."

He had sent Jumana on to Deir el Medina, telling her to warn the others that they might be late. Selim and Daoud were there; they could explain the site as well as he.

Since Emerson did not believe anyone could do anything

as well as he, Ramses knew his father was up to something. He didn't need to ask what it was. As they loaded themselves with knapsacks and several heavy coils of rope, he said only, "We're going on foot? It's a long way to the Cemetery of the Monkeys."

"A brisk hour's walk," Emerson declared. "No point in taking the horses, we'd have to leave them somewhere along the way, and I don't want the poor brutes standing round in the sun."

"You mean you don't want to go near Deir el Medina for fear Cyrus will spot us and ask where we're going. Father, what's the point of this?"

"I only want to make a preliminary survey."

The evasive tone would certainly have aroused his wife's suspicions. Ramses said, "Preliminary to what? You don't mean to give up Deir el Medina *and* Medinet Habu in favor of the western wadis, do you? And what about Cyrus? He isn't going to settle for workmen's houses while we're looking for queens' tombs."

Emerson's face took on a look of noble self-righteousness. "Cyrus is not up to the kind of survey we'll be doing. He might injure himself. Can't have that."

"We're doing him a kindness, really."

Emerson glanced at his solemn face and burst out laughing. "Glad you agree, my boy. I haven't made up my mind yet where we will be working. I just want to have another look round. Without," he added indignantly, "half a dozen people, including your mother, getting in my way."

Emerson moved at a rapid pace; he had insisted on carrying the heavier load, but it didn't slow him in the slightest. Though he did not pause, he greeted everyone he met and responded cheerfully to their questions. Several passersby asked where they were going. Emerson told them. Matching his father's long strides, Ramses realized Emerson didn't really expect to find Jamil's tomb by himself. He was hoping Jamil would show himself again.

"Do you think he'll be there?" he asked.

"Who? Oh. Hmph. He has been. He's bound to make a mistake sooner or later, and when he does we'll be ready for him."

"You don't know that the masked demon was he."

"Who else could it have been? The Gurnawis don't play silly tricks like that."

"Mother will find out, you know—especially if Jamil succeeds in bashing one of us with a boulder."

"Unlikely in the extreme," Emerson declared. "However . . . No one is a better companion than your mother—when she is in a friendly state of mind—but women do get in the way at times. Especially your mother."

Ramses grinned but saved his breath. He did not suffer from false modesty about his physical fitness, but keeping up with his father taxed even him. Emerson must have decided to take one of his famous "round-about-ways," for they were already climbing, along a steep, winding path that would eventually lead them behind Deir el Medina and the Valley of the Queens.

They had got a late start and Emerson was in a hurry. Once they had reached the highest part of the path they made good time over relatively level ground. Absorbed in thought, Ramses followed his father without speaking.

He didn't want to be here, or at Medinet Habu. If he'd had his way they would settle down for the season at Deir el Medina. He hadn't explained himself very eloquently, and apparently his father's fascination with temples prevented him from seeing what Ramses saw: a unique opportunity to learn about the lives of ordinary Egyptians, not pharaohs, not noblemen, but men who worked hard for a living, and their wives and children. The scraps of written material he had found contained work schedules and lists of supplies, and tantalizing hints of family relationships, friendly and not so friendly, extending over many generations. He was certain there were more papyri to be found; one of the men had mentioned coming across a similar cache some years earlier, near the place where this one had turned up. If his father would let him dig there . . .

He didn't want to be here, but he'd had no choice. Once Emerson got the bit in his teeth it was impossible to turn him aside, and wandering the western wadis alone was dangerous, even for an old hand like his father. Paths wound all over the place, marked in some places by tumbles of stone that marked the ruins of ancient huts, used by the necropolis guards or by workmen. Ramses could only marvel at his father's encyclopedic memory of the terrain; he did not pause before turning into a track that led downhill, following the eastern ridge of a deep wadi. When he finally stopped, they were only twenty feet from the valley floor, and Ramses saw a flight of rough stone stairs going down.

"Rest a bit," Emerson said, unstrapping his knapsack. He removed his coat, tossed it onto the ground, sat on it, and took his pipe from his pocket. Ramses followed his example, except for the pipe. He took advantage of the lull while his father fussed with the pipe to look round and try to get his bearings.

For the past half hour they had been going roughly southwest, and must now be near the mouth of one of the wadis that spread out northward from the plain. It wasn't the one they had visited twice before; this configuration was quite different from that of the Cemetery of the Monkeys. There was ample evidence of ancient occupation: several deep pits, too obvious to have been overlooked by modern tomb robbers, and more remains of ancient stone huts.

Once he had his pipe going, Emerson opened his knapsack and began fumbling in it. "Hmph," he said, as if the idea had just struck him. "I suppose I ought to have thought of bringing some water. Are you thirsty, my boy?"

"A little." It was the understatement of the day; his mouth was so dry it felt like sand. He unstrapped his own knapsack. "I asked Fatima for a few bottles of water. And a packet of sandwiches."

"Good thinking. No, no—" Emerson waved the bottle away. "You first."

Ramses took a long pull and watched, with the admiring vexation his father continued to inspire, as Emerson went on rooting round in his knapsack. He had flung his pith helmet aside and the sun beat down on his bare black head. His pipe lay beside him; it was still glowing, and Ramses remembered a story his mother had once told him, about Emerson putting a lighted pipe in his pocket. She had thought it very amusing.

"Ah," said Emerson, removing a long roll of paper from his knapsack. "Here it is. Hold this end."

Once the paper was unrolled and held flat by rocks, Emerson said, "I did this some years ago. Very rough, as you can see."

It was a map of the area, annotated in Emerson's decisive handwriting, and although it was obviously not to scale, it made the general layout of the wadis clear. They resembled the fingers of a hand that stretched out to the north, penetrating deep into the rising cliffs; below the flatter "palm" was a common entrance, very wide and fairly level, opening onto the plain below. Emerson had labeled the separate wadis with their Arabic names.

"We're here," Emerson went on, jabbing at the paper with the stem of his pipe. "We'll have a look at Wadi Siqqet e Zeide first. Hatshepsut's tomb is at the far end of it."

"What are these *x*'s?"

"Spots I thought worth investigating."

"You never got round to doing it?"

"There isn't enough time!" Emerson's voice rose. "There never will be. If I had ten lifetimes I couldn't do it all."

"Have a sandwich," Ramses said sympathetically. "I know how you feel, Father. We must just do the best we can."

"Don't talk like your mother," Emerson growled. He accepted a sandwich, but instead of biting into it he stared at the ground and said rapidly, "I've come round to your way of thinking, you know. The most important aspect of our profession is recording. At the rate the monuments are deteriorating, there won't be much left by the time your children are grown."

Considering that they aren't born yet, that will be a long time, Ramses thought.

The subject of children was one he and Nefret avoided, and so did everyone else in the family. Some of them, including his mother—and himself—knew that her failure to conceive again after the miscarriage she had suffered a few years earlier grieved her more than she would admit. He wanted a child, too, but his feelings weren't important, compared with hers.

His father appeared not to have noticed the gaffe, if it could be called that. He went on, in mounting passion, "But, confound it, leaving undiscovered tombs to the tender mercies of thieves is inviting further destruction. Finding them first is a variety of preservation, isn't it?"

"Yes, sir."

"Don't agree with everything I say!" Emerson shouted.

"No, sir."

"You do agree, though."

"Yes . . ." He cut off the "sir." Emerson's morose expression indicated that he was not in the mood for raillery. Ramses went on, "In this case we have an additional, equally defensible motive for exploring the area. One might even call it self-defense."

He hadn't succeeded in cheering his father. Emerson's brow darkened even more. "It's ridiculous," he grumbled. "I resent having to waste time tracking down a miserable little rat like Jamil."

Ramses understood how he felt. They had faced a number of formidable enemies in the past. To be defeated, even temporarily, by such a feeble adversary was what his father would call a damned insult. It is easier to trap a lion than a rat, though. He decided not to voice this comforting adage aloud. It sounded like something his mother might have said.

"We'll find him, Father," he said.

"Hmph. Yes. Er . . ." His father patted him awkwardly on the arm. "You'll get a chance at your chapels, my boy. I promise."

"But, Father, I don't want—"

"This way."

They located two pit tombs which had been ransacked in antiquity, many shards of pottery, and a number of hieratic inscriptions scratched onto the rock by necropolis inspectors who had visited the area in pharaonic times. Several of the names were known from similar graffiti in the Valley of the Kings. It was additional evidence that there were tombs, probably royal tombs, in the wadis. To Emerson's extreme annoyance, they found modern graffiti next to many of them: the initials "H. C." and the date "1916."

"Carter, curse him," he muttered.

"You shouldn't hold it against him just because he got here before you," Ramses said.

"I was here thirty years ago," Emerson retorted. "But I didn't scratch my name all over the scenery."

"It is a courtesy, Father, telling any who may follow that he has copied these inscriptions. I presume he did?"

"I would ask him if I could lay hands on him," Emerson snarled. "He wasn't in Cairo, he isn't in Luxor. Where the devil is he?"

"Off on some errand for the War Office, I presume. He said he was working for the intelligence department."

"Bah," said Emerson. "Ramses, I want copies of these graffiti. Carter doesn't understand the language. Yours are bound to be more accurate."

"You want me to do it now?" Ramses demanded.

"No, there won't be time. Another day."

Another day, another distraction, Ramses thought, concealing his annoyance. There was no man alive—or dead, for that matter—whom he admired more than his father, but sometimes Emerson's obstinacy rasped on his nerves. I'll try again to explain about Deir el Medina, he thought. Perhaps I didn't try hard enough. Perhaps if I tell him . . . He was thinking how to put it when he heard a strange sound. Clear and high, it might have been a bird's trill, but it was unusual to find a songbird this far from the cultivation.

He got to his feet and turned slowly, raking the cliffs with narrowed eyes. The sun was high, reflecting off the barren rocks, dazzling the vision.

"What—" Emerson began.

"Listen."

This time Emerson heard it too. He jumped up.

"There," Ramses said, pointing.

The figure was too far away and too high up to be distinct. Without taking his eyes off it, he knelt and got the binoculars out of his pack.

"Jamil?" Emerson asked hopefully.

"No." The small figure jumped into focus. "Goddamn it! It's Jumana. What the hell—"

Emerson cupped his hands round his mouth and let out a bellow whose reverberations brought down a shower of rock from the cliff.

"Did she hear me?" He picked up his coat and waved it like a flag.

"The entire Western Desert heard you," Ramses said. "She's seen us. She's coming. Good God, she'll break her neck if she doesn't slow down. Let's go and meet her."

Leaving their belongings, they hurried up the path they had recently descended. She descended even faster, slipping and sliding, waving her arms to maintain her balance. When she was ten feet above them she glissaded down the last slope, straight into Emerson's outstretched arms.

"Hurry," she gasped. "Quick. We must find him."

Her face glowed with heat and exertion. Scowling blackly, Emerson held her off at arm's length, and Ramses saw that she was wearing a belt like that of his mother, hung all round with various hard, lumpy objects. The only one he could identify was a canteen.

"Who?" he asked, since his father seemed incapable of speech. "Jamil?"

"No." She pushed her hair out of her eyes. "I followed . . . I didn't know . . . you were here . . ." Her breath gave out.

"Curse it," Emerson said. He swung her up into his arms and swore again as something—possibly the canteen—jabbed him in the ribs. He carried her back to the place where they had left their knapsacks, put her down on his coat, and offered her the water bottle.

"I have this," she said proudly, unhooking the canteen. "And other useful things. Like the Sitt Hakim."

"Wonderful," said Emerson, rubbing his side. "Now tell us who you followed. Cyrus?"

"Bertie." She wiped her chin and hung the canteen back on her belt. "I don't know how long he was gone before I realized. I asked one of the men; he said he saw Bertie walking very fast down the road away from Deir el Medina and—"

"How do you know he wasn't going home?" Emerson asked.

"Without telling his father or Reis Abu? He stole away, like a thief!"

"But why here?"

"He had been talking of how he wished he could find something wonderful for Mr. Vandergelt. When you did not come, we were wondering why, and Mr. Vandergelt said . . ." She stopped and thought, and when she went on, it was in Cyrus's very words and in a fairly good imitation of his accent. "' . . . he'd durned well better not find out you had snuck off looking for queens' tombs behind his back.' He was joking, but—"

"Hmph, yes," Emerson said guiltily. "The damned young fool! You've seen no sign of him?"

"No. I looked and I called him, over and over." She stood up and straightened her skirt. "We must find him. He may have fallen. Hurry!"

"Hold on a minute," said Emerson abstractedly. "No sense in rushing off in all directions. What do you think, Ramses?"

He didn't have to tell them what he thought, they were as

familiar with the terrain as he was. There were hundreds of square meters of broken country, around and above and below, split by crevices of all sizes and shapes. Locating one man in that wilderness would be hellishly difficult, especially if he had fallen and injured himself.

"I don't think he'd have gone over the gebel as Jumana did," Ramses answered. "He'd have come the way we came the other day; it's the only route he knows. He didn't enter this arm of the wadi or we'd have seen him. Unless he arrived long before we did . . . Father, why don't you sing out?"

Emerson obliged. Not even a bird answered. Jumana was dancing up and down with impatience, but Emerson's monumental calm kept her quiet. After calling twice more, without result, he said, "He'd have heard that if he were within earshot. All right, we can go on."

"The Cemetery of the Monkeys," Ramses muttered. "Yes, that's where he'd go. I could kick myself for making those clever remarks about missing queens. Which way? I can climb up and go across, while you—"

"No," Emerson said without hesitating. "You were right, he'd have gone the way we did before." He hoisted the pack onto his shoulders and started down the rough steps. "You next, Jumana. Watch your footing."

Once down, they crossed the wide mouth of the wadi and started up the path that led into the next narrow finger. Jumana would have bounded ahead if Emerson had not kept hold of her. Every few minutes he stopped and shouted Bertie's name. They had gone some distance, with the walls rising higher on either side, before there was a reply, faint and muffled, but unmistakably the sound of a human voice.

"Thank God," Ramses said sincerely. He cupped his hands around his mouth and yelled, "Bertie, is that you? Keep calling out!"

Bertie obeyed, but it took them a while to locate him. Sound echoed distractingly between the cliffs, and there wasn't a sign of him, though they scanned the rock surface with binoculars as well as the naked eye.

"He's up there somewhere," Emerson said, indicating a crevice that ran slantwise across the cliff face. "Yes—this is where he climbed." The marks where booted feet had slipped and scraped were fresh, white against the weathered stone. He shouted again. The response was close now, and the words were distinct.

"Foot's caught. I can't . . ."

"All right, I'm coming," Ramses called. He slipped off the knapsack, removed his coat, and picked up one of the coils of rope. "No, Jumana, you stay here. Hang on to her, Father."

"If she tries to follow you, I'll tie her up with the rest of the rope," Emerson said coolly. "Be careful."

Ramses nodded. It was an easy ascent, with lots of hand- and footholds, and a slight inward slope. The crevice narrowed and appeared to end about fifteen feet above him; he went on up, at an angle, till he reached a point where the opening was wide enough for him to swing himself into it. The floor of the cleft was almost horizontal here, and several feet deep, like a small natural platform.

"Down here," Bertie said.

Ramses switched on his pocket torch and shone it down. All he could see was Bertie's face. His body was jammed into the narrowest part of the crevice, like a cork in a bottle. "My God," he said. "How did you do that?"

Bertie's face was smeared with dust and sweat and streaked with blood, but he summoned up a rueful grin. "I slipped. It wasn't at all difficult; I could do it again anytime."

Ramses laughed. It wasn't going to be easy getting Bertie out, but it was a relief to find him alive and relatively un-damaged, and cool as ice. "If I lower a rope, can you grab hold of it?"

"I've got one arm free," Bertie said, raising it in a flippant wave. "The other one's stuck. And one of my boots is caught."

"Let's try this." Ramses tied a loop in the end of the rope and let it down. Bertie slid his arm through the noose and

Ramses pulled on the rope till the slipknot tightened. "Ready?"

"Slacken the rope a bit so I can get hold of it. Here, wait a minute. Are you hanging on to something? If I come popping out of here you may lose your balance."

There was nothing he could hang on to, no protuberance round which to tie the rope. He looped a section round his waist and knotted it. "I'm fine. Here we go."

He'd had to put the torch back in his pocket to use both hands for the rope. He couldn't see Bertie now, but he could hear his hard, difficult breathing. There was resistance at first, and a gasp of pain from the man below, but Ramses didn't dare stop, he could feel upward movement. He transferred his grip farther along the rope and heaved.

"That's done it," Bertie gasped. "Both hands out . . ."

"Good," Ramses said, recovering his balance. He'd almost fallen over, the release of resistance had been so sudden. Bertie's hands came into view. He was trying to pull himself up. His knuckles and the back of one hand were scraped raw.

Ramses helped him up onto the relatively level section and then leaned out. His father's requests for information and reassurance were reaching an ear-splitting pitch. They harmonized with Jumana's piercing soprano.

"It's all right. We're coming down," Ramses called.

"Thanks," Bertie said.

"What for?"

Bertie had unfastened the slipknot. He dug in his pocket for a handkerchief and passed it over his filthy face. "Well, for pulling me out. And for not saying something like 'I'm about to lower the poor idiot down.'"

"You aren't that. But I am going to lower you, unless you have violent objections."

"No. I've played the bloody fool once today, I won't do it again. How did you know I was here?"

He wanted a little more time. Holding the end of the rope,

Ramses decided he had better break it to him at once. "Jumana. She noticed you were missing and figured you'd come this way. Father and I heard her calling you, and we joined forces."

"Oh." He added bitterly, "Kind of her to rush to my rescue."

"This could have happened to anyone," Ramses said. "All right, let's get it over."

"Wait a minute. I don't want you to think I'm a complete fool. I wouldn't have risked climbing alone—I know I'm not much good at it—if I hadn't seen him. Just about here, leaning out and looking down at me. He didn't push me," Bertie added quickly, reading Ramses's expression. "I wouldn't want her to think that."

"The hell with what she thinks," Ramses said angrily. "Damn it, Bertie, you don't climb a rock face when there's someone up above who doesn't like you. I wouldn't have risked it."

"Yes, you would—if you'd seen what I saw. He was laughing, Ramses, and waving some object. I couldn't see it clearly, but it glittered. Like gold."

⁚

Six

I cannot recall ever seeing Cyrus Vandergelt so angry. Even Emerson sat in silence, without attempting to interrupt, while our old friend paced up and down uttering incoherent American ejaculations.

Nefret and I arrived at the house shortly after the others. From what I could make out, amid his cries of fury, Cyrus had met the other four on the homeward path. He had been searching for Bertie and Jumana for hours, after discovering that both had left Deir el Medina, and was at Medinet Habu, still in quest of them, when they appeared, with Ramses and Emerson supporting Bertie. Whether Cyrus had harbored the same suspicions that would have occurred to his wife upon finding two young persons of opposite genders unaccountably missing from their designated places, he never said.

Relief was immediately succeeded by outrage, as is usually the case. When Cyrus found out where they had been, a good deal of the outrage was directed at Emerson. At the latter's suggestion they had brought Bertie straight to our house, and it was obvious from their appearance that none of them had had the time, or perhaps the inclination, to make themselves tidy. Their dusty, sweat-stained garments were sufficient proof of a somewhat arduous day, but a quick yet comprehensive survey assured me that Bertie appeared to be

the only casualty. He had his foot up on a hassock and
Kadija was smearing it with her famous green ointment. Fatima ran in and out with plates of food—her invariable solution for all disasters; Gargery demanded to know what had
happened—Jumana tried to tell him; and Cyrus raved. It was
very busy and loud.

Nefret went to Ramses. He shook his head, smiling, in response to her unvoiced concern. I removed my hat, put it
neatly on a table, and proceeded to bring order out of chaos.

"Cyrus!" I said, rather emphatically.

"Of all the consarned, low-down . . ." He stopped and
stared at me. "Amelia. Where've you been? Why weren't
you here? Do you know what underhanded, contemptible
stunt this bunch of crooks played on us?"

"I am beginning to get an idea. Sit down and stop shouting, Cyrus. Fatima, will you please bring the tea tray? Thank
you. Let us now have a coherent narrative, from . . ." Jumana
was waving her hand in the air and bobbing up and down,
like an eager student volunteering to recite. I observed that
the jangling noise accompanying her movements came from
several articles attached to her belt. I was somewhat flattered
but not inclined to encourage her; she looked a little too
pleased with herself.

"Emerson," I said. Jumana subsided, pouting.

I had to shush Cyrus more than once during the course of
Emerson's tale, but the genial beverage, which I forced upon
everyone present, had its usual soothing effect—even on me.
I was extremely put out by Emerson's duplicity. However, I
confined my expressions of chagrin to a few reproachful
looks, which Emerson pretended not to see.

"All's well that ends well, eh, Peabody?" he inquired.

"Hmmm," I said. "Nefret?"

She was conferring with Kadija. "No broken bones," she
announced. "He was lucky. But he'll have to stay off that
foot for a few days."

"Lucky!" Cyrus burst out. "He had no business going off
like that. He—"

"Is not the only person present who has ever been guilty of reckless behavior," I interrupted.

Ramses gave me a wide, unself-conscious grin, and then sobered. "We'd have found him eventually, Cyrus, even without Jumana."

The girl must have been even more annoying than usual that day, or he would not have minimized her effort. We would certainly have looked for Bertie, but we might not have found him in time. It might well be said that the young man owed her his life.

"Who bandaged his hand?" Nefret asked.

"I wish everyone would stop talking about me in the third person," Bertie said stiffly. "Jumana—"

"Yes, I did it!" She jumped up, jangling. "You see, I have my belt of tools, too, like the Sitt Hakim! I washed his hand and bandaged it and I took care of him. He was very stupid to go there alone."

Bertie turned red, but he didn't have a chance to defend himself; he had not yet learned that in our circle it is necessary to shout in order to be heard. Emerson did it for him. Men always close ranks when women criticize one of them.

"And so were you, Jumana." Emerson slammed his cup down in the saucer. "Any man or woman, even the most experienced, could suffer an accident in that terrain, and die of exposure before he was found. No, young lady, don't talk back to me! Why didn't you tell Vandergelt where you were going?"

Jumana bowed her head. "I wanted to find him myself," she murmured.

"I see." Emerson's voice softened, and Bertie's face went even redder. Men are such innocents; they had taken her statement as a declaration of affectionate interest. I, who had once pointed out to Jumana that wealthy and powerful Cyrus Vandergelt would think well of anyone who looked after his adopted son, suspected that self-interest had been her primary motive.

"Enough of recriminations," I said. "We must—"

"I'm not finished recriminating," Cyrus declared. "Not by a damned sight. Excuse my language, ladies, but I've got a few words to say to my old pal here. Emerson, you deliberately and with malice aforethought pawned Deir el Medina off on me so you could do what I would have done if you hadn't told me not to do it! And by the Almighty, there is a tomb out there! We've got proof now."

Emerson looked sheepish and drank out of his cracked cup. Tea dribbled down the front of his shirt, but I cannot say its condition was appreciably worsened thereby.

"If we had found anything of interest, I would have let you in on it, Vandergelt," he mumbled. "I only wanted to—er—save you time and effort."

"Oh. All right, then," Cyrus said, mollified. "But now we know there is a tomb—"

"I'm afraid not, Cyrus," Ramses said. "Jamil may not be the most intelligent opponent we've ever faced, but he isn't stupid enough to give away the location of the tomb—if there is one."

"The gold Bertie saw—" Cyrus began.

"He said it glittered like gold," Ramses interrupted impatiently. "Hasn't it occurred to you that the boy has been deliberately leading us astray?"

"It had occurred to me, of course," I said.

Ramses's sober face relaxed into a grin and Emerson snarled wordlessly. "Where is the tomb, then?" Cyrus demanded.

"Like Ramses, I am not convinced there is one," I replied. "I can think of a number of reasons why Jamil might want to lead us on a wild-goose chase. 'He only does it to annoy, because he knows it teases.' Or he may want to lure us into a trap. It is wild country, and Bertie's accident today is a grim reminder of what can happen if he catches one of us alone."

Jumana lifted her chin and stared defiantly at me. The rather pathetic collection of tools on her belt jingled as she shifted position. I wondered if she had also acquired a parasol.

"He didn't mean to hurt Bertie," she declared. "It was an accident."

"That's right," Bertie said quickly.

"Perhaps he didn't intend to," I said. "But the result might have been disastrous. He's been watching us—spying on us."

"Damnation!" Emerson exclaimed. "Jumana—Bertie—all of you—don't take any more chances, do you hear? Even if Jamil appears decked out in the Double Crown and the full regalia of a pharaoh, blowing kisses, don't follow him."

"Here!" Cyrus exclaimed, his eyes brightening. "Do you think it's a royal tomb he's found?"

"Good Gad, Vandergelt, is that all you can think of?" Emerson gave him a rueful smile. "I thought of it, too, I admit. But there won't be a king's tomb in that area. My point is that none of us must go into a remote area alone. It is too dangerous, as Bertie discovered today."

"Oh." Cyrus glanced apologetically at Bertie. "Sorry, son, I was forgetting about your foot. Guess I'd better get you home. I'll go to the Castle and send the carriage."

"I can ride," Bertie said, trying to push himself to his feet.

"Take Risha," Ramses said, before any of us could voice an objection. "Jamad can go with you and bring him back. Here, let me give you a hand."

"Don't put your weight on that foot," Nefret called, as they left the room, Bertie hopping and leaning on Ramses's arm. Neither of them replied. Closing ranks, I thought. Closing ranks!

"A word of advice, if I may, Cyrus," I said.

He had been about to go after them. He stopped and turned to me. From his expression and that of my husband I suspected one of them was about to make a sarcastic comment, so I went on before either could do so. "Don't treat him like a child. He is a grown man and must make his own decisions. He did it for you, you know."

"I know." Cyrus tugged at his goatee. He turned a challenging look on Emerson. "So, old buddy, where are we going tomorrow?"

Emerson mumbled something.

"Hey?" said Cyrus, cupping his hand round his ear.

"Not," I said, "to the Cemetery of the Monkeys. We will meet you at Deir el Medina tomorrow, Cyrus. All of us."

As soon as Cyrus had taken his departure, Emerson fled to the bath chamber. He was well aware that this was only a temporary refuge; after arranging a few domestic matters, I followed him. I had intended to sit on the edge of the bath but he was splashing the water all about, so I leaned against the wall instead. Emerson gave me a cheerful smile.

"Did you have a pleasant day, my love?" he inquired.

"Quite pleasant. Emerson, why do you do this sort of thing? You know I will find out in the end."

"Certainly I know. I enjoy stirring you up, Peabody. And you enjoy ferreting out my evil schemes and scolding me." He got to his feet.

I always say there is nothing like a vigorous out-of-door life to keep a person in excellent physical condition. Emerson had changed very little since the days when I had first known him—except of course for the absence of the beard that had hidden his firm chin and strong jaw. His stalwart form was as trim, the pull of muscle across his broad shoulders just as distracting.

"I will not be distracted, Emerson," I informed him.

"No?" He stepped out of the bath and reached for me. He has very long arms.

After a time I said, "Turn round and let me dry your back."

"I can think of another way of—"

"No, Emerson! I am soaking wet already and we have a great deal to do if we are to get everything ready for tomorrow. I sent a message to Selim, inviting him to dinner."

"Good thought," said Emerson, sufficiently distracted by this reminder to release me. "I wonder what he will say about the latest development."

Seated next to me—a delicate attention I always paid him when he condescended to favor us with his company—Selim listened in frowning silence to Emerson's account of the day's adventure. Then he shook his head.

"I am surprised, Emerson, that you should have been so thoughtless," he said severely. "The temples and the workmen's village are more important than searching for tombs in that dangerous place. And you, Ramses, ought not have let him go."

Emerson had become accustomed to Selim's occasional criticisms, but having his own words quoted back at him silenced him momentarily. Ramses said meekly, "You are absolutely right, Selim, but when the Father of Curses speaks, the whole world obeys."

"Huh," said Selim, just as Abdullah might have done. A thought occurred to him, and he said in a milder voice, "Well, perhaps it was meant to be. Had you not gone there, Mr. Bertie and that foolish girl might have come to harm."

"That's one way of looking at it," Emerson agreed, as Jumana glared at her cousin.

"As for Jamil," Selim continued, returning Jumana's glare with interest, "he has caused us enough trouble and kept us from our work. Leave him to me."

Even Emerson was silenced by that flat demand, which had been delivered with a dignity and authority as great as Abdullah's had been. Selim was becoming more and more like his father, his handsome, strongly defined features framed by a neatly trimmed beard and mustache. Perhaps it is not surprising that I should have dreamed of Abdullah that night.

He was waiting for me in the place we both loved best, the top of the cliff above Deir el Bahri, where the path went on to the Valley of the Kings; and the sun was rising over the eastern mountains. As I mounted the last steep slope, I wondered why I was beginning to find the ascent as difficult as I would have done in waking life. If it was a touch of realism, it was one I could have done without. I was extremely short of breath when Abdullah gave me his hand and assisted me to attain the summit.

"They are all well in England," he said. "My next grandchild grows strong in the womb of her mother."

"A girl this time?" I panted.

Abdullah nodded. "Sit down, Sitt, and rest. Yes, it is a girl; that is already determined."

"Er—speaking of grandchildren, Abdullah . . ."

He threw his head back and laughed heartily. As always in these dreams, he was youthfully handsome, without a single gray thread in his beard; his laughter was as merry as Selim's.

"What about them, Sitt?"

"You aren't going to tell me, are you?"

"There is a time for all things, Sitt Hakim. When that time comes you will be among the first to know. How could it be otherwise?"

Annoyed as I was at his teasing, I could not help smiling a little. He had said "when," not "if"! That was hopeful. "I expect I will," I said. "How could it be otherwise?"

"There are other things I will tell you: The boy who is in France is safe still, but David is troubled because he feels he should be here with you. Do not let him come. The underwater boats will sink many ships this winter. You are wise to stay in Egypt until that danger is over."

Having recovered my breath, I rose from the extremely lumpy rock on which I had been sitting and stood beside him, watching the slow spread of sunlight across the landscape. Below us the columns of Hatshepsut's temple were ivory-pale in the morning shadows.

"I know better than to press you when you are determined to keep silent," I grumbled. "But you haven't said anything about our current plans. Where is that cursed boy, Abdullah, and what are we going to do about him?"

"It is a matter of shame to me that Jamil is a member of my family." Abdullah's face was as stern as a bronze mask.

"He will be punished, Sitt, but not by you. Leave him to me. Do not take foolish chances, here or elsewhere."

"Where else would I be? If you are referring to the submarine menace, we have already decided . . . Curse it, Abdullah, you are trying to get me off the track again. Where is the confounded tomb?"

"It would be tangling the web of the future to tell you that," Abdullah said dreamily. "Now, Sitt, do not swear. It will come right in the end, though not, perhaps, as you expect."

He took my hand and held it for a moment. Then he turned away.

"Wait," I said. "Please."

"No more questions, Sitt. I have told you all I am allowed."

"I only wondered how you liked your new tomb."

Abdullah turned back to face me. "It is well enough."

"Is that all you can say? David designed the structure, you know, and Selim got the men to work as soon as you asked me for it."

"I should not have had to ask," said Abdullah, sounding as sulky as Sennia.

It was so like him—so human—so like a man! Laughing, I threw my arms around him in an impetuous embrace. It was the first time I had ever done so, and for the first time he held me close—only for a moment, before he gently loosened my hands and stepped back.

"Is there anything else you would like?" I asked.

"No." The corners of his mouth twitched, and he said, "It is a very fine tomb, Sitt. Fine enough for a pasha."

I did not follow him. I never had. Something held me back; perhaps it was the sure knowledge that I would see him again, or the comfort I always gained from speaking with him, even when he was at his most irritatingly vague.

"Good-bye for now," I called. "Maassalameh, my friend."

I had, of course, arrived at the logical solution to our dilemma—or, to be more accurate, Emerson and Cyrus's impractical plan. I had said nothing to Emerson, for in my opinion he did not deserve my confidence after playing such a trick on me. He was therefore in a state of happy ignorance when we got to Deir el Medina, where we found Cyrus and Abu and their crew awaiting us. Bertie was not there; as I had expected she would, Katherine wanted to keep him under her wing for a few days. Sennia had gone off to her lessons with less fuss than usual, since she looked forward to "taking care of Bertie."

We all gathered round Emerson, and a sizable audience we were: Selim and Daoud, Cyrus and Abu, Jumana, Nefret, Ramses, and of course the Great Cat of Re, who had climbed up onto Ramses's shoulder and was staring at Emerson with round green eyes. I waited until Emerson had drawn a deep breath and opened his mouth before I spoke.

"The solution to our problem is obvious."

Caught off-balance, figuratively speaking, Emerson forgot what he had been about to say. "I . . . Curse it, Peabody, what are you talking about? What problem? We have no problem. We—"

"Several problems, I should have said. First, the distinct possibility that your plan will enrage M. Daressy and result in our being forbidden to work in Egypt. Second, the fact that although Bertie has become a competent supervisor, he knows nothing of hieratic and cannot cope with the inscribed materials we have been finding. Third, Ramses's desire to continue working here. Are you so indifferent to the feelings of your son, Emerson, that you will ride roughshod over them? I had not supposed you would be so unkind."

I managed to get through this entire speech without interruption, since I had learned the trick of pausing for breath, not at the end of sentences, but at random intervals the listeners did not expect. Emerson would not have been reluctant to interrupt at any interval; but as he explained later, my tone of voice warned him he had better not. And by the time I had finished, the alteration of his expression assured me that the last point, at least, had made the desired impression.

He turned to his son, his handsome features sober. "Do you feel that strongly about it, Ramses? You know I would never . . . Why didn't you tell me?"

"He did tell you," I said in exasperation. "You didn't listen."

"It's all right, Father," Ramses said quickly. "Perhaps I didn't express myself clearly enough."

"Clearly enough for *me* to understand," I said with a sniff. "Never mind. My solution is very simple. Cyrus and we are both shorthanded. I suggest we combine forces and focus on one site—this one—dividing the responsibility. Cyrus can have the tombs; we will take the village. M. Daressy can have no objection to our expanding our workforce."

Cyrus, who had listened in gloomy silence to what he expected would be the failure of his hopes, immediately cheered up. "You mean it?" he exclaimed.

"Certainly," I replied, returning his smile. "Naturally we will assist one another should anything of particular interest turn up which would demand additional manpower."

Emerson had been thoroughly humbled. He loved his son dearly—though I do not believe he had ever actually said so—and was ready to accept any penance I proposed—until I added that last sentence. It livened him up considerably. He turned on me with a shout.

"Confound it, Amelia! I see through you. You are bored with sifting rubbish. You are after those tombs yourself."

"I have just now proposed handing that part of our concession over to Cyrus, Emerson," I reminded him. "Do you agree?"

"Oh." Emerson rubbed his chin. "Well . . ."

"It's a durned good idea," Cyrus declared. "Just what I'd have expected you to come up with, Amelia. What do you say, old pal? Shake on it?"

Instead of taking Cyrus's outstretched hand, Emerson turned to his son. "Is that acceptable to you, Ramses? Be honest."

"I think it is an excellent plan, Father. Honestly," he added.

"In that case . . ." Emerson seized Cyrus's hand in a firm grip. "It is agreed."

"Perhaps we should sign a written agreement," I suggested. "In case M. Daressy inquires."

"No, ma'am, that won't be necessary," Cyrus declared. "Emerson's word is good enough for me."

"The word of the Father of Curses," Daoud said, "is stronger than another man's oath."

I believe I may be excused for feeling a trifle smug. Ramses was pleased and so was Cyrus; Nefret was happy because Ramses was happy; even Selim condescended to commend me. The only one who was not thoroughly delighted with the arrangement was Emerson, and I felt certain that his main objection was that I had thought of it first.

I will say for Emerson that he does not hold a grudge. Having agreed, he immediately began issuing orders.

"The first thing for you to do, Vandergelt," he declared, "is to produce a proper survey of the slope and the location of the tombs, and see that it is published. Good Gad, if you only do that, you will have made a great contribution. Everybody from Wilkinson to Schiaparelli has found tombs—"

"The royal architect Kha," Cyrus murmured longingly. "Much as I'd like a royal tomb, I'd settle for a find like that. Sealed up and undisturbed for over three thousand years, the wooden door still latched, jam-packed with furniture and linen and . . ."

"Pay attention," Emerson said forcibly. "The survey is the first priority. Our cursed predecessors never published their notes, if they bothered to make any, so you will have to begin afresh. Some of the tombs are known and open, but not all, and a certain amount of clearance . . ."

Cyrus began to fidget, and I said, "Quite right, Emerson, we all understand."

"And," said Emerson, raising his voice, "you will have to shut down your dig at Medinet Habu. Anything that has been exposed will be at risk from weather and vandals. We will go round there later and see what needs to be done."

Leaving Selim in charge, we set out for the temple after luncheon. It was a mild, mellow afternoon, with bright sunlight and a faint breeze stirring; one of Mr. Cook's tours was making a late day of it, strolling about the temple precincts and taking photographs with their little cameras. Emerson glowered at the tourists. They did look a trifle ridiculous in their pristine pith helmets and veils, their faces crimson with sunburn. Some of them were all hung round with straps supporting field glasses, canteens, pocket compasses, and other accoutrements that probably made them feel very professional.

"Some of them have got acetylene or magnesium lamps," Emerson grumbled. "Confound it, don't they know they mustn't use them?"

"Possibly not," I replied.

"Then I will tell them. Come, let's see if any of the louts have invaded our temple. Smoking up the wall surfaces, scratching their wretched names . . ."

Mumbling, he strode off toward a group that was staring up at the empty windows of the upper stories of the tower, and as I followed, hoping to avert a nasty scene, I heard the guide lecturing. "This tower, sirs and madams, was the harem of the great Ramses, where he enjoyed himself with his beautiful concubines. The floors have fallen, so you cannot go up to see the reliefs on the walls, but they show the king reclining on a soft couch while the concubines caress—"

"Wrong!" Emerson shouted. "Curse it, Nazir, you know better than that! Why are you telling these idiots such lies?"

The tourists let out little squeals of surprise; several of the ladies got behind their husbands. The sight of Emerson in a rage, advancing in great bounds, was enough to terrify the timid. Nazir, who was accustomed to him, only grinned and shook his head.

"It is what they want to hear, Father of Curses," he said in Arabic.

"Oh, bah," said Emerson. "Don't let them use those damned magnesium torches, that's all."

He pushed through the crowd and headed straight for the Saite chapels, with the rest of us following close on his heels. I was distressed to observe that his fears had been justified. Several persons, coolly ignoring the ropes and No Trepass signs that enclosed the work area, were passing in and out of the chapel. There was a flash of light from the interior as a magnesium flare went off. Emerson began to run.

"Hurry and catch him up, Ramses," I panted. "Don't let him hit anyone!"

"All right, Mother." Ramses was the only one of us who could cover ground as quickly as his father. It was as well I had anticipated the worst; we found them inside the lovely little chapel of Amenirdis, confronting a trio of tourists. Ramses had managed to get between them and his father, who was cursing at the top of his lungs.

"Damnation!" I said. "It's the confounded Albions again. What do they want?"

"A spot of sight-seeing, one must suppose," Nefret answered. She went to Emerson and slipped her arm through his. "Good afternoon, everyone."

None of the Albions appeared perturbed by Emerson's tirade. To judge by his broad apple-cheeked smile, Mr. Albion had enjoyed every profane word. "He sure can cuss," he observed admiringly. "Not proper in the presence of a lady, though."

Mrs. Albion, hands folded and face composed, emitted a genteel cough. Emerson looked a little sheepish. "I didn't say a word that could—"

"What got you riled up?" Albion inquired curiously.

Emerson drew a deep breath. Fearing another tirade, Ramses said quickly, "For one thing, sir, this area is out of bounds to tourists. Didn't you see the signs?"

"I wanted to examine the reliefs," said Sebastian Albion. He was leaning against them, another archaeological sin in Emerson's book.

"Stand up straight, Mr. Sebastian," I ordered. He obeyed instantly, his eyes widening. I went on, "Touching or leaning

against the walls mars the paint. Magnesium flares give off
smoke which damages the reliefs. You risk a bad fall wandering round in the dark. Cyrus, I thought you were going to
repair the floor."

"Hadn't got around to it," Cyrus admitted. "Thought the
signs would keep people out."

"We assumed the prohibition did not apply to us," said
Mrs. Albion coldly.

"You were mistaken," said Emerson. "Out, everyone."

"The Cook's people are leaving," I added. "You had better
hurry if you want to go with them."

"We didn't come with them." Albion hopped nimbly over
the rope while Emerson, endeavoring to make up for his
rudeness to a lady, held it down for Mrs. Albion. He got not
so much as a murmur of thanks, but the younger Mr. Albion
squared his shoulders and began to apologize.

"You are quite right, madam, I of all people ought to have
known better than to risk damage to the reliefs. We were also
wrong to ignore the barriers, but, you see, we had heard you
were working at Medinet Habu, but when we arrived no one
was here, and my father—"

"Hmmm, yes," said Emerson, scowling at the older man.

We started back toward the gate, with Emerson herding
Mr. and Mrs. Albion ahead of him, and Nefret accompany-
ing them, in case Emerson started to be rude. I followed with
Jumana and Ramses and Mr. Sebastian Albion.

"I would appreciate the opportunity to examine those reliefs and perhaps take a few photographs," the latter said. "If
you could spare the time to explain them, it would be a great
favor. At your convenience, of course."

"We will be working elsewhere for a time," I said. He had
addressed Ramses, not me, but Ramses's mouth was set in
that way of his and he was obviously not inclined to be co-
operative. "How much longer are you planning to remain in
Luxor?"

"Indefinitely, Mrs. Emerson. I suppose you have heard
about the resumption of submarine warfare? In any case, we

had planned to spend the entire winter in Egypt. I am thinking of doing some excavating."

"You had better stop thinking of it," I said. "Unless you can obtain permission from the Service des Antiquités."

"Is that really necessary? There's hardly anyone working here at present. The Valley of the Kings, for instance—"

"That is out of the question," I said sharply. "Few expeditions are in the field at this time, but most of the sites have been allocated. Lord Carnarvon holds the firman for the Valley of the Kings, and I assure you that the authorities would come down hard on anyone who began digging there."

Instead of appearing abashed, the young man gave us a supercilious smile. "Thank you for the advice. We will have to see, won't we?"

"I trust we won't see you digging in the Valley," Ramses said. "The Service des Antiquités is not the only one who would come down hard on you."

The only response was a shrug.

"Goodness, Ramses, but you were brusque with young Mr. Albion," I remarked, after we had seen the party on its way back to their hotel and had mounted our noble steeds.

"Was he? Good," said Emerson. "Don't want people of that sort bothering us."

Ramses glanced back at Jumana, who was talking to Nefret. "I haven't told you what he said about Jumana the other evening."

He repeated the offensive remark. Cyrus turned red with indignation and Emerson growled, "Damn the young swine! Why didn't you tell me? I would have—"

"So would I, if Nefret hadn't stopped me," Ramses said. "I took pains to make the position clear. There's been no harm done."

"And there won't be any," Cyrus declared.

"Quite right," I said. "What did you think of his absurd proposal of excavating in the Valley of the Kings?"

"I was surprised," Ramses admitted. "Visitors sometime

fall into the error of supposing they can dig wherever they like, but he ought to have known better. Was he trying to provoke us?"

"You're almost as suspicious-minded as your mother," said Cyrus.

"My ma," Ramses corrected. "That's how Mr. Albion referred to her the other evening. Father, how would you like being addressed as Pa?"

"Not very much," Emerson grunted.

"You are taking them too seriously," I insisted. "They are rather silly and somewhat annoying, and we will have as little to do with them as possible. Have you decided what needs to be done here, Emerson?"

"What needs to be done," said Emerson grumpily, "is lock the whole place up and shoot any damned tourist who tries to get in. Yes, yes, Peabody, I know, it is an impractical suggestion. You made plans of the brickwork you found west of the chapel, Vandergelt? The men had better cover it up again, otherwise the bloody tourists will climb all over it and destroy what little is left."

"What about repairing the floor?" Cyrus asked. He was not anxious to waste time on that chore, but he was a conscientious individual.

"Leave it," Emerson said. "One of the damned tourists may fall in."

We started back toward the donkey park, where we had left the horses. Still chuckling over Emerson's humorous remark—I think it was supposed to be humorous—Cyrus remarked, "Bertie was in a pretty glum state of mind this morning. Hates being laid up. Is there any reason why he can't come out with us tomorrow?"

"Why not?" Emerson replied. "We can use another pair of hands, if only for keeping field notes."

"I suppose we could arrange a chair and footstool," I mused. "But in my opinion, Bertie ought to stay at home for a few more days."

"He won't stand for it," Ramses said. "I know Katherine; she'll drive him wild, and then he'll run off and do something foolish."

"You are speaking from personal experience, are you?" I inquired, smiling to indicate that it was just one of my little jokes.

I got an answering smile, and a quick kiss on the cheek. "Not at all, Mother. Will you excuse Nefret and me if we go on ahead?"

Risha was aching to run, and so was Moonlight; the slow pace of Cyrus's amiable mare was irksome for steeds of such mettle. So I nodded, and the two young people went off at a brisk trot.

"They sure are a fine-looking young pair," Cyrus said admiringly. Nefret had taken the remaining pins from her hair; it streamed out like a bright banner as Risha broke into a run and Moonlight, not to be outdone, stretched out to match his pace. "I'm not as jealous as I used to be, though," he went on. "Bertie is like a son to me. I'm gonna make him my heir, Amelia. After Cat, of course."

"Excellent, Cyrus," I said approvingly. "He has earned your approbation. I wouldn't mention it to anyone else, though, or the lad will be courted by every female fortune-hunter in Egypt. And if he knows of it, he will suspect the motives of every young lady who indicates interest."

"That's good advice, I reckon," Cyrus agreed.

Emerson's glazed stare indicated that he had stopped listening. He considers me far too prone to offer advice, and talk of courting bores him. "A stick," he said suddenly. "Get the boy a good stout stick, let him do whatever he likes."

"Don't be ridiculous, Emerson," I said.

At Cyrus's suggestion we dined informally at the Castle. Bertie was pleased to see us, and even more pleased when he was offered the chance to return to work. I examined his ankle; it was better; the swelling had gone down and there was only a little bruising. Everyone attributed this to Kadija's miraculous ointment, and such may well have been the case, though I had begun to wonder whether its greatest effectiveness came from the mind of the patient.

After dinner the young man hobbled off to the library with the others. I remained with Katherine to offer additional reassurances.

"I have set up a nice little shelter where Bertie will be perfectly comfortable, and if it proves necessary for him to work elsewhere on the site, we will make certain he does not exert himself. Jumana has taken it upon herself to look after him."

This last was not, perhaps, what Katherine wanted to hear. In my opinion her worries about a serious attachment were groundless as well as prejudiced. Bertie had not got over his interest in the girl, but she had given no evidence of reciprocating; she treated him rather like a slow-witted child. I gave Katherine a little lecture on the subject, adding, "After all, Katherine, there is nothing so destructive of romance than continued proximity."

Katherine pursed up her mouth. "It didn't work that way for Ramses and Nefret."

"That is a special case. Mark my words, working together will soon make Bertie and Jumana detest one another."

I had exaggerated a trifle, but over the next few days Bertie showed increasing evidence of impatience with Jumana. Being a man, he wanted to impress her with his strength and professional skill; being Jumana, she took advantage of his enforced helplessness to fuss over him. By moving his chair and table from one part of the site to another, we made it possible for him to assist with the surveying, at which task he was skilled, but he spent a good deal of the time sitting still. Watching Jumana bustle about, climbing nimbly up the hillside and dashing back down to readjust his sunshade, strained his temper considerably. Only his equable nature and inherent good manners prevented an explosion.

One mildly disquieting incident marred the productive happiness of the next few days. It had nothing to do with

Jamil, though as the Reader may well believe, I had not forgotten him. I did not suppose Jumana had heard from him, since I kept a close eye on her, but his very avoidance of her began to worry me. He needed money, if only for bare subsistence. Where was he getting it?

If it was from his friends and family in Gurneh, none of them would admit it. A wall of silence blocked Selim's inquiries.

"Some are speaking the truth, I think," he had said. "But with certain others, something has frozen their tongues. It is like the old days when the Master controlled the illegal antiquities business and all men went in fear of his wrath."

"Could it be?" Emerson asked me, after Selim had gone on his way.

"Impossible, Emerson."

"Why? We haven't heard from the . . . from him for weeks. We don't know where the devil he's got to."

"He would never interfere with our work, or tolerate a contemptible boy like Jamil."

We were seldom interrupted by visitors. However, one morning when I was investigating a ruined chapel up on the hillside—helping Cyrus with his plan of the tombs, as I had explained to Emerson—I saw a pair of horsemen approaching. Both were wearing the drab olive of military uniform. I made haste to scramble down the slope in the hope of heading them off before they ventured to approach Emerson.

I was too slow, or Emerson was too quick. When I reached them the two men had dismounted and were endeavoring to carry on a polite conversation with my husband. They were finding it heavy going.

"Allow me to repeat that there is nothing to see here," Emerson declared, hands on hips, feet apart, and brows thunderous. "This is an archaeological dig, and you are interrupting my work."

"But, sir . . ." One of the officers—for so their insignia proclaimed them—turned with visible relief to me. He was of something over medium height, his frame heavyset and his face square, particularly around the jaw. The hair exposed when he whipped off his pith helmet, which he did immediately upon seeing me, was a nondescript shade of brown, slightly darker than his carefully trimmed mustache.

"Mrs. Emerson!" he exclaimed. "I dare not hope that you remember me—I had the good fortune to be introduced to you last year in Cairo, by my colleague Woolley, of the Arab Bureau."

"Certainly I do, Major Cartright," I replied, before Emerson could say something rude about the Arab Bureau. "Mr. Woolley is an old friend. I was very sorry to hear he had been taken prisoner by the Ottomans."

"The fortunes of war, ma'am, the fortunes of war."

"Stupidity and ineptitude," Emerson declared. "Sailing up and down the coast in that distinctive yacht, trying to put agents ashore under the very noses of the Turks. He was bound to be caught sooner or later."

Cartright flushed angrily, but kept his temper. "Yes, sir. May I have the honor of introducing another admirer of yours—Lieutenant Algernon Chetwode."

I have never seen a countenance so prototypically English. Like his hair, the brave mustache was flaxen-fair; the lashes framing his blue eyes were so pale they were almost invisible, and his cheeks were as smooth as a girl's. They turned pink as he stuttered out a series of incoherent compliments.

"Can't express my pleasure . . . such an honor . . ."

"Yes, how nice," I said, and since they showed no intention of going away, I added, "I would offer to show you around, gentlemen, but as my husband mentioned, there is nothing here that would interest you. I presume you are on leave from Cairo? May I suggest the Valley of the Kings or the temple of Medinet Habu, which is in that direction."

"You are most kind, Mrs. Emerson," Cartright said, with a smile that showed he was well aware of my real motive. "We only dropped by to pay our respects. We had hoped—that is to say—is your son with you?"

Emerson's eyes narrowed and I felt a constriction in the

region of the diaphragm. Naturally and necessarily, Ramses's activities on behalf of the War Office had been a closely guarded secret. Had his courageous sacrifices been generally known, he would have been a hero; since they were not, he was regarded by many of our acquaintances in Cairo as a coward and a pacifist. (The two words being synonymous in the views of the ignorant.) There was hardly an officer in Cairo who would have spoken to him last year—and here were two of them actually seeking him out.

I might have been tempted to lie, but I could not; Ramses had seen us and was approaching. It was not in his nature to avoid a confrontation. Nefret had hold of his arm. She was biting her lip, a sure sign of worry or annoyance.

If young Lieutenant Chetwode had fawned over us, he did all but genuflect before Ramses. He paid no more attention to Nefret than courtesy demanded, which was in itself highly suspicious; most men paid attention to Nefret.

Unsmiling and composed, Ramses shook hands with both men. "On holiday, are you?" he inquired.

"A brief holiday," Cartright replied. "I have just got back from the Gaza front, and after I had reported to the general, he was good enough to give me a few days' leave."

"I'm sure you deserved it," I said politely.

"Ha," said Emerson. "What the devil are you people doing? You pushed the Turks across the Egyptian border early in January, and you've been squatting outside Gaza ever since. We need a victory in the Middle East, gentlemen; God knows the news on other fronts is bad enough. Why isn't General Murray pushing ahead toward Jerusalem?"

"I'm sure you know the terrain, sir," Cartright said deferentially. Glancing at me—a mere female, who presumably knew nothing about military matters—he explained, "The Turks are determined to hold Gaza; the town is heavily fortified and so are the ridges that run all the way from Gaza to Beersheba. It's a natural defensive line twenty-five miles long. Water is one of our major problems; we have to pump it from the sweet-water canal at Suez clear across the Sinai,

and the advance of the railroad has been delayed by difficult terrain. Intelligence is dreadfully vague at the moment.
Our agents find great difficulty in getting through, and their
aircraft—"

"Yes, yes," Emerson said impatiently. "But the longer you
delay, the more time the Turks will have to bring in rein-
forcements and dig more trenches. You'll have to hit Beersheba at the same time you attack Gaza. There's plenty of
water there."

"I'm sure General Murray would be interested in hearing
your views, sir," Cartright said.

I cleared my throat loudly, and Emerson recollected himself. "If he needs me to point out the obvious, his staff isn't
doing its job. Good day, gentlemen."

He took me firmly by the arm and stalked off, leaving the
two officers no choice but to mount and depart. "Hell and
damnation," he remarked.

"Quite," said Ramses, catching us up. "Extraordinarily
forthright, wasn't he?"

"Too forthright," Emerson muttered. "Why did he tell us
so much?"

Ramses's lips tightened. After a moment, he said, "There
is no reason why you should remember; but Cartright was
one of the three patriots with whom I had that rude encounter at the Turf Club two years ago. He was with the
Egyptian Army at the time."

"The man who struck you in the face while two others
held your arms?" I demanded indignantly. "Good Gad. If I'd
known that I would not have been so courteous."

"No, he was one of the ones who held me," Ramses corrected. "Something has brought about a radical change in his
attitude."

"We can guess what it is," Emerson grunted. "He's with
intelligence now, and someone has told him about you. Secret Service! Good Gad, they might as well shout their business from the rooftops."

I said, "The news of your heroism—" Ramses made a wry

face, and I went on firmly, "That is what it was, and I will call it what it was. But perhaps the information has not spread as widely as we suppose."

"I hope it has spread," Nefret said. She raised her chin defiantly. "I hope everyone knows."

None of us had to request elucidation of this statement. Nefret lived in constant fear of his becoming again involved in a mission like the one that had almost cost him his life two years ago. Accepting another assignment would have been dangerous enough even when his former activities were known only to a few—particularly when one of those few was the head of the Turkish Secret Service. It would have been suicidal if every intelligence officer in Cairo knew. As Ramses had once remarked, there is no point in being a spy if everybody knows you are one.

"I've told you before," Ramses said, addressing his wife in a voice that brought a flush to her cheeks, "that the subject is closed. May we drop it, please?"

"Quite," said Emerson quickly. Though he is, as his conduct proves, a firm believer in thrashing out differences of opinion on the spot and with vigor, disharmony between his beloved children upsets him. "We've wasted enough time on this nonsense. Back to work, eh?"

I had myself been a trifle surprised at the harshness of Ramses's tone. However, I did not suppose that his ill humor would last or that she would be unreceptive to an attempt at apology; and so it proved. Sometime later I happened to observe that neither was in sight; and since it was almost time for luncheon I entered the vestibule of the temple, where I had set up my little shelter. They were not there, but I heard a murmur of voices from behind one of the columns that separated the vestibule from the pronaos. It was a very nice column, with the head of the goddess Hathor instead of a capital. I moved forward to examine it more closely.

I did not tiptoe or try to walk silently, but neither of them was aware of my presence until they saw me. "Damnation!"

said Ramses, releasing her and turning rather red. "Er—I beg your pardon, Mother."

"I should rather beg yours, my dear. I didn't realize you were here. It is almost time for lunch."

"I'll get Father," said Ramses, retreating in haste. Nefret, who was trying to twist her loosened hair into a knot, let out one of her musical chuckles. "Were you afraid we had gone off to quarrel in private?"

"Not really. I presume you were admiring those nice heads of Hathor. I believe I heard Ramses repeat one of her charming epithets—'Golden One.'"

"If you heard," said Nefret, amused and not at all embarrassed, "you know he was addressing me."

"Very appropriate," I said. A ray of sunlight haloed the red gold of her locks. "Hathor was the goddess of love and beauty and—er—"

"Happiness." She looked up at the carved face. It might not have struck some people as the epitome of beauty, for the ears were those of a cow, one of the goddess's sacred animals. After so many years of viewing ancient Egyptian art, such elements had come to seem quite natural to us, however, and the other features were delicately rendered, the long hair curling over the shoulders. "Praising the Great Goddess, Lady of Turquoise, Mistress of the West," Nefret recited. She bowed gravely and deferentially.

I couldn't help myself. "What are you asking for?"

"Happiness," Nefret repeated.

"Then—it is all right, isn't it? Between you two?"

"Of course." She took my arm. "Let's eat."

Emerson kept us so busy that it was not until later in the week that I was able to make my annual pilgrimage to Abdullah's grave. I never felt any particular urgency about doing it, since I did not think of him as being there. I only went because . . . In fact, I do not know why. Le coeur a ses raisons que la raison ne connaît point.

On this occasion my primary purpose was to look at his

new monument. I had not seen it before, since Abdullah had not got round to mentioning that he would like one until just before we left Egypt the previous spring. The request had taken me by surprise; one would not have supposed that an immortal spirit—or, according to Emerson, a sentimental fantasy of my sleeping brain—would care about such things. Emerson raised no objection, however, and I had sent David's sketch and plan to Selim, asking him to proceed.

I meant to go alone, but Ramses saw me slipping out of the house and intercepted me. "I thought we agreed none of us would go off by ourselves, Mother."

"If I see Jamil wearing the Double Crown and blowing kisses I assure you I will not follow him."

Ramses was not amused or convinced. "Where are you going?"

"Only to the cemetery. I have not seen Abdullah's tomb."

"Oh. I haven't seen it either. May I come with you?"

Recognizing the uselessness of a refusal, I agreed. In point of fact, he was the only person to whose company I had no objection. He had been with me the day after Abdullah's funeral, and had helped me to bury over the grave the little amulets of Horus and Sekhmet, Anubis and Sobek—symbols of the ancient gods who guard the soul on the road to the West—in flagrant defiance of Abdullah's faith and my own. However, I had always suspected Abdullah had a secret, half-shamed belief in the old gods. Ramses's silent understanding had given me comfort, which I needed badly that day.

We went on foot, over the rocky ridges and across the stony expanse of the desert plain, Ramses slowing his long strides to match mine. The cemetery was on the north side of the village, not far from the mosque. It was all desert here, all baked earth and stony ground; neither tree nor flowering plant softened the starkness of the lonely graves. The tombs themselves were underground, their location indicated by low rectangular monuments of stone or brick, with upright stones at head and foot. The grave of a saint or sheikh of eminence might be marked by a simple structure crowned with a small cupola. There were only a few of such monuments in this humble cemetery; Abdullah's was conspicuous not only by the freshness of the stones that had been used in its construction but by the somewhat unusual design. It was the conventional four-sided building, but there was a subtle grace in its proportions, and the dome seemed to float, light as a bubble.

The sun was about to set. The rosy light warmed the white limestone of the walls, and from a mosque in a neighboring village came the first musical notes of the evening call to prayer.

"It will be dark shortly." Ramses spoke for the first time since we had left the house. "We mustn't stay long."

"No. I only want—"

I broke off with a catch of breath. It was somewhat uncanny to see any movement in that deserted place, and this figure, emerging from the dimness under the cupola, was human. We were still some distance away; I could not make out details, only the long galabeeyah and white turban, before it scuttled into concealment behind the walls of the mosque.

"Who was that?" I asked.

"I don't know. Did you bring a torch?"

"Certainly. I have all my accoutrements. Shall we follow him?"

"That wasn't Jamil. I don't see any point in chasing after the fellow. Let's just make certain he hasn't done any damage."

The disturbance of the sandy dust was the only sign that anyone other than we had come there. "There are a number of footprints," Ramses muttered, shining the torch around. "Overlapping. That's odd."

"Perhaps members of the family have come to pay their respects, or to pray," I suggested.

"Perhaps. Are you ready to go?"

I had intended to say a few words—think them, rather—but he was obviously uneasy, and really, what more was there to say when I had just had a long conversation with Abdullah? I acquiesced and let Ramses take my arm, since the dusk had thickened.

"I like the design," Ramses said as, with the aid of the torch, we picked a path around the standing monuments. "I hope Abdullah is pleased with it."

"Oh, yes. He was only annoyed because he had to ask. He implied that I ought to have thought of it myself."

"Ah," said Ramses noncommittally.

On the Thursday we were in the midst of our preparations for departure—complicated these days by Sennia and the Great Cat of Re—when a messenger arrived. Jumana had left for Deir el Medina, Ramses was explaining to the cat that he would prefer it did not accompany him, I was dealing with the customary delaying tactics from Sennia, and Emerson was stamping up and down demanding that we hurry. He took the note from Fatima.

"Well, what do you think of this?" he inquired. "Yusuf wants to see us."

"Us?" I echoed. "Who? Sennia, get your books together and GO."

"You and me. He says it's urgent. I wonder who wrote it for him?"

Ramses finished his conversation with the cat and put it down. "A public letter writer, perhaps. Shall Nefret and I come?"

Emerson stroked the cleft in his chin. "No, he said for us to come alone. Run along, we'll join you shortly."

"Unless something interesting develops," I amended.

"Something about Jamil, perhaps," Nefret said. "Do you suppose Yusuf knows where he's been hiding?"

"Let us hope so. It would be a relief to have that business over and done with. I ought to have made more of an effort to question Yusuf," I admitted.

"Don't be unkind to the poor old fellow," Nefret said. "He must have been suffering horribly, torn between his love for his son and his loyalty to you."

"It could be another trick," said Ramses. "Remember your warning, Father, not to go after the boy alone, even if he is wearing—"

"I won't be alone," Emerson said. "Your mother will be with me."

Ramses's heavy dark eyebrows tilted. "Don't forget your parasol, Mother."

"Certainly not. However, I expect Yusuf only wants sympathy and some medicine. It is the least I can do, and I ought to have done it before this."

I put together a little parcel for Yusuf, some of his favorite tobacco and a freshly baked assortment of Fatima's honey cakes, of which he was fond. I also took my medical kit. The others had gone by the time I had collected everything I needed. Emerson and I were soon on our way; but as we turned the horses onto the path that led by the tombs on the lower part of the hill of Sheikh Abd el Gurneh, I saw something that made me bring my little mare to a rude halt.

"Emerson! Look there!"

Where she had come from I could not tell—one of the tombs, perhaps—but the outlines of that trim figure were unmistakable. Only a few women in Luxor wore boots and divided skirts and only one other woman wore a belt jangling with objects.

Emerson, who had also stopped, let out an oath. "After her!" he exclaimed.

"Not so fast, my dear. We must follow at a distance and ascertain where she is going—and why. She has been in the village; if Yusuf admitted his intention of turning Jamil in, she may be on her way to warn him."

"Damnation," said Emerson. "How could she . . . Well, we will soon find out."

He had dismounted as he spoke. Hailing one of the villagers, he said, "Give me your galabeeyah."

"But, Father of Curses," the fellow began.

"Hand it over, I say." Emerson dispensed baksheesh with so lavish a hand that he was instantly obeyed. The jingle of coins attracted several other men. One of them was willing to part with his outer garment too. (I had selected the shortest and cleanest of them.)

Jumana was almost out of sight by then, trotting along with the agility I knew so well, but the delay had been necessary; she would have spotted us instantly if we had been in our usual clothing and on horseback. We got into our impromptu disguises, left the horses with one of the men, and hastened after the girl.

"She's heading back toward our house," Emerson said, looking uneasy. "Perhaps we are wrong, Peabody. She may have been paying a duty call on her father."

"Don't be such a sentimentalist, Emerson. She admitted she hadn't spoken to him for months—and why would she not tell us of her intentions, if they were innocent? She has deliberately deceived me, the treacherous little creature."

The truth of this soon became apparent. Shoulders hunched and bent, as if to make herself less conspicuous, Jumana cut off onto a rough track that wound around houses and hills toward the western cliffs south of Deir el Bahri. Once or twice she glanced over her shoulder. She must have seen us, but evidently our clumsy disguises were good enough to deceive, for she went on without pausing, scrambling nimbly up the rising slope at the base of the cliffs. I could see the temple, below and to our right, as we climbed; the colonnades and tumbled stones shone in the morning light.

Quickly as the girl moved, Emerson kept up without difficulty, his breathing even, his stride slower than his usual pace. Since my lower limbs were not much longer than Jumana's, I had to trot.

"Where the devil is she going?" I panted. "Curse the girl—"

"Save your breath," Emerson advised, offering me his

hand. "By Gad, Peabody, you don't suppose . . . That's where she's headed, though."

With the help of his strong arm I found the going easier, and was able to look about. I knew the place well. The previous year we had removed the golden statue of the god Amon-Re from its hidden shrine at the back of a shallow bay. Jamil was the original discoverer of that place. Could he have selected it as his hiding place? The shaft that led down to a small chamber cut out of the rock was only eight feet deep and it was unlikely that anyone would go there; the Gurnawis knew we had cleared the place of everything it contained.

Jumana stopped, her back to us, in the mouth of the little bay. Her head turned from side to side. Emerson pulled me down behind a heap of detritus. We dared not risk going closer; we were only twenty feet from Jumana, and there was no one else in sight.

She called out. "Jamil, are you there?" Her voice cracked with nervousness.

I heard nothing. She called again, "I am coming."

"We've got him now," Emerson whispered. "Let's go."

When I got to my feet, Jumana was no longer in sight. Emerson ran toward the opening of the bay. I ran after him.

The declivity was shallow and the morning sun shone directly into it. At its far end the shaft we had cleared gaped open, a black square against the rock. There was no sign of Jumana.

"Where is she?" I demanded.

"Never mind her. He can't have got out, there wasn't time." Kneeling on the rubble-strewn ground, Emerson took out his torch and shone it down into the shaft.

It was as empty as we had left it, and that in itself was confirmation of our theory. Sand and pebbles would have partially filled it unless someone had kept it clear. In the light of the torch I saw additional confirmation: a rough but sturdy wooden ladder.

Before I could stop him, Emerson, disdaining the ladder,

had lowered himself by his hands and dropped, landing with a thump of booted feet. Jamil must have heard that, even if he had not heard the sound of our approach.

"Damnation, Emerson," I exclaimed. "Wait for me!"

He had already proceeded into the short passage that led to the chamber. The roof was low; he would have to bend over, which would put his head at a particularly convenient level— convenient for a blow, that is—when he emerged. I dropped my parasol into the shaft and descended the ladder. Snatching up the parasol, I proceeded quickly into the passageway.

There was light at the end of it, but I could hear nothing, which did not lessen my anxiety; already Emerson might be unconscious and bleeding. I removed my little gun from my pocket.

It was plucked from my hand the moment I reached the end of the passage.

"I knew you'd be waving that damned pistol," Emerson remarked, helping me to rise. "He's not here, Peabody. He's been here, though."

He shone his torch round the small chamber. A pile of rugs, forming a rough pallet, tins of food, jars of water, and . . . I lifted the saucer that covered one of them. Beer. He had made himself comfortable.

"He has eluded us again," I said angrily. "How could she have warned him?"

"Obviously he was not in residence," Emerson replied. "That's all to the good, Peabody; if he wasn't here he can't have seen us. He will come back eventually—it's a cozy little den, isn't it? We'll go for the others and stake the place out. Once I get my hands on that girl I will make certain she cannot warn him." His large square teeth, bared in a snarl, shone white in the torchlight.

"Let us go," I said uneasily. "I am not at all comfortable here, Emerson."

"One of your famous premonitions?" He chuckled, but perhaps he had one, too, for he added, "I'll go first."

He waited in the shaft while I crawled through the passage.

The ladder was no longer there.

Before I could stop him, Emerson reached up and gripped the rim of the shaft with both hands. The muscles on his bare forearms tightened as he prepared to pull himself up.

"Watch out!" I shrieked, an instant too late. The heavy stick struck Emerson's arm, causing him to loosen his grip and fall down. I had heard the bone crack.

A trifle unnerved, I took out my pistol and fired twice. The bullets went ricocheting round the walls. The only response was a laugh. I had heard that laugh before, in the Gabbanat el-Qirud.

"A waste of ammunition," remarked Emerson, who was sitting on the floor with his back against the wall, cradling his left arm with his right. His face shone with perspiration.

"Don't move your arm," I ordered, fumbling with the implements hanging from my belt. "Confound it! From now on I will carry some bits of wood with me. Why did we clear the place so thoroughly? There is nothing to serve as a splint. I will go and—"

"Don't even think of it, Peabody. I might be able to lift you up with one arm, but as soon as your head is within range, he'll strike. He's got us in a pretty pickle, my dear."

"He cannot stay there all day," I said, and ducked my head as a rain of small stones descended.

"He appears to have another plan in mind," Emerson said coolly. More rocks fell, including a fist-sized boulder. It landed on my head, which was quite painful, since I was not wearing my pith helmet. "We had better get back into the tunnel," Emerson continued.

I rigged up a rough sling with my shirt, fastening it in place with safety pins from my sewing kit. It was the best I could do in a hurry. If we stayed where we were, one of us would be brained by a boulder eventually. It took Jamil a little while to get his next load of rocks collected; we made it into the passage before another shower descended.

"Well!" I said, drawing a deep breath. "Now we have time to think of a plan."

"Go right ahead," said Emerson through tightly set lips. "At the moment my mind is a blank."

"And no wonder, my dear. I am sure you are in considerable pain. Have a little brandy."

"My discomfort is more mental than physical," Emerson muttered, but he accepted the brandy and took a long swallow. "Peabody, this is ridiculous. We've been in uglier places before, with opponents far more dangerous than that miserable boy; and yet he's managed to get us in an exceedingly tight spot. No one knows where we are . . . except Jumana. Have we been so mistaken in her character? I can't believe she would connive in murder."

"No," I said. "She wouldn't." The strained voice, the odd, bent walk . . . "That wasn't Jumana, Emerson. It was Jamil."

Seven

When the citizens of Deir el Medina abandoned their houses they took their most valued possessions with them—except for the most valuable of all, the goods devoutly deposited with the dead. Looking for tombs was a gamble, with approximately the same odds as any game of chance. The great majority of them were empty and vandalized, but every now and then a lucky winner would find a prize, with some of the grave goods still intact, and the grand prize, the unrobbed tomb of a king or king's wife, was a will-o'-the-wisp that tantalized the imagination of every excavator, whether he admitted it or not. However slim the odds, the temptation to search for treasure was hard to resist, especially when the alternative was a clutter of unimpressive mud-brick walls, or the tedious tasks of measuring and recording.

Jumana was supposed to be helping Bertie and Cyrus finish the surveying, but Ramses wasn't surprised to see her halfway up the hillside, squatting, her head bent, her hands busy. He let out a shout that made Nefret jump and brought Jumana to her feet. She waved vigorously and started down.

"She shouldn't be doing that," he said in exasperation.

"Look at her, grinning and cavorting. She knows she is violating orders."

"Don't be too hard on her," Nefret said tolerantly. "Mother would be up there too. She's found something."

She was holding a small stela. It was not an unusual discovery; a good many of them had been found by earlier excavators, in or near the chapels of the tombs. She offered it to Ramses, raising shining eyes to him.

"You were told not to remove objects from their place," Ramses said severely. The way she was looking at him made him nervous.

"I tagged the place," Jumana protested. "As you showed me. I made the measurements, I know exactly where it should go on the plan. There is no chapel there, Ramses, it must have fallen from its place and tumbled down the hillside. See—isn't it pretty?"

Mollified, and regretting his hard tone, he took the stone from her. The curved top and straight sides, the rows of hieroglyphs that praised the deities worshiped by the male and female figures, were of a standard type, but the deities were somewhat unusual—two plump cats, facing each other across an offering table.

"I've seen other stelae from Deir el Medina that depict cats," he said. "They were identified with several goddesses, including Amon's wife Mut."

"Not with the Great Cat of Re?" Jumana asked.

"Not these." They were rather charming animals, fatter and less aloof than the usual lean Egyptian cat. He indicated the appropriate hieroglyphs. " 'Giving praise to the good and peaceful cat.' Well, maybe they are at that. They aren't named. But the Great Cat of Re wasn't peaceful, was he."

"They're delightful," Nefret said, nodding at Jumana. She got no response; Jumana was watching Ramses, breathless and expectant, waiting for a word of praise from him.

"They are," he conceded. "Let's take it to Bertie. Drawing it will be good practice for him."

"I would like to give it to the Little Bird," Jumana said, as they walked toward the shelter. "Her cat is getting fat, like these, and we could tell her one of them was the Great Cat of Re."

"We will have to wait for the Antiquities Department to decide which pieces we may keep," Ramses said. Feeling he had been a trifle harsh, he added, "It was kind of you to think of it, Jumana."

They greeted Bertie and handed over the stela, and Ramses said, "It's rather a charming piece. Why don't you try your hand at making a copy, Bertie? Unless you're busy with something else."

"I will do it," Jumana said. "I can—"

"Yes, I know you can, but I need you elsewhere."

Selim had set the men to work. He hailed Ramses, demanding his opinion of an unusual raised platform in the corner of the house they were excavating, and Ramses lost track of the time. It wasn't until Cyrus joined them and suggested they stop for luncheon that Ramses realized how late it was.

"Where're your ma and pa?" Cyrus asked with a grin.

"They haven't come?" He knew they hadn't; his father always made his presence known. "They went to see Yusuf; he sent a message asking for them. But they ought to be here by now."

Nefret's expressive face reflected his own uneasiness. "Were we right after all—about Yusuf and Jamil? I really didn't believe it, you know."

"Neither did I," Ramses admitted. He ran his fingers through his hair.

"Where is your hat?" Nefret asked.

"I don't know. Never mind my damned hat. Confound it, they've no business wandering off without informing us. What are we going to do?"

"Have lunch," Nefret said practically. "And wait a little longer."

Cyrus demanded to know what was going on, and after they had set out the food, Ramses told all of them about the message. Cyrus was unconcerned. "They can take care of themselves." Selim scowled. "If Yusuf knew, and did not tell me—"

"That's only a theory, Selim. We can't be certain what Yusuf wanted. Maybe it was Mother's notorious medical skills."

"He would be more likely to ask for hers than for mine," Nefret admitted. "The older men and women don't believe in my newfangled notions. But it shouldn't have taken them this long, even if Yusuf asked Father to perform an exorcism."

By the time they had finished the meal Ramses had come to a decision. "We had better try to find them. Assume the worst, as Mother says, and act on it."

"Where are you going to look?" Cyrus asked. "You don't know where they might be by now."

"Yusuf," Ramses said shortly. "If he has any information, I'll get it out of him."

Selim rose. "Daoud and I will come with you."

"Damn this foot!" Bertie burst out. "Look, it's almost healed, I can keep up."

"Not this time." Ramses's hand rested briefly on the other man's shoulder. "We don't need additional manpower—"

"No," said Daoud, folding his massive arms.

"No," Ramses repeated, nodding in acknowledgment. "Cyrus, you had better stay here. Jumana, come with us."

She stared at him, her eyes wide and dark. "You think I know something I have not told you? It is not true!"

"I haven't accused you of anything," Ramses said.

"Do let's go," Nefret exclaimed. "Why are we wasting time talking?"

They took the most direct route, past the temple and across the foothills, approaching the village from the south. Most of the inhabitants were enjoying their afternoon nap, but by the

time they reached Yusuf's house a few wakeful souls had
spotted them and run on ahead, so Yusuf was expecting them.

He was lying on the divan in the main room, covered with
a blanket, though the day was warm. It was the first time
Ramses had seen the old man since their arrival. The change
in him was distressing. The once plump jowls hung down in
loose folds, and his thin hands gripped the edge of the cov-
erlet. He shrank back as they all crowded into the room.
Ramses didn't blame him; they made a threatening assemblage: he and Nefret, Daoud looming like a monolith, Selim's face unyielding as walnut.

Nefret let out a little sound of pity and surprise, pushed
past the others, and bent over the old man. "Salaam
aleikhum, Uncle Yusuf. I regret we did not come before. We
did not know you were so ill."

Her low voice, sweet with sympathy, reproached the others and reassured Yusuf. "I am better, Nur Misur," he
croaked.

Ramses gestured Selim to remain silent. He couldn't
bully a pathetic specimen like Yusuf. Anyhow, Nefret's
methods were more likely to win him over. He looked
around for Jumana. She was behind Daoud, whose large
form hid all of her but her little boots.

"Was it the Sitt Hakim who made you better, Uncle
Yusuf?" Nefret asked. "What did she give you?"

"The Sitt Hakim? She has not been here. No one has been
here." Self-pity and resentment gave new life to his feeble
voice. "None of you came to ask about me."

"We are sorry, Uncle," Nefret said. "But the Sitt Hakim
did come, this morning. You sent her a message asking her
to come."

"I sent no message," Yusuf said sullenly. "Why should I?
You should have come without my asking."

Selim moved slightly, and again Ramses motioned him to
be quiet. Yusuf's resentment—justifiable resentment, Ramses had to admit—was genuine. There was no reason for him

to lie, since he knew there were dozens of witnesses who would have seen the elder Emersons had they been there.

From the doorway a harsh voice said, "He speaks the truth, Brother of Demons. The Sitt has not been here."

It was Yusuf's eldest wife, her voice accusatory, her face crumpled into innumerable wrinkles by age and indignation. She shoved at Daoud. "Get out, Daoud, and take her with you, the shameless creature. Why have you all come, like accusers, to trouble a sick old man?"

Daoud turned, in his ponderous fashion, and Jumana let out a little squeak. Her father's eyes rested briefly on her and shifted away.

"I'm sorry," Ramses said. "We are looking for my father and mother, who may be in trouble. It is true that Yusuf sent no message—that they did not come here?"

"It is true," the old woman snapped. "Ask anyone."

"Shall we go now?" Daoud asked nervously. According to Selim, his giant cousin feared only two things: the displeasure of the Father of Curses, and an angry old woman.

"We may as well," Ramses said.

Daoud was the first to go. Jumana followed, so closely she was treading on his heels. Ramses hesitated. He had meant to ask Yusuf about Jamil, but this disclosure had altered everything. His parents must have been intercepted or distracted before they reached Yusuf, lured away by a false message. There was no time to waste; the afternoon was passing.

"I'm sorry," he said again.

"I'll come back," Nefret promised the old man. "As soon as I can."

Yusuf did not reply. His eyes were closed.

The usual crowd had gathered outside. Selim, who had been talking with several of the men, turned to Ramses. "It is true, they did not come to this house. But Ahmed says Mahmud says his cousin Mohammed saw them this morning. They left their horses with him and gave him money."

"Which Mohammed?" Ramses demanded.

"His house is at the bottom of the hill, near the tomb of Ramose."

"Oh, that Mohammed. All right, let's find him."

They led the horses; the slope on this side was steep. Mohammed, who was stretched out in the shade peacefully sleeping, did not wake until Ramses shook him. "Ah," he said, rubbing his eyes, "you have come for the horses. I took good care of them, you see."

They were in the courtyard of an ancient tomb, shaded and well supplied with water. Ramses handed over baksheesh. "Yes, you did. When did the Father of Curses and the Sitt Hakim leave the horses?"

"Many hours ago." Mohammed yawned.

"They'd have come straight here," Nefret interposed, knowing, as did Ramses, that Mohammed's notions of time were vague.

"Probably. It's been at least six hours, then. Where did they go, Mohammed?"

"That way." A gesture indicated the direction—not up the hill, toward Yusuf's house, but northward.

"On foot?"

"How could they ride when they left the horses with me?"

Selim lost patience. "Don't try to be clever, Mohammed, because you are not. Why did they leave the horses and go on foot? What did they say to each other?"

"How should I know? They spoke in English, very fast." Another gigantic yawn concluded the speech.

A younger man, his beard just beginning to show, plucked at Selim's sleeve. "My father only thinks of baksheesh and sleep, Selim, but I can tell you what happened. The Father of Curses took his galabeeyah, and the Sitt took mine. It was because they saw someone. She said 'Look there,' and he looked and swore and then they took our clothes and went hurrying away, behind the tombs and around the hill."

"Your clothes?" Nefret repeated.

"Our galabeeyahs, my father's and mine. The Father of Curses paid well; but when the Sitt Hakim has finished with mine, I would like to have it back. I have only—"

"Did you see the person they were following?" Ramses interrupted.

"Oh, yes." The boy pointed. "It was she."

Jumana froze, her eyes focusing on the pointing finger. "He lies," she gasped.

"I do not lie. She wore the same clothing, boots and coat and a skirt, that blew out as she ran. Not trousers, as men wear. What other woman would wear such garments?"

"Several of us," Nefret said, catching hold of Jumana, who appeared ready to fly at her accuser. "We know it wasn't you, Jumana, you couldn't have got from here to Deir el Medina before we arrived."

Ramses rewarded the observant youth extravagantly and went after Selim, who was already running along the path the boy had indicated. It turned and rose, and there before them lay the length of the desert plain, covered with hillocks and hills, houses and villages and ruins—almost two miles long from Medinet Habu to the slopes of Drah abu'l Naga on the north. The sun was low over the western cliffs.

"Wait," Ramses called. Selim stopped, and the others came up to him.

"What can we do?" the reis asked, for the hopelessness of pursuit was evident to him as well. "It was hours ago that they were here. Even if one saw them—"

"He wouldn't be here either," Ramses cut in. "Or remember them. Father and his damned disguises!"

"The Father of Curses," said Daoud, his calm unshaken, "cannot be mistaken for any other man."

"That's true," Nefret agreed. "Not to mention Mother trotting along holding up the skirts of somebody else's galabeeyah. Ramses—Selim—let's just keep calm, shall we? We will spread the word, asking anyone who may have seen them to report to us; but that may take a while. Perhaps we can deduce where they might have gone." She turned to Jumana. "You know whom they were following, don't you?"

The girl's eyes fell. "Jamil?"

"It couldn't have been anyone else," Nefret said. "He's taller than you, but otherwise the resemblance between you is strong. Somehow he got hold of clothes like yours. He must have sent the message. I don't believe your father knew anything about it."

If it was meant as consolation, Jumana remained indifferent. "Why?" she demanded. "Why would Jamil do this?"

"Not to lead them to his tomb," Ramses said. He was too worried now to be considerate of her feelings. "Face the facts, Jumana. He meant to do them harm—and he must have succeeded, God knows how, or they would have been back before this. Can you think of anything—anything at all—that might help us to find them?"

"How could Jamil harm the Father of Curses?" She flinched back from Ramses and her eyes filled with tears. "No—wait—don't be angry. I am trying to think, trying to help. And I think there are only a few things he could do. He is not very strong, Jamil, or very brave; the Father of Curses could break him in two with one hand, and the Sitt Hakim is as fierce as a man. He would lead them to some place where he can play a dangerous trick on them with no danger to himself."

The sun was sinking. It would be dark in a few hours. "This isn't getting us anywhere," Ramses said, trying to keep his voice level. "There are too many places like that. If he's got in the habit of pushing people off cliffs, as Mother put it . . ."

"Can you visualize Jamil pushing Father?" Nefret demanded. "He'd have to back off twenty feet and run at Father—and then have another go at Mother, who would be peppering him with bullets while he ran."

Jumana gave her a look of surprise and reproach, but Ramses knew his wife's lighthearted comment was a valiant attempt to keep their spirits up and reassure them. It did help to relieve Ramses's anxiety a bit; the scene she had described was so ludicrous it brought a halfhearted smile to his face.

"You're right, though, Jumana," she went on. "He'd want some place away from people. Not toward the cultivation, but back that way, along the base of the cliffs. A place he could trick them into entering without exposing himself."

"But then," said Daoud, "they would come out again. How could he prevent them? Unless . . ."

Quick wits were not Daoud's most notable characteristic, but every now and then he confounded them all by reaching a conclusion that had escaped everyone else. They waited for him to continue.

"Unless it was a very narrow space," Daoud went on, his brow wrinkling. "With no other way out. Then, when they tried to come out, crawling or bent over, he could prevent them—standing to one side with a long heavy stick. If he was quick and lucky, one blow might be enough."

The simple words had created a vivid and very ugly picture. "You're talking about a tomb," Ramses said slowly. "Or a cave. Surely they wouldn't be stupid enough to enter an obvious trap—not both of them . . ." He caught Nefret's eye and threw up his hands. "Hell and damnation! They would, wouldn't they? Especially Mother. Daoud, you reason well, but there are hundreds of such places in the cliffs. We wouldn't know where to start looking. I'm going back and talk to Yusuf. There's an outside chance—"

"Wait—wait!" Jumana was bouncing on her toes, her face flushed with excitement. "I have remembered something—something Jamil said when we first met at Luxor. He was talking about the tomb of the princesses and how he had been cheated, and then he talked very fast and very angrily, saying that he had discovered two rich treasures and had nothing to show because everyone had cheated him of what was rightfully his, and—"

She paused to draw a long breath. Ramses was about to express his impatience with her dramatic, long-drawn-out narrative when Nefret said softly, "Let her tell it her way."

"I am trying to remember exactly what he said," Jumana explained. She hadn't missed Ramses's signs of impatience either. "These are the words, the exact words. 'They took it, the Inglizi, but I have taken it back; the dwelling place of a god is not too good for me, and they will never find me there, and someday . . .' It was then he threatened to kill you, Ramses, and I forgot what he said before because it made no sense and I was very worried and—"

"Ah, yes." Daoud nodded. So far as he was concerned, the matter was settled. "The shrine of Amon-Re. I should have thought of it."

"The place certainly fits your specifications," Ramses said. He was afraid to let his hopes rise. "I suppose it can't do any harm to have a look."

"Shall we go back for the horses?" Nefret asked.

"They went on foot," Ramses said. "We may find some trace of them along the way."

They took the most direct path, straight toward the western cliffs, over rising rocky ground interrupted by occasional outcroppings. Remembering the shrine chamber they had cleared the previous year, Ramses had to admit it would make an ideal spot for an ambush, assuming Jamil could trick them into entering the place. It might not have been difficult. They had thought they were following Jumana, and if they had believed Jamil was inside the man-made cavern, Emerson would not have hesitated to go down after him. And his mother would have followed, of course—"to protect him!" If they had found the place empty they would have returned to the shaft, which was perpendicular and not very deep. If he was standing on the bottom, Emerson's head would be less than two feet below the surface. The picture that formed in Ramses's mind was even uglier than the first: a long, heavy club crashing down on his father's bare head.

Their precipitate pace aroused the curiosity of the people they encountered. Several of them followed along, in case something of interest might occur. Questions assailed them. "Had something happened? Where were they going?" Ramses didn't answer; he wanted to swat at them, as he would have swatted flies. Receiving no replies, one of them suggested, "Are you looking for the Father of Curses, then? He was—"

The word ended in a gurgle as Selim spun round and caught him by the throat. "You saw him? When? Why didn't you say so?"

Plucking at his fingers, the luckless man gasped, "You did not ask, Selim."

Selim loosened his grip and Ramses apologized in the usual way. Clutching a handful of coins and swelling with pride at being the center of attention, their informant explained that he had seen the Father of Curses and the Sitt Hakim early that morning, when he was on his way to work. They had been wearing Egyptian dress, but, the fellow added, the Father of Curses could not be mistaken for any other man. He had been tempted to follow, but he was late for his work and they were going too fast. Yes, that way, toward Deir el Bahri.

He and several of the other men trailed along, speculating and discussing the matter. The sun was low and the shallow, well-remembered bay was deep in shadow. Ramses thought he saw a darker shadow, slim and supple as a snake, move rapidly along the broken ground to the south. He might have imagined it, and just then it was the least of his concerns.

One look into the shaft told him they had come to the right place. It was four feet deep in rubble—not the drift of sand and random bits of rock that might have accumulated naturally, but new fill, broken stone. Not far from the opening lay a rough wooden ladder and a crumpled basket.

"My God," Nefret gasped. "He was filling in the shaft. They must be . . . Mother! Father, can you hear me?"

The uneven surface of the fill moved, shifted, subsided. Using language he had never before employed in their presence, Selim fell flat on the ground, reached down and snatched a handful of chips. "They are under it! They are still alive, they are moving! Hurry—Daoud—"

"Hold on," Ramses said, ducking to avoid the chips Selim had flung frantically over his shoulder. "There's the basket Jamil must have used. Leave it to Daoud."

"Yes," said Daoud placidly. "There is no hurry. Look." Another shift of the stone surface resulted in a further subsistence—no more than an inch, but now Ramses saw what Daoud's calmer mind had grasped. Someone was digging the stone out from below, a little at a time.

"They will be in the passage," Daoud went on, climbing down into the shaft and taking the basket Selim handed him. "We will soon have them out."

There wasn't anything they could do to help Daoud except empty the basket as soon as he handed it up. Ramses fought the urge to join him in the shaft, but only one person could work efficiently in the narrow space. It was not long, though it seemed an eternity to the anxious watchers, before a break in the solid wall of the shaft became visible—the squared-off lintel of the entrance to the side passage.

It was filled to the top with broken stone.

Ramses lost the last remnants of his calm. "Father!" he shouted at the top of his lungs. "Mother, for God's sake—"

Daoud stopped digging. In the silence Ramses heard sounds of activity behind that ominous blockage. An irregular gap, less than two inches deep, appeared, and an eerily distorted, very irritated voice was heard.

"Ramses, is that you? I trust you did not allow him to escape. Is Daoud with you? He will have to empty the entire shaft, the cursed stones keep trickling down into the passage. Though 'trickle' is perhaps an inappropriate word."

After Ramses had drawn his first full breath in what felt like hours, he persuaded his garrulous mother to retreat farther down the passage. She continued to shout instructions and questions, and they shouted questions back at her—a fairly futile exercise, since Daoud had gone back to work with renewed energy and the crash and rattle of stone drowned out most of the words. Ramses shouted along with the rest of them. He had been utterly taken aback by the in-

tensity of his relief when he heard his mother's voice, and a
distant bellow from Emerson. This wasn't the first time they
had been in trouble, not by a long shot, and he had always
worried about them, but for some reason he had never fully
realized how much he loved and needed them. The very
qualities that sometimes irritated him were the qualities he
would miss most: his mother's infuriating self-confidence
and awful aphorisms, his father's belligerence and awful
temper. After all the adventures they had survived with their
usual aplomb, it would be horribly ironic if they met their final defeat (he couldn't even think the other word) at the
hands of the most contemptible opponent they had ever
faced.

I'm getting to be as superstitious as Mother, he thought. It
hasn't happened. It isn't going to happen.

His mother's half-heard orders had provided enough information to save valuable time. Some of their followers ran
off and came back with enough wood to make a litter as well
as a splint for Emerson's arm. The light of several torches
brightened the increasing darkness and one overly enthusiastic helper got a basketful of rock square on the chin as he
leaned over the shaft offering unnecessary advice.

As soon as the space was clear enough, Ramses dropped
down and crawled into the passage. It was half-filled with
bits of stone, which sloped down toward the far end. His
mother hadn't sat waiting to be rescued; she had scooped the
stuff out from below as Jamil dumped it in above. She hadn't
been able to keep up with him, but that was his mother for
you—"every little bit helps," she would have told herself,
and, "Never give up hope." Something caught in his throat.
He hurried on toward the square opening at the far end,
which glowed with faint light.

He took in the scene in a single glance, by the light of the
failing torch—the pile of rugs on which Emerson was lying,
the jars, the stores of food—and his mother, sitting on the
floor with her back against the wall, dredging peas out of a
tin with her fingers.

"Ah, there you are, my dear," she said. "And Nefret too? How nice."

Her face was filthy, her hair gray with stone dust. Arms and shoulders were bare and as dirty as her face; the garment that more or less covered the upper part of her body had narrow ruffled straps, yards of lace, and several little pink bows.

Ramses was unable to speak or move. Nefret had gone at once to Emerson and was examining his arm. She let out a choked laugh. "She's used the ribs and shaft of the parasol for a splint!"

"Once again proving, if proof were needed, the all-round usefulness of a good stout parasol," said his mother.

Peas went flying as Ramses snatched her up and hugged her.

⋮

"**A**ll's well that ends well," I remarked, sipping my whiskey and soda.

The axiom was trite, I confess, but I do not believe it deserved the general grumble of disapproval it received. They were all there on the veranda, even Katherine. Dinner was going to be very late, since Fatima had been too agitated to instruct the cook when she learned that not only we, but Ramses and Nefret and Daoud and Selim, had vanished into thin air, somewhere between Sheikh Abd el Gurneh and the western cliffs. Cyrus and Bertie had waited less than an hour before going in pursuit; finding the horses still in Mohammed's charge and with no idea of where to look next, they had returned to the house in the hope that some or all of us had returned.

I cannot say that anyone behaved sensibly. Cyrus had sent for his wife, Sennia demanded that she be allowed to take the Great Cat of Re out to look for Ramses, and Gargery had to be forcibly restrained from dashing wildly out of the house waving a pistol. His grumbles, on the monotonous theme of "going off like that without me" were the loudest of all.

"Do be still, Gargery," I said sternly. "And the rest of you. We had no choice but to act at once."

"Quite," said Emerson, who was having some difficulty smoking his pipe and drinking his whiskey with only one serviceable arm. Nefret had tended to him; he had a nice neat cast and a proper sling. Nefret had admitted, in confidence, that she had made the cast twice as heavy and thick as was usual, since she knew he would keep hitting it against things. I saw the logic of this, though I knew it would mean a few more shirts ruined. I had had to cut a long slit in the sleeve of the one he was wearing so he could get it over the cast.

"Well, mebbe so," Cyrus conceded. "But you four should have left word with someone. You knew we'd be worried."

Ramses began, "I'm very—"

"Sorry be damned," said his father gruffly. "For all you knew, there was not a moment to lose. Ramses, my boy—er—thank you. Again."

Ramses's thin brown face broke into a smile. "It wasn't me, Father, it was Daoud and Jumana. Sherlock Holmes couldn't have done better."

Daoud beamed. "Who is Sherlock Holmes?" he asked.

"The greatest detective who ever lived," Ramses replied. None of us laughed, for fear of hurting Daoud's feelings, but Ramses directed another smile at me. "Except for Mother."

Then we could laugh. I joined in as heartily as the others, my heart swelling with affection.

"Sennia, it is long past your bedtime," I said. "Off you go."

She had to give everyone a good-night kiss and of course she had to have the last word. "The Great Cat of Re would have found you."

"Ha," I said, but I said it under my breath. The kitten had grown very fat and lazy. Curled up on Ramses's lap, it resembled a shapeless bundle of spotted gray fur.

After Sennia had gone I took another cucumber sandwich. I was ravenous, for the peas and the foie gras that had preceded them had done very little to assuage the hunger resulting from long hours of strenuous manual labor.

"Let us now," I said, "discuss what we have learned. It has not been wasted effort, though we did let Jamil get away from us."

"I haven't learned a blamed thing except that you two are incorrigible," Cyrus grumbled.

"Not at all, Cyrus. First, there is the interesting matter of Jamil's costume. He was not wearing Jumana's clothes. They would have been far too small for him. He cannot have purchased them because . . . Need I explain my reasoning?"

"No," Katherine said. "Aside from the question of how he could pay for them, I can't see him going into one of the shops and trying on blouses and skirts."

"That is right. We will leave that matter for the moment. I think I know the answer, and it can easily be proved. The second clue . . . Ramses, at one time you were able to recall the entire contents of a crowded storeroom some hours after you had seen it. Do you remember what was in Jamil's hideout?"

"Rugs, several jars . . . I guess I wasn't paying attention. Sorry, Mother."

"Quite understandable, my dear," I said. His impulsive embrace had touched me deeply, even if it had hurt my back. To see my imperturbable son forget all else in the joy of finding his parents alive and well assured me that his affection was sincere and profound.

"Fortunately I had ample time to inspect the place," I went on. "It was well stocked, but the most interesting items were the tins of food. European food—peas and beans and cabbage, beef, even a tin of foie gras. Someone supplied him with those delicacies, or with the money to purchase them. No, Jumana, I know it wasn't you."

I knew because I had been careful to keep all the cash in the house under lock and key. Trust is a beautiful thing, but when someone has done you an injury, you are a fool if you give him the chance to do you another.

"It is beginning to look as if he *has* found another tomb," Ramses said thoughtfully. "It's the only way he could lay his hands on that much money, by selling some of the artifacts. Mother, what did you do with that cosmetic jar you bought in Cairo? I'd like to have a closer look at it."

"Wait until after dinner," I said, rising with a suppressed groan. Those long hours on hands and knees in the passage, pulling the rubble out, had taken their toll on my back, and ruined a good pair of leather gloves.

The Vandergelts stayed, of course. Wild horses could not have dragged Cyrus away, and nothing made Fatima happier than having more people to feed. Some of us were rather inclined to gobble, I am afraid; but I noticed that Bertie was not eating with his usual healthy appetite. Under cover of the animated speculations about another tomb, I said softly, "Are you feeling well, Bertie? How is your ankle?"

"It's fine. I could walk or climb with no trouble, if everyone would stop fussing over me." Repenting his surly tone almost at once, he gave me an apologetic smile. "You told me last year you'd let me take a hand in your next adventure, remember? I haven't done a bl——blasted thing to help! It's nobody's fault but mine, I know that; I'm so confounded clumsy and stupid——"

"Now don't say that, Bertie. Anyone could suffer an accident like yours, and we are still a long way from a solution to this matter. Who knows, your opportunity may come at any moment."

The corners of his mouth drooped. "Yes, ma'am, I hope so. I've been sitting in that chair staring at the same scenery for so long, it's driving me crazy. I swear, I know every crack in that cliff face and every brick in those house walls."

"We will have another look at your foot, Nefret and I," I promised. "Perhaps with a little strapping you can begin to move about more."

As soon as we had finished dinner we retired to the drawing room, and I went to fetch the cosmetic jar and lid and the other odds and ends I had purchased from Aslimi. Emerson arranged the lamps to give the maximum amount of light and Ramses took the jar in his long fingers.

"There *was* a cartouche," he said, after a moment. "I think I can make out a few lines." He turned the jar from side to side, so that the light came at it from different angles. "Paper and pencil, Nefret, please."

The sketch he produced was, I confess, something of a letdown. There was a great expanse of blank paper and a few random lines, some horizontal, some perpendicular, some curved. Ramses studied it for a few moments and then began filling in the missing spaces, connecting one section to another, as one does in a certain kind of child's puzzle. Finally he put the pencil down. "That's all I can be certain of. It's enough, though."

Not to me, I thought, studying the hypothetical hieroglyphs in puzzlement. There were only a few: a long, thin, squared-off sign, the jagged line of the water hieroglyph, and a pair of curving horns.

"Not to me," said Emerson.

"There is only one royal cartouche that contains those particular signs," Ramses said. "To the best of my knowledge, that is. This is how the rest of it looks." He completed the name and Emerson let out a gasp.

"Shepenwepet. By the Almighty, the boy has found one of the Divine Wives of Amon!"

Eight

We sat up late that night, going over and over the astonishing revelation—for none of us doubted Ramses's reconstruction of the cartouche. In the end we were forced to the conclusion that there was absolutely no way of knowing where in the immense Theban necropolis Jamil's hypothetical tomb might be. The cosmetic pot in itself told us nothing, except that Jamil was not as stupid as we had believed.

"It is a common error," I admitted, in chagrin, "to assume that because someone is uneducated and illiterate he is necessarily ignorant. There are ways of acquiring knowledge other than by reading. Jamil had worked for a number of Egyptologists and he knew a great deal about tomb robbing—more than we know, I expect. He had sense enough to realize that such a cartouche would arouse speculation, so he removed it, even though he lost money thereby. Are you certain it was done recently, Ramses, not in ancient times, by someone who wanted to reuse the jar?"

Ramses was certain. The little pot was not an essential part of the funerary equipment, like a canopic jar or a sarcophagus. Besides, the marks were fresh. The patina—

Emerson had cut him off at that point, remarking that we would take his word for it.

The other bits and pieces I had purchased from Aslimi were even less informative. As we all knew, the same techniques and motifs had been used throughout pharaonic history. They might not have come from the same place as the jar; there was no way of dating them.

"So where are we gonna look next?" Cyrus asked hopefully. "The western wadis again?"

"We certainly are not going off on a series of random searches," Emerson replied, extracting his pipe and tobacco pouch from his shirt pocket. "Damnation," he added, acknowledging the difficulty of proceeding with the process.

"Let me do that for you, my dear." I took them from him.

Bertie coughed deprecatingly. "I may be on the wrong track altogether, but if I were trying to conceal something I wouldn't hang about the place howling like a banshee and making a spectacle of myself."

"I agree," Ramses said. "That's the one area we can forget about. If he wants us to go there, it's because there's nothing to find."

The men all nodded. I hoped they were right, since I had not much enjoyed our excursions to that remote region, but I was not entirely convinced. Jamil obviously enjoyed taunting people, and youth suffers, among other weaknesses, from overconfidence. It might amuse the wretched boy to lead us to the general area and watch us wear ourselves out looking for a well-concealed entrance.

I had to admit that thus far his confidence had been justified; he had outwitted us on every occasion.

Emerson announced that we would return to Deir el Medina next morning. "We will finish that plan of yours, Bertie," he said. "Fine job, my boy. There are only a few more details to be added."

"Tomorrow's Friday," Cyrus objected. "My men have the day off, and you ought to rest, Emerson."

"We can finish the surveying without the men," Emerson said dogmatically. "And I have no intention of allowing a minor injury to keep me from my usual activities—all my usual activities."

Nor did it. I wished Nefret had not made the cast quite so heavy.

We managed to get off next morning without Sennia or the Great Cat of Re. Nefret did not accompany us either. I had suggested—tactfully, as is my habit—that she might want to give a little luncheon party, since she had not had the opportunity to entertain our friends in her new abode. Under threat of losing our custom, Abdul Hadi had actually finished a dining table and several chairs. She readily consented, but added with a knowing smile, "I won't ask what you are up to, Mother, since I know you enjoy your little surprises."

Early morning in Luxor, particularly at that season of the year, is always beautifully cool and stimulating. I was even more keenly aware of it that day, after those long hours in the stifling darkness of the buried chamber. Truth compels me to admit that I had wondered at times whether I would ever again behold the shining cliffs of western Thebes and feel the morning breeze against my face. Logic had informed me that Jamil could not continue pouring stones into the shaft indefinitely, but the space in the passage and the chamber itself was limited, and so was the air.

I had not, and would not, confess this weakness to any other. After all, it had turned out right in the end.

When we arrived at Deir el Medina, Bertie was working on his plan, and Selim had also turned up. He was not as devout as his Uncle Daoud, who always attended Friday services when he could.

"That is very well done, Bertie," I exclaimed. "Obviously you didn't spend all the time staring at the cliffs! But where is Cyrus? Didn't he come with you?"

"Up there." Bertie gestured. "I offered to go with him, but he said—"

"Damnation!" Emerson exclaimed loudly. Cyrus was high on the hillside, north of the area where most of the tombs were located. Hearing Emerson's shout, he straightened and waved.

"What's he doing up there?" Ramses asked.

"He wanted to have a look at the tombs of the Saite princesses," Bertie explained.

"Why, for Heaven's sake?" I demanded. "They aren't the original tombs of the princesses—the God's Wives, to be more precise—or even their reburials. Two of their sarcophagi were—"

"Yes, yes, Peabody," said Emerson. "Damned old fool climbing around up there . . ." He set off toward the slope with his usual brisk stride.

Ramses caught my eye, nodded, and went trotting after him. The rest of us followed more slowly. Bertie was determined to accompany us, so I walked with him, giving him little suggestions as to where to place his feet.

The shafts—tombs, I should say—were not in the main cemetery on the western hill, but on the northern slope, closer to the temple, so we did not have far to go. We found Emerson on his hands and knees—one hand and both knees, that is—peering down into a dark opening while Ramses directed his torch into it. It did not look much like a tomb entrance; the edges were broken and irregular.

"Are you sure this is it?" I inquired. "It doesn't look like a tomb entrance."

"Of course I'm sure" was the querulous reply. A chunk of rock broke off from under his hand. "Curse it," said Emerson, recovering his balance without difficulty. "The whole place is falling in. Nobody has been down there for a while."

"Which one of the princesses' tombs is it?" Cyrus asked eagerly.

Emerson got to his feet. "None, as a matter of fact. This is the tomb where they found the reused sarcophagus of Ankhnesneferibre. Another sarcophagus was found nearby."

"Here," said Ramses, a little distance away.

We must have looked somewhat absurd clustered round that hole in the ground peering intently at nothing. There was nothing to be seen, not even rubble. The shaft was fairly clear, but so deep, the light of our torches did not reach the bottom.

"Nobody has been down there either," Ramses said. "Not since—1885, wasn't it, that the sarcophagus was removed?"

Emerson grunted agreement. "I cannot imagine what prompted this performance, Vandergelt," he said severely. "You might have done yourself an injury."

"Idle curiosity," said Cyrus with a sheepish grin.

"The view is worth the climb," Bertie said, shading his eyes with his hand.

We were about halfway up the sloping ground that ended at the base of a precipitous cliff. It dropped abruptly to the level; opposite lay another high range of hills, and in the cleft between them we could see the Theban plain, misty green in the morning light, stretching down toward the distant sparkle of the river.

"Quite beautiful," I agreed. "Now that we have seen it, shall we go? Nefret is expecting us for luncheon, and I want to call on Yusuf sometime today."

We retraced our steps, down the hill toward the temple. Emerson, who had disdained assistance from Ramses, allowed me to take his arm, under the impression that he was assisting me. "Are you planning to question Yusuf?" he inquired. "I suppose we ought to."

"I will interrogate him, yes—subtly and indirectly—but my primary motive is to be of help to the poor old fellow. I ought to have gone before."

"Hmph," said Emerson. It was an expression of doubt or derision, but I did not know whether he was being sarcastic about my motives or my ability to carry out a subtle interrogation. I did not ask.

"I will come with you to see Yusuf," Selim announced.

"I would rather you did not, Selim. In fact," I added, inspecting my escort, "I don't want any of you to come with me. Goodness gracious, the five of you looming over him would frighten the poor old man into a fit."

"I guess you don't need Bertie and me," Cyrus conceded. "We may as well go home and get spiffed up for the party."

"Nefret will not expect you to dress, Cyrus," I assured him. "Emerson won't bother."

"Selim will," said Cyrus, directing a grin at the young man. "Can't let him outshine the rest of us."

Selim remained grave. "I will only do what is right. The Father of Curses does what is right in his eyes."

"Well said." Cyrus gave him a friendly slap on the back. "Don't let Amelia go by herself, Emerson. Lord only knows what she might get up to."

"What nonsense!" I exclaimed. "I am only going to examine Yusuf and prescribe—"

"My house is not far from Yusuf's," Selim said. "We will sit in the courtyard, Ramses and the Father of Curses and I, and keep watch."

However, Yusuf was not at home. That elderly harridan his wife informed me that he had gone to the mosque. She did not know when he would be back.

"He cannot be as feeble as I feared, then," I remarked. "He is able to be up and about?"

"Yes." No thanks to you, her hostile stare added.

"Give him this." I extracted a bottle from my medical bag. It was a harmless concoction of sugar water with a few herbs added to give it piquancy. Such placebos can be as effective as medicine in certain cases, if the sufferer believes in them. "He is not to take it all at once," I added. "This much . . ." I measured with my fingers on the bottle. "Morning and night. I will come round tomorrow or the next day to see how he is getting on."

Her wrinkled face softened a trifle. "Thank you, Sitt Hakim. I will do as you say."

My reception by Selim's wives was much more enthusiastic. They were both young and pretty and I must confess—though I do not approve of polygamy—that they seemed to get on more like affectionate sisters than rivals. Selim was an indulgent husband, who had become a convert to certain Western ways; with his encouragement, both had attended school. They offered me a seat and brought tea and coffee, with which they had already supplied Ramses and Emerson.

"You may as well have something," said my son, who was sitting on a bench pretending he had been there the whole time. (In fact, he had been watching Yusuf's house; I had caught a glimpse of him ducking back into concealment as I approached.) "Selim will be a while; he is changing into proper attire for the luncheon."

"You weren't long," said Emerson. "Wasn't Yusuf there?"

"He was at the mosque. At least, so I was told."

"He spends too much time in prayer for a man with nothing on his conscience," said my cynical spouse.

Selim finally emerged looking very handsome in a striped silk vest and cream-colored robe, and we bade the ladies farewell with thanks for their hospitality.

Nefret met us at the door of her house. I thought she looked a trifle fussed, and expected to hear of some minor domestic disaster. Then the cause of the disaster appeared and flung herself at Ramses.

"I couldn't refuse her," Nefret whispered. "She wanted so badly to come."

"It is very difficult to refuse Sennia when she is in one of her moods," I said resignedly as Sennia, beaming and beruffled from neck to hem, hugged Emerson and Selim. "I presume this means Horus and the Great Cat of Re are also lunching with us?"

"Not actually at the table," Nefret said, dimpling. "At least I hope not."

"And where is Gargery?"

Nefret gestured helplessly. "In the kitchen with Fatima. He insisted on arranging the whole affair and he has been bullying everyone, including me! Shall I ask him to sit down with us?"

"He won't. He is very firm about keeping us in our place. He will listen to every word we say, though."

The arrival of the Vandergelts interrupted the conversation. Everyone went on into the drawing room; but Nefret drew me aside long enough to say in a low voice, "I looked in my wardrobe this morning, Mother. Several things are missing."

"Ah. I thought as much. I will deal with the matter, my dear. Just leave it to me."

"I always do, Mother."

The Great Cat of Re, now approximately the size of a melon, had to be removed from Ramses claw by claw before we could proceed to the dining room. I had not seen the room since the furniture was delivered, and some of the others had not seen it at all. The effect was extremely attractive—fine old rugs on the floor, a few antique chests, and the table itself, spread with one of the woven cloths Nefret had purchased in Luxor and with the Spode dinnerware that had been a wedding present from Cyrus and Katherine.

Amid exclamations of admiration we seated ourselves, and Gargery, in full buttling attire, poured the wine. I might have expected he would jump at the chance to appear at a formal meal; he considered Emerson and me very remiss in carrying out our social duties. He then stood back, stiffly alert, while the two young Egyptian girls served the food.

Most people would have been unnerved by his critical stare, not to mention the lecture he had undoubtedly delivered beforehand. Ghazela, the sturdy fourteen-year-old, was unaffected, except for occasional fits of giggles, but Najia crept about like a ghost, letting Ghazela do most of the work. The birthmark was not nearly so prominent. Nefret must have given her some cosmetic that helped to conceal it.

It is almost impossible to keep conversation at a meaningless social level with our lot, and the interesting events of the previous day were fresh in everyone's mind. I knew Sennia would introduce the subject if Gargery did not find some means of doing so.

The child had coolly taken a chair next to Emerson and was cutting up his food for him, over his feeble protests.

"Tell me again how you hurt your arm," she demanded. "You made me go to bed last night before I heard the whole story and it is very important that I know all the facts."

"And why is that?" I inquired, amused at her precise speech.

"So that I can help you, of course."

Gargery coughed. His coughs are very expressive. This one indicated emphatic agreement.

Emerson glanced at me. I shrugged. Keeping the matter secret was now impossible.

"Well, you see . . ." he began.

Gargery had not heard the entire story either. In his interest he so forgot himself as to edge closer and closer to the table, until he was hovering over Emerson like a vulture. Emerson turned with a scowl. "Gargery, may I beg you to fill the glasses? If it isn't too much trouble."

"Not at all, sir," said Gargery, backing off. "I must say, sir and madam, that I can find no fault in your actions."

"Good of you to say so," said Emerson, snatching the bottle from him. Gargery snatched it back.

"It might have occurred to you, perhaps," he continued, splashing wine into the glasses, "to drop odds and ends along the way, to mark your trail."

"Like the poor children in the fairy tale," Sennia added approvingly.

"We hadn't any odds and ends," I explained, recognizing the start of one of those digressions that can, in our family, go on interminably. "Anyhow, it is over and done with. Thanks to the quick wits of Daoud, and Jumana's excellent memory, we were found in time."

Sennia demanded a detailed account of that, too, which Nefret gave. Jumana had spoken very little all morning and she did not add to the story, but Sennia's praise of her cleverness brought a smile to her solemn face. "I should have remembered before," she said modestly. "It was what Daoud said that made me think of it."

"Memory," I remarked, "is capricious and aberrant. It is

not surprising that the import of Jamil's remarks should have escaped you until a dire emergency recalled them to your mind. Without your assistance we might have perished in the trap he set for us."

I had kept a close if casual eye on Najia, who had become increasingly clumsy and uncomfortable. When she slipped out of the room, observed only by me, I immediately rose.

"Nefret, will you come with me? The rest of you stay here. That includes *you*, Gargery."

She had gone straight through the kitchen and out into the courtyard, and was, when I caught sight of her, trying to open the back gate. The unfortunate creature was already in a frightful state of nerves; her shaking hands could not work the latch. When I called to her to stop, she crumpled to the ground, her hands over her face, her body shaking with sobs.

We lifted her up and half carried her to a bench, and then Nefret waved me to stand back.

"She's afraid of you, Mother."

"Afraid of *me*? Good Gad, why?"

"Let me talk to her." Her gentle voice and reassurances finally succeeded in calming the girl. She raised a face sticky with tears.

"I meant no harm. He told me I was beautiful—"

I was trying my best not to appear threatening, but the sight of me set her off again.

"I know you meant no harm, Najia," Nefret said. "The Sitt Hakim knows that too. What was the harm in writing a message to his sister, and in borrowing my clothes? What else did you give him?"

She had not much to give, and she had given that, gladly and humbly. He had told her that he loved her, that the disfigurement did not mar her beauty in his eyes. She had never thought to attract any man, much less one as young and handsome. When he asked the loan of a few of Nefret's clothes, to play a joke on one of his friends, she had seen nothing wrong. Not until she heard how he had used that disguise did she realize she had been an unwitting accomplice to attempted murder.

Another pitiful tale of man's perfidy! I determined on the spot that she should not suffer for it. Seating myself next to her on the bench, I spoke quietly and firmly.

"No one else knows of this, Najia, and no one will ever learn the truth from us. Wipe your eyes . . ." I gave her my handkerchief. "And go home. We will tell the others you were taken ill."

"But when my shame is known . . ." She faltered. ". . . no man will ever want me. My father will—"

"He will do nothing and no one will know unless you are fool enough to confess." Distress had weakened her wits, which had never been very strong; I gave over trying to get her to see sense, and asserted the full force of a stronger will. "Say nothing to anyone. That is an order from me, the Sitt Hakim. We will take care of you—and find you a husband, if that is what you want. You know we can do what we promise."

"Yes—yes, it is true." She threw herself at Nefret's feet. "How can you forgive me? You were so kind, and I betrayed you."

"For pity's sake, stop crying," I said impatiently. My handkerchief was stained, not only with tears but with some brownish substance; the birthmark, wiped clean, stood out strong as ever. "Run along and remember that the word of the Sitt Hakim is stronger than another man's oath."

"That's 'the word of the Father of Curses,' isn't it?" Nefret remarked, as the girl scampered off, still swabbing at her face. "I don't see how we can keep all of it secret, though. Someone is bound to suspect it was my clothing Jamil wore. They'd have been a tight fit, but not as tight as Jumana's. Especially the boots. I hope they pinched horribly."

"He probably cut the toes out or slit the heels," I said absently. "Some people must be told some part of the truth, but it is the girl's dishonor, as men call it, that we must hide. We

may have to buy a husband for her," I added in disgust.
"That seems to be all she cares about."

"She and a good many other women of all nationalities,"
said Nefret. "Do you think she knows more than she told
us?"

"Jamil is too wily to give away useful information. He
even lied to his sister. What worries me," I continued, as we
strolled slowly back toward the kitchen, "is how many others he may have seduced from their duty—literally and figuratively. I fear, Nefret, that the wretched boy has caused a
rift in his family that may never be mended."

Emerson took a brighter view. I told him the whole sad story
later, when we were alone, knowing his chivalrous heart
would respond sympathetically to the girl's plight. After
cursing Jamil with admirable eloquence, he calmed down
and said, "We've eliminated two of the boy's allies. How
many more can he have?"

"Some of the younger men, perhaps. There are a few who
would see nothing wrong in a spot of tomb robbing. And he
seems to have a way with women."

"He selected a victim who would be particularly susceptible to flattery," said Emerson with a curl of his lips. "Grrr!
As for the men, yesterday's events must end any influence
he might have had with them. None of the Gurnawis would
dare become involved with a murderous attack on *us*."

"That is probably true," I agreed.

"There's another angle we haven't considered fully,"
Emerson went on. "He had made himself very comfortable.
I cannot see our lad abandoning his cozy little den unless he
had another hiding place prepared."

"That is also true, and no help whatever," I said.

"I thought you were the one who insists we must look on
the bright side, Peabody. We are whittling away his assets,
one by one, and his repeated failures to damage us will lead
him, sooner or later, into a false move."

"Such as trying to murder us again?"

Emerson let out a shout of laughter and threw his arm round me. "Precisely. It is time for tea. Let us go down. Are the children joining us?"

"If you mean Nefret and Ramses, the answer is no. I suggested they might like to have tea alone for a change."

"Why should they?" Emerson asked in surprise.

"Really, Emerson, you of all people should not have to ask that question."

"Oh," said Emerson.

"Jumana and Sennia will be with us. That should be entertainment enough for you."

They were on the veranda, sitting side by side and looking very pleased with themselves.

"Only see what Jumana has given me," Sennia shouted.

"Unless the Museum takes it," Jumana warned.

"Yes, you said that, but I know Mr. Quibell will let me have it, he is a very kind man."

It was the little stela with the two cats which I had seen Bertie copying. I admired it all over again, while Emerson smiled sentimentally at the two. Sennia had not been an admirer of Jumana's, perhaps because she was aware of Jumana's admiration of Ramses. I gave Jumana credit for wanting to win Sennia's friendship. A present is a sure way of influencing a young child in one's favor.

Fatima brought the tea and Emerson settled down with his pipe, and I began looking through the post. There was a several days' accumulation of letters and messages, which I sorted, putting aside the ones directed to Nefret or Ramses, and opening the envelopes addressed to Emerson before I handed them to him.

"Howard Carter, by G—— by heaven," Emerson exclaimed, extracting one of the letters. "High time we heard from him. Listen to this, Peabody, he says he won't be coming to Luxor for—"

He looked up and stopped speaking in mid-syllable. "Peabody? What is it?"

"Nothing," I said, forcing a smile. Sennia, quick to catch every nuance, especially the ones one hoped she would miss, demanded, "Is something the matter, Aunt Amelia?"

"Nothing," I repeated. "Have another biscuit, my dear."

I handed Emerson the missive that had occasioned my lapse. It was a telegram, addressed to Ramses and bearing the stamp of the C-in-C of the Egypt Expeditionary Force.

We had to wait until dinnertime to find out what was in the cursed thing. I think that if I had not been watching him, Emerson would have ripped it open—and if he had not been watching me, I might have done the same. Delivering it immediately to the addressee was also out of the question; if we had rushed off, Sennia would have been alarmed by our urgency. As Emerson later confessed, the telegram felt as if it were burning a hole in the pocket where he had placed it. Fortunately for his nerves and mine, the children came early in order to say good night to Sennia before she went to bed.

"Whiskey and soda, my boy?" Emerson asked, his manly voice gruff with the effort it cost him to keep from shouting and/or swearing.

"Thank you, sir." Emerson's perturbation would have been obvious even to an individual less perceptive than his son. "I see you and Mother are already one ahead of me."

"Two," I said. "Yes, yes, Sennia, you have already kissed everybody; now run along."

Darkness had fallen; the night breeze rustled the leaves. The lamps, enclosed in glass, burned with a steady flame. "What's wrong, Mother?" Nefret asked. "Has something happened to Katherine or Cyrus or—"

"No, my dear; and your question is a salutary reminder of one of my favorite aphorisms—"

"Don't say it, Peabody!" Emerson exclaimed.

"If you insist, Emerson. This is such a minor difficulty, compared with others, that we ought to be humbly grateful for—"

"And don't paraphrase, either. Here." Emerson handed the telegram to his son.

"Hmmm," said Ramses, inspecting the envelope.

"Open it this instant!" I exclaimed.

He put the glass down before he did so, remarking in his usual cool voice, "Have you two been hoarding this all afternoon? I am surprised you should get yourself worked up over . . ." His voice checked briefly, and then he read the message aloud. "'Your assistance required in important matter. Please report soonest.' Good of him to say 'please.'"

"Smith," Emerson said through his teeth.

"No. It is signed by Cartright. You remember he—"

"That visit was a reconnaissance," I said. "Though I cannot explain what he learned from it."

"Are you going to answer it?" Nefret demanded.

"Courtesy requires an answer, surely." He took up a sheet of paper and a pencil. Nefret, looking over his shoulder, read the message as he wrote it. "Sorry cannot comply. Needed here."

"Ah," said Emerson.

"Thank you, darling," Nefret murmured.

"What for? Can't leave Luxor, can I, with Jamil on the loose?" His voice changed; he sounded exactly like his father when he went on. "And I don't jump when someone like Cartright cracks the whip."

"I'll send Ali to the telegraph office at once," Nefret said. She picked up the paper; hesitated for a moment; then took the pencil and crossed out a word.

Ramses laughed. "Quite right. I'm not at all sorry."

The following day brought a discovery that kept us fully occupied for a time—a cache of mummies, several in their original wooden coffins. To Cyrus's annoyance we found them, not in a tomb but in the cellar of one of the houses.

The rock-cut space, which had served for storage, had been enlarged just enough to contain the remains. They were arranged neatly but so tightly that it was impossible to enter the small chamber. Squatting on the steps, Emerson moved his torch slowly over the assemblage. One detail after another emerged from the darkness: the calm face of a woman, crowned with a painted diadem; the brightly colored form of a hawk-headed god; a still form uncoffined and wrapped in intricate patterns of bandages.

"Roman," said Emerson.

"How do you know?" Cyrus demanded, from the top of the stairs. "Let me have a look."

Emerson and I went up and gave Cyrus the torch. "The cartonnage masks are unquestionably first century," Emerson said. His enthusiasm had faded as soon as he realized this, for he is not interested in Greek and Roman Egypt. "Can't be more precise about the date until we have a closer look. Come up from there, Vandergelt, and let's get them out. The local thieves will tear the coffins and mummies to pieces if we leave them unguarded."

Cyrus scrambled up the rough steps and passed the torch on to Ramses. "Pretty fancy coffins," he said enviously. "In good condition, too. Maybe there's more stuff at the back . . ."

"I couldn't see anything," said Ramses, returning to us. "They are definitely Roman or very late Ptolemaic. The most important question is what they are doing here. The settlement was abandoned after the Twenty-first Dynasty, when conditions became unsettled, and the inhabitants moved to the greater security of Medinet Habu, with its stout walls. This discovery may force us to reexamine our assumptions about—"

"Quite," said his father. Ramses had almost given up his old verbosity, but archaeological enthusiasm sometimes inspired him to lecture. "Er—we will discuss the historical implications at another time, my boy. Just now we need to concentrate on a somewhat tricky problem of excavation. How do you suggest we proceed?"

I left them to it, and joined Cyrus. "They are only Roman mummies, Cyrus," I said, in an effort to console him. "And commoners, too."

"A Roman mummy is better than nothing," Cyrus grumbled. "I swear to goodness, Amelia, I feel as if I'm under some kind of curse. You folks were good enough to let me have the tombs here, and where do we find the first burials? In the town! Unless Emerson needs me, I'm going back up the hill."

I watched with some uneasiness as he stalked off, kicking at pebbles. One could only hope temper would not lead him into carelessness. Another accident was the last thing we needed.

Thanks to Emerson's meticulous methodology, we were all day clearing the cellar. Nefret and Jumana took photographs at every stage of the way and Ramses found an inscription that gave an exact date for at least one of the interments: the seventh year of the emperor Claudius. There was not much for me to do and I was tempted to join Cyrus in his search for tombs, but since I knew Emerson would take a poor view of that, I remained, watching and thinking.

I had not given up my intention of speaking with Yusuf. He had been doing his best to avoid us, which was suspicious in itself; his frequent visits to the mosque were also suspicious, though not necessarily for the reason Emerson had mentioned. Repetition of the daily prayers is one of the Five Pillars of Islam, but a man may pray wherever he chances to be. Jamil would not dare come to the house. They would have to meet elsewhere.

I decided to wait until evening, after the sunset time for prayer, before paying my visit. If Jamil had been reluctant to show his face near the village before this, he would be even more wary now. He would wait until after dark before meeting his father.

I did not explain my intentions to Emerson until later that day. Bertie and Cyrus, who was still sulking a bit, had set off for home, and Emerson was down in the cellar with the last of the mummies. He did not want to come up, but I insisted.

His initial reaction was skeptical. "There are a good many ifs in your theory, Peabody. It may be a complete waste of time."

"If we succeed in proving Yusuf innocent of complicity, it will not be a waste of time," I retorted. "What was it you said about whittling away Jamil's supports?"

"Oh, bah," said Emerson. He cast a longing look at his mummies, which Selim was loading onto a cart. "Careful with that, Selim."

"Emerson, please pay attention."

"What? Oh. It can't do any harm, I suppose. Tomorrow."

"Today. We must strike while the iron is hot." Eyes fixed on Selim, Emerson tried to pull away from my grasp of his sleeve. "If you won't go with me, I will go alone," I added.

As I had expected, this drew his attention back to me. His brows drew together. "No, you will not. What's this about irons? Another of your confounded aphorisms?"

"A very apt one, my dear. Yusuf must have learned of Jamil's latest and most serious crime. We must talk with him, and reinforce the gravity of the matter, before the boy has a chance to tell his version, which will be a pack of lies but which a doting father might believe."

"Hmph." Emerson fingered the cleft in his chin. "Oh, very well. But not until I have seen our find safely back at the house."

"Selim and Daoud could manage it perfectly well, as you know. However, there is no hurry. It won't be dark for another hour."

With a little encouragement from me, the carts were loaded in good time and we set off for home, where the men carried our new acquisitions into the storeroom. The shelves were filling with a variety of objects, none as impressive as the new coffins, but, Ramses assured me, of much greater interest. Emerson studied them with satisfaction.

"Time for tea, eh?"

"No, Emerson, we must go at once. As I told you—"

"You've told all of us, so don't do it again. Come on then."

"Do you mean us to come, Mother?" Nefret asked.

"Yes. We will employ a combination of intimidation—Emerson and Ramses—and gentle persuasion—you and I and Jumana."

Emerson snorted in derision—presumably at the idea of me employing gentle persuasion. Jumana gave me an apprehensive look.

"But, Sitt Hakim—"

"No objections, if you please." I added, in a kindlier tone, "You were of great assistance yesterday. If your father does possess information about Jamil, you may be able to add something. If he does not—well, in my opinion it is high time he got over his annoyance with you. We may not be able to effect a complete reconciliation today, but it will be a beginning. You would like to be reconciled with him, wouldn't you?"

"He is my father," the girl said in a low voice. "I did not leave him, it was he who told me to leave."

"I am sure he has regretted that, Jumana. Words spoken in anger—"

"Damnation, Peabody!" Emerson shouted. "This is no time for more of your meddling in other people's feelings. Let's get it over."

The luminous dusk of Upper Egypt had fallen when we climbed the hill toward Yusuf's house. The first stars shone in the eastern sky and the afterglow flushed the cliffs; pale gray ghosts of smoke, swaying in the evening breeze, rose from the cooking fires.

We were met at the door by Mahira, whose scowl made her look even more like a medieval witch.

"It is high time you came. What did you do to my husband?"

"What do you mean?" I asked.

She hurried us through the house, talking all the while. "It was the medicine you gave him. At first he was better, but this morning . . ." She flung open the door of the old man's room. "See for yourself. He has been like this all day."

The lamp she carried showed the form on the bed. Yusuf was twisting and twitching and talking to himself—or rather, to Someone else—repeating the same words over and over. "Lead us in the right way of those to whom you have shown mercy . . ."

"He's delirious," Nefret whispered, her eyes shining with pity. "What did you give him, Mother?"

"Sugar water. It is not delirium, but nervous excitability. Speak to him, Emerson."

Emerson hesitated for only a moment. Like another, he is not above quoting Scripture for his own purposes. His sonorous voice rolled out in the words of the fathah, the first sureh of the Koran, from which Yusuf had quoted. "In the name of God, the merciful and gracious. Praise be to God, the Lord of the Worlds."

Yusuf sat up with a galvanic start. His wild eyes gleamed like those of an animal. "So," he said. "It is you, Father of Curses. Have you come to punish me because my silence might have caused your death and that of the Sitt Hakim?"

"Good Gad, no," exclaimed Emerson, shocked into English.

"The Father of Curses is also merciful and gracious," I explained, hoping this did not sound blasphemous. "We are here to help you—and Jamil, if we can. Where is he?"

"Is it the truth? It is the truth, you do not lie. You do not seek his life?"

We had to listen to quite a lot of this sort of thing and repeat the same reassurances several times. In psychological terms it was quite therapeutic for Yusuf, though rather tiresome for us. My diagnosis had been correct; his indisposition was not physical but mental, and the news of Jamil's latest assault on us, which he had undoubtedly heard that morning, had left him torn between loyalty and affection, unable to decide what to do.

"I will take you to him," Yusuf quavered. "We meet, at different times, in the cemetery near the mosque. He will be there tonight, when the moon rises."

"Abdullah's tomb," I said. "Praying at that holy place was an excuse for meeting your son?"

My resentment must have shown in my voice. The old man shrank back. "It was not an excuse. I prayed there. That my brother Abdullah would forgive me and ask God to forgive me."

He had ignored Jumana as if she were invisible. This did not seem the proper time for a little lecture on the subject of forgiving one's daughter.

The cemetery was on the north side of the hill, on a space of level ground. Over the cliff floated a silver orb, flooding the landscape with light. Abdullah's monument shone like snow.

On the edge of the cemetery, still in the shadow of the hill, Yusuf stopped. "Let me go ahead. Let me talk to him. I will tell him he must give himself up."

"Go on then," said Emerson.

He waited until the old man was out of earshot before muttering, "I don't share Yusuf's confidence in his power of persuasion. Peabody, give me that pistol of yours—I know you have it, so don't pretend you don't."

I did not hesitate to do so. I had been practicing with the confounded weapon for years without attaining the degree of skill Emerson possesses.

"No," Jumana whispered. "Please, you said you would not kill him."

"Couldn't kill a rabbit with this thing," said Emerson contemptuously. "If he bolts, a few warning shots should stop him. Worst comes to worst, I'll shoot him in the leg."

Yusuf made no attempt to conceal himself. Standing full in the moonlight several yards from the tomb, he called out, "It is I, Jamil, your father. Come out and speak with me."

Though he spoke softly, we heard every word. The cemetery was silent and deserted. Few people came there at any time, and none came after nightfall. It was one of the safest places Jamil could have chosen.

After a moment the boy emerged from the entrance to the tomb. "Are you afraid to come closer, my father? The spirits of the dead do not trouble the living."

He was in Egyptian clothing, a dark robe and carelessly wound turban. His face was the image of his sister's now that he had shaved off his mustache; he looked very young and very harmless. But there was a knife thrust through his sash, and in his right hand he carried a long stick.

"The spirit of my revered brother Abdullah troubles *me,*" the old man retorted. "We have dishonored him, Jamil, but it is not too late to seek forgiveness. Come with me to the Father of Curses, who will help you."

Jamil's pretty face twisted into a grimace of pure hate. His head turned from side to side, his eyes searching every shadow. Whether he saw us or only deduced our presence I will never know; but he raised the stick to his shoulder, holding it as one might hold a rifle. It *was* a rifle—Yusuf's antique weapon, his most prized possession.

Yusuf cried out. "No, Jamil! You said you would not fire it unless one attacked you. Put it down."

Emerson stepped out into the moonlight. "Drop it, Jamil," he called. "Yusuf, get away from him."

Aiming my pistol at the ground in front of Jamil, he took a long step forward. If he meant to say more or do more, he did not have the chance. A loud explosion rent the air and the darkness was reddened by fire. Somewhat belatedly I tried to fling myself in front of Nefret.

"Dear God," Ramses whispered. "The damned gun exploded. I was afraid it would someday, he must be—"

Emerson was running toward the crumpled form. By the time we reached Jamil there were two crumpled forms. Yusuf had bent over his son, shrieked, and dropped like a stone.

Jamil was still alive. When I saw the ruin that remained of his face I could only pray he would not live long. His one remaining eye rolled from side to side and focused. Sounds whistled through his broken teeth.

"Jumana. Sister. Is our father—"

After one horrified look at Jamil, Nefret had known there was nothing she could do. Kneeling by the old man, her hand on his bared breast, she said, "It is his heart. We must get him to the house."

"Heart," Jamil said faintly. "I killed him. My father. Sister—listen—the tomb—"

Jumana leaned closer. Shock had deprived her even of tears. "Do you want to tell me where it is? Speak, then, and go to God having done that last kindness."

"Kindness." I think he was trying to laugh. It was a dreadful sound, bubbling with blood. Then he said, with a last burst of strength, "The fools. It was there, before their eyes. In the hand of the god."

Yusuf lived only long enough to take the hand of his daughter (placed in his by me) and murmur a few unintelligible words. A sentimentalist might say he had died of a broken heart. In scientific terms he had succumbed to the same heart ailment from which Abdullah had suffered in his last years. We left Ramses to stand guard over Jamil, and Emerson carried Yusuf's wasted body back to his house. I looked back as we walked away. The lovely shape of Abdullah's tomb was outlined by moonlight and shadow. In the deeper shadows of the doorway, nothing moved.

There was not much we could do for the afflicted family. Indeed, the angry looks directed at us by some of its members indicated that our best course was to leave them alone.

The whole ghastly business had taken far less time than I had realized—less than half an hour from start to finish—but explanations and changes of clothing delayed the longed-for moment when we could settle down on the veranda.

Ramses was the last to join us. Though the tightness of his mouth betrayed his distress, he was his usual phlegmatic self when he replied to our questions. "I left him with his cousins. They made it clear I was not wanted. Where is Sennia?"

"I sent her to bed," I replied, as Emerson pressed a glass of whiskey into his son's hand. "She made quite a fuss, and Horus tried to bite me."

"Jumana?" was Ramses's next question.

"She finally broke down, but not until Fatima took her in a motherly embrace. Perhaps," I mused, "I emphasized too strongly the virtue of a stiff upper lip."

"What a pity," Nefret said softly. "The family was once so strong and proud and united."

"The greater pity," said Ramses, "is Jamil. If he had turned his unique talent to archaeology he might have been happy and successful. How does one account for such men?"

"Don't start a philosophical discussion," Emerson growled. "I cannot account for them and neither can your mother, though she will try if you give her half a chance. The family will get over this in time, and so will Jumana. Time heals . . ." Realizing he had been on the verge of committing an aphorism, he caught himself and went on, "Was he trying to tell us, at the end, where the tomb is located, or was he still taunting us? 'In the hand of the god!'"

Yusuf's funeral took place next day, as Moslem custom decreed. Naturally we all attended. When we saw the second shrouded body, Emerson muttered, "They wouldn't have the audacity to put him in Abdullah's tomb, would they? By Gad, the old fellow would rise up and forbid it."

I didn't doubt that he would. Had he not said, "Leave him to me"? Call it fate, call it accident; yet vicious as the boy had been, I was glad he had not met his death at our hands.

Selim had seen to the arrangements, as he told us later. Father and son were interred in another of the family sepulchres—an underground chamber where they could sit upright, awaiting the call of the angels of death. We took our departure before the opening was closed.

Cyrus got all fired up, as he admitted in his quaint American slang, by Jamil's last words. "It was there, before our eyes? In the Cemetery of the Monkeys? What hand of what god?"

"One cannot place much credence in the words of a dying man," I informed him. "Especially a man who spent his entire life trying to deceive."

So we went back to work at Deir el Medina—all of us except Jumana. The horrors of that night had been too much. She took to her bed, and refused to eat or respond to my attempts to reason with her. The only person who could rouse her was Sennia. She knew that Jumana had lost both brother and father, though of course we had spared her the dreadful details, and the good little creature spent hours reading to her and talking with her.

It was on the Tuesday, if memory serves, that we received a message from Howard Carter, asking us to join him for dinner that evening at the Winter Palace.

"So he's back in Luxor," Emerson said. "We'll go. I have a number of questions for him."

It was a diversion we all needed, and I must confess that my spirits lifted as I assumed my favorite crimson evening frock and fastened on my diamond earrings. The pleasure derived from dressing in one's best may be a weakness of women; in my opinion men would be better off if they could indulge in it.

No shadow of foreboding darkened my thoughts as the boat bore us smoothly across the shimmering water. It ought to have done. The first person we saw when we entered the elegant lobby of the hotel was the man we had known as "Smith"—the Honorable Bracegirdle-Boisdragon, who had tried on several occasions to get Ramses back into the intelligence services.

There was no way of avoiding him without downright

rudeness. This consideration might not have deterred Emerson but for the fact that "Smith" was accompanied by an attractive lady of a certain age, wearing elegant mourning. Smith introduced her as his sister, Mrs. Bayes, who was visiting Egypt for the first time, and she immediately burst into raptures about the country, the antiquities, and the great honor of making our acquaintance. She had heard so much about us.

"Have you indeed?" I said, giving Smith a sharp look.

"She is reading the Professor's *History* and has reached Volume Three," said Smith blandly.

"It was Algie's excitement about Egypt that induced me to come," Mrs. Bayes explained. She gave her brother a sickeningly fond look. She is putting it on, I thought to myself; that cold fish of a man is incapable of inspiring such adoration.

"It was courageous of you to risk the sea voyage at this time," I said.

The lady's face took on an expression of gentle melancholy. "When one has lost that being who is all the world to one, one becomes resigned to whatever fate may offer."

Emerson let out a loud "Hmph," turned it into a cough, and glanced at me. He objects to my "pompous aphorisms," as he terms them, and this was certainly in the same category. I could have put it better, though.

"I am very sorry," I said. "Was it a recent loss?"

"Fairly recent. But," said Mrs. Bayes, smiling at her "brother," who was patting her hand with a look of concern, "I promised Algie not to dwell on that. I am determined to enjoy these new experiences to the full, and they have been delightful. Algie has been a splendid guide. He knows the antiquities so well!"

"A sister's fondness exaggerates," said Smith with a modest cough. "I may claim, however, to be exceedingly keen. My interest was aroused during my first visit to Luxor—perhaps you do me the honor of remembering our meeting at that time . . ."

He transferred his gaze to Ramses and Nefret.

"Very well," said Ramses. Nefret, her lips forming a line almost as thin as Smith's, said nothing.

"We must not keep you from your dinner," I said. "It has been a pleasure to meet you, Mrs. Bayes. Enjoy the rest of your stay."

"Aren't you dining here?" the lady asked innocently.

"No," I said, and took Emerson's arm. "Good night."

I led our little party out of the hotel.

"What about Carter?" Ramses asked.

"I would be very much surprised to find that Howard is here. Smith sent the message."

"I wonder what he wants," Nefret muttered. She had very tight hold of Ramses's arm. "If he thinks he can—"

"Not now, Nefret," I said firmly.

"Where are we going?" Emerson asked. "I want my dinner."

"The Luxor will suit, I believe. We must have a little chat before he tracks us down again."

Emerson waved away the carriages that sought our custom. It is only a short walk from the Winter Palace to the Luxor, and it was a lovely evening, the dark sky star-strewn and the air fresh. The scent of night-blooming jasmine tried (in vain) to counter the other scents of Luxor, but even these had a certain charm—the smell of cooking fires and camel dung; of unwashed donkeys, camels, and humans.

We were greeted with pleasure and seated at one of the best tables in the dining salon. After consulting with Ramses, Emerson ordered a bottle of wine and then shoved his plate aside and planted both elbows on the table, a habit of which I have given up trying to break him.

"You think he will follow us here, do you?" he inquired.

"Yes. What other reason could he have for being in Luxor?"

"It may be a perfectly innocent reason," Ramses said. "Do you suppose the lady is really his sister?"

"Possibly," I replied, studying the menu. "Men of his sort are not above using personal relationships for their own purposes. It was only her presence that prevented your father from being rude. I believe I will start with lentil soup. They make it very well here. Nefret?"

"I don't care. Mother, how can you think about food, when you know that bas—— that man is after Ramses again?"

"He can't make me do anything I don't want to do," Ramses said, somewhat sharply. "You are getting yourself into a rage about nothing, Nefret. There is no inducement they could offer that would make me change my mind."

"Damn right," said Emerson. "Who's he working for anyhow? I can't get all these departments and bureaus and agencies straight in my mind. Not that I care to," he added.

"Nobody's got them straight," Ramses said with a wry smile. "At one time there were four separate intelligence groups, and the police. I believe they've been reorganized, but there is still a certain amount of infighting between the civilian branch, which reports to the high commissioner and the Foreign Office, and the military branches, who are under the C-in-C—that's General Murray—in Cairo. The Admiralty has, or had, its own group. God knows where Smith fits in."

"I don't give a damn where he fits in," Nefret declared. "So long as you aren't in it with him."

I was tempted to intervene, for her voice had risen and Ramses's eyes had narrowed—sure signs, in both cases, of rising temper. Considering the scrapes we often got into—Nefret included—her almost hysterical fear of this particular danger might have seemed exaggerated, but I understood. In our other adventures we worked as a family. Well . . . most of the time. In these he was alone, with every man's hand against him. I told myself to leave it to them. It was not my role to interfere—unless it became necessary.

"The devil with Smith, eh?" said Emerson, whose fond paternal brow had furrowed. He is such a hopeless sentimentalist, he hates to see the children exchange hard words; whereas I, who understand the human heart better, knew that little disagreements are natural and healthy. On this occasion his remark had the desired effect. The lines of tension left Nefret's face and she smiled affectionately at Emerson.

"Quite right, Father. Let us drink to it: The devil with Mr. Smith!"

He had at least enough courtesy to allow us to finish our dinner in peace. The waiter was hovering, waiting to remove our plates, when he approached us. The lady was not with him.

"Will you allow me to offer you a liqueur or a glass of brandy?" he asked.

"I don't want any damned brandy," said Emerson, glowering. "Or a conversation with you."

"I think you had better, Professor."

Emerson's face brightened. "Is that a threat?" he asked hopefully.

I had once before observed in Smith the rudiments of a sense of humor. Amusement narrowed his eyes and he shook his head emphatically. "Good Lord, no. Threatening you, Professor Emerson, is tantamount to teasing a tiger. However, I am sure you will want to hear what I have to say, and if I am mistaken, you will—er—take whatever steps occur to you. May I sit down?"

"Oh, I suppose so," Emerson grumbled. "Just be quick about it. You want Ramses for some other filthy job, I suppose. He has already refused. What makes you suppose that you can change his mind?"

"He is wanted," Smith said quietly. "And I think he will change his mind."

Nefret caught hold of Ramses's hand. Ramses gave her a quick glance from under lowered lids, and although his controlled countenance did not change, I knew he had misunderstood, and resented, the gesture. It was not one of possessiveness but of fear—the unreasoning panic of a child reaching out for comfort in a dark room.

"He will," Smith went on, "because he won't want to see

a close friend face a firing squad. Someone closer than a friend, in fact. A kinsman."

There was no doubt as to whom he meant. Nefret's face turned pale, Emerson's turned red. "Don't speak, Emerson," I exclaimed. "Don't anyone speak until he has explained what he means."

"You know *who* I mean," Smith said, with that thin, satisfied smirk I remembered so well. "He has turned traitor. Gone over to the enemy."

From Manuscript H

Nefret had told herself there was no reason to be apprehensive. She had Ramses's word, and he would not break it. But because she was so intensely aware of the emotions he succeeded in concealing from almost everyone but her, she had sensed his growing restlessness and feelings of guilt at going on with his work while friends and kin were fighting and dying. He wouldn't fight, but his unique skills could be of use without violating his pacifist principles, and there was one appeal he would find impossible to resist: danger to her or his parents or a friend. It was difficult to classify the enigmatic, eccentric individual who was Emerson's half brother, but whether he was friend or foe—over the years he had been both—they were indebted to him.

Emerson's sun-browned face was almost as expressionless as that of his son, and when he spoke, it was in a soft purring voice. "That's a lie."

Smith leaned forward. "Then prove it."

"I thought it was Ramses you wanted," said Emerson, in the same soft voice.

"It is. May I explain?"

"You had damned well better," said Emerson. "Peabody, my dear, would you care for a whiskey and soda?"

Nefret had never been certain precisely how her mother-in-law felt about the man who had pursued her so ardently all those years; obviously she cared enough about him to resent the accusation. Her gray eyes had a hard, almost metallic shine.

"No," she said. "Thank you. Mr. Smith, how did you find out?"

"Find out what?"

She was too clever to be tricked into an admission. "Whatever it is you know."

Smith gave her a nod of grudging admiration. "If you are referring to my knowledge of the—er—relationship between you and the individual in question, I—uh— Please, Mrs. Emerson, won't you let me offer you something to drink?"

"No. There were a good many people present the evening we ourselves learned of that relationship," she went on thoughtfully. "Military persons. One of them overheard our conversation and reported it to you?"

"Only a few words of the conversation, but they were enough to arouse his curiosity. Eventually the word got back to me, and aroused *my* curiosity. It took my associate in England a while to find the proof—birth and death certificates, records of certain financial transactions—you know the procedure. I haven't told anyone else, Mrs. Emerson."

"No, you hoard information like coins, paying it out only when you can gain something" was the furious response. "Do not expect thanks for your discretion from us."

"Never mind, Mother," Ramses said. "That isn't the issue now. He's won the first round. Perhaps we should let him explain further."

It was a damning story. A few weeks earlier, a man calling himself Ismail Pasha had appeared in Constantinople. The word soon spread among the faithful: he had been an infidel, a high-ranking member of the British Secret Service, who had come over to the true religion and the right cause. He had been seen in public with German officers and also with Enver and the other members of the ruling triumvirate, richly dressed and clanking with jewels. He had prayed at the mosques, and on at least two occasions he had addressed the crowd with an eloquence that brought them to their knees. For surely no one could be so familiar with the words of the Prophet unless he himself was a holy man!

Shortly thereafter, one of the local agents in British pay was caught and executed. It was pure luck that the others in the group got away. Sethos was one of the few who knew of that particular network; he had been sent to Constantinople to meet with its members.

"That isn't proof of anything," Emerson declared.

"No," Smith agreed. "However, he has not been heard from since. Attempts to contact him through the usual channels have received no response. His assumed name is interesting, too, don't you think?"

"Ismail is a very common name," Emerson said.

"The name of the son of Abraham by his handmaiden Hagar, who was cast out into the wilderness, lest he challenge the position of Abraham's legitimate son," Smith said, his thin lips curving in a cynical smile. " 'His hand will be against every man and every man's hand will be against him.' "

"I believe I am better acquainted with Holy Writ than you," Nefret's mother-in-law said with a sniff. "God saved Ismael and blessed him and promised to make him—er—fruitful."

"Confound it, Peabody, will you stop talking about the Bible?" Emerson was trying not to shout; the words squeezed between his lips like rumbles of distant thunder. "Prove it, you say. How?"

"That should be obvious." Smith knew he had won. He leaned back in his chair. "Ismail Pasha is now in Gaza. Find him. You will know if he is the man we believe him to be—or that he is not. If he is that man, and you can bring back evidence that he is a prisoner or under duress, we will take steps to free him—unless you can do the job yourself."

"That's rather a tall order," said Emerson. "Even for us."

"You mistook my meaning, Professor. That's the trouble with English, it is too imprecise about pronouns."

"So," said Emerson, after a long moment. "You want Ramses to go after the fellow. Alone."

"It's the only way, Professor. You surely don't suppose that the four of you could cross enemy lines in disguise? Individually you are only too recognizable; as a group you are unmistakable. It's a job for one man, and there is only one man who can maintain a convincing disguise long enough to do the job."

They were all looking at Ramses, waiting for him to speak; Emerson caught himself on the verge of a heated reply and remained silent, possibly because his wife had administered an admonitory kick under the table. Ramses turned his head and met Nefret's eyes.

They had been over this subject many times, with Nefret continuing to demand promises and reassurances and Ramses increasingly resentful of her refusal to accept his given word. There was no need for speech now; she knew what he wanted to do, what he felt he must do, and she knew that the decision was hers.

She had the means to hold him. A few sentences, a few words . . . She released her grip on his hand. Her fingers had left white marks.

"I've always felt that Ismail was unfairly treated," she said, shaping the words with care so her voice wouldn't tremble. "God won't take a hand this time, so . . . so someone else must."

:

PART TWO

. .

Gateway to
Gaza

Nine

We arrived in Cairo on a misty gray morning. The city was swathed in fog and there was not a breath of air stirring. The feeling of oppression was not solely physical. We had had to leave our friends to cope with Jumana's grief and Cyrus's frustration—for that enigmatic clue of Jamil's was driving him to distraction. I had made him promise on his solemn oath that he would not go wandering round the wilderness looking for Jamil's tomb. He had given his word; but his hands were behind his back and I suspected he had his fingers crossed. Although Katherine did not reproach me, I knew she wondered how we could abandon her at such a time.

Emerson had pointed out that *I* need not abandon her. Not only was there no need for me to go to Cairo, my presence there would add unnecessary difficulties to an already difficult situation. The summons had been for—

"For Ramses," I said, cutting into his tirade with the skill of long experience. "You weren't asked either."

"If you think," Emerson announced loudly, "that I am going to let the boy go off alone to face that pack of wolves from the War Office—"

"My sentiments exactly," I said.

Upon which, Emerson burst out laughing and pulled me

into a close embrace. "Peabody, when you put your chin out and give me that steely stare, I know I've lost the argument."

"You wanted me to come. Admit it."

"Mmmf," said Emerson, his lips against mine.

We caught the evening train and went straight to Shepheard's. The sufragi on duty greeted us like the old acquaintances we were, and asked what he could do for us.

"Breakfast," I said, while Emerson divested himself of various articles of clothing and tossed them around the room. Emerson had not been in favor of staying over, but even he admitted that we could not dismiss this request as brusquely as we had done with the War Office's other attempts to bring Ramses back into the service, and catch the first train back to Luxor.

"Emphatically not," said Ramses. "Smith told us virtually nothing, but they wouldn't have sent for me unless they have some idea as to how to locate him. We must try to find him, Father. If he is a prisoner—"

"If?" Emerson exclaimed. "Do you believe he is a turncoat and a traitor?"

Once upon a time Emerson's intimidating scowl would have reduced Ramses to silence. Now he met those narrowed blue orbs squarely and smiled a little. "It's odd to hear you defend him, Father. Good God, I don't want to believe it either! But the man is an enigma—embittered, cynical, and unpredictable."

"Hmph," said Emerson. "Well. The sooner we find out what Murray has to say, the better. Shall we go?"

"General Murray?" I repeated. "What has he to do with this? You haven't even made an appointment."

"You know my policy, Peabody—go straight to the top and avoid underlings. He will see me whenever I damn well decide to see him," said Emerson. "Are you ready, Ramses?"

I would have insisted upon accompanying them if I had believed there was the slightest chance the general would allow me or Nefret to take part in the discussion. Men are singularly limited in their views about women, and military men are even worse.

I handed Emerson his coat—he would have walked out of the room in his shirtsleeves if I had not—and helped him into it. "Come straight back here," I ordered.

"Mph," said Emerson.

"Yes, of course," said Ramses, smiling at Nefret.

From Manuscript H

Murray kept them waiting for half an hour. It wasn't long, considering his busy schedule and the fact that he had not expected them, but Emerson took it as a personal affront. He was in an extreme state of annoyance by the time they were ushered into the General's office, and he expressed his feelings with his usual candor.

"What the devil do you mean by letting us cool our heels all that time? It was damned inconvenient for us to come just now. You had better have a good reason for interrupting my work."

Murray was losing his hair. The high forehead added to the length of his face, which was set in stern lines, but the mouth under the neatly trimmed graying mustache twitched as Emerson spoke. Ramses had heard that Murray had had a nervous breakdown in 1915, after serving as chief of staff to the British Expeditionary Force. An encounter with Emerson wasn't going to do his nerves much good.

"I did not ask you here, Professor Emerson," he said stiffly.

The office was comfortably, almost luxuriously, furnished, with deep leather chairs and Oriental rugs. The wide windows behind the desk offered a view of palm trees and gardens. The fog had cleared; it was going to be a fine day.

"No?" Emerson sat down and took out his pipe. "Well, if it wasn't you, it was one of your flunkies, and you ought to know about it. What sort of administrator are you?"

Murray began fumbling through the papers on his desk. Emerson's tactics were brutal but effective; the general's hands were shaking with rage. He couldn't bully a civilian, especially one of Emerson's eminence, as he would have done a military subordinate—but how he wanted to! After a moment of hard breathing, he selected one paper from among the rest, stared at it, and rang for an aide. A whispered conversation took place. Ramses, whose hearing was excellent, caught only a few words: ". . . devil he thinks he's doing . . ."

"Didn't your mother teach you that it is rude to whisper when other persons are present?" Emerson inquired, tossing a burned match onto the floor.

Murray's complexion was that of a man who spends most of his time indoors. His pale cheeks reddened. "Professor Emerson, I did not ask to speak with you, but so long as you are here I can spare you a few minutes, in order to emphasize the seriousness of the situation. From now on you will be taking orders from someone else."

Oh, Lord, Ramses thought, is the man a natural idiot, or hasn't he heard about Father? The last sentence had the effect he had known it would. Emerson's eyes narrowed, and when he spoke it was in the quiet purring voice his acquaintances had learned to dread.

"The only person from whom my son takes orders is me, General. I don't take them from anyone—except him."

Ramses's jaw dropped. His father had deferred to him on a few occasions—to his utter astonishment—but this was the first time he had paid him such a compliment.

"When the situation demands it," Emerson added. "We may as well leave, Ramses."

The door opened. Murray transferred his bulging stare to the newcomer. Not Smith. Cartright. "Why didn't you tell me they were coming?" the general demanded.

"I didn't know, sir. The last I heard from them was a curt telegram denying my request for their assistance. I had planned to go to Luxor in person within the next few days."

Ramses caught his father's questioning eye. Evidently the same doubt had entered Emerson's mind. If this lot didn't know of Smith's visit, he wasn't going to bring it up. He shook his head slightly, and Emerson settled back into his chair. "So," he purred, "is this the person from whom my son is to take orders?"

"You misunderstood, Professor," Cartright said quickly. "We are asking for his help, not demanding it."

"He did say 'please,' " Ramses reminded his father. "Perhaps we ought to listen to what he has to say."

⁝

Emerson stamped into the room, flung himself into a chair, and took out his pipe. Nefret had left his thumb and fingers free of the cast, and by now he was using both hands, against her advice and my orders. The weight of the cast did not seem to bother him in the slightest. He proceeded to tamp tobacco into the pipe, making an even greater mess than usual. Ramses followed, his face unreadable. That withdrawn, "stone pharaoh" look was his reaction to bad news, just as poorly repressed fury was his father's.

"Well?" I demanded. "What happened?"

Ramses's features relaxed into a smile. "Father threatened to punch General Murray on the jaw."

"Ah," I said. "Well, that was only to be expected if the general accused your—er—Sethos of treachery."

"Bastard," said Emerson, round the stem of his pipe. I knew he was not referring to his brother.

"Stop swearing and tell me what transpired."

"I will swear if I like," Emerson said sullenly. "Murray would drive a nun to profanity."

Nefret held out her hand to Ramses. He went at once to her and took her hand in his.

"You had better let me tell it, Father. It appears there was a problem of miscommunication. Murray wasn't expecting us, and he was not at all pleased to have us turn up. He knew about the matter, but if we had asked for an appointment, in the usual way, the request would have been passed on to his chief of staff, who would have passed it on to the head of military intelligence in Cairo, who is—"

"Boisdragon-Bracegirdle," I exclaimed.

"No, Mother. My old acquaintance, Captain, now Major, Cartright."

"How extraordinary. It was on this business he telegraphed you in that brusque fashion? Then what does Brace—curse it, Smith—have to do with this?"

"I don't know, and I didn't ask," Ramses said. "There is something odd about this business, and until we can make sense of it, the less we say the better. It may be only a question of interservice jealousy. That has caused more trouble than the enemy."

"How much does Murray know?" I asked.

Emerson was still muttering curses, so Ramses answered the question. "He made no reference to our relationship with Sethos. Smith may have been telling the truth there. They know I've met him, though, and that I have had ample opportunity to observe him. It was Cartright who convinced Murray that I was the best man to track Sethos down. They've had trouble getting agents into and out of Turkish territory. None of their own people can pass as an Arab, and the locals they've recruited are unreliable and untrained."

Emerson had got himself under control. "They're a bunch of bumbling incompetents," he declared. "Sometimes it takes weeks for information about Turkish movements to reach them, via the indirect channels they employ. They got the news about Sethos fast enough, though. I suggested to Murray that he might be a prisoner instead of a traitor, and that swine Murray—"

"That was when Father tried to hit him," said Ramses, with a grin. "Cartright got us out of Murray's office in a hurry."

"I cannot believe Sethos passed on vital information willingly," I exclaimed.

From behind a cloud of vile-smelling smoke, Emerson said, "The alternatives are almost as unpleasant, my dear."

"Alternatives? I can only think of one." I got up and moved to the window, where the air was not so thick. "Emerson, that pipe—"

"It calms my nerves, Peabody. However, anything to please you." He knocked the thing out into a receptacle, sending sparks flying. "Torture is one possibility, certainly, though I don't see how they could make a public spectacle of him if he was injured and under duress. There are other ways of forcing an individual to speak. Are you certain Margaret Minton is in France?"

"What a horrible idea!" I cried. "That the villains would use the threat of harm to the woman he loves!"

"It is a well-established technique, not only in the service but in popular fiction," said Ramses.

"I beg, Ramses, that you will refrain from inappropriate attempts to be humorous. I will set about ascertaining Margaret's present whereabouts as soon as is possible."

"I beg your pardon, Mother," Ramses said. He was still holding Nefret's hand, running his fingers lightly over her wrist. "Such inquiries would take too long and would probably be inconclusive. There is one sure way of learning the truth. Ismail Pasha is now in Gaza. I'm going there to try and find him."

I was conscious of a sinking feeling at the pit of my stomach. "I thoroughly disapprove, Ramses. You are too well known to the enemy. Let them find someone else."

"I must go, Mother. I can't leave it to someone else. You don't understand." He looked from me to Nefret; and on her face I saw the same dawning horror that I felt on my own.

"They ordered you to kill him," she whispered. "Is that it?"

"That is how the Great Game is played." Ramses's voice was hard, his expression withdrawn. "Assassination, deception, corruption—nothing is too vile if it can be labeled patriotism. Whether he is guilty or under duress, he can give away vital information. Cartright wouldn't tell me what that information is, but it is obviously enough to make him extremely dangerous."

I cleared my throat. "You agreed, of course."

Ramses came to me with his long strides and bent to kiss my cheek. It was a rare gesture for him, and I took it as the compliment he intended. "I would have done, Mother, if I had supposed they'd believe me. Murray would have; he hasn't imagination enough to suppose anyone would dare disregard his orders, and he doesn't know the man he wants me to assassinate is my uncle. Not that that little matter would bother him."

" 'If thy hand offend thee, cut it off,' " I murmured.

I ought to have known better than to quote Scripture when Emerson was already in a vile humor. His heavy brows drew together, but before he could bellow, Ramses spoke again. "Cartright knows me well enough to suspect I would balk at assassination, so we arrived at a compromise. I will get a look at Ismail Pasha and ascertain whether he is Sethos, and whether he is being used by the Turks against his will."

"Rather a tall order, that," I remarked.

"The first part shouldn't be difficult. He'll be showing himself in public, as he did in Constantinople. I only hope he hasn't altered his appearance so much I can't recognize him."

"And then what?" Nefret demanded.

Ramses shrugged. "One can't plan very far ahead when there are so many unknowns in the equation. I'm not counting on anything except making a preliminary reconnaissance. Depending on what I learn, if anything, we'll decide what to do next."

"Can you get in and out of the city undetected?" I asked, endeavoring to conceal my concern.

"Oh, I think so. The trouble is, Cartright insisted I take someone else with me."

"It's safer for two than for one," Nefret said hopefully.

"Not when one of the two is fresh out of the nursery,"

Emerson growled. "Fair, young, speaks Arabic like a text-book, stammering with excitement at the prospect of playing spy . . ." Emerson summed it up with an emphatic "Damnation!" and went back to filling his pipe.

"He can't be that bad," Nefret protested.

"Ha! D'you remember Lieutenant Chetwode?"

"Oh dear," I said. "Not that ingenuous baby-faced young man who came to Deir el Medina with Cartright?"

"Cartright claims he is his best man," Ramses said. "He must be older and less ingenuous than he looks, since he has been in intelligence for over two years."

"Doing what?" Nefret demanded. "Sitting behind a desk filing reports?"

"What does it matter?" Emerson said. "His assignment is not to assist Ramses but to make sure he does what he has said he will do. That bastard Cartright doesn't trust him."

Nefret let out an indignant expletive. I said judiciously, "He does have a nasty suspicious mind. To be sure, a sensible individual, which Ramses is not, would go into hiding for a few days and then report that he had determined that Ismail Pasha was not the man they are after. Perhaps if I were to have a little chat with General Murray—"

"No, Mother," Ramses said, politely but emphatically. "He wouldn't have approved the scheme if I had not agreed to take Chetwode with me. He's a likable boy, and not as hopeless as Father makes him sound. It'll be all right."

"Every time you say that, something disastrous occurs," I exclaimed.

"Now, Mother, don't exaggerate. It doesn't always." He was back to normal, his smile broad and carefree, but the concern of a mother informed me he was holding something back.

"What other orders do you have?" I asked.

Emerson, who had been deep in thought, looked up. "Oh, nothing much," he said sarcastically. "Scout the Turkish defenses, look for weak points, and while you're at it, sound out the governor to see if he would accept a bribe."

"Hold your fire, Mother, I've no intention of doing anything of the sort," Ramses said quickly. "The chaps in charge still labor under the delusion that 'Johnny Turk' is a white-livered coward. You'd think they'd have learned better after Rafah and Gallipoli."

"But the military mind is slow to accept new ideas," I agreed. "Are they planning a direct assault on Gaza?"

"I have not been taken into their confidence," Ramses said dryly. "I'd bribe the damned governor if I could. It would save countless lives."

"You can't," Emerson said positively. "Anyhow, von Kressenstein is the one in command of the Gaza defenses. He'd have you shot if you offered him a bribe. Stick to your primary aim, my boy, and get the hell out of Gaza as soon as you can."

"Yes, sir," Ramses said.

"When do you leave?" Nefret asked steadily.

"It will take a while to make the necessary arrangements," Ramses said. She gave him a reproachful look, and he went on, "I'm not being deliberately evasive, dear. I need to learn all I can about our present dispositions in south Palestine before I decide on the best way of getting into the city. Then there's the little matter of transport. They've pushed the rail lines as far as Rafah, but most of the traffic is military, and if I tried to pass as a British officer, it would mean being subject to orders from people who didn't know who I was, or letting too many military types in on the secret. I don't want even Cartright to know my plans: I politely refused several of his suggestions."

"You don't trust him?" I asked.

Ramses began pacing restlessly up and down the room. "I don't trust any of the bas—— any of them. I still don't know how Bracegirdle-Boisdragon fits into this; he's made no further attempt to communicate with us, and when I posed a carefully phrased question to Cartright, he stiffly informed me that I was taking orders from him and no one else."

"It's the usual interservice rivalry, as I said," remarked

Emerson, with a curling lip. "They keep more secrets from one another than from the enemy."

Ramses shrugged. He had said all he was going to say on the subject.

"What makes them suppose Sethos—if it is he—will stay in Gaza?" I asked. "Ramses, you won't go haring off to Constantinople or Jerusalem after him?"

"Even if he's left by the time I arrive, there will be news of him. We'll just have to wait and see."

He was being deliberately evasive now, and we all knew it. He was right, though; it was impossible to plan ahead.

For the next several days we were all busy about our different affairs. At my insistence, we kept up the pretense that we were in Cairo for personal reasons—a little holiday away from the family, the need to do a little research at the Museum. We dined out every evening, at one of the hotels, with as carefree a mien as we could manage, and if Emerson shouted at the waiters more often than usual, no one thought anything of it.

I remember one of those evenings with a particular poignancy. We were lingering over coffee after an excellent dinner at Shepheard's and listening to the orchestra render a selection from *The Merry Widow*. Emerson came out of his fog of frowning introspection when he heard the familiar strains of the waltz, and asked if I would like to dance. I pointed out to him that the dancing had not yet begun. It did soon thereafter, and several couples took the floor. Emerson asked me again, and I pointed out to him that the tune was not a waltz. It was another of the ballads that had become popular in the past few years—the kind of song Ramses had once described as tools of the warmonger, with their sentimental references to love and duty and sacrifice. I knew this one very well. Nefret had played it the night we got the news of the death in battle of our beloved nephew Johnny.

Ramses rose and offered Nefret his hand. I don't know what had moved him to want to dance to that song; perhaps the memory of Johnny, who had loved music and gaiety and laughter, perhaps a sudden need to take her in his arms. In my opinion the new dances were not nearly so pretty as the waltz, but they certainly offered the opportunity for close embraces.

It was always a pleasure to watch them dance together, they moved with such matching grace, even in the clumsy (in my opinion) two-step. She was wearing a gown of pale blue voile printed with little flowers, a copy of a favorite garment of Ramses's that had been worn to shreds and discarded. Her skirts floated out as he turned her.

My sentimental husband cleared his throat and reached for my hand. There was no need for speech; we were both thinking the same thoughts: of Johnny, only one of the millions of gallant young men who were lost forever; and of another young man, even dearer, who was about to disappear into the dark underworld of war. Would we ever see our children dance together again?

"Yes," I said emphatically.

So closely attuned are my dear Emerson and I (some of the time) that he required no explanation. He squeezed my hand. "Yes," he repeated. "How are your arrangements coming along, Peabody?"

"Very well. And yours?"

"I will be ready when the time comes."

Ramses was in and out at odd hours; all he would say, when I questioned him, was that he was exploring various sources of information. He spent a good deal of time alone with Nefret. I did not begrudge them this, but I could not help asking her, one morning when we were alone, whether he had told her anything I wasn't supposed to know.

"If I had promised not to tell you, I wouldn't," she said with a smile that took any possible sting out of the words. "But there's nothing."

"Are you all right, Nefret?"

"Yes, of course. Why do you ask?"

"You are too calm. More than calm—serene. Misty-eyed."

"Good Gad, Mother!" She burst out laughing. "You do have a way with words. Perhaps I've become a fatalist. If I could go with him I would, but I'm beginning to realize—finally!—that my whining and my clinging only make it harder for him. There are some dangers one must face alone."

"True," I said thoughtfully. "However, there is nothing wrong with attempting to minimize the danger if one can."

"You've got something in mind, haven't you?" She looked alarmed. "Mother, don't tell me unless you want Ramses to know. We keep nothing from one another."

"And quite right, too. Perhaps I had better not, then. He would only fuss. Fear not, my dear, I won't do anything that might endanger him."

I had not expected Ramses would give us much notice of his departure, so I went ahead with my own schemes as quickly as was possible. Sure enough, my son turned up one afternoon in time for tea, with the news that he would be leaving immediately.

"There's a new batch of Labour Corps 'volunteers' going off tomorrow. I'll stay with them as far as Rafah, where I am to meet Chetwode."

At the beginning of the war, Britain had promised the Egyptians they would not be asked to take part in the conflict. That promise, like so many others, had been broken. Some of the poor fellows who made up the Labour Corps had volunteered, but most had been conscripted by local magistrates to fill their quotas. I didn't doubt Ramses could blend in perfectly; for a man who had played the parts of beggars, camel drivers, and mad dervishes, a peasant from Upper Egypt presented no difficulty. It sounded like a very uncomfortable method of getting where he wanted to go, but there was no use asking Ramses to explain.

"Ah," I said. "In that case, we had better start packing."

Ramses must have known there wasn't a hope of persuading us to remain in Cairo, but he tried.

"Mother, too many people already know about this supposedly secret expedition. The three of you marching purposefully on Gaza will be a dead giveaway. You're too well known, especially Father."

"Ah, but we will be in disguise," Emerson said.

Emerson loves disguises, and is not allowed to indulge in them as often as he would like; he looked so pleased, his lips parted in a broad smile, his blue eyes shining, that Ramses hadn't the heart to object. Instead he gave me a critical look. "You've worked it all out, haven't you, Mother? Nefret, why didn't you tell me about this?"

"She knew nothing of it," I said quickly. "I couldn't ask her to keep secrets from you, now could I?"

"Oh, God." Indignation and reluctant amusement mingled on his face, to be replaced by remorse. He went to Nefret and took her hands in his. "I'm sorry, sweetheart."

"Your apology is, for once, appropriate." She looked up at him with a smile. "I accept it. Mother only told me she had the situation well in hand. I didn't ask for details. I trusted her, and I suggest you do the same."

"Don't worry, my dear," I said cheerfully. "Your father and I have it worked out. He has a dear old friend in Khan Yunus—"

"Of course," Ramses said resignedly. "Mahmud ibn Rafid. Is there any place in the Middle East where Father doesn't have a 'dear old friend'?"

"Not many," said Emerson, smoking. "Khan Yunus is only ten miles south of Gaza, and Mahmud owns a villa there." He chuckled. "When he told me 'My house is your house,' he may not have meant it literally, but he cannot object if I take him up on the offer. He's scampered off to Damascus, so that will be all right. It is quite a comfortable house. Even your mother will be pleased with it."

I doubted that very much, but at such a time I would have settled into a cave or a tent in order to be nearby when Ramses carried out his hazardous mission. "Quite," I murmured. "Emerson, I presume you have made the other arrangements we discussed? I cannot think of anything I dislike more than a long journey by camel, but there seems to be no alternative."

"Ah, but there is," Emerson said. Self-satisfaction is too weak a word for the emotion that illumined his countenance and swelled his broad chest. "I will give you three guesses, Peabody."

A hideous sense of foreboding came over me. "Oh, no, Emerson. Please. Don't tell me—"

"Yes, my dear. I have acquired a new motorcar." Avoiding my stricken expression, he turned to Ramses and explained. "It's a splendid vehicle, my boy, one of the T Model Ford Light cars the military has been using. It has—"

"How did you—uh—acquire it?" Ramses asked.

"Ah, well, you know my methods," said Emerson with a grin.

"You stole it!"

"No. Well. Not exactly. It has—"

"You can't drive it yourself, you know," I interrupted. This obvious fact had occurred to me once I got over my initial consternation, and it cheered me quite a lot. "Think how absurd you would look at the wheel, in turban and caftan."

"I have considered that," said Emerson, with great dignity. "You said you would leave the problem of transport to me."

"Hmmmm. Frankly, I do not see how we can drive all that distance without getting bogged down in sand dunes and blowing up tires; but if all goes well—"

"It won't," Ramses muttered.

"If it does, we should arrive within a few days of one another. Mind this, Ramses; you are to report yourself to us before you go to Gaza. You know where we will be. For our own peace of mind and for safety's sake, we want to be made cognizant of your plans. Have I your word?"

"Yes." He hesitated for a moment, and then shrugged. "You'll have to follow the road, so I suppose the worst that can happen is that you'll break down and be forced to accept help from the military. Speaking of peace of mind, I would like to be made cognizant of *your* plans. Is Father to be a

wealthy aristocrat—a wealthy, *bearded* aristocrat—and
Mother his favorite wife?"

"No, that is Nefret," I explained. "I am the older wife."

Ramses exchanged bemused glances with Nefret. Her
open-mouthed astonishment convinced him, had he doubted
it, that she had known nothing of my scheme. He laughed a
little, and shook his head.

"Mother, you never cease to amaze me. I hope you enjoy
yourself. As the older wife you will be in a position to bully
Nefret—and Father."

"Ha," said Emerson meaningfully.

Ramses was gone next morning. When Nefret joined us for
breakfast she was a trifle hollow-eyed and pale, but that
might have been a normal reaction to such a hard parting. I
did not feel I had the right to ask what they had said to one
another—my sympathetic imagination supplied a good deal
of the dialogue—but I did venture to inquire whether Ramses had been angry about our following him.

"Resigned, rather," Nefret said, toying with her toast.

"Eat something," I ordered. "We are leaving in an hour
and it will be a long, hard day. The first of many, I fear."

"Not at all," said Emerson. "The T Model Ford Light
car—"

"I don't want to hear about it, Emerson. Eat your breakfast."

"I have," said Emerson indignantly. "You are the one who
is delaying us."

To have left the hotel in disguise or in the vehicle Emerson had acquired would have aroused speculation. We went
by cab to Atiyeh, the village where the northern branch of
Abdullah's family lived, and there we found no other than
Selim awaiting our arrival. He was disappointed when I
failed to register surprise at seeing him.

"It was logical," I explained. "Once I learned of the motorcar. I am pleased, Emerson, that you didn't insist on driving it yourself."

"I had a number of reasons for bringing Selim along, all of them excellent, and all of them, you will claim, obvious to you. Let us not waste time discussing the subject. Is the car ready, Selim?"

"Yes, Father of Curses. It is," Selim said enthusiastically, "a wonderful motorcar. It has—"

"What about supplies?" I asked.

"Everything is in order, Sitt Hakim," Selim said. He looked doubtfully at the piles of personal luggage I had brought. "I think there will be room."

There was, but just barely. Nefret and I would have to sit on some of the parcels and put our feet on others. There was not even space on top of the vehicle, where Selim had fastened several long planks.

The whole village gathered to wave good-bye and shout blessings. It would have been impossible to conceal our expedition, whose ostensible purpose was to examine certain ruins in the Sinai. Selim had asked them not to speak of it, and since they all knew about Emerson's frequent disputes with the Antiquities Department, they assumed we were planning to excavate without official permission. Sooner or later someone would tell the story, as a good joke on the authorities, but as Emerson philosophically remarked, it didn't matter much; by the time the gossip reached General Murray, it would be too late to stop us.

As an additional precaution we waited until we were well away from the village before we assumed our disguises. Emerson's consisted of shirt and trousers, an elegant long vest and flowing robe, and, of course, a beard. Instead of a tarboosh or turban, he covered his head with a khafiyeh—the flattering headdress worn by the desert people that frames the face in folds of cloth and is held in place by a twisted cord. It shadowed those distinctive features more effectively than a turban and protected the back of his neck from the sun.

Nefret and I bundled ourselves up in the inconvenient and

uncomfortable ensembles worn by Moslem ladies when they travel abroad. Ramses always said that if a disguise is to be successful, it must be accurate in every detail, so Nefret and I were dressed from the skin out in appropriate garments: a shirt and a pair of very full trousers, with a long vest, called a yelek, over them; and over the yelek a gibbeh; and over the gibbeh the additional layers of the traveling costume—a large loose gown called a tob, a face veil that reaches nearly to the feet—and on top of it all a voluminous habarah of black silk which conceals the head and the hands as well as everything else.

Emerson and Selim both stared when Nefret removed the scarf that had covered her head; I had dyed her hair before we left the hotel, and it made quite a difference in her appearance.

"What did you do that for?" Emerson demanded. "Her hair will be covered."

"Not from other women in the household," I replied, applying brown coloring to Nefret's smooth cheeks. "And one must always be prepared for accidents. That red-gold hair is too distinctive."

Selim nodded and grinned. He was in a state of boyish exuberance, flattered by Emerson's confidence and looking forward to the adventure. He had not been told of Ramses's mission, nor of our real purpose. That did not matter. He had complete faith in Emerson—and, I believe I may say, in me—and rather fancied himself as a conspirator.

I can best sum up that journey by saying that camels might have been worse. Without Selim's expertise and Emerson's strength we could never have got through. The first part of the trip was not too bad, for the Corps of Engineers had improved the roads from Cairo to the Canal. We crossed it at Kantara, on one of the pontoon bridges, and it was here we met our first and only check by the military. Huddled in the tonneau amid piles of parcels, enveloped in muffling garments that concealed everything except our eyes, Nefret and I waited in suspense while Emerson produced a set of papers and handed them to Selim, who passed them over to the officer. Staring straight ahead, arms folded and brow dark, Emerson was a model of arrogant indignation. He did not move an inch, even when the officer handed the papers back and saluted.

"How did you get those?" I asked, sotto voce.

"I will explain later," Emerson grunted, as Selim sent the car bumping over the bridge.

We camped that night in a little oasis not far from the road, and a great relief it was to stretch our cramped limbs and remove several layers of clothing.

"We are making excellent time," Emerson announced, as Selim got a fire started and Nefret and I sat by the little tent he had set up. So far I could not fault Emerson's arrangements, though I was inclined to attribute some of them to Selim. Emerson would never have thought of the tent. Concealed in its shadow, away from the flickering firelight, we allowed ourselves the luxury of removing not only the face veil and habarah but the tob and gibbeh. The air had cooled rapidly after the sun set, as it always does in the desert.

Selim insisted upon doing the cooking, and while he arranged his pots and pans, Emerson produced the set of papers he had shown the officer. I studied them with a surprise I was unable to conceal. They bore the signature of none other than the high commissioner, Sir Reginald Wingate, and testified to the moral character and loyalty of Sheikh Ahmed Mohammed ibn Aziz.

"Where did you get these?" I demanded. "Not from Wingate?"

"Good Gad, no." Emerson began digging around in the luggage. "What did you do with my pipe?"

"I didn't do anything with it since I didn't know you had brought it," I retorted. "Isn't a meerschaum out of character?"

"The devil with that," said Emerson, extracting pipe and tobacco pouch. "As for the papers, you will never guess how I got them."

"A forger?" inquired Nefret, scanning the papers I had handed her by the light of the flickering flames. "A very skilled forger. You know a good many of them, I expect."

Emerson went about filling his pipe. "The ones with whom I am acquainted specialize in antiquities," he replied. "I required a different sort of expertise. So I paid a visit to Ibrahim el-Gharbi."

"The procurer?" I gasped. "But, Emerson, you called him—"

"A vile trafficker in human flesh. A good phrase, that," said Emerson, puffing. "According to Ramses, el-Gharbi can be useful if one takes everything he says with a strong seasoning of skepticism, and he has connections with every illegal business in Cairo. At the moment he is open to reason. He wants to get out of that prison camp."

"I hope you didn't promise you would arrange his release in exchange for these papers," I said severely. "The end does not justify the means."

"I made no promises" was the evasive reply. "But we owe the rascal, Peabody. It was through el-Gharbi, or rather one of his sources, that I was able to—er—acquire the motorcar. He also gave me the name of the man who forges official papers for him, and a chit telling him to comply with my request. Good, aren't they?"

"Let us hope all our difficulties will be so easily solved," I said.

"Don't be such a pessimist, Peabody," said Emerson. "Aren't you the one who keeps telling me to enjoy the moment, without worrying about what the future may bring? What could be more enjoyable than this?"

I could have mentioned quite a number of things, but it was pleasant to sit round the fire with the fresh breeze of the desert cooling our faces and the blazing stars of the desert shining down. The infinite eyes of God—and nowhere in that vast wasteland to hide from them.

Fortunately my conscience was perfectly clear.

It was to be our last peaceful hour for several days. From Romani on, the road surface worsened, and we encountered a great deal of traffic. Heavy lorries lumbered past, loaded with supplies; troops of soldiers plodded through the sand. They gave us curious glances, but no one ventured to address us. The magnificent presence of Emerson, his nose jutting out from the spreading blackness of his beard, was imposing enough to win respect, and the presence of two veiled females forbade interference. The men had been warned to leave Moslem women strictly alone. Squeezed uncomfortably in our nest of baggage, Nefret and I looked enviously at the troops of cavalry that occasionally contested our right of way. Most of them were Australians or New Zealanders, and a splendid-looking lot of men they were.

It was after we passed el-Arish, the farthest advance of the railroad, that the real trouble began. Men were working on the tracks and our unusual group had begun to attract undesirable attention. Emerson, who thinks he knows everything—and usually does—declared he knew of another path that would lead us through the Wadi el-Arish and into Palestine from the southwest.

There had been fighting at Maghdaba, some twenty miles south of el-Arish, and the ground was strewn with the debris of battle, including the pathetic remains of horses and camels. After the second tire blew I began to worry about supplies. We were down to our last three cans of petrol, and the water was running low. The bed of the wadi was rough but not impassable; Selim kept turning and swerving, trying, as I supposed, to avoid the worst bumps. He could not avoid all of them; holding Nefret in a firm embrace, I began to wonder how the devil we were to get out of the cursed canyon. It was one of the longest wadis in the region, stretching all the way down into the desert. Suddenly there was a shout from Emerson.

"There!" he cried, pointing. "Left, Selim."

I took one appalled look at the slope, littered with boulders, and shrieked, "Stop!"

Selim did, of course. When faced with conflicting orders from Emerson and me, he knew whose command to obey. Emerson turned and shot me an outraged glare. "What's the matter with you, Peabody? There is no easier way out of the wadi for another five miles, and—"

"Easier? Well, Emerson, I will take your word for it, but I am not going to be bounced up that incline. Nefret and I will ascend on foot. Get out of those clothes, Nefret."

I began stripping off my own garments as I spoke. Flushed with heat but perfectly composed, Nefret said meekly, "Yes, Mother," and followed my example.

The men raised all sorts of objections. Emerson declared, "You can't climb in those clothes!" and Selim, deeply offended, assured us that he was perfectly capable of getting the confounded motorcar up the slope without difficulty. Naturally I ignored these complaints. After fumbling about, I located one of the bundles I had brought and took out two pairs of boots.

"What the devil," Emerson began.

"I believe in being prepared for all possible contingencies," I replied. "And as you see, it is as well I was! Hoist up your trousers, Nefret, and tuck the ends into your boots. Now then, I think we can manage; are you ready, my dear?"

Nefret grinned. "As Ramses has often said, you never cease to amaze me, Mother. Yes, I'm ready."

It was not a difficult climb—there was even a path of sorts, winding back and forth across the slope. We were able to remain upright most of the time, without having to resort to four-limbed progress. When we reached the top we saw before us a baked, barren landscape that shimmered with sunlight; but the hot air dried the perspiration that had coated our bodies, and it was wonderful to be out of those layers of clothing.

Nefret peered down into the wadi. "Selim has backed the car up," she said. "They see us—the Professor is waving us to get out of the way—they're coming . . . Oh dear. I don't think I can watch."

It was impossible not to, though. Amid crashes and thumps and the groans of various bits of the machinery, the vehicle thundered up the slope. Even louder than the other noises were the enthusiastic whoops of Emerson, bouncing up and down and grinning from ear to ear. When Selim stopped, on a fairly level stretch of ground, Nefret and I ran toward the car.

"There, you see?" Emerson demanded. "I told you it would be all right."

"One of the tires is flat," I remarked.

Emerson waved this aside. "We'll have it mended in a jiffy."

Selim managed to mend the tire, despite Emerson's attempts at advice and assistance. We passed round the water bottle, resumed our costumes, and started again.

I will draw a veil over the succeeding hours. I lost count of the number of times we got stuck in a sand dune. On several occasions Selim was able to back up and go at it again; at other times he had to lay the planks down and Emerson had to push from behind. He had removed all his extraneous garments, and shouted encouragement to Selim as the wheels spun and sent sand spraying over him. His head was bare, his fine linen shirt was torn and smeared with oil; in short, he was having a wonderful time.

As the sun sank westward, it became apparent that we were not going to make it back to the coastal road that day. Bathed in perspiration, muffled in fabric, I was considering methods of murdering Emerson, and perhaps Selim as well, when I saw ahead a few spindly palm trees.

"There it is," Emerson said happily. "I thought I remembered the location."

"You thought?" I repeated.

It was not much of an oasis, but there was water, brackish and muddy, but enough to allow us to sponge our faces and limbs. "Your little shortcut has only cost a day," I remarked, as we sat round the small fire. "So far."

"We'll be back on the main road tomorrow," Emerson said. "And in Khan Yunus by nightfall."

"So you say." I looked at Nefret, who was sitting cross-legged on the ground eating sardines out of a tin. "I will have to dye your skin again, Nefret. What with sand and perspiration, most of it is gone. And you, Emerson—"

"What's wrong with my appearance?" Emerson demanded, running his hand through his beard and sprinkling his sardines with sand.

"Shall I have a disguise, Sitt Hakim?" Selim asked hopefully.

"You might shave your beard," I said.

Selim went pale and clutched at his treasured beard. I repented my cruelty almost at once. "I was joking, Selim. You are not known in this region; I do not believe a disguise is necessary."

One can easily comprehend how the Israelites felt when, after toiling through the arid wilderness, they beheld before them the green pastures and fertile fields of the Promised Land. (I did not mention this charming idea to Emerson, since he does not believe in the Exodus and would have given me a long boring lecture about it.)

All was fresh and emerald green, with the brilliant scarlet spots of poppies dotting the landscape. Winter was passing and summer was yet to come; the air was fresh and cool, the sky a cerulean cloudless vault; wildflowers grew in profusion: anemones and lilies, wild purple iris and sweet peas of all shades, from golden yellow to rosy mauve.

Yet the signs of war were everywhere. Every now and again an aircraft would drone overhead, and sometimes its passage was followed by an explosion and a cloud of dust.

None of the bombs came close to us, but I was glad of the veil that covered my face. Since that air raid in London I had a tendency to flinch at explosions.

We did not want to spend another night on the road, so we started early and went on with scarcely a pause until late afternoon. As the sun blazoned the western sky with flaming color we came to the outskirts of Khan Yunus. An old city of the Philistines, like Gaza, it was a garden spot indeed, with flowers everywhere and fig and orange trees heavy with fruit. Selim propelled the motorcar skillfully through the narrow streets, and I realized that our arrival would not go unnoticed by the military. Since the enemy had withdrawn without a battle, the town had been spared destruction, and our brave fellows were enjoying the amenities of the suk and the picturesque winding lanes. In the center of the main square, a group of field engineers was at work improving the old well. According to Emerson, Mahmud's house was on one side of this square.

Unlike the city mansions with which I was acquainted, this one did not face directly onto the street. Instead we saw a high, featureless wall of stone covered with crumbling plaster and a double-leaved door wide enough to be called a gate. Heavy and banded with iron, it stood ajar, and from the litter that had blown up against it I had the impression it had not been closed for quite a while.

Selim got out and shoved at it. Emerson maintained his stately persona, looking neither to right nor left. I leaned forward and spoke softly. "It is an unusual arrangement, Emerson. More like a khan or caravansary. And the gate is wide enough for—"

"Camels," said Emerson, sotto voce and without turning his head. "Some of the old villain's caravans carry merchandise that cannot be unloaded in the open street. Be quiet, Peabody, you have not been given permission to speak."

After shoving with all his strength, Selim got the rusted hinges to move. When the gates creaked open we saw an unpaved courtyard and a group of men, women, naked babies, chickens, goats, and a sheep gathered in the courtyard. All, except for the chickens, stared in stupefaction. Obviously we had not been expected.

They were members of a family that had been charged by Mahmud to look after the place; they had taken advantage of his absence to move in and make themselves at home. Our appearance threw them into a total panic. Emerson's curses soon sorted them out, and they scattered in all directions to carry out his orders. Once the babies, goats, and sheep had been removed, Selim drove the car into the courtyard and closed the gates. I did not doubt the military authorities would soon be informed of our arrival, and could only hope that Emerson's forged papers would convince them of our bona fides. There was no use worrying about it. We would deal with unexpected setbacks in our usual efficient fashion.

Straight ahead, forming one side of the courtyard, was the house itself. The living quarters were on the first floor, with storage and work areas underneath. The barred and closely screened windows on one side of the facade must be those of the haremlik; on the other side, stone steps led up to the carved arches of the mak'ad, a reception room that was open to the court so that the owner of the house could see approaching visitors—male visitors. The mak'ad was not used by the women of the household.

Obeying a brusque gesture from Emerson, who was reveling in his role, Nefret and I gathered up our voluminous skirts and went through a side door and up a flight of narrow stairs to the haremlik.

We were followed by several women, squawking like the chickens as they made excuses and offered assistance. I could see I had a long job ahead of me getting the place in proper order. The basic plan was comfortable if somewhat old-fashioned, with a bath chamber and a number of small cubicles surrounding a handsome salon, or ka'ah, a lofty chamber with an arched ceiling and tiled floor. One end was raised, with rugs covering the floor, and two divans. I cannot describe to persons of fastidious tastes (as my Readers certainly are) the condition of the place. It was all I could do to refrain from rolling up my sleeves and seizing a broom. Since this was impossible, I threw myself into my role as elderly harridan and began shouting out directions. I doubt the flustered females had ever moved so fast. The rugs and cushions were removed to be beaten and fumigated, the floor was swept and scrubbed, the dust and cobwebs covering all the flat surfaces were removed. When the room was habitable, and we had been supplied with a jug of warm water, I sent the whole lot of them off to the bath chamber, assuring them I would come soon to make certain they had cleaned it thoroughly.

Nefret had remained modestly silent; her Arabic was less fluent than mine. I wondered what Ramses would think of the transformation in her appearance. She had darkened her skin a shade or two, and her hair was now a pretty shade of russet brown. The cornflower-blue eyes could not be concealed, but they could be explained by the assumption that she was of light-skinned Circassian or Berber ancestry. There were a good many girls of that complexion in Turkish harems.

"You certainly look like an old man's darling," I remarked in French. We had decided it was safer to use that language, even in private conversation, in case we were overheard.

Nefret made a face and plucked at the embroidered gibbeh that covered several other layers of garments. "I don't smell like one. I'd give anything for a bath and a change of clothing."

"So would I. It will have to wait. But you may as well remove the gibbeh and freshen up a bit. Curse it, here are some of the women come back."

They had brought our luggage, including the mats on which I intended we should sit and sleep. Emerson had howled at the amount of baggage I had considered necessary—he would have gone off to Timbuktu with only the clothes on his back—but I absolutely refused to share my bed with the interesting variety of insect life that I had good reason to expect. The women spread the mats over the divans and unpacked a few more things, including my traveling tea set, which included a silver kettle and a spirit lamp. (This had produced a particularly sarcastic string of remarks from Emerson.)

I was preparing an emphatic speech of dismissal for the ladies when the appearance of Emerson spared me that effort. The women at once fled, drawing folds of their garments over their faces, and closed the doors.

Hands on hips, feet apart, Emerson inspected the room and us with a lordly sneer. He looked magnificent! I repressed the thrill of admiration that ran through my limbs, since it was unlikely I could do anything about it for some time. Regret was mitigated by the presence of the beard. It looked splendid, but I knew how it would feel—like a bramble bush.

"Well, this is very pleasant," he remarked.

"French, Emerson," I said.

"Merde," said Emerson, whose command of that language is limited. He does know most of the swearwords, though.

"I have ordered dinner to be brought here," he went on. "It is a condescension on my part, but I am an uxorious, indulgent husband. You will serve me kneeling, of course."

"Don't get carried away, Emerson," I warned.

"En français, ma chérie, s'il vous plaît," said Emerson, grinning broadly. He went on in his version of that language, with occasional lapses into English when his vocabulary failed him. "Selim is in a condition because of the motorcar. He injured the—er—bonnet when he passed it between the gate."

Through the window I could hear Selim's voice, raised in vehement commentary, and understood enough to comprehend that he was trying to sort out the servant situation. I deduced that dinner would be late.

"Well, we are here," I remarked, "and although some of our habits will undoubtedly strike the servants as peculiar, they won't think much about it. But how is Ramses to reach us? He can't come here as himself."

"He knows that," Emerson said. "Give the boy credit."

"We must do something about the mashrabiya screens, Emerson. I cannot see an infernal thing out the window."

"Vous êtes en la harem, ma chérie," said Emerson, smirking. "Les dames non pouvait—pourraint—(curse it!) voir dans le aperture."

I understood his meaning, despite his atrocious grammar. Some of our windows opened onto the courtyard; it would not have been proper for strangers to see a woman looking out.

After his little exercise of wit, Emerson admitted we would be well advised to get the screens loose, so that we would have warning of unexpected visitors. It took all three of us to do the job, since we did not want to remove them entirely. With the aid of strips of fabric cut from the hangings, we managed to secure them so they would not flap but could be opened without difficulty.

Dinner finally arrived. It was very bad, so I assumed Selim had not been able to find a skilled cook. We ate sitting cross-legged round the platter of rice and mutton. Though mats had been placed in the adjoining cubicles, we decided to spend the night in the ka'ah. What the servants thought of this I cannot imagine (or rather, I prefer not to imagine). Emerson considered it best that we should not separate, however.

Next morning Selim, now in undisputed charge of the household, relegated the extraneous members of the family to the house they had originally occupied, and went off to hire several more servants, including a cook. The patriarch of the small clan we retained in the post of doorkeeper.

After breakfast (warmed-up rice and mutton) Emerson went out to visit the coffeeshops and listen to the local gossip. I saw no reason why we could not have visited the suk, properly veiled and escorted, but Emerson declared it would be an unnecessary risk, and Nefret produced an even more conclusive argument.

"What if he should come while we were out?"

She was right, but the morning dragged on, with nothing to do except bully the servants and familiarize ourselves with the rooms of the harem. We were able to bathe for the first time since we had left Cairo, and a great relief it was.

In the course of my exploration, I discovered several secret passages with peepholes in the walls, used by the master to spy on his women. Many of the older mansions in the region had such devices, as well as escape tunnels and hidden rooms. There were three of the latter in the haremlik, two mere cubbyholes in the wall and the third a large hiding place under the floor. The trapdoor covering it was concealed by matting. It had been designed for hiding objects, not people, since it was less than four feet high and there was no means of ventilation, and it was, as I had expected, empty. Mahmud would not have left anything of value.

Emerson returned with nothing to report, except that the town was full of soldiers, which we already knew. We were lingering over luncheon when there were sounds of a disturbance without. Emerson hurried to the door; when it opened I heard someone say in Arabic, "There is a person here, lord—I could not keep him away—"

Emerson let out a strangled cough, and a voice I knew well murmured deprecatingly, "Lord, your slave begs your mercy, it is not his fault he did not come before this, he was detained by the cursed British and made to dig holes—see, see how his hands are bleeding!"

A thump followed, as if of knees hitting the floor.

My curiosity could not be contained. Nefret was already at the door, peeping out.

Emerson stood staring down openmouthed at the form crouching at his feet. Ramses's curly black head was bare and what I could see of his skin was almost as dark as his hair. I could see quite a lot of it.

His voice rose in a wail. "They took my clothes, lord, the fine clothing you gave me, my gibbeh and my sudarayee and my tarboosh and my shoes, and my—"

"God curse them," said Emerson, recovering himself. "Come in, then, and tell me."

Ramses straightened, smirking like a favored servant who has talked his way out of a beating; but the old man who had escorted him there croaked, "Into the harem, Effendi?"

Emerson drew himself up and skewered the presumptuous fellow with a fierce stare. "Did not the Prophet say, when he brought to his daughter the gift of a male slave, that she need not veil herself, for there was none present save her father and a slave?"

This interesting theological reference may have been too abstruse for the servant, but Emerson's stare got the point across. "Come," he added to Ramses.

Nefret and I quickly retreated from the door and Emerson propelled Ramses through it with a hard shove. "Now," he said loudly, in Arabic, "make your excuses to your mistress."

He slammed the door and Ramses looked quizzically from me to Nefret. "Which?"

"Me," Nefret said breathlessly. "I'm the new favorite, aren't I?"

"Speak French," I said warningly.

Neither of them heard me, I believe. Nefret was staring at him as if she had never seen him before—which, in a way, she had not, for to the best of my knowledge this was a new role for Ramses, and when Ramses played a part he did it thoroughly. He was wearing only a pair of dirty cotton drawers and he had stained his body a rich dark brown. I observed several raw marks across his bare back, and remembered that I had heard one of the officers explain that "a few cuts of the whip" were advisable when dealing with recalcitrant members of the Labour Corps.

Nefret had seen them too. She let out a little cry and threw herself into his arms.

They made a picturesque tableau as they clung to one another, framed by the pointed arch of the alcove—his dark, muscular body and her slender, yielding form in its gold-embroidered blue velvet gibbeh. "Story pictures" were popular with a certain school of painting, and it was not difficult to think of a title for this one. "The Slave and the Sultan's Favorite," or "A Tryst with Death," or—

Emerson let out a sound rather like one the sultan might have made if he had come upon such a scene, and the two drew apart.

"Careless," I said softly. "I stopped up several peepholes in the walls, but I doubt I found them all."

Ramses dropped to his knees in front of me and clasped his hands. "Your forgiveness, honored lady."

"Yes, all right, just don't do it again." I added, just as softly, "I, too, am relieved to see you, my dear. What next?"

"I can't stay. You had better send me on an errand—and find me some clothes," he added, looking up at me with a smile. His thin dark face and cheerful grin and the curls clustering untidily round his forehead filled me with a strong desire to shake him. Men actually enjoy this sort of thing! So do I, if truth be told, but only when I am allowed to take an active part. It is the waiting I find so difficult, particularly when one waits for news of a loved one.

"When will we see you again?" I asked.

"I don't know. I am to rendezvous with Chetwode this evening and go on to Gaza with him. Two days, perhaps three. I'll come here as soon as we've finished the job, I promise."

He kissed my hands and my feet and rose. "Is there a bab-sirr?" he asked Emerson. "I may want to use it next time."

"A secret door? Oh, yes. Mahmud has too many enemies to do without that little convenience. I'll show you, and get you some clothes."

Ramses nodded. He turned to his wife. She stood as still as a prettily dressed doll, lips parted and braceleted arms folded over her breast. Ramses knelt and bowed his head.

"Don't worry," he whispered. "It will be all right."

She put out her hand, as if to touch his hair, but stopped herself in time. "Come straight here after . . ."

"As soon as I can." He took her hands and raised them to his lips.

From Manuscript H

Ramses hadn't told her the part that worried him most. He shared that information with his father, as they tried to find him something to wear.

"I met Chetwode in Rafah, as we had arranged. He's not awfully good at this sort of thing; his jaw dropped down to his chest when a filthy 'Gyppie' edged up to him and gave him the word we'd agreed upon."

"Curse it," said Emerson. "Can't you go off on your own—leave him behind?"

"They'd stop me before I got out of Khan Yunus. You haven't heard the worst of it. General Chetwode, the commander of the Desert Column, is our lad's uncle. I was dragged off to his office, where I was required to report to him and his chief of field intelligence."

"Hell and damnation! Who else knows about your 'secret' mission?"

"God knows." Ramses picked up a shirt, grinned, and put it aside. "Mother would say He does. If the word has come down the chain of command, Chetwode's superior Dobell must also have been informed. There's nothing here I can use, Father."

"What about that parcel you asked me to bring along?"

"I'll take it with me, but I don't want to wear those things in Khan Yunus. Selim must have a change of clothing he'll lend me."

"You mean to let him in on this?" Emerson asked.

"How much does he know?"

"Only that we are obviously bent on mischief of some sort. Selim doesn't ask questions."

"He deserves to be told—some of it, at any rate. It's a

poor return for his friendship and loyalty to be treated as if he were not completely trustworthy. Especially," Ramses added bitterly, "when every idiot and his bloody uncle knows. I think Selim may have spotted me when I arrived; he gave me a very fishy look when I was arguing with the doorman."

Selim had spotted him, but not, as he was careful to explain, because of any inadequacy in Ramses's disguise. "Who else could it be, though?" he demanded. "I do not ask questions of the Father of Curses, but I expected you would join the others sooner or later."

"You must have wondered what this is all about, though." The clothes Selim had given him would suit well enough; Arab garments were not designed to be form-fitting.

Selim folded his arms and said stiffly, "It is not my place to wonder."

Ramses grinned and slapped him on the back. "You sound exactly like your father. I and another man are going into Gaza, Selim. There have been rumors about a certain Ismail Pasha—that he's a British agent who has gone over to the enemy. Since I am, er, acquainted with the gentleman in question, they are sending me to get a look at Ismail and find out whether the rumors are true."

"Acquainted," Selim repeated. "Ah. Is it possible, Ramses, that I am also, er, acquainted with him?"

"You can't go with me," Ramses said. He hadn't answered the question. Selim accepted this with a shrug and a nod, and Ramses went on, "Thank you for the clothes. I'll try to return them in good condition."

"Tonight's the night, then," Emerson said.

"Yes. Chetwode—our Chetwode—and I are meeting after nightfall in an abandoned house in Dir el Balah, just north of here. I hope to God he can find it. It will take me a while to get there by roundabout ways, since I don't want to be recruited by some lad looking for laborers. I had better go. Do you want to send me on my way with a few curses and kicks, Selim?"

Selim did not return his smile. "If you say I should. Be careful. Do not take foolish chances."

"As your father would have said. I'll try not to. Watch over them, Selim."

Chetwode was late. He stood squinting into the darkness of the half-ruined building, his form outlined against the starry sky. Ramses waited only long enough to make sure the other man was alone before he moved out of the shadows.

"Didn't they teach you not to make a target of yourself in an open doorway?" he asked caustically.

"Since it was you—"

"You hoped it was me. Get out of that uniform and put these on."

He made certain he had covered Chetwode's face, neck, hands, and forearms with the dark dye, and got all his hair concealed under the turban. There wasn't anything he could do about the blue eyes that looked trustingly into his, but when the boy grinned, cheerful as a hound pup, the expanse of healthy white teeth was another reason to remind him to keep his mouth shut. Patiently Ramses went over it again.

"If anybody speaks to you, drool and babble and bob your head. Idiots are under the protection of God. Stick close to me . . ." He hesitated, gripped by one of those illogical premonitions—or maybe it wasn't so illogical, under the circumstances. "Stick close unless I tell you otherwise. If I tell you to run, do it, without arguing and without looking back. That's an order. If you disobey I'll see that you face a court-martial."

"But if we're separated—"

"I'll find you if I can. If I can't, you'll have to make your own way back to our lines. Don't wait for me or go looking for me."

Chetwode's face was as easy to read as a page of print. Some of the sentences read: "One doesn't abandon a comrade." "You can count on me, old chap, to the death." Or something equally trite. Ramses sighed and offered another

cliché. "One of us has to get back with the information
we've collected. We know we're laying our lives on the line;
that is part of the job."

Chetwode's tight lips parted. "Oh. Yes, that's right. You
can count on me, old chap—"

"Good. One more thing. Hand over that pistol."

Ramses had every intention of searching him if he denied
carrying a weapon, but the young fool didn't even try to
bluster it out. His hand flew to his waist.

"What if we have to shoot it out?" he demanded.

"If it comes to that, we'll have a hundred men shooting
back at us. Hand it over, or I'll leave you behind."

Chetwode looked from his stern face to his clenched fist
and got the point. Slowly and reluctantly he unbuckled the
belt fastened round his waist under his shirt and gave it and
the holster to Ramses.

Ramses removed the shells and added the empty gun to
the pile of abandoned clothing, which he covered with a few
loose stones. "Now shut up and watch where you're going."

The boy wouldn't shut up. He'd memorized the directions
that Ramses had ignored, since he didn't need them, and
kept up a breathless, whispered monologue: "Keep to the
north until the mosque bears 132; bearing 266 till we come
to the edge of a bog . . . is this . . . Oh, hell."

Ramses hauled him out. "One more word and I'll sink
you back into the muck. We're within a hundred feet of the
Turkish trenches. Don't open your mouth again until I tell
you you may."

"Sorry." He closed his mouth and nodded vigorously. The
starlight reflected in his eyes.

Ramses turned and led them along the edge of the bog.
The boy followed so close he kept treading on Ramses's
heels. I shouldn't have allowed this, Ramses thought in
silent fury. Goddamn Murray and Cartright and the rest of
them; the kid's doing his best, but I would spot him a mile
away, even if he were standing still with his face hidden. It
was that "Lords of Creation" look, shoulders stiff and jaw

squared—drilled into them from childhood, and almost impossible to eradicate.

The Turks had ringed the city round with trenches and breastworks. An intricate network of cactus hedges provided an additional defense. The series of ridges that ran from Gaza eastward to Beersheba were also fortified, but they had no trouble getting through. The defenders knew no attack was imminent; reconnaissance planes would have warned them of such preparations, even if they had not had busy little spies reporting back to Turkish HQ. The area between Gaza and Khan Yunus was peaceful. People came and went, tilling the fields, carrying produce to the British encampments, engaging in all the mercantile activities that spring up when new customers are available. It would have been impossible to keep tabs on all of them.

Once over the ridge, Ramses led his companion in a wide circle that brought them to a guard post just as the sun was rising. Chetwode had protested; he wanted to crawl romantically through the barbed wire and the cactus hedges.

"It's too hard on one's clothes," Ramses said shortly. He had learned from experience—and from that master thief, his uncle—that the best way of getting into a place where you weren't supposed to be was to walk boldly up and demand entrance. He had supplied himself with a convincing story—a sick, aged mother awaiting him—enough money to arouse cupidity without arousing suspicion, and a few bags of a substance he expected would serve better than money. Hashish wasn't hard to come by in Turkish areas, but the best varieties were expensive.

The noncommissioned officer in charge of the post didn't believe the pathetic story about the dying mother. Ramses had not expected he would; they then proceeded to the next stage of negotiation, which left him without a certain percentage of his money and his merchandise. It wasn't an outrageously high percentage; the NCO knew that if his victim started howling protests, it would have brought an officer to investigate—and demand his share.

Ramses had been in Gaza only once, in the summer of 1912, but he knew the place fairly well; he'd spent several days wandering around, enjoying the amenities of the suk and admiring the fine old mosques and making a brief, informal survey of the ancient remains, since he knew his father would expect one. There weren't many. For almost four thousand years the area between the Sinai and the Euphrates had been fought over, conquered and reconquered, destroyed and rebuilt. Egyptians, Assyrians, Phoenicians, Greeks, Romans, Saracens, and Crusaders had occupied Gaza in turn. It had been one of the five cities of the Philistines, the site of the great temple of Dagon, pulled down by Samson in his last and mightiest feat. (He'd got that information from his mother; his father didn't give much credence to anything in Scripture unless it could be confirmed by archaeological sources.) The most recent conquest had been by the Ottoman Sultan, Selim the First, in the sixteenth century; in revenge for the city's stubborn resistance he had let his troops sack and destroy a large part of it. However, by 1912 Gaza had become a prosperous town with almost forty thousand inhabitants. The population had spilled out beyond the walls, to north and south and east; the central city, raised on the accumulated debris of various levels of destruction, contained the administrative and commercial buildings, as well as the homes of wealthier citizens.

On the hill that rose from the center of the upper town stood the Great Mosque, formerly a Christian church built in the twelfth century. He had spent an enjoyable afternoon admiring the carvings and the magnificent gray marble columns. It was now being used as a powder magazine.

So much for the Great Mosque, Ramses thought. So much for the other architectural treasures of Gaza—the little church of St. Porphyry, an exquisite example of early Christian architecture, the beautiful ancient mosque of Hashim, even the remains of the old walls and their seven gates. Modern weapons were much more efficient than the older variety. One well-placed shell and the Great Mosque, with its delicate octagonal minaret, would be gone.

And so would hundreds, maybe thousands, of people.

The suk appeared to be as prosperous as ever, with stalls selling everything from handmade lace and the fine black pottery of the region to a variety of mouthwatering fruits and nuts and vegetables, whose discarded rinds and husks littered the ground. Ramses found a popular café, squatted genteelly, and ordered mint tea. The habitués were an inquisitive lot; they put him through a merciless but friendly interrogation, not leaving off until they had determined his name, place of origin, business, and ancestry, and had commiserated with him on the condition of his poor young brother. "He has blue eyes," said one observant man.

"His mother was Circassian," Ramses explained. "My father's favorite, until she died giving birth to him. My mother . . ."

It did not take long for Ramses to establish his bona fides as a seller of desirable merchandise. The town was full of men in uniform, strutting through the street with the arrogance of Europeans among natives. The most loquacious of their newfound friends, a middle-aged man with only one eye and a stump where his right hand had been, had a few pungent epithets for the Germans. "But," he added, "they are no worse than the Turks. God curse this war! Whoever wins we will be the losers. If Gaza is defended, our homes and livelihoods will be destroyed."

It was a good opening, and Ramses took advantage of it. His questions and comments brought out a spate of information, much of it highly inaccurate, and some more accurate descriptions of various public figures. Von Kressenstein, the German commander, was feared but respected; the governor was feared and loathed; the Turkish general was a fat pig who did nothing but sit in his fine house and eat. And so it went, until dusk grayed the sky and the party dispersed.

Ramses and Chetwode spent the night in the picturesque

ruins of what was locally known as Samson's tomb—actually a structure dating from the Middle Ages. Moonlight filtering through the broken walls and roof made baroque patterns on the ground, and the leaves of the ancient olive trees rustled in the night wind. As they ate the food purchased in the bazaar, Chetwode enlivened the meal with questions. He hadn't had a chance to talk all day, and it must be wearing on him.

"You didn't ask about Ismail Pasha," he said accusingly.

"One tries to avoid asking direct questions." Ramses tossed away a handful of orange peel and stretched out on the ground. "In this case it wasn't necessary. You were there; didn't you hear what they said about him?"

"Everybody was talking too fast," Chetwode said sullenly. "Anyhow, it's your job to locate the fellow."

The hero worship was wearing thin. Ramses couldn't have said why he was reluctant to share this bit of news; old habit, perhaps, or one of the Secret Service's basic rules: Don't tell anyone more than he needs to know. Maybe Chetwode did need to know this, if only to keep him from doing something impulsive.

"The holy infidel, as they call him, is going to pray at the mosque of Hashim tomorrow at midday," Ramses explained. "There will be quite a crowd, I expect. We'll go early and find a place where we can get a good long look at him."

"And then?"

"Then we make a quick and, let us hope, unobtrusive exit from Gaza."

"After only two days? Without—without doing anything?"

Ramses tried to hold on to his temper. Being responsible for this ingenuous youth was nerve-racking enough without having to deliver lectures on espionage. "You hadn't planned on an indefinite stay, had you? We have to assume that there are certain people here who keep tabs on newcomers. One of our amiable acquaintances at the coffeeshop could be an agent of the governor or the military."

"Really?"

"That's how the Turks operate. They don't trust anyone, and with good reason. They aren't well liked in these parts. Sooner or later our presence will be known, and some bright soul may decide it would be a good idea to question us. Then there are the press gangs. They're always looking for recruits. One more day is all we can risk." He yawned and wondered why he was bothering. "Get some rest."

"As soon as I finish this."

Ramses sat up with a start. Chetwode squatted by the ruined arch of the entrance, scribbling busily by moonlight on what appeared to be a folded piece of paper. "What the hell are you doing?"

"Making notes. I didn't recognize all the insignia of the men we saw, but if I describe them, our people can get a good idea which units—"

"Eat it."

"What?"

"Get rid of the goddamn paper!" Chetwode stared blankly at him. He got to his feet. "If you were caught and they found that on you, you'd be dead. Or wish you were. What other incriminating objects are you carrying?"

He snatched the paper from Chetwode. Hastily, eyes wide, the boy took a pouch from the breast of his robe. It contained sheets of paper, several pencils, a small pocket torch, and a tiny bottle containing two white pills.

"Christ, I should have searched you before we left," Ramses muttered, as he shredded the papers and stamped on the neatly sharpened pencils. "What's in the bottle? Cyanide, no doubt. The Secret Service loves cyanide."

"But if we're caught—"

"We had better be able to talk our way out of it, which we could not do if we were carrying British-made writing materials. As for these . . ." He ground the innocent-looking pills under his heel. "Were you planning to ask the governor's head torturer to hang on a minute while you fished round in your pouch for the bottle, opened it, and popped the pills into your mouth?"

Chetwode's head drooped. "It does sound ridiculous, when you put it that way. They told me—"

"Yes, all right. Look here, there are a number of ways we could have gone about this, including your uncle's idiotic suggestion that we wear captured Turkish uniforms and march into their headquarters demanding information."

"I don't see why—"

"Then I'll tell you why." Ramses lost the remains of his temper. "It's a miracle you haven't already been spotted. If I were picked up and questioned, they would probably do nothing worse than send me to the trenches, from which I would soon remove myself. If they caught you, it wouldn't take a trained officer more than ten seconds to identify you as an Englishman. It's not just your accent, it's the way you stand, and sit, and move and . . . everything about you!"

Chetwode bowed his head. "I didn't know I was that bad."

"All of you are. It's not your fault," he added, more kindly. "To pass convincingly as a native of the area, you have to live there and think in the language for years. This is the safest way, and I'm trying to minimize the risks. You've done fine so far, but you'll have to follow my orders and keep your notes in your head."

"Like you? All that"—he gestured at the scattered bits of paper—"was a waste of time, wasn't it? You've got it memorized."

He was back to the hero worship. It was almost worse than his brief attempts at independent thinking. But not as dangerous. Ramses shrugged. "It's a matter of practice."

"A little late for me to start now, I guess." He looked up with a rueful smile. "Sorry. I'll do everything you say from now on."

"Then get some sleep."

Chetwode couldn't keep quiet even when he slept. He snored. Lying awake, his hands under his head, Ramses was tempted to kick him, but his better nature prevailed. Let the fellow sleep. He wished he could. The night noises here weren't the same as the ones at home; his nerves twitched at every rustle in the weeds. Since sleep was impossible, he went over and over the conversations he had held that day, picking them apart, looking for hints he might have missed.

He got a little sleep, but not much, what with Chetwode's snores and the need to listen for suspicious sounds. At daybreak he roused his companion. Chetwode was uncharacteristically silent—sulking or brooding, or maybe fighting an attack of cold feet, for which Ramses wouldn't have blamed him.

Suddenly Chetwode said, "What if something goes wrong?"

"I told you. Run."

"That's not much of a plan," Chetwode said. His mouth twitched. Perhaps he was trying to smile.

Ramses came to a decision. One of the many worries that had prevented him from sleeping was the thought of his anxious family, waiting in Khan Yunus.

"If you make it out and I'm caught or killed," he said, "go to the house of Ibn Rafid in Khan Yunus. It's on the main square, the largest house in town—anyone can show you which it is. Leave a written message for . . ." He realized he didn't know the name Emerson was currently using. "For the present master of the house, telling him what happened to me."

"Is he one of us?" Chetwode asked.

"No." The boy's curiosity made him wonder if he'd done the right thing. The alternative would have been worse, though—leaving them in ignorance of his fate, possibly for days. They might even decide to invade Gaza looking for him. None of them was noted for patience; and if the worst happened, certain knowledge was better than false hope.

Chetwode asked no further questions.

After they had finished the bread and fruit left over from the previous night, Ramses led the other man on a circuitous route back toward the center of town. The mosque was near the Askalon Gate. Ramses found a coffeeshop—not the one they had visited the previous day—and they settled down to wait.

As the morning wore on, the cafés filled and people began to gather. It lacked half an hour till midday when the procession appeared. It was small but impressive, headed by half a dozen mounted men wearing baggy trousers and jackets heavy with tarnished gilt, and silken sashes wound round their waists. They were armed with long swords and pistols. The horses were splendid animals, their bridles and stirrups of silver. Not Turkish regulars; the personal guard of some important official. They cleared the way brutally but effectively, using the flats of their swords. Since he was a head taller than most of the spectators, Ramses could see reasonably well; there seemed to be another group of guards at the end of the procession. Between the guards were several horsemen: the governor, flashing with gold, his fleshy face set in a look of conscious piety; and, next to him, flanked by two officers in Turkish uniform . . .

Ramses got only a glimpse of a bearded profile and prominent, hawklike nose, before a gun went off, so close to his ear, it momentarily deafened him. He spun round and struck the weapon out of Chetwode's hand. The second shot went wild.

"You goddamned fool!"

Chetwode's lips moved. Ramses couldn't hear what he said; the people around them were screaming and shoving, some of them trying to reach the would-be assassin, others—the wiser majority—scampering for safety. There was no such thing as an innocent bystander in the eyes of Ottoman officials.

"Run!" Ramses yelled, and emphasized the order with a shove. Chetwode gave him a wild-eyed stare and dashed off. Ramses tripped one of the avengers who were closing in, knocked another one down, ducked under the outstretched arms of a third, and set out at a run toward the mosque.

"That's the man! Stop him!" someone shouted in Turkish. He heard the pound of hoofbeats behind him and threw him-

self aside in time to avoid being ridden down, but the brief
delay was fatal. When he got to his feet he was surrounded
by the gaudily uniformed guard, all heroically brandishing
their swords.

"No weapons," the officer ordered. "Take him alive."

Ramses considered his options. He could only think of
two, and neither held much appeal. He could cringe and
whine and deny guilt, or he could take on six men. It would
end the same in either case, so he decided to give himself the
satisfaction of hitting someone.

He had two of them on the ground and a third on his
knees, when a missile skimmed the side of his head, hard
enough to throw him off balance for a vital moment. Flat on
his back, with four of them pinning his arms and legs, he re-
considered his options. There didn't seem to be any.

The officer raked his men with a scornful eye. "Six
against one, and it took a lucky throw from a safe distance to
bring him down. Tie his hands, my brave fellows, or he may
yet escape you."

Not much chance of that, Ramses knew. The blow on the
head had left him slightly giddy and there was blood trickling down his face. After they had bound his hands behind
him, one of them looped a rope round his neck and fastened
it to the leader's saddle. Wonderful. One slip, on any of the
scraps of rotting fruit that littered the street, and he'd be
dragged, choking, until the officer decided to stop. The only
positive feature in an otherwise gloomy situation was that
Chetwode was nowhere in sight.

Hot sunlight beat down on the deserted square. No—not
quite deserted. The onlookers had fled and the guard must
have escorted the dignitaries to safety, but from the opposite
side of the square a rider was coming slowly toward them.
Ramses stared, hoping his eyes had deceived him, knowing
they hadn't. He'd believed his situation couldn't be any
worse. He had been wrong.

The rider had only a single escort, a servant who followed
at a respectful distance. His mount was superb—a roan stal-

lion, his tail and mane braided with bright ribbons. He was
an impressive specimen, too, a tall, heavily built man with
finely cut features and a neat gray beard. His robes were of
silk and on the front of his turban was a jewel of rubies and
emeralds, surmounted by a white egret feather. Even the
whip he held had a jeweled, enameled handle. He pulled up
next to Ramses and acknowledged the officer's respectful
salute with a casual movement of his hand.

"What is this?" he asked in Turkish.

"As you see, Sahin Pasha. We have captured the assassin."

So now he's a pasha, Ramses thought. What was the head
of the Turkish secret service doing in Gaza? His first and—
he had hoped—last encounter with this formidable individual had ended in the failure of Sahin's mission; it wouldn't
be surprising if he bore a grudge against the man who had
been partially responsible. Ramses could only pray the Turk
wouldn't recognize him. He was bareheaded, having lost his
khafiyeh during the fight, but in his filthy torn robes, bearded
and disheveled, he bore little resemblance to the man Sahin
had last seen—disheveled, admittedly, but clean-shaven and
in European clothing. He cringed and ducked his head.

"We are taking him to His Excellency the Kaimakam," the
officer went on.

"The governor? Why?"

"Because—because—why, because he is an assassin!
One of those fanatics who would rebel against our benevo-
lent rule, who—"

"No," Sahin said. The handle of the whip caught Ramses
under the chin and forced his head up. The Turk studied him
thoughtfully for a few seconds. Then he leaned down and
with a powerful jerk pulled the beard off, taking several
square inches of skin with it. Ramses straightened and met
the Turk's inquiring gaze. He was in for it now.

"Ah," Sahin Pasha said, and smiled. "I relieve you of your
prisoner, Bimbashi."

"But, Your Excellency—"

"He is an English spy. Espionage is my department, Bimbashi. Do you question my authority?" He beckoned his servant, who dismounted and untied the rope from the officer's saddle.

The officer didn't like what was happening. A direct refusal was more than he dared risk, but he ventured to protest. "You will need an escort, Excellency. He fights like a demon. It took six of my men—"

"No need for that," Sahin said affably. He raised his arm and brought the whip handle down.

Ten

It was a very pleasant dream. The surface on which he lay was soft and faintly perfumed. Above him arched a golden canopy—yellow silk, gilded by sunlight streaming through the gathered folds. He could hear birdsong and the crystalline tinkle of water.

The only discordant note was a headache of stupendous proportions. He raised his hand to his temple, and a familiar voice said, "Try this. I do not indulge, of course, but I keep it for certain of my guests."

It wasn't a dream. Ramses sat up. A few feet away, cross-legged on a pile of tasseled cushions, Sahin held out a glass half-filled with an amber liquid.

Ramses started to shake his head and thought better of it. "No, thank you," he mumbled in Turkish—the same language the other man had used.

"It is not drugged. But, as you like." His host placed the glass on a brass tray and reached for the mouthpiece of his water pipe. He smoked contentedly for a time, for all the world like a courteous host waiting for his guest to get his wits back.

It took a while. When the Turk's blow had landed, sinking him into unconsciousness, Ramses expected he would wake up in a dark, verminous cell, with various people holding various sharp, heavy, or red-hot implements. This room was airy and bright, probably the mandarah, the principal chamber where guests were received. The central part of the room was several inches lower than the rest, tiled in tasteful patterns of red and black and white, with a small fountain at one end. The alcove in which he was now sitting was draped with silk and floored with cushions. He was wearing only a shirt and drawers; they had removed his stained robe and dirty sandals, and cleaned the worst of the muck off his body. One wouldn't want those satin cushions smeared with rotten fruit and donkey dung.

"I regret the necessity of that," Sahin said, as Ramses explored the lump on his head with cautious fingers. "I knew you would not come willingly, and resistance might have caused you serious injury."

"How can I ever thank you?" Ramses inquired, slipping into English. The Turk laughed aloud.

"It is a pleasure to match wits with you again, my young friend. I was delighted to hear that against all my expectations you had survived that interesting affair outside Cairo, but I am uncertain as to the details. How did you manage it?"

Ramses considered the question. It was loaded with potential pitfalls, and the genial conversational tone, the comfortable surroundings, were designed to lower his guard. A new interrogation technique? He preferred it to the methods the Turks usually employed, but he would have to be careful.

"My affectionate family came to the rescue," he said, feeling certain that this information must have reached Sahin's ears. "You know my father."

"By reputation only. It is a formidable reputation. I hope one day to have the honor of meeting him. So he heard of your—er—dilemma—from your friend, whom I did not succeed in killing after all? I might have done, had you not spoiled my aim."

"Possibly."

Sahin drew the smoke deep into his lungs. "You also

spoiled a pretty little scheme which had been long in the making. What are you after now? Why are you here?"

"Just having a look round."

"I do admire the imprecision of the English language," Sahin said. "So useful when one wishes to avoid answering a question."

"Would you prefer to speak Turkish? I don't find it as easy to equivocate in that language."

Sahin's beard parted, showing his teeth. "I think you could equivocate in any language, my boy. In this case, it is a waste of time. You were caught in the act. A particularly futile act, I might add. In that jostling crowd you had little chance of killing him."

"I didn't succeed, did I?"

"You hit the governor," Sahin said, his smile broadening. "A flesh wound in a particularly awkward place. He's very annoyed with you."

No mention of anyone else. Did that mean Chetwode had got away? Good luck to the young fool, Ramses thought sourly. He had only been obeying orders. He put his head in his hands. Thinking about Chetwode worsened his headache.

"What can I offer you?" Sahin asked solicitously. "If you don't want brandy, what about coffee or mint tea?"

He clapped his hands. The servant who entered was so anxious to show the proper deference, he was bent over at the waist, his face only a few inches from the tray he carried. Obeying a brusque gesture from Sahin, he deposited it on a low table beside Ramses and backed out, still at a right angle. The heavy curtains closed after him. "Please help yourself," Sahin said. "They have not been drugged."

Ramses's throat was painfully dry, and he concluded it would be expedient to accept something. To refuse hospitality was an affront, and it was unlikely Sahin had ordered the drinks to be drugged. And what difference would it make if he had?

So he picked up the glass of tea and sipped it gratefully,

holding the hot glass by the rim, while the Turk smoked in pensive silence. Then he said suddenly, "I have a daughter."

"My felicitations," Ramses said, wondering what the devil this had to do with anything. "When did the happy event occur?"

"Eighteen years ago."

"Eighteen—"

"Yes, she should have been married long before this. It is not for lack of offers. She is beautiful, well born, and educated. She speaks and writes English. She is somewhat headstrong, but I believe you prefer women of that sort." He looked hopefully at Ramses, who had begun to feel like Alice. What sort of rabbit hole had he fallen into? Surely Sahin Pasha didn't mean . . . Silence seemed the safest course.

"The war cannot last forever," the Turk went on. "We will not always be enemies. You have the qualities I would like in a son."

"But . . ." Ramses tried to think of a tactful way of refusing this flattering and appalling suggestion. He blurted out, "I'm already married!"

"I know that. But if you were to embrace Islam, you could take another wife. I don't recommend more. It requires a brave man to manage two women, but three are six times as much trouble as two, and four—"

"You're joking."

Sahin's mouth stretched wider. "Am I? It is in the best tradition of our people and yours—forging an alliance through marriage. Think it over. The alternative is far less attractive."

"What is the alternative?"

"Surely you need not ask. Imprisonment, a considerable degree of discomfort, and eventually a trip to Constantinople, where you will have to face several persons who know you as one of our most dangerous opponents." He leaned forward, his face lengthening. "They will execute you, my young friend, publicly and painfully, as an English spy, but before they kill you they will try to find out everything you know. I consider torture an unreliable means of extracting information, but I fear my enlightened views are not shared by the others in my service. I am offering you a chance to escape that fate. You are no assassin. You came here for another reason. I can protect you from a death that will cause your wife and your parents much grief if you confide in me and prove your sincerity by the alliance I have offered. I assure you, the girl is quite presentable."

Increasingly bewildered, but reminded of his manners, Ramses said, "I am sure she is a pearl of rare beauty and a worthy child of her father. You would think less of me, however, if I betrayed my beliefs and my country for a woman, however desirable."

"You would not be the first Englishman to do so."

He fixed Ramses with a steady stare and Ramses considered how to respond. He wasn't feeling very clever; insane questions kept popping into his head and it was all he could do to keep from blurting them out. "Anybody I know?" or "You wouldn't be referring to my uncle, would you?" He wondered if there had been some drug in the tea after all, or if it was only the blow on the head that was clouding his thinking. Sahin couldn't be serious. He was playing some sort of game and Ramses hadn't the foggiest notion what he was really after.

"There have been several," Ramses began. His voice echoed oddly inside his head. He tried to put the glass down. It tipped, spilling the rest of the tea across the floor. "Was that really necessary?" he asked thickly.

"A lesson, which you have not yet learned, it seems," Sahin replied equably. "Never trust anyone's word. Now come along like a good lad. I don't want to hurt you."

He clapped his hands. Two men entered. "Gently, gently," Sahin crooned, as they pulled Ramses to his feet and half led, half dragged him out of the room, up a few steps and down a few, through the mazelike series of rooms and corridors that were typical of such houses. He was vaguely aware of staring faces, as indistinct as ghosts, and of soft exclamations. Eventually they escorted him down a long flight of stairs. The smell came up to meet him—wet stone, and mold, and the sickly sweetness of something rotten.

There were three doors along the short passage, heavy wood banded with iron. Two were closed. They took him into the third room, a stone-walled box barely six feet square and six high. Rodent bones and a thin layer of straw, liquescent with decay, littered the floor. The cell contained a rough wooden bench along one wall, a few crude earthenware vessels, and several sets of chains held by staples driven deep into floor and wall. Working with silent efficiency, as if they had gone through the procedure many times, the two guards deposited Ramses on the bench. Too dizzy to sit upright, he toppled forward; one of them had to hold him while the other raised his arms and locked the fetters round his wrists. They chained his feet, too, and then left.

"Faugh," said Sahin Pasha, wrinkling his nose. "It's even worse than I remembered. This house is a temporary loan, from a colleague of mine; my own prisons are more civilized. I will return in the morning to see if you have changed your mind."

He drew his elegant robes tightly about him so they wouldn't touch the filthy wall and backed away. The door slammed shut. The hinges creaked horribly. They would, of course.

Ramses sat with his head bowed, breathing steadily and slowly, hoping he wasn't going to be sick. Gradually he got his stomach under control and strength began to return to his limbs. Cautiously he tested the fetters. The iron cuffs had simply snapped into place, they could probably be opened without a key, but his hands were a yard apart and each chain was less than six inches long. He entertained himself for a while banging and rubbing the cuffs against the stone wall but succeeded only in scraping his knuckles.

He leaned back, overcoming an instinctive reluctance to touch the slimy stone of the wall. His mother would have added several other adjectives—hard, cold, wet, dank, crawling with curious insects that were gathering to investigate a new source of nourishment. A few of them had already found his feet. He smiled wryly. His mother would also inform him, in that brisk way of hers, that he'd got himself into a pretty mess this time. No weapons, no useful tools concealed in his boots or clothing. They had even found the needle-thin knife he'd hidden under a dirty bandage wrapped round his forearm. And all for nothing. He was no wiser about the identity of "the holy infidel."

He closed his eyes and summoned up the image of that bearded face and arrogant nose. He had a good visual memory, but he hadn't seen enough for a positive identification. Remembering the innumerable times he had failed to recognize his exasperating uncle, he had known a single glance wouldn't be enough. He had counted on being able to observe Ismail longer, watching for a familiar gesture or movement, hearing his voice. The man had been closely guarded, but it might have been a guard of honor. Sahin hadn't actually confirmed or denied anything, he had only made a few ambiguous references to turncoats.

It had been a restless night and a tiring day. He fell into a waking doze, jerked upright by the pressure of the shackles against his scraped hands whenever deeper sleep loosened his muscles. Dream images floated through his mind: Nefret, first and last and always, her blue eyes tender with concern or blazing with fury—at him, for being stupid enough to fall into this trap. It had been a trap; he had been lied to, used, cold-bloodedly, for the sole purpose of getting that innocent-looking assassin into Gaza. Cartright and his superiors must have known there was a good chance both of them would be caught or killed if Chetwode carried out his orders . . . The trap, a cage as big as a drawing room, swathed in folds of golden silk that didn't quite conceal the rusty bars; soft cushions under him, and a girl in his arms, a girl with long black hair that snaked round his hands, and tightened and hardened into fetters.

When he opened his eyes, he thought for a moment he must still be dreaming. The face close to his was a disconcerting blend of Sahin's strong features and the round-cheeked houri who had nestled in his embrace. But the pain in his hands was real, and so was the pocket torch whose beam wavered wildly before she put it down on the bench beside him. He sat up straighter and started to speak. She put her hand over his lips.

"Don't speak, don't cry out," she whispered in English. "I will help you escape."

Her hand was soft and plump and perfumed. Her hair was black; it had been twisted into a knot, but long strands had escaped to hang limply over her forehead. Her nose was her father's, large and curved, and her mouth was the same shape, though it was now tremulous and, he noticed, carefully painted. There could be no doubt of her identity. Was this another trick of Sahin's—a version of cat and mouse, raising hopes of escape before dashing them, with his daughter as the very visible alternative to re-imprisonment?

Her palm and fingers slid slowly across his mouth. "Why?" he asked softly.

"Don't ask questions!" Her voice was thin with nervousness. She straightened, and he saw she was wearing the enveloping black tob over a rather frivolous pink frock of European style.

It took her a while to open the manacles. Under the perfume that wafted round her, Ramses could sense the fear that made her hands shake and soaked her with sweat.

The iron circles finally parted. He had lost all track of time in the eternal darkness, but he must have been there for hours. Slowly he lowered his aching arms and flexed his hands. She was kneeling, working at the chain around his feet. He bent over and pushed her hands away. "I'll do it. Hold the torch. How do they work?"

"You have to push . . . here . . ." A shaking finger indicated the spot. "And pull this at the same time. They're rusty, stiff . . ."

The chains clinked and he swore under his breath. They were making too much noise and taking too much time. It was too damned quiet. Hadn't Sahin left a guard? Maybe it wasn't a trick after all. If her father had set it up, she was putting on a very convincing show of fear. As soon as he stood, she thrust a bundle at him.

"Put it on. Hurry!"

The caftan was probably one of Sahin's. It was of fine wool and far too costly for someone who wanted to be inconspicuous, but since he had no choice in the matter, he put it on, and wound the woolen scarf over his head and face. The last item in the bundle was a knife. She'd thought of everything—except a belt. He slashed a strip off the bottom of the caftan, tied it round his waist, and slipped the knife through the makeshift sash.

She let him precede her to the door but stayed so close behind him he could hear her agitated breathing. She'd left the door ajar. Ramses swept the torch in a hasty circuit, half expecting to see Sahin's grin and a heavily armed guard; but the corridor was empty.

"That way." She extended a shaking arm over his shoulder.

"I know. Is there anyone in the other cells?"

"What does it matter? Hurry!"

She pushed at him, but he stood firm. "Is there?"

"No!"

The light of the torch showed that the doors were not barred or bolted, but he couldn't leave without making certain. He eased them open, one after the other, just far enough to look inside. Despite his care, the hinges gave off a series of groans, echoed, on a higher note, by the girl. She tugged at his arm.

Ramses let himself be drawn away. The cells had been unoccupied except by a family of rats that had set up housekeeping in a pile of moldy straw. She led the way now, tiptoeing, her black skirts raised. Ramses followed her up the stone steps and through a mazelike series of narrow passages and small storerooms. She certainly knew her way around the cellars. He doubted very much that she had explored them herself.

But they had met no one and seen no one when she finally stopped by a wooden door and tugged at the handle. Somehow Ramses was not surprised when the portal swung silently open. Stars shone bright overhead, illumining a walled courtyard. It was strictly utilitarian; no fountain, no flowers, only weeds and piles of trash. They were at the back of the villa, near the kitchens. He looked up, scanning the night sky, and found the Dipper and the North Star. It would be light in a few hours. Time was definitely of the essence, but there was one question he had to ask.

He turned to the girl. "Who helped you?"

"No one helped me! I did it myself, all of it. I saw you today when they brought you in, and I . . . There is no time for this. You must hurry."

"But how did you know—"

"No questions! It won't be easy to find your way out of the city. I must show you where—"

"No, go back to your rooms before you are missed. I know where I am now."

She put her hands on his arms. "A horse. I will get one for you."

"Why don't you just paint a target on my back?" Ramses inquired, and immediately felt guilty when her mouth quivered pathetically. Her face was so close he could see the kohl lining her eyes. She'd made herself up as if for an assignation, and that absurd pink frock was probably one of her best.

"I'm sorry," he whispered, and although every moment counted now, he racked his brain to remember a few pleasing platitudes. "You have saved my life. I will never forget—"

His breath came out in a grunt as she threw herself against him. "We will meet again one day," she gasped. "You can never be mine, but your image will be enshrined in my heart!"

"I forgot that one," Ramses muttered. She was a well-

rounded armful, soft and warm and heavy, and there seemed
to be only one way of getting her to stop talking.

So he kissed her, thoroughly but somewhat absentmind-
edly, and then detached the clinging arms and propelled her
through the open door.

"Through that gate," she panted. "Turn to the left—"

"Yes, right. Uh—God bless you."

He pulled the door shut and headed, not for the gate, but
for the wall to his right. How long would it be before they
discovered he was gone, and warned the defenders that an
English spy was on the loose? Maybe not for hours. Maybe
a lot sooner. He couldn't take the chance of waiting until
morning and strolling out the way he had come.

Once over the wall, he found himself in a typical Middle
Eastern street, narrow, dusty, and extremely dark. His suspicions had been incorrect; there was no one lurking outside
the gate.

He had exaggerated a trifle when he told the girl he knew
where he was, but it didn't take long to orient himself. The
lacy, domed minaret of the Great Mosque pricked the moonlit sky to the southwest. He was near the Serai, then, the governor's palace, and the quickest way out of town was
westward.

It took him longer than he had hoped. He had to avoid the
main east-west street, which was well lighted, with men
standing guard at the entrances to official buildings. The
lanes wound in illogical curves, and twice he had to climb a
wall to avoid patrols. Luckily the marching men made
enough noise to warn him of their approach.

Three miles of sand dunes separated Gaza from the
Mediterranean. There was plenty of cover—the ruins of the
ancient seaport of Gaza—and the picket lines were widely
spaced, since their primary purpose was to guard against
agents who might be landed from the sea. The first pallid
light of dawn was showing in the east before Ramses waded
out into the water. He had hoped to "borrow" a fishing boat
under cover of darkness, but it was too late now; a boat

would be seen and fired upon. With a heartfelt groan, he shed Sahin's caftan and began to swim.

∴

"**H**e's all right," Nefret said. "Believe me. I always know when he isn't."

I wanted to believe her. The bond between them was so strong that she had always been able to sense, not so much danger—Ramses was in trouble a good deal of the time— but an imminent threat to his life. She didn't look as if she had slept well, though. None of us had. It had been almost twenty-four hours since we got the word that Ramses had been captured and we had spent most of that time discussing what we should do about it. Emerson does not bear waiting well. By late afternoon he had walked a good ten miles, pacing back and forth across the tiled floor of the saloon.

"We cannot act yet," I insisted, for the tenth time. "Give him a little more time. He's got himself out of worse situations, and at least we know he was alive when he was last seen. Emerson, for pity's sake, stop pacing. What you need is a nice hot cup of tea. Help me, Nefret."

Emerson said he did not need the confounded tea, but I needed something to do and so, in my considered opinion, did Nefret. The confidence she had expressed to us had not rendered her indifferent to the fate of one dearer to her than life itself; her breath came quick and fast, and her hands shook so badly I had to prepare the tea myself.

Suddenly she sprang up. It was anticipation, not fear, that had made her tremble—the unbearable, final moments of waiting for an event greatly desired. As she turned toward the door, it opened, and there he stood. There was no mistaking him, though he was wearing a British uniform, and the brim of his pith helmet shadowed his face.

I had not really been worried. Nefret's instincts had never been wrong. All the same, I felt as if a set of stiff rods had been removed from my back and limbs.

"Ah," said Emerson, trying to appear unconcerned. "I had begun to believe I might have to go looking for you."

"I had begun to think so too." Ramses removed his hat and unbuckled the belt with its attached holster. "You'll never believe . . . Nefret!"

Her face had gone dead-white. Ramses sprang to catch her as she crumpled. He held her to him in a close embrace, with her head resting on his shoulder. "Nefret—sweetheart—darling, say something!"

"There is no need for such a fuss," I assured him. "It's only a swoon. Put her down."

"She's never swooned in her life!" Ignoring my sensible suggestion, he dropped onto the divan, holding her tightly. Uttering incoherent ejaculations, Emerson snatched one of her limp hands and began slapping it. I selected a clean cup, poured tea, and added several heaping spoonfuls of sugar.

A moment or two later Nefret stirred. "What happened?" she asked weakly.

"You swooned," Emerson said in a hoarse voice.

"I've never swooned in my life!" Her color was back to normal and indignation brightened her blue eyes. "Put me down."

"It was my fault," Ramses said wretchedly. "I shouldn't have burst in like that. I suppose you thought . . . Are you sure you're all right?"

She smiled up into his anxious face. "I can think of something that would complete the cure."

I have no objection to public displays of affection between married persons or those about to be wed, but I did not want Ramses distracted. I said firmly, "A nice hot cup of tea," and took it to her.

Nefret pushed it away. "Give it to Ramses. He looks as if he needs it more than I do."

"I'm all right. Just a little tired. I haven't had much sleep in the past forty-eight hours."

"Did you come in through the secret door?" Emerson asked.

Ramses shook his head. He had acquired a few more scrapes and bruises, including a sizable lump on his temple. "There's no need for secrecy now. The job is blown, Father. A complete disaster from start to finish."

Nefret studied him critically. "It would be nice if just once you could come back from one of your expeditions unbruised and unbloodied."

"It wasn't my fault," Ramses said defensively.

"According to Chetwode, you heroically took on ten men so that he could get away," Emerson said.

"So he's been here. It was only six," Ramses added.

"Hmph," said Emerson. "Yes, he's been here, and our cover is also blown. He insisted on delivering his message in person, and if he didn't know my identity when he came, he does now. I—er—I forgot myself when he broke the news that you had been captured and were in 'the merciless grip of the most dangerous man in the Ottoman Empire,' as he put it. The fellow has something of a melodramatic streak."

"Hmmm," said Ramses. "So he lingered long enough to see that, did he?"

"He claimed he had hoped to come to your assistance, but the odds were too great, and he was obliged to follow your orders. It was at this point that your mother and Nefret came rushing in—"

"We were in one of the secret passages," I explained. "Very useful devices. The news that a British officer had come here with a message naturally aroused our interest, so we—"

"Also forgot yourselves," said Emerson.

"My dear, the damage was already done. Lieutenant Chetwode did not seem at all surprised when we popped out of that cupboard."

"He's going to put you in for a DSO," Nefret said.

"How nice," said Ramses, with sardonic amusement. "So you sat here drinking tea while, for all you knew, I was undergoing hideous tortures?"

"We were discussing what steps to take in order to rescue

you," I explained. "And how to go about them in the most efficient manner."

"I know, Mother. I was joking."

"I would be the last to deny that a touch of humor is seldom amiss," I said. "However . . . Lieutenant Chetwode told us what transpired up till the time he ran away. So you need not repeat that part."

"Did he happen to mention that we would have made it out without running or any other inconvenience if he hadn't tried to shoot Ismail Pasha?"

Nefret gasped and Emerson swore, and I said evenly, "I take it he did not succeed?"

"No. He hadn't a chance of killing him. The governor's considerable bulk was in the way and there was a good deal of commotion. It was my fault, really," Ramses went on wearily. "I suspected he was armed and took one pistol away from him before we left. I should have had the sense to realize Cartright would anticipate that and provide him with a second weapon. I didn't search him. I ought to have done."

"Stop berating yourself and tell us what happened," I said. "From the beginning, please, and in proper order."

His narrative agreed for the most part with the one Chetwode had given us, up to the point where Chetwode had fired at the suspect. He had then fled—obeying Ramses's order, as he had claimed.

"I did tell him to run," Ramses admitted. "The damage was done, and in the confusion no one could tell which of us had fired. The governor's guards went after me and matters went as one might have expected. I got on reasonably well until someone threw a stone. They were about to escort me to the governor when who should appear but . . . This is the part you'll find hard to believe."

In his youth Ramses had been appallingly verbose and given to an excessive use of adverbs, adjectives, and other descriptive flourishes. I had found this extremely exasperating, but the sparse, uninformative narrative style that was now his habit sometimes vexed me even more. Admittedly, the events themselves were enough to hold us spellbound; no one uttered a word until he had finished.

"So," I said. "He attempted at first to win you over with kind treatment and flattering words. When you refused to tell him what he wanted to know, he chained you to the wall of a cell and left you. You managed to free yourself, found the guard had left his post, and escaped. As simple as that."

"You have often told me," said Ramses, "to stick to the facts, avoiding rhetorical flourishes and—"

"Curse it," I exclaimed.

"Er, hmph," said Emerson loudly, while Nefret laughed and Ramses gave me one of his most charming smiles. "What about another nice cup of tea, Peabody? And you, my boy. Perhaps just a few words of additional explanation—"

"There was a woman involved," I said. "Wasn't there? Who?"

Ramses's smile died a quick death. "You'd have been burned at the stake in the seventeenth century."

"Quite possibly," I agreed, taking the cup Emerson handed me. "Again, Ramses, from the beginning."

So we were treated to a description of Sahin Pasha's beautiful, desirable daughter, and the pasha's remarkable offer. Once he had been forced to speak, Ramses made an entertaining story of it, and even Emerson grinned reluctantly when Ramses quoted the Turk's comments about multiple wives.

"Excellent advice, my boy. It's cursed strange, though. He couldn't have been serious."

"You think not?" Nefret asked. It was the first time she had spoken since Ramses began his story. He gave her a quick look and shook his head.

"He couldn't have supposed I would agree—or keep my word if I did."

"Oh, you'd have kept your word," Nefret murmured.

"I didn't give it. It does seem to me," Ramses said emphatically, "that I am entitled to some credit for preferring torture and death to infidelity. She was a damned attractive girl, too."

"Now, now, don't quarrel," I said. "It was the girl who helped you escape?"

Ramses nodded. "There was no way I could get those chains off by myself. She's an efficient little creature," he added thoughtfully. "She'd brought me a caftan and head-cloth, and even a knife. She also offered to steal a horse for me, but I pointed out—somewhat rudely, now that I think about it—that it would only have made me more conspicuous."

Nefret looked as if she wanted to say something—I knew what it was—but she restrained herself. It was Emerson who voiced the same thought that had, of course, occurred to me.

"He let you go. The girl was acting under his orders or with his cooperation."

"That idea had, of course, occurred to me," I said. "But it doesn't make sense. He might have intervened to take you from the governor's men, but why would he connive in your escape so soon thereafter?"

"Damned if I know," Ramses said. "No doubt you are prepared to speculate, Mother. It is a useful process that clears away the underbrush in the thickets of deduction."

I did not at all mind his teasing me. It was such a relief to have him back with us, alive and relatively undamaged. "Certainly," I said. "Let us begin with the assumption that he intended to save your life. If he had not taken you from the governor's guards you would have been treated far less courteously."

"I would be extremely surprised to discover that Sahin Bey—Pasha, I should say—acted out of kindness," Ramses said. "He had an ulterior motive, and I doubt it was finding a husband for his daughter."

"Why, then?" Emerson grunted. "If he wants to turn his coat and come over to us—unlikely on the face of it—he wouldn't need a good word from you. The War Office would sell their souls and those of all their mothers and grandmothers to get the head of the Turkish secret service on our side."

Ramses scratched absently at the scraped flesh on his jaw. "I agree, Father."

"All the same, HQ must be notified."

"I've already done so. Why do you suppose I'm wearing this bloody damned uniform? I was in the water long enough to wash the dye off my skin, but I hadn't any clothes except the bare necessities, and I'd never have got to General Chetwode looking the way I did." Ramses added, "I expect the officer I waylaid holds a bit of a grudge; I had to borrow his uniform without his consent. He oughtn't wander so far from camp."

Emerson knew his son too well to misinterpret his light-hearted manner. "What did General Chetwode say?"

Ramses shrugged. "What could he say but 'Bad luck, old boy, glad you made it back after all'? Our Chetwode had already left for Cairo to make his report."

"He was in something of a hurry to get out of town, wasn't he?" Emerson mused. "How much did you tell the general?"

"I am not telling anyone any more than I have to," Ramses said tightly. "Nobody is telling *me* anything. I'll be damned if I can understand who is actually running this stunt. Apparently General Chetwode didn't know what his nephew intended to do, he was only told we were going to investigate and reconnoiter. I didn't mention the girl, or Sahin's proposition. The general is under the impression that I cleverly escaped all by my little self. I'm sorry, I ought to have come here straightaway, but—"

"Bah," said Emerson gruffly. "You did what you had to do. I still say the girl couldn't have managed it on her own. The young, spoiled daughter of an aristocrat, raised in the harem—"

"She'd been exposed to Western ideas and Western schooling," Ramses interrupted. "Your basic point is well taken, however. Someone helped her, but it need not have been her father."

"Ah," said Emerson.

"I'm sorry, Father. I ought to have made a greater effort to find him."

"Don't be absurd," I said forcibly. "You could not have eluded recapture for long, and if you had not turned up, your father would have gone into Gaza looking for you."

"Perhaps I ought to have let him go in my place." Ramses leaned back against the cushions and closed his eyes. The dark stains of exhaustion under his eyes were very visible. "I made a thorough muckup of the whole business. I'm sorry . . ."

Nefret was sitting cross-legged on the divan next to him. She stood up, the bracelets on her ankles and wrists jingling musically. "Stop saying you're sorry!"

"Quite right," Emerson exclaimed. "I am the one who should apologize, my boy, for badgering you. Go and get some rest."

Ramses sat up, propping his heavy head with his hands. "It might have been him. There wasn't time to get a good look. I couldn't determine whether the soldiers were guarding a prisoner or protecting a holy man. But the mere fact that I am here, and not in Sahin's cell, is a strong indication that Sethos is in Gaza. Unless that is what we are meant to believe . . . Sorry. I seem to be adding to the deadwood instead of clearing it away."

"You didn't have time to question the girl, I suppose," I said. "And don't say you're sorry again!"

Ramses summoned up a feeble grin. "Yes, Mother. I did ask who had helped her. She claimed no one had, that it was all her doing."

"She lied," I said. "Quite understandable; she wanted the credit and your—er—gratitude."

Ramses shook his head. "I don't think so. Her fear was genuine. You know how Sethos operates. If it was he who arranged my escape, he'd have found a way of supplying her with everything she needed while leaving her with the impression that the whole thing had been her idea."

"But how did he manage it?" I demanded. "He had less than twelve hours to come up with a plan and carry it out. He must have known the identity of Sahin's prisoner, for surely he would not have taken such a risk for a stranger. How did he find out it was you?"

"That question hadn't occurred to me." Ramses sat up straighter. "And it may be significant. Could that have been why Sahin didn't pop me into his little cell straightaway? Damn it, yes! He put me on display—beardless and bareheaded, easily recognizable—and when they did take me downstairs they paraded me through most of the house first. If Sethos was staying in the same house . . ." His brief animation faded. "It still doesn't answer the most important questions."

"Yes, yes," Emerson said gruffly. "We'll talk about it later. Take him away, Nefret."

Ramses got slowly to his feet. "Take me where?"

"To my little private cubicle," Nefret said, drawing his arm over her shoulders.

"Are there any peepholes in the walls?"

"Probably. Does it matter?"

"That depends." He smiled down into her upturned face and brushed her cheek with his fingertips.

"I don't suppose it does matter," I admitted. "By this time everyone in town will know we have dealings with British officers, and that we may not be what we seem. I do strongly urge, however, that you rest instead of—er—"

"Of course, Mother." Nefret turned her head and gave me a bewitching smile.

"That was an extremely impertinent and unsolicited bit of advice," Emerson said, after they had left the room. "She'll look after him. And—er—cheer him up. The boy is too hard on himself."

"He always has been," I said, taking no notice of the criticism. "It wasn't his fault, it was the fault of the confounded War Office. Shall I begin packing?"

"No, my dear. What's your hurry?"

"I would have supposed," I said, with a certain amount of sarcasm, "that you would want to go in pursuit of the conscienceless villain who sent your son to risk torture and death."

"All in due course, Peabody. We went to considerable trouble to get this close to Gaza, and I'm damned if I am going to leave before I've learned what we came here to learn."

"And how do you propose to do that?"

"We could wait for him to come to us. That is your favorite method of investigation, I believe."

"You mean Sethos, I suppose."

"Sethos or anyone else who decides we are a threat to his plans." He settled himself on the divan and beckoned to me. "Come and sit by me, my love. We've had little enough privacy these past few days."

I acceded at once, but as his strong arm wrapped round me and drew me close to his side, I felt obliged to remind him of the peepholes. Emerson only chuckled. "It is time I paid a few attentions to my elder wife. Give me a kiss."

"In English?" I exclaimed.

"Kisses are a universal language," said Emerson.

I was so touched by this poetic sentiment, I suffered the prickles of the beard without objection. When I had got my breath back, I said suspiciously, "You are in a very cheerful mood, I must say. What are you concealing from me?"

"I have no intention of concealing anything from you, my dear. I didn't want to keep Ramses from his bed—er—his rest any longer; but he made an interesting point. If Sethos was staying in the same house . . . He must have been, mustn't he? Not only did he know Ramses's identity, but he had access to the girl. Now listen closely, Peabody . . ."

"Yes, my dear." I rubbed my stinging cheek.

"He wouldn't have approached her as Ismail Pasha. It would have been an unnecessary risk. He disguised himself as someone else . . . and I know who."

"Well, so do I."

"Confound it," Emerson shouted, removing his arm and

fixing me with an evil glare. "You're doing it again! You always claim you—"

"But, my dear, it is obvious."

"Oh? Then you tell me. Or shall we play our old game, each of us writing the answer and sealing it in an envelope?"

We had played this little game often, and I will admit, in the pages of my private journal, that I had maneuvered Emerson into committing himself first on certain occasions when I was not entirely certain of my conclusions. On this occasion I did not hesitate.

"Why, my dear, I think we are past that childish sort of competition. I will be happy to tell you. He disguised himself as Sahin Pasha."

Emerson let out a whoop of laughter. He sobered almost at once, however, and began stroking his beard. "Really, Peabody, that is deuced ingenious. But . . . No, it is impossible. What led you to that remarkable deduction?"

"Your turn next," I said playfully. "Whom did you suspect?"

"I need my pipe," Emerson muttered. "What did you do with it?"

I hadn't done anything with it. Muttering to himself, Emerson rummaged through his voluminous garments until he located the thing and his tobacco pouch. I helped him to light the pipe, keeping a wary eye out for sparks in his beard.

"Well," said Emerson, settling back onto the divan and puffing away with enjoyment. "Where were we?"

"You were about to tell me whom you suspected of being Sethos."

The comfort of his beloved pipe had given Emerson new courage. "The servant," he said decidedly.

"The fellow who brought the tea? It was drugged, Emerson."

"Well, of course. It would have been a dead giveaway for him to ignore his master's orders. People don't look at servants," Emerson went on. "And Sahin had borrowed the house and, one must suppose, the staff from someone else."

"It isn't like Sethos to choose such an inconspicuous role."

"No, he much prefers to make a spectacle of himself. It would be a coup much to his taste to take over the role of someone as well known as Sahin."

He looked so chagrined that I felt obliged to offer his vanity a little encouragement. Husbands appreciate these gestures.

"There are some things I don't understand, though," I said. "How could Sethos deceive Sahin's men and his household and even his daughter?"

"Oh, that," said Emerson, with a dismissive wave of his hand. "Sethos has fooled more observant individuals than a handful of dull-witted guards. The girl may have seen very little of her father; I don't suppose Sahin was the sort of papa who plays games with his children."

"Well, perhaps I am wrong," I said handsomely. "Without knowing more about the household than we do, it is impossible to know for certain how he managed it."

"I don't know how he managed it," Emerson admitted. "Or what is behind all this maneuvering. But I have a feeling—yes, my dear, call it a premonition if you like—I have a feeling we will hear from my eccentric—er—acquaintance before too long. And since it appears that far too many people know our identities already, we may as well leave off pretending to be respectable Moslems. What do you say I borrow a bottle of whiskey from one of our chaps?"

"I have considered the advantages and disadvantages of abandoning our masquerade, and in my opinion the advantages outweigh the disadvantages. The people we were trying to keep in the dark already know the truth, and the presence of the famous Father of Curses can only inspire respect from others. However, there is no need for you to borrow anything." I reached behind the cushions and drew out the parcel I had kept in my personal charge during that long, wearisome journey. It was a large and rather lumpy parcel, as I knew to my sorrow, since I had sat on it most of the way.

"Good Gad!" said Emerson, as I extracted the bottle, which I had wrapped in certain articles of clothing.

"We will have to use plain water or drink it neat, like Cyrus. The gasogene was too large, and fragile besides."

Emerson's smile faded. "What else have you got in there?" he asked suspiciously.

"Trousers, shirts, and boots for me and Nefret—you saw them the other day—my knife, and hers—my belt of tools—and—"

"No!" Emerson exclaimed, his eyes bulging.

"You cannot suppose I would venture into danger without it." I had spread the articles out on the divan. I added my parasol.

Emerson's lips writhed, but the light of forlorn hope lingered in his eyes. "Please. Tell me it isn't . . ."

I took hold of the handle and gave it a twist and a pull. "My sword parasol, yes. The one you were kind enough to give me."

Emerson reached for the bottle.

We did not see the children again that evening. When they joined us for breakfast, I was pleased to observe that Ramses looked more rested. He was wearing the uniform shirt and trousers, but with the shirt open and his feet bare, the hated military look was diminished. He was in full agreement with my decision that we might as well abandon our disguises.

"I didn't suppose Mother would stand being confined to the harem for long," he remarked, selecting a piece of fruit from the tray.

"It is too inconvenient," I explained. "We were running out of excuses for admitting strange men to our quarters. I haven't spoken with Selim for days, and in my opinion a council of war is imperative. We must plan our next move."

"Next move?" Ramses's eyebrows tilted up at the corners. "Surely that's obvious. There's no point in your staying on here."

The pronoun did not escape me, but I said only, "That is

one of the things we must discuss. Let us ask Selim to join us. Perhaps he can find you something else to wear, Ramses. I brought a change of clothing for us, but not for you."

"Oh, I don't know," Nefret drawled. "I like those short trousers. You ought to wear them all the time. Father, too."

Emerson does have well-shaped lower limbs, but he is rather shy about it. He coughed and looked away. Ramses, less self-conscious than his father, laughed and said, "I ought to return them to their owner, along with the rest of his things. Never mind that now; let's have Selim up."

Selim was delighted to accept the invitation. Settling himself comfortably on a cushion, he looked round with an air of approval. "This is good. We have not been able to talk. Now tell me everything. What happened in Gaza, Ramses?"

He had known of Ramses's safe return—had, in fact, been the first to know, for he had recognized him at once. Ramses had not lingered to chat, being anxious to reassure us, so he had to go over the whole business again for Selim.

"Ah," said that young man interestedly. "Is she beautiful?"

Everyone laughed, and Ramses repeated what Sahin had said about multiple wives.

"I have not found it so," said Selim, looking a trifle smug. "She is a brave girl, to take the risk of freeing you. I hope she does not suffer for it."

"So do I," Ramses said briefly.

I knew then what I had only suspected before. He meant to go back to Gaza. His mission had not been accomplished, and the fate of that girl would haunt him until he made sure she was safe.

Selim was unable to add anything to our own deductions, such as they were, but he was of the opinion that Ismail Pasha must be Sethos. "So what shall we do now?" he inquired.

"We will wait a day or two for the news of our presence to spread," replied Emerson. "If Sethos has not communicated with us by then, we'll go in after him."

"Father!" Ramses exclaimed.

"Now, my boy, don't waste your breath. You mean to go; don't deny it. If my—er—if he is being held against his will, he must be freed. If he has turned traitor—which," Emerson said grimly, "is seeming more and more likely—he must be taken prisoner by us."

"Why do you consider it more likely?" I demanded hotly. "You said before—"

"He couldn't have managed Ramses's escape if he were a closely guarded prisoner," Emerson replied, with equal heat. "Don't try to defend him, Peabody, or I will begin to wonder whether you have got over your—"

"Please, Emerson!"

"Father has the right idea." Nefret's quiet voice reminded both of us that we were in danger of getting off the subject. "Traitor or captive, we must get him out of Gaza."

Ramses turned appalled eyes on her. "What do you mean, we? I admit I didn't succeed, but that was because Chetwode mucked things up. One person has a better chance than three . . . four . . . five . . . Good God, Father, you can't—"

"I believe I can," said Emerson. "More safely than you, Ramses. Do you suppose Sahin won't have everyone in Gaza looking for a man of your description?"

"But how—"

Emerson held up one hand, demanding silence, and reached with the other into his pocket. "I have another set of papers," he announced proudly.

They were a good deal more impressive than the first set—spattered with blobs of crimson sealing wax, framed in ornate curlicues, and with quite a lot of gilt. The script was equally ornamental; it looked like Arabic, but I could make nothing of it. I handed the papers to Ramses.

"Turkish," he muttered. "Father, do you have any idea what this says?"

"No," said Emerson placidly. "Is there more coffee?"

"But—but—" Ramses ran one hand through his tumbled curls and brandished the papers in front of Emerson's nose. "Were you planning to use these to get into Gaza? For all

you knew, it might be a denunciation of you, or—or somebody's laundry list!"

"Is it?" Emerson inquired.

Nefret served him and Ramses with fresh cups of the
Turkish coffee she brewed so expertly, and Ramses inspected the papers again.

"No," he admitted. "They appear to be in order—so far as
I can tell. I've never been privileged to see a direct order
from the Sublime Porte, signed by the sultan himself."

"Few have," said Emerson, and sipped his coffee. "Ah—
excellent. Thank you, Nefret. I didn't suppose el-Gharbi
would play me false, but the very look of those documents is
enough to overawe most people, especially since literacy
is—"

"El-Gharbi," Ramses broke in. "I might have known.
What did you promise him in return?"

"My goodwill," said Emerson, with an evil smile.

Ramses was not quite himself, and the effect of the stun-
ning surprises his father had administered showed on his
face, together with evidence of another, equally strong emotion. "So," he said, trying without complete success to control his voice, "if I had not come back you would have
marched up to the Turkish lines with a set of papers you
couldn't read and a broken arm and—"

"And your mother," said Emerson.

He was, I believe, attempting to lighten the emotional atmosphere with a touch of humor. His comment did not have
that effect. Ramses went pale, and I said firmly, "Quite right.
All for one and one for all—that is our motto, is it not? You
would have taken equal or greater risks for any of us, Ramses. Now that that is settled, let us get back to business. Are
those papers adequate for the purpose your father had in
mind?"

"Is my name on them?" Selim demanded.

"No one else's name is on them," Emerson replied. "If an
honorable sheikh, a friend of the sultan's, decides to take his
servants—"

"And wives," I said.

"Bah," said Emerson. "He can take anyone he likes, I suppose. Do be quiet, all of you. I haven't decided yet how to go about this. It might be better to make my way through the lines under cover of darkness."

"With one arm in a cast," said Ramses under his breath.

Emerson inspected the cast irritably. "I don't see why I need it. My arm itches like fury. Nefret—"

"No, Father. Absolutely not." She moved closer to Ramses, her shoulder against his. "We don't have to come to a decision immediately. In fact, it would be the height of folly to go rushing into action until we know more. It's all very well to say that Sethos must be in Gaza because only he could have got Ramses away, but we can't be certain of that, can we? The most sensible course is to give him a chance to communicate with us, as Father suggested."

And keep Ramses with her a few days longer. "I agree," I said. "It behooves us, then, to make our presence known. Shall we pay a little visit to the suk, Nefret? Gracious, it will be good to get out of this house."

Ramses's limited wardrobe, and the fact that he had, as he remarked, seen enough of bloody Khan Yunus, made him agreeable to my suggestion that he remain in the house. Selim stayed with him. We left them deep in conversation, some of which had to do with Sahin's interesting daughter.

Squashed into the tonneau of the motorcar and half-buried in bundles, I had not seen much of the town when we arrived. It had only one structure of artistic interest, a fine thirteenth-century mosque. With a few exceptions the houses were small and mean, and the suk had not much to offer. However, the gardens made up for the general squalor. Some of them were enclosed by the same thick cactus hedges that surrounded the town, very curious in appearance and more effective than any fence or wall. It was a veritable garden spot, where every variety of fruit and vegetable was grown. Fig and almond trees, orange and pomegranate waved leafy branches.

We strolled for an hour or so, admiring the luxuriant vegetation, and purchased a few articles of clothing for Ramses in the bazaar. By the time we returned to the house I felt certain our presence had been noted by the entire population of Khan Yunus. Nefret and I were wearing our European garments. Emerson was bareheaded, but he had declined to abandon his comfortable caftan, or his beard. (I meant to attend to the beard in due course.) Our presence occasioned considerable curiosity but less surprise than I had anticipated; and as we crossed the square, Emerson was accosted by a ragged individual who addressed him by name and demanded baksheesh.

The fellow was tall for an Arab and well built; I thought for a moment Emerson was going to grab hold of his beard. But then he saw, as did I, that one of the extended arms had no hand, and that the sleeve hung empty from the elbow.

"It is too soon to hear from *him,* Emerson," I said as we walked away, followed by the loud blessings of the beggar.

"No, it isn't. We might have spared ourselves this little stroll; the word of our presence had already spread. Otherwise," Emerson added, stroking his beard fondly, "that chap wouldn't have recognized me."

"But how did it get about?" Nefret demanded, quickening her pace.

"Any one, or all, of a number of ways," I replied. "The servants have been gossiping and speculating about us ever since we arrived. There are undoubtedly informers in Khan Yunus who report to the Turks or the British; some probably sell the same information to both. Lieutenant Chetwode . . . Don't be in such a rush, my dear; Selim is with Ramses, he won't let anyone get near him."

Ramses was asleep, curled up like a cat on the cushions of the divan. Squatting by the door, his knife in his hand, Selim was obviously disappointed to see us instead of the assassin he had hoped for.

"No one came," he said regretfully.

"But someone might have." I patted his shoulder. "Thank you, Selim, for guarding him."

"It is my duty and my pleasure," said Selim. "Now I will go and see what that fool of a cook is doing to our lunch."

We had several callers that afternoon. All of them wanted to sell us something.

Our visit to the suk had aroused the mercenary instincts of every entrepreneur within a twenty-mile radius. It was customary for sellers of choice merchandise to bring it to the house of wealthy individuals, especially to the ladies of the harem. Female brokers are employed for this latter errand, but since we were known to be infidel English persons, we were attended by the merchants themselves, who spread out their silks and jewels, carpets and brassware, for our inspection. One of them, more canny than the rest, had several antiquities for sale, including a fine scarab of Seti I. The area had been in Egyptian hands for a long period of time, Gaza being one of the cities mentioned in documents of the fourteenth century B.C. Arms folded and lips set in a sneer, Emerson refused to violate his rule of never buying from dealers, but I saw the acquisitive gleam in his eyes and bought the scarab and a remarkably well preserved Phoenician vessel.

After that I told Selim we would receive no more callers for a while, and Emerson got out the whiskey. We were using the ka'ah of the harem as our sitting room; I had got it in a state of relative cleanliness, which could not be said of other apartments in the house. Ramses had just opened the whiskey when Selim came hurrying into the room.

"There is a man," he panted. "An officer. He asks—"

"I'll do my own asking. Stand out of the way." The officer had followed him. I recognized the voice and the square, flushed face that peered over Selim's shoulder. Selim didn't budge.

Emerson took the pipe from his mouth. "Ah. Major Cartright, as I live and breathe. May I remind you that you don't give the orders here? Ask politely."

Cartright got the word out, though it almost choked him. "Please!"

Selim stepped aside, folding his arms. Cartright marched in. Emerson pointed out, in the same mild voice, that there were ladies present and Cartright removed his hat with a muttered apology.

"That's more like it," said Emerson. He sipped appreciatively at his whiskey. "Well? Don't stand there gaping, you must have something to say."

Emerson was doing his best to be annoying, and no one can do it better than Emerson. Cartright swallowed several words he knew better than to pronounce, and took a long breath. "Send—that is, will you please send that man away?"

"No," said Emerson. "But I will do my best to prevent him from using his knife on you. You are either very complacent or very courageous to show your face after the filthy trick you played."

Still standing—for no one had invited him to sit—Cartright took out a handkerchief and wiped his perspiring brow. "Mrs. Emerson—I appeal to you. May I be allowed to speak?"

He was looking at me, not at Nefret, whose tight lips and crimson cheeks must have told him he could not expect any consideration from her. I nodded. "Are you going to claim you knew nothing about Chetwode's plan?"

"Chetwode is a bloo——is a young idiot!" his superior exclaimed heatedly. "I didn't know, Mrs. Emerson, and that is the truth."

Ramses spoke for the first time. "On your word as an officer and a gentleman?"

The irony went unnoticed by Cartright. "Yes! I was appalled when I learned what Chetwode had done. He has been relieved of duty and will be punished appropriately. Do you believe me?"

"Since you have given your word, we have no choice but to do so," said Ramses, eyebrows raised and tilted. "Was that the only reason you came, to express your regrets?"

"Regrets!" Nefret exclaimed. "That is somewhat inadequate, Major. Do you know what happened to my husband after—"

"He doesn't," Ramses said, giving her a warning look. "I expect that is why he is here, to find out. I did make my report, Cartright, to General Chetwode."

"I know, he forwarded it immediately, and I . . ." He cast a longing glance at the bottle of whiskey. "My relief, believe me, was inexpressible. But he gave me few details—which was quite in order, quite right of you to tell him no more than was necessary."

"A basic rule of the Service," said Ramses, in his even, pleasant voice. "You are, I suppose, entitled to know more. In a nutshell, then, I don't know whether Ismail Pasha is the man you want or not. Chetwode didn't give me time enough to make a determination. I was taken prisoner, as Chetwode was good enough to inform my family, but I managed to free myself later that night." Forestalling further questions, he added, "That's all I can tell you. Chetwode's futile attack has made it virtually impossible for anyone to get near Ismail Pasha. They will guard him even more closely from now on."

Cartright nodded grudgingly. "We certainly can't try the same stunt again. Not for a while. I suppose you'll be returning to Cairo at once, then. I will make the necessary arrangements."

"We will make our own arrangements," said Emerson. "When we are ready."

The finality of his tone, and the inimical looks Cartright was getting from everyone in the room, should have convinced him that there was nothing more to be said. No one had offered him a whiskey or even a seat. Yet he lingered, shifting his weight nervously from one foot to the other.

"Look here, old boy," he exclaimed. "This is off the

record, you know—but by Gad, that was well done! Chetwode was man enough to admit that you risked yourself to
help him escape—and then to break yourself loose from a
Turkish prison, and get through their lines . . . It was—confound it, it was deuced well done."

"Oh, you know the Turks," Ramses said. "Careless beggars."

"All the same, I—er—" Military discipline or an inadequate vocabulary brought him to a stuttering stop. He
straightened and snapped off a crisp salute. Ramses did not
return it, but he nodded in acknowledgment, the corners of
his mouth compressed.

"How absurd military persons are," I remarked, after Cartright had marched stiffly out and Selim had slammed the
door.

"Don't underestimate him," Ramses said softly.

"I don't," said Emerson. "He was trying to find out how
long we mean to remain here. Perhaps I ought to have come
up with an excuse for staying on, but I couldn't think of one
offhand; this isn't the place one would choose for a holiday,
and there are no archaeological remains of any interest."

"Good Gad," I exclaimed indignantly. "Do you think he is
still suspicious of us? How insulting!"

Ramses laughed and rose, taking my empty glass from
my hand. "You ought to consider it a compliment, Mother.
'Suspicious' is perhaps too strong a word, but a good intelligence officer doesn't take chances with people whose behavior is, shall we say, unpredictable. It poses a bit of a
problem. If we don't start making arrangements to leave
within the next day or two, he will assume we're planning
something underhanded and place us under surveillance.
That's what I would do."

"Quite," Emerson agreed. "Damnation! It doesn't give us
much time. Let us hope my—er—Sethos makes his move
soon. Since you are on your feet, Ramses, another whiskey
here, if you please. How long till dinner, Selim? That refreshing little episode has given me quite an appetite."

"I do not know, Emerson. I have been at the door all afternoon, and the cook—"

"Yes, yes, my boy, that is quite all right. See what you can do to hurry him up, eh? You need not stand guard, we won't have any more visitors tonight."

In that he was mistaken. Not long after Selim had taken himself off, the aged doorman shuffled in to announce that another merchant had called. He had a carpet for sale, a very fine carpet, a silk carpet, a—

"Tell him to go away," said Emerson. "We don't want any carpets."

The man bowed and wandered out. He was too late and too ineffectual to intercept the seller of carpets, however. The fellow had followed him.

He was a tall man with a grizzled beard and a squint. The roll of carpet was slung over his shoulder. Taking hold of the door, he shut it in the doorkeeper's face, lowered the rug to the floor, seized one end, and heaved.

A rich tapestry of crimson and azure and gold unrolled, and from the end rolled a human form—a female form, wearing a rather tasteless and very crumpled frock of bright pink silk. Coughing and choking, it raised dirty hands to its eyes and rubbed them.

"Christ Almighty," said my son in a strangled voice.

I was too thunderstruck to object to this expletive, and the others were equally stupefied. Naturally I was the first to recover. I looked from the girl, who seemed to be suffering nothing worse than the effects of being bundled up in a rug smelling of camel, to the merchant, who stood with hands on hips staring at me.

"Back again, are you?" I inquired unnecessarily.

"Not from the dead this time," said Sethos. "I have brought you a little gift."

"In a rug?"

"It worked for Cleopatra," said my brother-in-law. The unfortunate female sneezed violently. Automatically I handed her a handkerchief.

"I'm leaving her in your care for a few days," Sethos went on. "Make certain no one gets to her."

Without further ado, he turned and strode toward the door. Emerson made a leap for him, caught him by the arm and spun him round, so vigorously that he staggered.

"Not so fast. You have a lot of explaining to do."

Instead of trying to free himself from the hand that gripped his shoulder, Sethos stared at Emerson's left sleeve, which had fallen back, exposing the cast.

"How did that happen?" he asked.

"An encounter with a tomb robber in Luxor," Emerson replied. "One of yours?"

"At present I have no business arrangements in Luxor. It's like you," he added in exasperation, "to go dashing into a war zone with a broken arm. Just sit tight for a few days, all of you. I can't explain now; lowly merchants do not linger to chat with customers."

"Then we will meet you elsewhere," I said firmly. "Later this evening. Where and when?"

"For God's sake, Amelia, be reasonable! There's a noose round my neck and it's getting tighter by the minute. If my absence is discovered . . . Oh, very well. I'll try to meet you tomorrow night. Midnight—romantic, isn't it?—at the ruined house in Dir el Balah. Ramses knows it."

"What?" Ramses tore his horrified gaze from the "gift." "Yes, I know it. What the devil—"

"Later. You shouldn't have any trouble for another day or two. Oh—I almost forgot. You owe me four hundred and twenty piastres. That's four and a half Turkish pounds," he added helpfully. "Quite a bargain."

After he had bowed himself out, I was at leisure to turn my attention to the young woman. Nefret had led her to the divan and was helping her smooth the tangled strands of her long hair.

"Would you like to freshen up a bit before we chat?" I inquired.

"For God's sake, Mother, this isn't a social encounter!"

Ramses burst out. "You let him get away without answering any questions, let's hear what she has to say."

She raised reproachful black eyes to his face. "Are you angry? I thought you would be happy to see me."

"He is," said Nefret. A dimple appeared at the corner of her mouth. "He just has an odd way of showing it. Mother, get her something to drink."

"Thank you, I would like that. And something to clean my face and hands."

She had the instincts of a lady, at any rate. The requested objects having been supplied, she wiped her face, and drank deeply of the cold tea. I had to keep telling Ramses to be quiet; he was fairly hopping with annoyance, but we owed the girl a little time to recover from her unusual and uncomfortable trip.

"Now," I said, after she had refreshed herself, "perhaps you can tell us, Miss . . . What is your name? Ramses didn't mention it."

"We were never properly introduced," Ramses said through his teeth.

"Esin."

"How do you do."

"How do you do," she repeated. "Are you *his* mother?"

Another one, I thought. Ramses has that effect on susceptible young women. I had suspected as much, even from Ramses's expurgated version of their encounter; the way she pronounced the masculine pronoun was a dead giveaway.

"Yes," I said. "And this is *his* father, Professor Emerson. And *his* wife."

"How do you do," the girl said, with only the barest nod for Emerson. She examined Nefret carefully, and her dirty face fell.

"Anyhow, I am glad to be here," she said with a sigh. "My father has been very angry since you escaped."

"Did he blame you?" Ramses asked.

"No, he thinks I am too stupid and too afraid of him." She took another sip of tea. "He wanted to blame Ismail Pasha, but he could not, since they were together all that evening, and when Ismail Pasha went to his rooms, my father put guards at the door. To protect him from assassins, he said."

"Then how did he—"

Nefret motioned Ramses to be silent. "How well do you know Ismail Pasha?" she asked.

"I talked often with him. He is an Englishman, you know. I liked talking to him; he treated me like a person, not a woman, and let me practice my English and told me I was a clever girl." She finished her tea and leaned back against the cushions.

"I'm surprised your father let you talk freely with other men," Nefret prodded.

"He could not stop me." Her dark eyes flashed. "In Constantinople many women are working now because of the war. I helped with the Red Crescent, rolling bandages. It was wonderful! We talked about sensible things, books and what was in the newspapers, and many new ideas. And we wore corsets and short skirts!"

"I heard about that," Nefret said. "Didn't the government issue an order demanding that Moslem women lengthen their skirts, discard corsets, and wear thicker veils?"

"They had to take back the order," said this young advocate of women's rights complacently. "We made them do it. The girls at the telephone company and the post office threatened to strike, and the ladies said they would not work for the Red Crescent anymore. But my father said I was keeping bad company, and made me come to Gaza with him, and it was so dull there. He tried to make me stay in the harem, but I got out whenever I could; it was fun, hiding from the men and exploring places where I was not supposed to be."

"The cellars," Ramses murmured, visibly chagrined. He had underestimated her, and so had the rest of us. I had a sudden image of Esin face-to-face with Emmeline and Christabel Pankhurst.

Emerson had been listening in silence, his mouth ajar.

Now he cleared his throat and said, "What about your father, child? He will be worried about you. Did you leave a message for him?"

"No, why should I? He doesn't care about me, I am only a piece of property to him. I have lived in England; I won't go back to the veil and the harem and the selling of women. When Ismail Pasha told me my father had captured an English spy, I wanted to see him, so I hid myself in the mandarah, hoping they would bring you there—and they did! My father told them to take off your filthy clothing so they would not stain his cushions, and when they did, I saw that you were very beautiful."

Nefret choked. "I'm glad you find this amusing," Ramses said sourly.

"It is not amusing," the girl insisted. "It is sad and very romantic. I did not know who you were, and when my father said he would give me to you I was happy, because you were so beautiful and so brave, and then—then you said you were already married and my heart cracked in two, because I knew an English gentleman would never be unfaithful—"

"That's quite enough of that," said Ramses to his wife, who had covered her mouth with her hands in an attempt to muffle her laughter.

"Quite," I said, getting a grip on myself. The conversation had been extraordinary. "Nefret, take the—er—young lady off to the bath chamber and get her some clean clothing. That rug is absolutely filthy."

"Don't say anything important until I get back," Nefret ordered.

The girl got to her feet. "Are you still angry with me?" she asked Ramses.

"Good Lord, no. I—er—I owe you a great deal. More than I realized." He smiled at her, and a blissful answering smile spread across her face.

"You owe me nothing. I will treasure the memory of that kiss forever, even if you can never be mine."

After Nefret had removed the girl, the rest of us sat in silence, reflecting upon what we had learned. We were, in my opinion, becoming somewhat overburdened with strong-minded young women. I fixed a critical gaze upon my son.

"The kiss was, perhaps, a mistake."

"It seemed the least I could do, Mother."

I think he was teasing me. One cannot always be sure with Ramses. I trusted he would find Nefret's comments equally entertaining.

"A kindly error, however," I conceded. "We will not speak of it again."

"Extraordinary young woman," said Emerson. He added gloomily, "I suppose we're stuck with her."

"For the time being," I agreed. "And we certainly cannot complain, considering what we owe her. We were dead wrong about her. She managed the whole business by herself."

"With a few hints from Ismail Pasha," said Ramses. "Don't give me that steely stare, Mother. I am not denying her intelligence and her courage, but I would be willing to wager that she went rushing off to her sympathetic English friend as soon as they removed my—er—beautiful self to the cells, and opened her heart to him. That gave him his opening, and no one is better at putting ideas into people's heads. I can almost hear him, can't you? 'The cruelties of war . . . too young to die . . . your father forced against his will to destroy a gallant enemy . . . in his heart he'd be grateful to be relieved of that grim duty . . . ' "

"She does seem to be a romantic young person," I said. "And clever enough to work out the details, with, perhaps, a suggestion or two from Sethos. He had probably explored the house, including the cells—'just in case.' Like myself, he believes in anticipating potential dangers. Nor would he have had any difficulty in persuading her to run away with him, to join the individual who had made such an impression on her susceptible heart."

"Now, Mother," Ramses protested. "She was bored and restless, and annoyed with her father for dragging her off to

Gaza, and fascinated by Sethos. It wouldn't have required more than that."

"Hmm," I said. "Admittedly *her* motives are less important than his. Why did he do it? Surely not to rescue a damsel in distress."

"Not Sethos," said Emerson—who might have been fool enough to do just that. "He means to use her against her father, somehow or other. It would be confounded embarrassing for Sahin Bey—oh, very well, Pasha—to admit he had lost his daughter to the enemy. What would he be willing to give to get her back?"

"We cannot be party to any such scheme," I declared. "I will not force a young woman against her will, no matter what is offered in exchange."

"Not even Sethos?" Ramses's eyes were on the unlit cigarette he was rolling between his long fingers.

"Oh, good Gad," I said.

Eleven

The night passed without incident, but in some discomfort. I felt it incumbent upon myself to keep the girl with me. She had been removed suddenly from her home and was in the company of strangers; a motherly presence would comfort her—and prevent her from leaving us, in case she changed her mind. Emerson attempted to convince *me* to change *my* mind, declaring that my habit of foreseeing difficulties that never arose had become, as he put it, deuced inconvenient. Unable to prevail, he went off to one of the small sleeping chambers in a considerable state of aggravation.

Esin proved to be a noisy companion, breathing heavily through her nose and changing position every few minutes. However, there is a silver lining to every cloud; wakefulness gave me ample time for reflection. The situation had become even more confusing than before, and the possible permutations were manifold. If we did not make preparations to depart, Cartright might decide to place us under house arrest or remove us by force—for our own good, as he would explain. I did not trust him one inch, or believe in his protestations. Heaven only knew what Sethos would do next. I had never believed he was a traitor; I did not believe it now, though his real purpose was still a mystery. He had not exaggerated, however, when he spoke of a noose round his neck; a turncoat is automatically under suspicion, and Sahin, an old hand at the Game, was probably watching his every move. Ramses's suggestion that Sethos had taken the girl as a possible bargaining counter, in case he was arrested, made a horribly convincing theory; in fact, it was the only reason I could think of why he might have taken that risk. Sahin Pasha was another unpredictable factor. What would he do when he discovered his daughter was missing?

By morning I had formulated my plans. I explained them to the others over breakfast.

"I am having serious doubts as to the advisability of our remaining here. Let us at least behave as if our departure were imminent."

"Start packing, you mean?" Nefret asked, her brow furrowed.

"It would certainly do no harm if each of us made up a little bundle of basic necessities. What I meant, however, was that we should shop for items we would need on a journey and inspect the motorcar to make certain it is in good order."

"It is in good order," Selim declared, in some indignation.

"I am sure it is, Selim. But you could pretend it was not, couldn't you—that some repairs were needed? That would give us a reasonable excuse to stay on for another day."

"Yes, I could do that," Selim agreed. His eyes shone in anticipation of an interesting vehicular challenge. "These people know nothing of motorcars. I could take off the—"

"No, no, you mustn't take anything off! I want to be ready to leave at a moment's notice, if we have to."

"Not having one of your famous premonitions, are you?" Emerson inquired, his eyes narrowing. "Because if you are—"

"You don't want me to tell you about it. I am only trying to anticipate every contingency, Emerson. That is not superstition, it is simply good sense. We must stay here until tomorrow at the earliest, so that we can confer with Sethos, and we don't want some helpful military person dropping by to inquire into our plans."

"How far do you want to go?" Selim asked. "If it is more than five miles, we will need more petrol."

"What else will we need?"

I made a little list. Our guest, who had not spoken except to bid us good morning, said, "Am I to go with you?"

I leaned back and gave her my full attention. A bath and a change of clothing, into one of "the favorite's" silk robes, had improved her appearance considerably, and I had braided her hair myself. One could not have called her pretty, her features were too strong, but she was a handsome girl, in her way. Selim kept sneaking sidelong glances at her.

"We aren't going anywhere just yet," I replied. "As for taking you back to Cairo with us, that depends on a number of factors that are as yet unknown."

"We can't do anything else," said Emerson. "She has placed herself in our hands and we owe her our protection."

Esin's admiring gaze indicated her appreciation of this noble sentiment, which was, I should add, entirely sincere. It wasn't that simple, of course; men fix on words like honor and decency and noblesse oblige, and lose sight of the important issues. My chivalrous husband would never consent to an exchange, even if the life at stake was that of his own brother. I had not decided what I would do if the situation arose. We would not be selling the girl into slavery, only returning her to a father who had always treated her indulgently . . .

Sufficient unto the day is the evil thereof, I reminded myself. We must hope that the hard decision did not arise. The likelihood of Sahin's agreeing to an exchange of any kind was slight, I thought. Pride and duty—two more of those masculine catchwords—would forbid it, and he would not fear for her safety if we were looking after her.

"Speaking of that—I refer to my husband's statement that you placed yourself in our hands," I said. "Did you? Were you aware that you were being brought to us?"

"Oh, yes." She transferred her admiring gaze to Ramses.

"Did you not say you were in my debt—that you would protect me from my father's wrath?"

"Did you?" Nefret inquired sweetly.

Ramses's beleaguered gaze moved from the girl to Nefret and back. "I—uh—to be honest, I don't remember what the hell I said!"

"If you did not say it, you meant it," Esin declared. "No Englishman would leave a woman to suffer for a service she had done him."

"But you said your father didn't suspect you," Ramses protested.

"He was beginning to. That is what Ismail Pasha told me."

"Ah," I said. "So he offered to help you."

Her forehead wrinkled. "I think that is how it was. But I did most of it myself. I had to find my own way out of the house. That was not so hard, I know all the secret passages and cellars, but then I had to go to the place he told me about, the tomb of a saint that is outside the wall of the Serai. It is not far, but I was very frightened, and I had to wait a long time before the rug merchant came with his cart, and then he was stopped at the guard post and I could hear them talking and laughing and I was afraid they would search the cart. But they did not. It was a long bumpy ride and I could not breathe very well, and—"

"You were very courageous," I interrupted, for I had heard enough. The essentials of the story had been told. It sounded as if Ramses had been correct about Sethos's devious methods.

The various schemes I had proposed kept us busy all day. Selim spent a good deal of the time underneath the motorcar, surrounded by a fascinated audience, including the babies and the goats. From time to time he emerged, sweating and oil-stained, to report progress and bask in the admiration of the beholders. We could have got the petrol from an independent businessman—there was a thriving black market on all military items—but Emerson decided that we might just as well ask the authorities for it. It required only four hours for his request to be approved. Clearly, they were anxious to be rid of us.

By evening our plans had been completed. I had whiled away the hours exploring the rest of the house. It was like many others I had visited, with nothing of particular interest except for even more secret passages and hidden chambers than usual. Mahmud or one of his ancestors appeared to have had little faith in his government, his associates, and his wives.

According to Ramses, we should allow at least an hour to reach the spot Sethos had indicated. When we gathered in the ka'ah for a light evening repast, we discussed who should go. Naturally I intended to make one of the party, and Emerson was set on confronting his infuriating brother. Someone had to stay with the girl, we all agreed to that—Nefret with a caustic "I'm always the one"—but Selim and Ramses could not decide which of them should go and which should remain with the two young women. It lacked half an hour till the time we were to leave, and we were still discussing the matter, when a horrible, ululating howl broke the silence of the quiet night. The mashrabiya screen was ajar and I heard the words quite clearly:

"O unbelievers, prepare for death! O ye unrighteous, who walk in darkness pursued by afrits and . . ." The speech ended in an anticlimactic squawk.

In a body we rushed to the window and flung the screen open. In the moonlight I saw a dark mass huddled outside the gate, and Selim, his shoulder braced against it. Realizing they had been discovered, the invaders began battering at the gate.

I tried, too late, to catch hold of Ramses, who had climbed over the sill. He dropped to the ground and reached Selim as the gate gave way. Selim's knife flashed. Ramses had snatched up a lever or spanner as he ran past the motorcar; he swung his arm, and a scream from one of the attackers wavered into silence.

"Quick!" Emerson exclaimed. "Out the bab-sirr, all of you."

"Be damned to that!" I shrieked, for my blood was up. "'Now who will stand on either hand, And keep the bridge with—'"

"Me," said Emerson. "Curse it, Peabody, get the girls out of here. You know what to do."

He was already halfway out the window, lowering himself by one hand.

The fighting instincts of the Peabodys were not easily controlled; but the confidence he had placed in me enabled me to master them. I expected some objection from Nefret, but she made none. Pausing only long enough to collect the bundles we had packed earlier, we fled down the stairs and through the rooms of the ground floor toward the small chamber that contained the secret door. Esin had spoken only once: "Is it my father?"

"I don't know. Be quiet and hurry."

The house was deserted. The servants who lived in had run away or were in hiding. One could hardly blame them for refusing to become involved in the affairs of strangers. No doubt the local authorities, such as they were, felt the same. I hoped the uproar at the gate would attract the attention of the military police, but by the time they arrived it might be too late.

Nefret had not spoken at all. We both had our torches; she held the light steady while I searched for the catch Emerson had shown me. It was stiff with disuse, but finally it yielded. The panel swung open, and we all crowded into the space beyond. The passage went through the thick wall of the house. It was ten feet long and less than two feet wide; we had to go single-file, our bundles bumping against the walls. At the end was a wooden door. It was not bolted or locked; one simply pressed a handle to release the latch, which was presumably less visible from the other side.

I did not know what lay beyond that door. This was as far as I had gone with Emerson.

"Go ahead," Nefret whispered. "What are you waiting for?"

Her face gleamed with perspiration. Esin's eyes were wide with terror and her breath came in short gasps. I was as anxious as they to get out of that cramped place; it was like standing in an upright coffin, with dust clogging the nostrils and a strange, sour smell. Many generations of rodents must have lived and died in that passage; their bones had crunched under our feet as we walked.

"I am waiting for the men to join us," I replied. "We cannot take the risk of being separated. Since I do not know whether they will follow us through the bab-sirr or come round to the back, we had better remain where we are. Put out the torch, Nefret. I expect they will be along shortly."

My confidence was not assumed. With the aid of Emerson's strength, they should be able to close and barricade the gate and beat a strategic retreat. However, it is difficult to estimate time in the dark; we waited, breathing with difficulty, for what seemed like hours, before hinges creaked and a square of paler darkness opened before me.

"Don't shoot," said a familiar voice.

I tucked my pistol back into my pocket. "I couldn't be sure it was you," I explained. "Are Ramses and Selim—"

"All present and accounted for," said Ramses breathlessly. "We can't stay here, they'll be looking for us. Let's go."

"Where?" I demanded, squeezing through a narrow aperture and a curtain of thorny vines.

"We have an appointment at midnight, I believe. I am all the more anxious now to hear what the . . . fellow has to say. Damn these cactuses," Emerson added.

They formed a hedge a few feet away. The wall of the house rose sheer and windowless behind us. Nefret and Esin followed me out and Emerson closed the panel, which was of wood painted to resemble the plastered surface of which it formed a part.

"Lead on," I said.

The narrow lane into which we had emerged led back to the square, but it was obvious we could not go that way; from the sounds of it, a full-scale riot was in progress. A tongue of fire shot up. Someone usually sets fire to something during these affairs, which, once started, go on of their own momentum—especially when there are interested parties fanning the flames. As we retreated in the opposite direction, I heard the same high-pitched shriek of "unbelievers."

It was fortunate that we had explored the town earlier. Cactus hedges and high walls formed barricades that had to be got round, and twice the sight of men waving torches forced us to retreat in haste. It was quite exciting. However, we found ourselves at last in the open countryside. The moon shone brightly down on fields of waving grain and groves of orange and fig trees.

Moonlight is good for lovers but it is cursed inconvenient for fugitives. We kept to the shadows whenever we could, and once the sound of approaching hoofbeats made us dive for cover in a ditch. After the small troop had galloped past, I said to Emerson, "They were our fellows, Australians and New Zealanders. Perhaps we ought to have stopped them."

"Do you want to explain this evening's events—and her—to General Chetwode?" Emerson demanded.

It was a rhetorical question, and he did not wait for an answer.

The distance was less than two miles, but I would never have found the place without a guide. The small hamlet had long been abandoned and the majority of the houses had collapsed into shapeless piles of stone. One or two of them still retained their walls and parts of the roof. There was no sign of life in the half-ruined structure to which Ramses led us.

"We are a trifle late," I whispered. "Perhaps he has left."

"If he isn't there, I will go to Gaza and drag him out by his collar," Emerson muttered.

He wasn't there. Ramses, who had insisted on searching the place before we entered, returned to report this fact. "It's not that late," he added. "Give him time."

"I suppose we can't expect punctuality under these circumstances," Emerson admitted. "This is as good a place as any to rest; we may as well make ourselves comfortable. What have you got in that bundle, Peabody?"

"Only the bare necessities, I fear. Water, of course, and my first-aid kit. Did any of you incur injuries that require attention?"

"Nothing to speak of," Emerson said. He let out a soft laugh. "Your quotation was apropos. The damned fools tried to crowd in all at once. 'In yon straight path a thousand may well be stopped by three,' as the *Lays of Ancient Rome* so poetically expresses it. We pushed them back, got the gate closed, and shoved a cart up against it. Then, unlike Horatius and his comrades, we retreated in good order. Selim wanted to stay and fight on, but I dragged him away."

"It was a good fight," Selim said reminiscently.

He reached for the water bottle, which was passing round, and I said with a sigh of exasperation, "All right, Selim, let me see your hand. Why didn't you tell me you had been wounded?"

"It is nothing," said Selim. "It will heal. I do not need anything on it."

He meant antiseptics. Men are strange creatures; he had taken a cut on the side of his wrist which had bled copiously and must have hurt quite a lot, but I had to speak sternly to him before he let me swab it with alcohol.

It was a relief to rest our weary limbs. Esin was half asleep already, stretched out on a patch of ground Selim had gallantly swept clean of pebbles, with her head on one of the bundles. "Biscuit, anyone?" I inquired, extracting the packet from my parcel.

Emerson chuckled. "What, no whiskey? My dear girl, packing those bundles was a brilliant thought, but I have come to expect no less of you." We were sitting side by side in a darkish corner, so he gave me a quick demonstration of approval.

"How long can we stay here without being discovered?" I asked.

"It's safe enough," Ramses replied. "The locals think the place is haunted."

"By you?" Nefret asked.

"I encouraged the idea. I wonder . . ." He went to the darkest corner of the place and shifted a few stones. After a moment he said, "No, it's not here—the pistol I took from Chetwode. He must have collected it on his way back."

"Pity," said Emerson. "We may want a weapon before the night is over. Ah, well, we usually manage without one."

"Yes, sir," Ramses agreed. He went back to Nefret and sat down. She leaned her head against his shoulder and he put his arm round her. "Darling, why don't you stretch out and sleep for a while? It's beginning to look as if he—"

He broke off with a hiss of breath, his head turning alertly, and raised a finger to his lips. Ramses's acute hearing had prompted one of Daoud's more memorable sayings: "He can hear a whisper across the Nile." We froze, holding our breaths. Ramses rose and drifted toward the door, silent as a shadow in his dark galabeeyah.

Someone was coming. He walked quietly but not noiselessly. I heard a twig snap and then a form appeared in the ragged moonlit aperture of the door. The silhouette was that of a tall man wearing a turban and a long robe. He leaned forward, peering into the darkness, his arms raised in greeting or defense. One sleeve hung limp from the elbow.

Ramses seized the fellow in a tight grip and clapped a hand over his mouth. "Hell and damnation," Emerson exclaimed, surging to his feet. "Bring him in. Keep him quiet. He must be the bastard who was howling out anathemas against the unbelievers; I thought that voice was familiar! If he's led that pack of jackals here . . . We need a gag, Peabody. Tear up some extraneous garment or other."

"I do not possess any extraneous garments, Emerson. Hit him over the head."

The prisoner, who had been quiescent until then, was gal-

vanized into frantic movement. He managed to wrench
Ramses's hand from his face.

"For God's sake, don't be hasty!"

The words were English. The accent was refined. The
voice was not that of Sethos.

Ramses lowered his hand but did not release his hold.
"Who the hell are you?" he demanded.

"A friend. That is the conventional reply, I believe. I really
am, though."

It had been a long time, but the well-bred drawl, with its
undercurrent of amusement, struck a chord of memory.

"Let him go, Ramses," I said. "You remember Sir Edward
Washington, Sethos's aide and co-conspirator?"

"I am flattered, Mrs. Emerson." Sir Edward removed himself from Ramses's loosened grasp and made me an elegant
bow. "How very good it is to see you again. And the Professor . . ." Another bow. "Nefret—do forgive the liberty—
beautiful as ever . . . Selim, my friend . . . And I see you
have the young lady safe. Well done."

Ramses switched on his torch and stared incredulously at
the tatterdemalion figure. Sir Edward bowed again, with the
mocking grace that was peculiarly his.

"By God, it is," Ramses muttered. "How the devil—"

"Never mind that now, Ramses," I interrupted. "Sir Edward, are you here in lieu of your chief?"

"Straight to the point as always, Mrs. Emerson. You are
right to remind me we ought not waste time. The answer to
your question is no. I have been waiting for him."

"Good Gad," Emerson exclaimed, recovering from his
understandable surprise. "I never expected to see you again,
Sir Edward; the last I heard, you were in . . ." He broke off,
staring at the empty sleeve.

"France," said Sir Edward coolly. "As you see, I have returned to private life."

"Did you follow us?" I asked.

"Only until you were safely out of the metropolis. Didn't

you hear me encouraging the riot? Kept everybody busy and happy and out of your way."

"Oh," said Emerson.

"I came straight on after that," Sir Edward continued blithely. "It was a safe assumption that you would keep the appointment."

"But *he* didn't," Emerson said. "Why not?"

Sir Edward scratched his side, murmured a genteel apology, and said, "He may have been unable to get away. Sahin's been watching him closely, especially since Ramses escaped. There's no use staying here any longer."

"Where shall we go, then?" I inquired. "In my opinion it would be inadvisable for us to return to Khan Yunus until we are apprised of conditions there. Some of Sahin's men may be lurking. Or were those assertive individuals not his men?"

"I assumed they were. Don't tell me you have another set of enemies after you!"

"There would be nothing new in that," said Ramses. "Have you anyplace in mind, Sir Edward?"

Sir Edward hesitated. Under the skillful makeup and the ingrained dirt and the wisps of beard I could see the lines of worry and indecision that marked his face. Then he shrugged, with all his old insouciance. "I know a place, yes. It's a good ten miles away, too far for the ladies to walk. We'll need transportation."

"I will go back and get the motorcar," Selim offered.

"Too risky," Emerson said at once.

"And too conspicuous," Sir Edward added. "We'll have to borrow a few quadrupeds. Ramses, my lad, have you ever stolen a horse?"

"As a matter of fact, he has," I replied.

"I don't know why I bothered to ask," Sir Edward muttered. "There's a picket line a mile south of here. Ramses and Selim—no, Professor, not you. Someone must stay with the ladies."

"This lady is going with you," Nefret said.

From Manuscript H

There was only one sentry. The enemy wasn't in the habit of sending out raiding parties, and local horse thieves had learned not to tangle with the men of the Desert Column. Trees and growing crops gave plenty of cover, and the moon was down. They crawled close enough to hear the snores of the men who lay rolled in their blankets beyond the line of horses. Sir Edward brought his mouth against Ramses's ear.

"I'm beginning to think this was a bad idea."

Ramses had been of that opinion from the start. Some of the straitlaced British officers considered the ANZACs an unruly lot, impatient of discipline, who didn't even know how to ride properly. Personally he would have preferred to have a whole troop of fox-hunting Englishmen after him than a few of these hard-bitten colonials.

Bad idea or not, it had to be done. The girl couldn't manage a ten-mile hike, and he was concerned about his mother, who would drop in her tracks rather than admit the task was beyond her. Anyhow, they had to get under cover before morning. It would take too long for the slower members of the party to walk that distance.

They had planned what they had to do, and he thought they could manage it, with a little luck—and Nefret's help. He had had to overrule Sir Edward, and his own instincts, when she announced she was coming with them; common sense told him that her help would be invaluable. She was an excellent rider, and she had an uncanny knack with animals.

Dealing with the sentry was his job. It wasn't difficult; the poor devil was tired and not expecting trouble. Ramses took him from behind with an arm across his throat, hit him hard in the pit of the stomach, and chopped him across the back of the neck as he toppled forward. By the time he had dragged the limp body under a tree, Nefret was moving down the string of horses, whispering in their ears and stroking their necks. When she reached the last in line, she untied the rope that passed through their bridles.

So far there had been no sound except a few soft, interested whickers from the intrigued equines. Now they had to move fast and noisily. Nefret scrambled onto one of the horses while Selim gave Sir Edward a hand up and mounted another. Except for Nefret's mount, the animals were stirring uneasily. One of the sleeping men sat up. Ramses tossed the dangling reins over the lead horse's neck and vaulted onto its back. It turned its head to give him an astonished stare.

"Wrong man, I know," Ramses said in a conversational voice. "Think of it as a temporary inconvenience."

There wasn't time to adjust the stirrups. He dug his bare heels into the animal's flanks and urged it into a trot. It responded to the touch or the English voice, or both. The entire camp was now awake; shouts and curses echoed through the night, and someone fired a rifle. Someone else let out a stream of oaths directed at the idiot who had fired it. By that time the entire group of horses was in motion, following their leader and urged on by Nefret, who brought up the rear yelling and smacking assorted equine rumps with a leafy branch. Her hair had come loose from its scarf; it streamed out behind her, silvered by starlight. Sir Edward was hanging on, though he didn't look happy. Selim looked very happy. This was the sort of adventure he had had in mind all along, a wild ride with the enemy in hot pursuit.

The pursuit consisted of one trooper, running as fast as his long legs would carry him, waving his arms and calling out. The horses broke into a gallop and the plaintive cries of "Mary! Mary, love, come back!" faded into the night.

A real and vindictive pursuit would not be long delayed, however. They did not slacken speed until they were near the ruins where the others were ready and waiting. None of them wasted time in conversation, though Ramses saw the look of resignation on his mother's face. She was not an enthusiastic horsewoman, and was accustomed to the smooth gait of their Arabians.

"Sorry, Mother," he said, offering his hands to help her mount. "Will you be all right?"

"Certainly." It was the answer he had expected.

Esin couldn't manage it, though. She had ridden only in England, with a proper lady's saddle. Declining Selim's eager offer of assistance, Nefret mounted the girl in front of her.

"We're leaving a trail a blind man could follow," Sir Edward said, as they started off two by two. "And now we've got the Australians after us."

"This was your idea," Ramses pointed out.

"So it was. I hope I'll live long enough to regret it."

The clipped accent sounded odd from that vagabond figure. There hadn't been time for Ramses to assimilate Sir Edward's sudden reappearance, and there were a hundred questions he wanted to ask.

"What are you doing here? I was under the impression that you had given up a life of crime."

"I can't imagine what gave you that impression" was Sir Edward's bland reply. "But my present job isn't criminal in nature. People give other people medals for doing it."

"Usually after the 'other people' are dead."

Sir Edward let that one pass. Ramses tried another tack.

"Why is Sethos in Gaza? He's no traitor, I'm certain of that now, but what the hell is he after?"

"You'll have to ask him that."

They reached their destination just before dawn. Ramses had expected a tumbledown ruin or a mean little house; instead he saw high walls rising up against the paling sky like those of a castle or a fortress. The heavy gates were closed. Sir Edward called out and after an interval one of the leaves of the gate opened and a man peered out. He let out an exclamation when he saw the group.

"They are friends," Sir Edward said. "Friends of the Master."

He led the way into an open courtyard with a well in the center and a roofed arcade on the right side. It *was* a fortress, and a strong one. The walls were twelve feet high and eight feet thick. A small two-storied structure within the enclosure must be the living quarters.

"Go ahead into the house," their host said, indicating this building. "Straight through and up the stairs to the salon. I'm afraid you'll find us ill-prepared for guests, but Mustafa and I will see what can be done in the way of food and drink."

He drew the other man aside. Leaving his father to assist his mother, and Selim the girl, Ramses edged toward the pair. He caught only two words: "No message?" and saw Mustafa shake his head.

Mustafa looked like the sort of man who would be employed by Sethos—burly, black-bearded as a pirate, and wary. He shot a suspicious look at Ramses, and Sir Edward turned.

"This is the notorious—er—famous Brother of Demons, Mustafa," he said in Arabic. "You have heard of him."

"Ah!" Mustafa held out a hand. "We will shake hands as the English do, eh? It is an honor to meet you. And so the others are . . . ?"

"The even more notorious Father of Curses and his family," Ramses said. "If you will forgive me for failing in courtesy, may I suggest that there are important matters to be dealt with before we exchange additional compliments? The horses, for instance. Their owners will want them back."

Mustafa threw his head back and let out a bellow of laughter. "You stole them? Well done. They will fetch a good price."

"Control your mercantile instincts, Mustafa," said Sir Edward. "They must be returned eventually. We—er—borrowed them from the Australians."

"Hmmm." Mustafa stroked his beard. "A pity. But you are right, the Australians are fierce fighters and they love their horses."

Ramses stroked the friendly muzzle that had come to rest on his shoulder. "Take care of them, will you, Mustafa? Rub them down and water them."

"If you have handled that to your satisfaction," said Sir Edward, "shall we go in? Your mother will be waiting in the salon for us."

"No, she won't," Ramses said.

⋮

The salon was an elegantly appointed apartment at the front of the house. I recognized Sethos's refined tastes in the furnishings—cushioned divans, carved screens, and low tables of brass and copper—but it was clear at a glance that this was a bachelor establishment. There was a bird's nest in one of the window embrasures, and dust covered every flat surface.

"Dear me," I said. "This won't do. Let us see what the rest of the house is like."

"He told us to wait here," Nefret said. She was supporting Esin, who looked as if she was at the limit of her strength.

"I have no intention of waiting for a man to make the necessary arrangements," I replied. "That girl should be in bed. Let us find one."

Two of the small rooms behind the salon had obviously been used as sleeping chambers. Various articles of masculine attire hung over chairs and chests. The beds were brass, in the European style, rather at odds with the rest of the furnishings, but with comfortable mattresses and sheets and pillows. Selim and I straightened the crumpled bedding and put Esin on the bed. I did not bother removing her clothing, since it did not appear that the sheets had been changed for several weeks.

Sir Edward and Ramses were in the salon when we returned to that room.

"Did you find what you were looking for?" the former inquired politely.

"I found a bed—yours, I believe—and got Miss Sahin tucked in. The poor child was worn out. Now, where is the kitchen? A nice hot cup of tea would be just the thing."

"Mustafa is making tea," Sir Edward said.

"Does he know about boiling the water long enough? Perhaps I had better go and—"

Sir Edward took the liberty of seizing me by the arm. "He knows. He knows! Mrs. Emerson, please sit down. I can't until you do, and I am dead on my feet."

"Oh, very well." I selected one of the divans that did not have evidence of avian activity. Sir Edward collapsed onto another with a long sigh and Ramses took his place next to Nefret.

Emerson was still prowling about the room. "Ha!" he exclaimed, opening a cabinet. "My—er—old acquaintance does himself well. Claret, 'pon my word, and an excellent vintage too. It isn't whiskey, Peabody, but would you care for a drop?"

"Not at this time of day," I replied. "Ah—here is Mustafa with the tea tray. Just put it here, if you please. I will pour."

He had slopped it all over the tray, of course. As he stood back, fixing me with a bold, curious stare, I had one of those moments of utter disorientation: the tea tray, set out in proper English style—that would be Sir Edward's influence—the black-bearded ruffian who had served it; the filthy, ragged beggar who was Sir Edward; and the rest of us in a motley array of garments, from Nefret's neat but crumpled trousers and coat to Emerson's torn silken robes.

However, the situation was no more bizarre than many in which we had found ourselves.

Mustafa said suddenly, "You are the Sitt Hakim? I have a little sore, here on my—"

"Later, my friend," I said graciously. Nefret hid her face against Ramses's shoulder and Emerson shouted, "Good Gad! Even here! Curse it, Peabody!"

Mustafa retreated, visibly impressed by the volume of Emerson's voice. I persuaded Emerson to sit down and take out his pipe. It soothed him; it usually did.

"I don't know where you are all going to sleep," Sir Edward muttered.

"At the moment my brain is too active to let me rest, Sir Edward," I informed him. "We need to know where we stand. First and most important, where is Sethos? Did you expect him to be here?"

"I hoped for a message, at least. He usually finds a way to let me know if there is any change in his plans. When I saw him yesterday morning—"

"You were in Gaza? Goodness gracious, you all seem to walk in and out of the place as you please."

Whether he would have confided in us under different circumstances I cannot say. It may have been exhaustion that loosened his tongue.

"The fortifications are like a sieve for a single man, if he knows where the holes are. Once inside I—and our other couriers—form part of the adoring mob that presses round the holy man asking for his blessing."

"So he can pass messages to you, and you to him," I prompted.

"Something like that," Sir Edward said evasively. "I knew he planned to get Sahin's daughter away. I'd have talked him out of it if I could, or at least tried to persuade him not to go back to Gaza. Sahin was bound to suspect he'd had a hand in the business and clamp down on him even more closely. I think that is what has happened."

"Can you send someone to find out?" I asked.

Emerson cleared his throat. "My papers—"

"No," Ramses and I said in the same breath.

"What papers?" Sir Edward demanded, his eyes widening.

Proudly Emerson drew them forth and handed them to Sir Edward. The sun was well up now; the gilt sparkled impressively in the light.

"I can't read Turkish," Sir Edward said blankly.

"Ramses can." Emerson's pipe had gone out. He struck a match. "He says they are perfectly in order."

"Yes, very well, but you can't—you can't just walk up to the trenches and—"

"No, it will take some preparation," Emerson admitted.

"That is quite right," I said, seeing in my mind's eye the preparations Emerson was planning. Camels, servants, gold-trimmed robes, and a huge scimitar . . . He would so enjoy it, and sheer effrontery might allow him to carry it off. For a while.

"Admirable," Sir Edward murmured. He sounded more horrified than admiring. "Sir, give me a chance to use our regular channels first."

"An excellent idea," I said, before Emerson could object. "Sir Edward, I am curious to know how—"

"I beg you will excuse the interruption, Mrs. Emerson, but could we postpone the interrogation for a few hours?" Sir Edward rubbed his eyes. "I need to rest, even if you don't, and there are a few domestic matters I must attend to."

"Certainly. Just show me where you keep the clean sheets."

It was the final straw for poor Sir Edward. "I— Oh, Lord. I don't know that there are any, Mrs. Emerson."

"If there were, where would they be? Come," I said in a kindly manner, "let's just have a look. It won't take long."

The others declared they would stretch out on the divans, and Sir Edward and I went off on what he clearly believed was a hopeless quest. Eventually we found a cupboard that contained linens of various kinds. I selected a few. Sir Edward, always the gentleman, took the pile from me. I allowed him to do so, though he had a little difficulty getting hold of it.

"I was sorry to see that," I said, with the lightest possible touch of his arm. "It was in France that it happened, I suppose."

"Ypres." He spoke curtly, avoiding my eyes. Pity he would not accept; acknowledgment of his sacrifice was owed him, and I felt obliged to make it.

"It must have been dreadful. I am so sorry."

"What, womanly sympathy from you, Mrs. Emerson? A touch out of character, isn't it?"

"It is sincere."

"I know." His rigid features relaxed. "I am sorry too, for speaking rudely. It's not so bad, you know. It got me out of the army, which was all to the good. I had become somewhat disenchanted."

"Can nothing be done about an artificial limb?"

"Oh, yes. I've got quite a good one. It broadens my repertoire of disguises to a remarkable extent. I'm thinking of attaching a bayonet, or perhaps a hook."

I patted him on the shoulder. "Splendid," I said heartily.

"Or a parasol," said Sir Edward. His smile was that of the charming debonair gentleman I had known.

I was to remember that smile for a long time. When I woke from a brief but refreshing nap, he was gone—from the house and from the grounds and, I feared, back into the powder keg that was Gaza.

It took me a while to discover this. I had decided to sleep on one of the divans rather than go to the trouble of making up a bed which, if events continued to unfold, I might never occupy. When I went to look in at Esin, I almost fell over Selim, who was stretched out across her threshold. I left him there, since that was where he had chosen to be, and went back to the salon. Ramses and Nefret lay side by side, his arm round her and her head on his shoulder. I stood for a moment watching them. One of Ramses's eyes opened and regarded me quizzically.

"All's well," I reported, and tiptoed toward the divan where Emerson lay.

I did not mean to sleep for more than an hour, but even as I reclined the skies were darkening, and the gentle murmur of rain must have lulled me. It was the sound of heavy footsteps that woke me—the running steps of a person in haste. I sat up with a start and reached into my nearest pocket. It was the wrong pocket. I was fumbling in another, trying to locate my little pistol, when a man burst into the room and came to a stop. He was breathing heavily and water poured from his soaked garments.

Emerson was thrashing around and muttering, as he always does when he is suddenly aroused, but Ramses was on his feet, alert and ready. The newcomer, too breathless to speak, held out empty hands in the universal gesture of conciliation. I could not see him clearly, the room was rather dark. I knew him, though.

"Ah," I said. "So here you are at last. It is all right, Ramses."

"No—it—isn't." Sethos got it out one word at a time. "Where's—Edward?"

"He isn't here?" I asked.

"No."

Emerson had finally got his wits together. "It's you, is it?" he demanded, squinting through the gloom. "High bloody time."

"Bloody too late," said Sethos, beginning to control his breath. "Did Edward tell you where—"

"We were not even aware of his departure," I replied. "Please compose yourself so that we can converse rationally."

"And get out of those wet clothes," Nefret said.

"What, here and now?"

Ramses had lighted several of the lamps. Sethos threw his shoulders back and tried to look as if he were in command of the situation, but he was a wretched figure, every garment saturated and even his beard dripping.

"A chill can bring on malaria," Nefret said calmly. "Get them off at once. I'll ask Mustafa to make tea."

"And something to eat," I called after her, as she hastened from the room.

"And something to wear," said my brother-in-law resignedly. He pulled off the sodden lump of his turban and the fez round which it had been wrapped. "This is as far as I am prepared to go, Amelia, while you remain in the room."

Anxious as I was to hold the long-delayed discussion—urgent as were the questions to be asked and answered—

physical needs took precedence. Sethos had had malaria be-fore. It would be extremely inconvenient if he came down with it again.

"Come with me," I ordered, and led the way out of the room.

Selim, still lying romantically across the girl's threshold, woke instantly when we approached—and no wonder, on that hard floor. He sprang up, reaching for his knife.

"He is a friend, Selim," I said. "Perhaps you would be good enough to help him change his wet clothing."

"I do not require a damned valet," Sethos snarled.

"Selim isn't a valet. You require assistance, and that is what you are about to get. Follow me, both of you."

A large cupboard in the other bedroom contained an ex-tensive wardrobe, ranging from abas and galabeeyahs to a nice tweed suit that Sethos had borrowed from Ramses the year before. I left them to it, and returned to the salon. Mustafa had scraped together a rather extraordinary meal—tinned tongue and bread and fruit, and, of course, tea. Before long, Selim and Sethos joined us, the latter in dry garments, his unruly hair still damp.

"Well, this is cozy," said Sethos, with a decidedly sar-donic inflection. "A jolly little family gathering. I've been chasing you across the countryside all night."

"Were you at the rendezvous?" I asked.

"Not until after you'd left. Would you like to know what happened?"

"Very much so," said Emerson, with a snap of his teeth.

"I had to make a run for it," Sethos explained. "I—er—miscalculated a trifle, you see. I didn't expect Sahin would move so quickly or so decisively. He's a very efficient man, with a well-organized network of supporters hereabouts. It didn't take him long to find out you were in Khan Yunus. You weren't exactly discreet, were you?"

"The disclosure of our true identities was unavoidable," I said. "And if I may say so, criticism from you is unwar-ranted, under the circumstances."

"Possibly," Sethos admitted. "If I may continue my narrative?"

"Pray do," I said.

"As I was about to say, the disappearance of his daughter hit him hard and he acted instantly. He sent orders to attack your house. There was a chance the girl was with you. If she wasn't, he hoped to acquire a hostage—one or all of you."

"How do you know all that?" I asked.

"He told me." Sethos had been eating ravenously, between sentences. He swallowed a bite of fruit and went on, "We had one of those friendly little chats—you know what they're like, Ramses. He explained in detail what he meant to do, and added, more in sorrow than in anger, that he was going to lock me up, since he had been forced to the conclusion that my conversion was not sincere."

He bit into a piece of bread. The pause was for effect, as I knew; the man could not resist making a dramatic story of it.

"So you hit him?" Ramses was as intrigued as the rest of us. "What with?"

"Not my fist, I assure you. He was waiting for that. I was nibbling daintily on a nectarine. I shoved it in his face. He was trying to claw the pulp out of his eyes and spit it out of his mouth when I broke his water pipe over his head. It made a frightful mess and rather a loud noise, so I didn't wait to tie him up. I calculated I had about sixty seconds before a servant got nerve enough to investigate, so I started running—straight out of the house and past the guards. If you don't have time to be cautious, speed and effrontery are your only hope. It was a spectacle dreadful enough to throw most people into a panic," he added with a grin. "The holy infidel, waving his arms and screaming broken phrases from the Koran. Nobody tried to stop me. Religious frenzy is dangerous. I kept running, divesting myself of my elegant ornaments as I went and scattering them about the streets, to the additional confusion of those I encountered. I presented the last—a very handsome emerald brooch, which I hated to give up—to the officer in command of one of the guard posts. With my blessing. May I have more tea?"

Ramses was the first to break the fascinated silence. "I'm a bloody amateur," he murmured. "Excuse me, Mother."

"You haven't done so badly," his uncle conceded. "This last escapade wasn't well thought out, though. You ought to have had a means of escape arranged before you shot at me."

"You don't suppose Ramses would do such a thing!" Nefret said indignantly.

"Now, now, keep calm. I did not suppose my affectionate nephew really intended to kill me. I credited him with realizing that an attack on me, presumably by my erstwhile employers, would establish me as a bona fide traitor. I didn't expect he would go so far as to let himself be caught. That was a complication I did not need."

"Accept my apologies," said Ramses, scowling at his uncle. Sethos did have a gift for turning people against him.

"Who was it, then, if it wasn't you?"

"A fellow named Chetwode. He's the general's nephew. His superior is a man named Cartright."

"Oh, that lot. How did you—"

"Never mind that now," I interrupted. "If we keep getting off onto side issues we will never make sense of this business. What happened after you left Gaza?"

"I decided I had better go to Khan Yunus and warn you."

"You might have thought of that earlier," Emerson grumbled.

"I told you, I didn't know what Sahin intended to do until he informed me. I barely made it out of the city before his men came boiling out in hot pursuit; I had to lie low in the hills until they tired of looking for me." He took a cigarette from the tin Ramses offered him and lit it before he went on. "By the time I got to Khan Yunus, all hell had broken loose. The army was on the scene, trying to suppress the riot, without the vaguest idea of who had started it or why. Your place had been broken into, and some of the locals were taking advantage of the confusion to carry off anything they could lay their hands on."

"The motorcar!" Selim exclaimed. "Did they damage it?"

"I wasn't given the opportunity to examine it," Sethos said dryly. "I hung about trying to look harmless until the military got things more or less under control. You hadn't shown yourselves, so I could only hope Edward had warned you in time for you to escape. It was after midnight by then. I had the devil of a time getting out of town, since I had to avoid not only soldiers looking for rioters but rioters who might be Sahin's lads. The whole bloody countryside was aroused—looking for a pack of horse thieves, as the sergeant who collared me explained. I was not in possession of a horse, so he let me go. You people really excel at stirring up trouble! I pushed on and, of course, found the ruined house deserted. You'd been there—you left an empty biscuit tin— and so had several horses. So I came on here. I couldn't think where else you might have gone. It took a while, since I was on foot."

I observed the faintest tremor in the hand that extinguished his cigarette. It was not the only sign of fatigue; his voice was flat and his face was drawn.

"You had better get some sleep," I said. "We will talk again later."

"As you command, Sitt Hakim." He got slowly to his feet. "Is someone sleeping in my bed?"

"Miss Sahin is in one of the beds. I will make up the other one for you."

"There is no need for that."

"Clearly it is not an amenity to which you are accustomed. I will do it anyhow. Come along."

What I wanted, as the Reader must have surmised, was a private chat. Even Emerson realized the reasonableness of this, though he did not much like it. He had never completely conquered his jealousy of his brother, baseless though it was—on my side, at any rate.

"Allow me to give you a little laudanum," I said. "You won't sleep without it, you are too tired and too on edge."

"Are you afraid I'll sneak out of the house?" He watched me unfold one of the sheets and then took hold of the other end. "I have better sense than that. If Edward isn't back by nightfall, I will have to take steps, but I cannot function efficiently without sleep."

He had tucked the sheet in any which way. I remade that end of the bed. Our eyes met, and he smiled a little; he was thinking, as was I, what an oddly domestic scene this was. "I don't need your laudanum," he went on, removing a container from one of the shelves.

"How long have you been taking that?" I asked, as he swallowed a small white pill.

"Weeks. Months." He stretched out on the bed. "It works quickly, so if you have any questions—which you undoubtedly do—talk fast."

"I only wanted to ask about Margaret. Have you heard from her?"

He hadn't expected such a harmless subject. "Margaret? No, not for months. I couldn't very well carry on a frequent correspondence, could I?"

"Does she know what you are doing?"

"She knows everything about me." He closed his eyes.

"Including—"

"Everything."

"You have complete confidence in her, then. Are you going to marry her?"

Sethos opened his eyes and clasped his hands behind his head. "You aren't going to leave me in peace until I invite you into my innermost heart, are you? The question is not whether I am going to marry her, but whether she will consent to marry me. I asked her. I hadn't intended to, it—er—came into my head at a particularly—er—personal moment. She said no."

"A flat, unconditional no?"

"There were conditions. You can guess what they were.

She was in the right. I told her—I promised her—this would be my last assignment. As it well may be."

"Not in the way you mean," I said firmly. "We are here, and on the job! We could be more useful, however, if you would tell me the purpose of your mission. What are you after?"

"Sahin." His eyelids drooped. The sedative had loosened his tongue. "He's their best man. Their only good man. Once he's out of the way, we can proceed with . . . He loves the girl. I didn't know that. I thought he'd go to some lengths to get her back, but I didn't realize . . . Paternal affection isn't one of my strong points. I told you about Maryam, didn't I?"

"Who?" I had to repeat the question. He was half asleep, wandering a little in his mind.

"Maryam. Molly. That's the name you knew . . . She's gone."

"Dead?" I gasped. "Your daughter?"

"No. Gone. Left. Ran away. Hates me. Because of her mother. She's living proof of heredity. Got the worst of both parents. Poor little devil . . . She is, you know. Amelia . . ."

"It's all right," I said softly, taking the hand that groped for mine. "Everything will be all right. Sleep now."

I sat by him until his hand relaxed and the lines on his face smoothed out. I had intended—oh, I admit it—to take advantage of his drowsy state to wring information out of him, but I had not expected revelations so intimate, so personal, so painful.

His daughter had been fourteen years of age when I knew her. She must be sixteen now. Her mother had been Sethos's lover and partner in crime; but her tigerish affection had turned to jealous hatred when she realized his heart belonged to another. (Me, in fact, or so he claimed.) She tried several times to kill me and succeeded in assassinating one of my dearest friends before she met her end at the hands of those who had been an instant too late to save him.

How much of that terrible story did the child know? If she blamed her father for her mother's death, she could not know the whole truth. He had not even been present when she died, and she had led a life of crime and depravity before she met Sethos. A moralist might hold him guilty of failing to redeem her, but in my opinion even a saint, which Sethos was not, would have found Bertha hard going.

I do not believe that the dead hand of heredity is the sole determinant of character. Remembering Molly as I had last seen her, looking even younger than her actual age, the picture of freckled, childish innocence . . . But she hadn't looked so innocent the day I found her in Ramses's room with her dress half off—by her own act, I should add. If I had not happened to be passing by—if Ramses had not had the good sense to summon me at once—or if he had been another kind of man, the kind of man she hoped he was—he might have found himself in an extremely interesting situation.

That proved nothing. She had not deliberately set out to seduce or shame him; she had been young and foolish and infatuated. My heart swelled with pity, for her and for the man who lay sleeping on the bed, his face pale and drawn with fatigue. He had not known how much he loved her until he lost her, and he blamed himself. How wonderful it would be if I could bring father and child together again!

It was a happy thought, but not practical—for the present, at any rate. We had to get through the current difficulty first. With a sigh I slipped my hand from his and tiptoed out of the room.

"Well?" Emerson demanded. "You've been the devil of a long time. How much were you able to get out of him?"

"We were right about him, of course," I replied, seating myself next to him as his gesture invited. "He is no traitor. His mission was to remove Sahin Bey—Pasha."

"Kill him, you mean?" Ramses asked.

"He didn't say. But surely Sethos would not—"

"Sahin is a dangerous enemy and this is wartime. However," Ramses said thoughtfully, "the same purpose would be served if Sahin Pasha were to be disgraced and removed from his position. In the last week he's lost me, his daughter, and now Ismail Pasha, whose flight will prove to their satisfaction that he was a British spy. Careless, to say the least!"

"More than careless," Emerson exclaimed. "Highly suspicious, to say the least! With that lot, you are guilty until proven innocent. By Gad, my boy, I believe you are right. It's like Sethos to concoct such a devious scheme. If the Turks believe, as they well may, that Sahin Pasha has been a double agent all along, they will have to reorganize their entire intelligence network. It could take months."

"And in the meantime they would be without their best and cleverest man," I added. "Sethos said that once Sahin was out of the way, they could proceed with . . . something."

"What?"

"He didn't say."

"And who is 'they'?" Nefret asked. "Who is he working for? Not Cartright and 'that lot'?"

"He—er—didn't say."

Emerson brought his fist down on the table, rattling the crockery. "What did he say? Good Gad, you were with him for almost three quarters of an hour."

"How do you know that?" I demanded. "You haven't a watch."

This time my attempt to distract him and put him on the defensive did not succeed. "Just answer the question, Peabody. What were you talking about all that while?"

"Personal matters. Oh, Emerson, for pity's sake, don't grind your teeth. I wanted to make certain he was asleep before I left him. The man is on the edge of nervous collapse. He has been living for months under conditions of intolerable strain. He must not be allowed to return to Gaza."

"He wouldn't be such a fool," Emerson muttered.

"He would if he believed Sir Edward had gone there to look for him."

"*He* wouldn't be such a fool," Emerson declared.

"He would if he believed his leader was in danger. They have been friends for a long time. I am going to talk to Mustafa; perhaps Sir Edward said something to him. And I promised to treat his sore . . . Ah, there you are, Esin. You had a good long rest."

"Yes." Rubbing sleepy eyes, she took a seat on the divan next to Ramses. "What has happened? Has my father—"

"Nothing has happened. You are perfectly safe. Are you hungry? There must be something left on that tray. Excuse me. I won't be long."

Ramses accompanied me. I had expected he or his father would do so, and on the whole I preferred Ramses to Emerson. His questions were not likely to be so provocative.

"I thought I'd better come along in case Mustafa's sore is located in a place Father would prefer you didn't examine," he explained.

"That is highly unlikely."

"I was joking, Mother."

"I know, my dear."

The skies were still overcast but the rain had stopped. It dripped in mournful cadence from the eaves of the arcades around the courtyard. I allowed Ramses to take my arm.

"I am of the opinion that you are right about Sethos's intentions," I said. "It was clever of you to reason it out."

"Too clever, perhaps? I'd hate to think my mind works along the same lines as his."

"Whatever his original intentions, they have almost certainly had the effect you described. Goodness, but this is a dreary place. There doesn't seem to be a soul about. Mustafa?"

"He's probably with the horses," Ramses said.

Mustafa heard our voices and emerged from the shed. "I was talking to the horses," he said. "They are fine animals. Is there something you lack, Sitt Hakim?"

"Not at the moment. I want to talk to you, Mustafa. And treat your sore . . . Where is it?"

Mustafa sat down on a bench and held out his foot. It was bare and callused and very dirty.

"You will have to wash it first," I said.

"Wash?" Mustafa repeated in astonishment.

Ramses, who appeared to be enjoying himself very much, fetched a bucket of water and we persuaded Mustafa to put his foot into it. I had brought a bar of Pear's soap with me, since I knew that commodity is not common in houses of the region. After a vigorous scrubbing the sore was apparent— an infected big toe, which he must have stubbed and then neglected. The alcohol made Mustafa's eyes pop.

"I am going to bandage your foot," I said, applying gauze and sticking plaster liberally. "But you must keep it clean. Change the bandage every day and wash it."

"Is that all?" Mustafa asked.

"That should—"

Ramses coughed loudly. "Will you say the proper words, Mother, or shall I?"

"Incantations are more in your line than mine," I replied in English. "Proceed."

Once that essential part of the treatment was completed, Mustafa was satisfied, and I got down to business.

"Did Sir Edward tell you where he was going?"

"No." Mustafa held up his foot and studied the bandage. "He took the mule."

"You have a mule?"

"Two. He took one."

"Did he say when he would be back?"

"No." Mustafa cogitated, his brow furrowing. "He said . . . what was it? Something about whiskey. That he would bring it to the Father of Curses."

"He's gone to Khan Yunus," Ramses said, as we left Mustafa admiring his bandaged foot.

"Not to Gaza?"

"Father is right, he wouldn't be such a fool. Not unless he had proof that Sethos was still there." He took hold of my arm and stopped me. "I don't believe we want to discuss Sahin Pasha in front of the girl, do we?"

"It would be wiser not to, I believe. The feelings of young persons are notoriously changeable. She is angry with him now, but if she believed he was in danger—"

"Yes, Mother, that is precisely what I had in mind."

When we returned to the salon Nefret looked up from the paper on which she was drawing. "Esin wanted to know about the latest fashions," she explained. "How is Mustafa's sore . . . whatever?"

"His toe," I replied. "A slight infection. Where is Emerson?"

"He said he was going to sit with Sethos." She chuckled. "I think he's looking for tobacco. He's run out."

Emerson did not find any tobacco. He came back looking even more perturbed than deprivation of that unhealthy substance could explain.

"Is he still sleeping?" I asked.

"Yes. He—er—doesn't look well."

"He isn't well."

"Is someone sick?" Esin asked.

I realized she was unaware of the latest arrival. "A—er—friend of ours. You know him as Ismail Pasha."

"He is here?" She jumped up and clapped her hands to her cheeks. "Why? Did my father send him? Has he come to take me back?"

"Goodness, but you have a one-track mind," I said. "He is a fugitive too. Your father became suspicious of him and he ran away."

"Oh." She thought it over and her face brightened. "Then I must thank him. He risked himself for me!"

"He is, after all, a gallant Englishman," Ramses drawled. "Much braver and more chivalrous than I."

"But you are younger and more beautiful," said Esin.

That took care of Ramses. He said no more.

The rest of us kept up a desultory conversation and the minutes dragged slowly by. There was much we could not say in Esin's presence, and I couldn't think of a reasonable excuse for getting rid of her. Sending her off to bed wouldn't work; she had slept most of the day.

Except for Selim, the rest of us had not. I persuaded Nefret to lie down and took Esin off into a corner so our voices would not disturb her. We found a common interest in women's rights, and I told her all about the suffrage movement and how I had marched with the suffragists and been seized by a large constable. She declared that she would have done the same, and kicked the constable as well.

Emerson sat in brooding silence, smoking Ramses's cigarettes and slipping out of the room periodically to look in on his brother. Ramses brooded too, over Nefret, sitting quietly beside her with his eyes fixed on her face. After a while I took Esin with me to the kitchen and showed her how to make tea. It was the first time she had ever performed such a menial chore, I believe. She was certainly clumsy enough. However, we got the tray upstairs without disaster.

Late in the afternoon the sun made its appearance, and shortly afterward Sethos made his. He was in a vile mood, which I had expected, and he had shaved his beard, which I had not expected. The strange gray-green eyes swept the room in a contemptuous and comprehensive survey. "Everybody here?" he inquired in his most offensive tone. "How nice."

I knew what concerned him most and I hastened to give him the news that would relieve his mind. "We believe Sir Edward has not gone to Gaza but to Khan Yunus."

"Oh?" He rubbed his chin. "Let us hope you are right."

"I am certain of it," I said. "Tea?"

"No." He flung himself down on the divan.

"You had better have some. Take it to him, Esin." I handed her the cup. "Lemon, no sugar, isn't that right?"

His eyes met mine and his tight mouth turned up at this reminder of the last time we had taken tea together. Unfortunately it reminded Emerson too. He knew what had happened at that meeting, for of course I had confided fully in him.

However, he confined his comments to a wordless grumble.

"Are you really Ismail Pasha?" the girl asked doubtfully. She stood beside him, the cup held carefully in both hands.

Sethos rose and took it from her. A smile transformed his haggard face, and the cultivated charm slipped onto him like a cloak. "Is it the absence of the beard that confused you? I am indeed the same man, and I am relieved to find you well and safe. My friends have looked after you?"

The charm was a little tattered, but it was good enough for Esin. "Oh, yes, but I was frightened for a while; there was fighting and we had to run away."

"Tell me about it," Sethos murmured.

Her account was accurate, on the whole, though she made a thrilling tale of it. Sethos listened attentively, his mobile countenance expressing admiration, astonishment, and distress at appropriate intervals, but I could tell she had not his complete attention. He was listening and waiting—as were we all.

The sunlight deepened to amber and then faded into gray, and there was still no sign of Sir Edward. Ramses lighted the lamps. I was about to suggest we do something about supper when the long-awaited sound of footsteps was heard and Sir Edward came into the room. In that first moment he had eyes only for his chief. Had I doubted the warmth of their friendship, the looks of relief on both faces would have proved it. Being English, they did not express their feelings.

"It's good to see you, sir," Sir Edward said coolly. "Mustafa told me you were here."

"*You* ought to have been here" was the equally cool reply. "Sit down and have a cup of tea."

"It's cold," I said, inspecting the sad dregs.

"I'll take it anyhow." Sir Edward dropped heavily onto the divan next to Emerson. "Sorry, Professor, I wasn't able to get your whiskey. The house—"

"Then we will have to settle for claret," said Sethos, going to the wine cabinet. "My supplies have become somewhat depleted. Amelia?"

"Yes," I said, answering both the spoken question and the unspoken order. "Esin, I suggest you—er—go to your room and rest."

"I don't need to rest," said the young person. "I am not tired."

"Then help Selim find us something to eat."

I gave Selim a wink and a nod. As a rule this was all Selim needed, but this time I had to give him a little poke, for he was not looking at me. His intent black eyes were fixed on Sethos.

"Your pardon, Sitt Hakim," he said, starting.

I repeated the suggestion. He nodded obediently, and got Esin to go with him by requesting the details of her daring escape from her father's house. "Such courage," I heard him say, as they left the room. "Such cleverness!"

Sethos turned from the cabinet, the bottle in one hand and the corkscrew in the other. "Report," he said curtly.

"The town's quiet," Sir Edward said. "Less damage than I had expected. The house is guarded by several soldiers and they're scouring the countryside looking for you people. According to the worthy citizens of Khan Yunus, you simply vanished into thin air, like the djinn you are reputed to be. The military hasn't accepted that, though." He took the glass Sethos handed him and went on, "They haven't made up their minds whether you were abducted by force or went off on your own, for purposes of your own. Either way, they want you."

Ramses took the bottle from Sethos, who had neglected the rest of us in his concern for his aide, and poured wine for Nefret and me.

"What about Gaza?" Sethos asked.

"The place is shut up tighter than a prison." Sir Edward sipped his wine appreciatively. "I made contact with one of our lads—Hassan. He'd just got back from an attempt to enter the city by his usual route, but what he saw made him veer off. They're stopping everyone."

"Shutting the barn door after the horse is stolen," I said with a smile.

"Ha," said Emerson, motioning Ramses to fill his glass. "Any news of Sahin Pasha?"

Sir Edward shook his head, and Sethos said, "It will take them a while to decide how to deal with him. The most sensible course of action would be to execute him and announce he'd been assassinated by the vile British."

"That was your plan, then," I said. "To make him appear guilty of treason."

"I didn't have a plan when I started out," Sethos said snappishly. "My orders were to remove him—pleasant little euphemism, isn't it? One learns to take advantage of unexpected events. We were damned lucky. All of us."

"It took more than luck," Ramses said grudgingly. His uncle gave him a mocking bow.

"Selim can't keep the girl away for long," I said. "And I certainly don't want her to know her father may be under arrest and facing death. We must decide what we are going to do with her."

"Quite right, Amelia," said my brother-in-law. "You'll have to take her back to Cairo, and the sooner, the better. The sooner you are all back in Cairo, the better."

"What about you?" I asked. "And Sir Edward?"

"Don't concern yourself about us. As soon as it's light I want you all to return to Khan Yunus. That will stop them searching the whole damned neighborhood and finding this place, which wouldn't be convenient for me. Make your preparations to leave Khan Yunus and get the hell away. You'll have to come up with some story to explain the girl. The military mustn't know who she is, or take her from you."

"As if I would leave a girl of eighteen with a troop of soldiers," I said with a sniff. "What do we do with her when we reach Cairo?"

"Take her to an address I will give you." He glanced at Ramses. "Memorize it; don't write it down."

"That's it, then," said Emerson, hearing Selim and Esin returning. "You have nothing more to tell us?"

Sethos made sure we had no chance to ask for more. After a scratch meal he went off with Sir Edward, instructing us to get our gear together and be ready for an early departure. We did not see him again until morning.

It was still dark when we gathered in the courtyard, with only the light of our torches to guide our steps. The horses were waiting.

"Good-bye," said Sethos. "A safe journey."

He shook Emerson's hand and mine. "When will we see you again?" I asked.

"When you least expect me, Amelia dear. That's my trademark." He smiled at me. "You'll hear from me soon, I promise. Good-bye, Nefret. Try and keep Ramses out of mischief."

"I always do." She stood on tiptoe and kissed him on the cheek. "Take care of yourself. Sir Edward, try and keep him out of mischief."

"Don't I get a kiss?" that gentleman inquired.

She laughed at him, and gave him her hand. "Good luck. And thank you."

We reached Khan Yunus by midmorning and went at once to the house, followed by a throng of idlers. The gate was closed, and there were two soldiers guarding it. They snapped to attention, rifles raised, when they saw us, and then one of them exclaimed, "It's them!"

"Grammar, young man," I said. "It is indeed we. Let us pass, if you please."

Selim went at once to his beloved motorcar. "They have stolen two of the tires!" he cried in anguished tones.

"That's easily remedied," said Emerson, helping me to dismount. "Come along, Selim, you can play with the motorcar later."

A quick inspection assured us that the house was deserted

and that a good many items were missing, including the best part of "the favorite's" elegant wardrobe. "Can't be helped," said Emerson. "Lucky we had everything we needed with us. Let us go to the mak'ad. I expect we will be receiving a visit soon."

"Yes, our arrival will have been reported," I agreed. "Esin, I want you to stay here in the harem."

"Why?" she demanded.

"You are an enemy alien," Nefret said. "If the soldiers find out you are here, they will take you away."

I hadn't intended to be quite so blunt about it, but the warning had the desired effect. Esin's rounded cheeks paled.

"We won't let them take you," Ramses said quickly. "Just stay out of sight and keep quiet."

"I would very much like a bath," I said. "But that will have to wait until we round up a few of the servants. In the meantime, what about a nice hot cup of tea?"

The inefficiency of the military was disappointing. It took them an hour to react to the news that we had returned. The open arches of the mak'ad constituted an excellent observation post; we were sipping a second cup of tea when he burst into the courtyard, kicked an unfortunate chicken out of his path, and came to a stop, staring. Emerson leaned over the rail and called to him.

"Up here, Cartright. Join us."

"We ought to have expected it would be he," I remarked. "He appears to be in quite an unhappy frame of mind."

Cartright took the stairs two at a time. His face was flushed and his mustache looked as if he had been chewing on it.

"You're here," he gasped. "All of you."

"Obviously," I replied. "Nefret, is there more hot water? I believe Major Cartright could do with a cup of tea. Do sit down, Major."

The young man collapsed onto a chair and passed a hand-kerchief over his face. "Where have you been? We've been searching for days."

"Not that long, surely," I said. "Drink your tea. We have decided to take advantage of your kind offer to facilitate our return to Cairo. We will need petrol, water, food, and two new tires. Is there anything else, Emerson?"

Leaning against the wall, arms folded and lips twitching, Emerson shook his head. "Not that I know of. Continue, Peabody, you seem to have the situation well in hand."

"We would like to leave tomorrow morning," I explained. "You seem to have frightened our servants away. Persuade—persuade, I said—them to return. We have clothing to be washed and meals to be prepared."

"Mrs. Emerson . . . please." Cartright waved away the cup I had offered. "Just stop talking, will you? Professor, I want to know where the devil—"

"Language, language," said Emerson. "There are ladies present. As for answering your questions, sir, I am not subject to your orders."

"General Chetwode—"

"Nor his. I will report to whom I see fit and when I see fit. In Cairo, to be precise. Are you going to get us the supplies we need or must I go over your head?"

"I . . . yes. That is, I will get them. And go with you."

"There won't be room in the motorcar," said Emerson with finality. "Oh—I almost forgot. The horses. Fine animals. They are in the stable."

Cartright sat bolt upright. "Then it was you who . . . One of the troopers swore there was a woman in the party, but—"

"Me," said Nefret with a smile. "The poor boy wants his Mary back, I expect. Tell him she has been well cared for and that I thank him for the loan."

"That is all you have to say?" His frowning visage turned from Nefret to Emerson.

"It is all any of us have to say," Emerson assured him. "When may we expect those supplies?"

Major Cartright's countenance underwent a series of contortions. He had been sorely tried, but knew perfectly well that any attempt to detain Emerson against his will would result in an uproar that would reverberate through every level of British officialdom.

"I'm not certain I can obtain everything you need today," he muttered.

"Oh, I think you can," said Emerson, showing his teeth.

"Yes, sir. Then . . . I will see you in Cairo?" He looked at Ramses, who had remained silent.

"No doubt," said Ramses.

"You are the one he would like to question," I said, after Cartright had taken his departure. "I expect he will go haring off to General Chetwode and demand we be held here."

"Chetwode has no authority to detain us," said Emerson. He rubbed irritably at the cast, which was looking somewhat the worse for wear. "Nefret, can't I have this cursed thing off?"

"Not yet, Father. As soon as we get to Cairo I'll have a look at it."

Selim returned from his inspection of the motorcar to report that everything seemed to be in order, and went off to commandeer some household assistance, since I did not suppose Major Cartright would consider that matter worthy of his attention. It had begun to rain, so we retreated into the room behind the open mak'ad, where we had left our baggage.

"We may as well unpack our bundles," I said. "What with all our comings and goings, I have lost track of precisely what we still have. I gave my bar of soap to Mustafa, but here is my medical kit and my parasol—"

"You won't need that, Mrs. Emerson. You will not be leaving the house just yet."

I had missed one of the secret rooms. Unlike the makhba under the floor of the harem, this was a small hidden chamber whose door resembled that of a wall cupboard. He looked much the same as he had when I had seen him before, a big man with a grizzled beard and shoulders almost as impressive as those of Emerson. He had a pistol in one hand and a knife in the other.

"Sahin Pasha, I presume," I said, after a slight catch of breath. "We ought to have anticipated that a clever man would comprehend the gravity of his predicament and escape before he could be apprehended. On the run, are you?"

"One might call it that. Now, if you don't mind—"

"Coming here was also a clever move," I mused. "There is a saying that the safest place for a criminal is in the police station."

"Is there? No, my young friend, don't take another step. I want all of you close together."

Ramses stopped. "You daren't use that gun," he said. "The sound of a shot will bring the servants and a dozen soldiers."

"If I am forced to fire, there will be more than one shot and by the time your assistants arrive it will be too late for some of you. There is no need for that. All I want is my daughter."

"Let us discuss this calmly," I said. "How do you propose to get her away from here, against her will, without killing all of us, which is, as you must see, impractical?"

A rather jolly rumble of laughter emerged from his parted lips. "Mrs. Emerson, it is a pleasure to meet you at last. I know you are hoping that your fascinating conversation will distract me. It won't. But since you ask, I have already dealt with Esin. She is lying bound and gagged on the divan in the ka'ah. I found this hiding place last night. As soon as I have persuaded you to enter it, I will take her and go."

"Go where?" I demanded. "Back into the lion's den? You are being unrealistic if you believe you can convince your erstwhile friends that you are still to be trusted."

The man's strong jaw hardened. "I will prove my good faith by returning, with my daughter."

It would require more than that. He knew it, and so did I. But if he could recapture the prisoner he had let escape . . . If he could herd us one by one into the secret room, leaving Ramses till last . . .

"Go on," Sahin said, gesturing with the pistol. "You first, Mrs. Emerson."

"No," I exclaimed. "Emerson, do you see what—"

"It's all right, Mother," Ramses said quietly. "I think he's bluffing. I wonder how many bullets are left in that pistol? Enough to stop all of us?"

"A good point." Emerson nodded. "I call your bluff, sir. We are not sheep, to be herded into a pen. The girl stays with us, but we will give you . . . oh, let us say an hour . . . to get away."

They measured one another, two men of commanding presence and stature. The Turk said slowly, "You would do that?"

"As the lesser of two evils. Your usefulness to your government has been destroyed. This way no one will be injured. You can trust us to look after the child, and when the war is over you may be reunited with her."

"The word of an Englishman?" Sahin Pasha murmured.

"Don't be foolish," Ramses said urgently. "There are two—four, I mean—of us. Hand over the gun."

Sahin smiled wryly. "Four? Ah well, it seems I have no choice. You were correct. The gun isn't loaded. I had to fight my way out of Gaza."

"Drop it, then," Ramses said. He took a step forward and held out his hand. "Or give it to me."

His eyes were fixed on the pistol. It might be a double bluff; we could not be certain, with a man so crafty. Sahin held it out—and then the knife flashed and Ramses stumbled back and fell, blood spurting from his side. Nefret flung herself down beside him.

"You never learn, do you?" Sahin shook his head regretfully. "You really ought to give up this line of work, my boy."

Emerson had not stirred. "Nefret?" he asked softly.

Her quick surgeon's hands had slowed the flow of blood. "It's . . . not too bad," she said.

"But now, you see, there are only three of you," Sahin said. "And I lied when I said the gun was not loaded. Do I take the ladies on next?"

"Yes," I said, and swung my parasol. It was one of my

better efforts, if I do say so. The gun flew out of Sahin's hand and fell with a clatter onto the tiled floor.

"Ah," Emerson breathed. "Well done, Peabody. Get the gun."

"Take my parasol, then." I pulled out the little sword and forced the weapon into Emerson's hand. Sahin Pasha let out a guffaw. Emerson swore, but he got the blade up just in time to parry a wicked cut at his good arm.

"I lied again," said the Turk, grinning. "The gun is empty."

"We will see about that," I replied. I pointed the weapon out the window and squeezed the trigger. There was no explosion, only a click. "Curse it," I remarked.

"This is so entertaining I hate to end it," said Sahin Pasha. "Professor, I admire you, I respect you, and I do not want to injure you. Anyhow, my reputation would never be the same if I overcame a man armed with a parasol who has only one serviceable arm. I accept your offer. Put down the . . ." A gurgle of amusement escaped him. "The umbrella."

"Oh, come, don't insult my intelligence," said Emerson in exasperation. "You have no intention of giving yourself up, and I have no intention of allowing you to take my son prisoner again. I cannot imagine how you could accomplish it, but I do not underestimate you. En garde."

Ramses pulled himself to a sitting position. "Be careful, Father. He doesn't—"

"Fight like a gentleman? Well, well. Neither do I."

He bent his knee and lunged. A cry of alarm escaped me. It was almost certainly the most ineffective move he could have made. The blade of the sword was only three inches longer than that of Sahin's knife. The Turk didn't even bother to parry it. One quick step backward took him out of range, and as Emerson straightened, staggering a little, the Turk's knife drove at his side.

It sank with a crunch into the plaster encasing Emerson's raised forearm and stuck, just long enough. Emerson dropped the parasol and hit the other man in the stomach. Rather below the stomach, to be accurate.

"Oh, Emerson," I gasped. "Oh, my dear! That was magnificent!"

"Most ungentlemanly," said my husband, contemplating the writhing, wheezing form of his foe. "But I was never much good with a parasol."

The capture of the chief of the Turkish secret service ended any doubts the military might have entertained about letting us leave. General Chetwode himself called to congratulate us, accompanied by several of his staff. We had quite a time getting rid of them.

"Medals again," Emerson grumbled. "They seem to think we intended this all along."

"You encouraged them to think so," Ramses said. At Nefret's insistence he was reclining on one of the divans. She had had to put a few stitches into the cut, which had bled copiously. "It was inspired lying, Father."

"At least we got a bottle of whiskey out of them," Emerson said complacently. "Much more useful than medals. Here, my boy, this will put a little color into your face."

"I would like some too," said Esin.

"Spirits are not suitable for young ladies," I said, sipping my own whiskey appreciatively. It had been quite a busy day, what with one thing and another, and I was not in a good humor with the girl. After we freed her she carried on quite extravagantly, and she had accepted the news of her father's capture with unbecoming equanimity.

"Aren't you at all concerned about your father?" I asked. "What will happen to him?"

"He is a prisoner of war," Emerson said. "Do you want to see him before we leave? I can probably arrange that."

"No." She shivered. "He tried to take me away. He says he loves me, but he will not allow me to do what I want. Is that love?"

"Sometimes," Nefret said.

The silence that followed was broken by a penetrating shriek from outside the house. I could not make out all the words, but there were references to the will of Allah and the blessings of various prophets, up to and including the greatest, that is, Mohammed. When Sir Edward had arrived on the scene, I did not know, but he must have seen the military go off with their prisoner. This was his farewell to us, and none of us doubted that his chief would soon be informed of the news.

Emerson smiled. "Clever beggar, isn't he?"

Selim, who had missed all the excitement and was still brooding about it, said under his breath, "Beggar. Yes. He is a clever man. And so is—" He broke off, with a glance at me.

"We will talk about it later, Selim," I said, as softly as he had done.

"As you say, Sitt. So—it is over?"

"Yes. It is over."

PART THREE

· ·

The Hand of the God

Twelve

Sped on by every assistance the military could provide, we reached Cairo in less than two days. Selim left us off at Shepheard's just in time for tea. He was to take the motorcar on to a prearranged location and leave it. What would become of it after that I did not know and did not ask; I was only happy to be rid of the thing, for I had feared Emerson— and Selim—would want to keep it. They did want to, very badly; but Emerson admitted it might be a trifle difficult to explain how we had acquired it.

The terrace was crowded, and our appearance aroused a certain amount of ill-bred attention, even from acquaintances who ought not have been surprised at anything we did. I heard Mrs. Pettigrew's trumpeting voice address her husband: "There are the Emersons again, Hector, looking even more disreputable than usual. It is positively embarrassing to be acquainted with them." I waved my parasol at her in a conspicuous manner.

There was some justice in her description; two days' motoring on military roads does not improve an individual's appearance, and our wardrobes had been deficient to start with. However, Ramses and Emerson in Arab dress, Nefret and I in sadly crumpled European attire, and Esin, enveloped in veils, as Nefret's maidservant, occasioned no comment from the well-trained staff of Shepheard's, and I was not surprised to learn our old rooms had been reserved for us. The luggage we had left was brought to us, so for the first time in days we were able to clean up and dress in proper clothing. There were a number of messages, most of them from Cyrus or Katherine, asking when we would return to Luxor. They had no news to report, except that Jumana was still sulking (Katherine's word) or grieving (Cyrus's).

"We had better take the train tomorrow night," I said.

Emerson grunted. He had not found the message he hoped for.

"What's your hurry, Peabody? I thought you'd want to shop and do your usual social round."

"Replenishment of certain supplies would be expedient," I agreed. "But I can accomplish that tomorrow. What do you say, Nefret? Do you want to spend some time at the hospital?"

Nefret was watching Ramses, who had taken up the latest issue of the *Egyptian Gazette*. "I may run in for an hour or so, Mother, but I would just as soon go on to Luxor at once. Ramses?"

"I am ready whenever you are" was the reply.

"Is Ramses concealing something?" Emerson asked, when he and I were alone. "I expected he would be anxious to get back to work, but he sounded almost indifferent."

"I am pleased to find you more sensitive to your son's feelings, Emerson. In this case I can interpret them for you."

"Pray do," said Emerson coldly.

"He was only exhibiting his usual consideration for the opinions of others, particularly those of Nefret. In fact I believe he would like to put this whole business behind him. You know," I continued, sorting garments that required washing, "that when he is in the thick of the action, he rather enjoys it. He doesn't have time to think about what he is doing. Later, when there is leisure for introspection, his overly active conscience reproaches him for employing and even enjoying violence. He is—"

"I'm sorry I asked," Emerson snarled. "I might have known you'd start talking psychology. When are you going to deliver the girl? I'm not sure I like that part of it. How do we know those bastards won't bully or mistreat her?"

"That is another thing that is bothering Ramses," I said. "And do not berate me for talking psychology—you are as sentimental about the girl as he is. As for me, I shall be glad to be rid of the responsibility. You may rest assured, however, that I will not leave her until I am certain she will be treated kindly. I will take her to Ismailiya first thing tomorrow morning."

Emerson did not accompany us. He was afraid Esin would cry and plead. I thought she might too, so I did not attempt to change his mind. I could not dissuade Ramses from coming, however. He had that stubborn set to his mouth.

Esin was wearing one of Nefret's frocks. She was somewhat stouter than Nefret, but this dress had a loose fit and an adjustable belt. It did not become her. I had not told her what was in store for her, in part because I do not believe in anticipating trouble and in part because I wasn't certain myself. It all depended on what, and whom, we found at that address in Ismailiya.

It looked respectable, at any rate—a house set in its own gardens, built in the European style of the previous century. Esin let Ramses help her out of the cab and looked admiringly at the house.

"It is very modern. Are we paying a visit?"

"Yes," I said.

The door was opened by a manservant, who led us into a nicely furnished sitting room. We were expected, it seemed; he had not asked our names, and we had only been waiting a few minutes before a lady entered the room—the lady Smith had introduced as his sister.

"Mrs. Bayes!" I exclaimed. "So you are—"

"Very pleased to see you again," the lady cut in smoothly. "Mr. Emerson, a pleasure. And this is Miss Sahin? Welcome, my dear. Did Mrs. Emerson tell you you are to stay with me for a while?"

"Am I? Must I?" She gave Ramses an imploring look. "Am I a prisoner of war too?"

"Not in the least," Mrs. Bayes said heartily. "You are an honored guest. Come along and I will show you your room. I think you will like it. I know you came away in a hurry, so perhaps later we can shop for some new clothes. There are many fine shops in the Muski."

"I saw them," Esin said slowly. She looked from Mrs. Bayes, who was holding out her hand and smiling sweetly, to me—I bared my teeth, not nearly so sweetly—and then to Ramses. "I am to go with her? Will I see you again?"

He had known it would be easier for her, and for me, if he was there to reassure her. I saw him brace himself for a round of comforting clichés.

"You must have known you could not stay with us, Esin. Mrs. Bayes will take good care of you, and one day . . . one day . . . uh . . ."

"We will meet again? You will not forget me?"

"Never," Ramses assured her.

"I will never forget you." She extended her hand at an awkward angle. Resignedly, Ramses kissed it. "One never knows what the future will bring, Esin," he said. "We will think of you often, and if you ever need our help, you have only to ask."

Her black eyes took on a dreamy look. "I read a book, an English book, where the lady sent a red rose to the man she loved, the man she had given up for duty. If I send you a rose, will you come?"

Ramses gathered himself for a final, valiant effort. "From the ends of the earth, Esin."

Mrs. Bayes had followed the exchange with poorly concealed amusement. "Well done," she murmured, and put a friendly arm round Esin. "Do not prolong the pain of farewell, my dear. Will you two wait here, please? Someone wishes to speak with you."

She led the girl out. Ramses blew out his breath. "Is it all right, do you think? Mrs. Bayes seems kind."

"And she has a sense of humor. That is a good sign. You did splendidly, Ramses."

The servant entered with a tray and poured coffee. "Very conventional," I said, accepting the cup he handed me. "Do you want to guess the identity of the person who wishes to speak to us?"

"No need to guess," Ramses said. "He's been behind this all along."

It was indeed the Honorable Algernon Bracegirdle-Boisdragon whom the servant ushered in. He came straight to me, his hands extended, his thin lips stretched in a smile. "Mrs. Emerson. What can I say?"

"A great deal, I trust. I do not know that I care to take your hand."

"I cannot say I blame you." He turned to Ramses, who had risen, and his smile faded. "Sit down, please. I heard of your injury. You may not want to take my hand either, but I must express my thanks and admiration. You accomplished everything we hoped, and more."

"It wasn't I, as you are well aware," Ramses said. "You knew when you sent me after Ismail Pasha that he was no traitor. He was acting with your knowledge and under your orders."

"The danger to him was real," the other man said soberly. "Military intelligence knew nothing of our plans. Call it interservice rivalry if you like, but they can't be trusted, and they disapprove of what they consider our unorthodox methods."

"So," I said, "your group is distinct from all those departments with confusing initials and meaningless numbers?"

"They are confusing, aren't they?" Smith agreed with a sardonic smile. "MO, EMSIB, MIa, b, and c . . . We don't go in for that sort of thing, Mrs. Emerson. Ours is a long and honorable history, going all the way to the sixteenth century. Cardinal Wolsey and Thomas Cromwell—"

"The Tudors, of course," I said with a sniff. "They *would* be the ones to foster spying and subterfuge. Spare us the history lesson, please."

"As you like. You are correct in assuming that our mutual friend was following our agenda. He had several purposes; removing Sahin Pasha was only one of them. Another was to investigate the network in Constantinople. We had warned MI that the man running that group was a double agent. They didn't believe us. Sethos got rid of the fellow by persuading the Turks that he had betrayed them—which was true. The trouble with him is that he plays his roles too well! I learned that my bumble-headed counterparts in military intelligence were planning to assassinate him. The only way of preventing that was to persuade you to go after him. If I had told them who he was and what he was doing, the word would have spread, and sooner or later it would have reached the ears of the enemy."

Ramses shook his head doubtfully. "Your solution was somewhat chancy. What if they hadn't accepted me?"

Smith leaned forward, his hands clasped. "You continue to astonish me. Surely you know that your reputation is second only to that of your—that of Sethos. There's not an intelligence officer in Egypt who wouldn't give his right hand to enlist you. Cartright is an ass—military to the core, and he's held a grudge against you since you fooled him several years ago, but he knew you were the only man who could get into Gaza undetected."

"And get Lieutenant Chetwode in. I did wonder," Ramses said deliberately, "whether the whole point of that operation was to convince the Turks of the genuineness of Ismail's conversion."

Under his steady gaze, Smith shifted uncomfortably. "You don't trust any of us, do you? The only way that scheme could have succeeded was to have the Turks identify you and/or Chetwode as British agents. Believe it or not, we don't risk our people so callously."

"Not when they are as valuable as my son," I said.

"Touché, Mrs. Emerson. You are correct, of course. Cartright's group isn't especially subtle; they wanted Ismail dead, and they were willing to hazard two men to accomplish it. To do them justice, none of them has the least idea of the difficulties involved in operating behind enemy lines; they still think of Johnny Turk as incompetent and cowardly."

"But you knew," I snapped. "And you let them send Ramses—"

"I had every confidence in his ability to get in and out undetected."

"I'm flattered," said Ramses, his lip curling.

"Easy for me to say, you mean? You have every right to feel that way. But the last I heard, Cartright had agreed to your proposal of a reconnaissance and nothing more. It never occurred to me that even Cartright would be stupid enough to go ahead with his little assassination attempt. And, naturally, I assumed you would come back with information that would prove Ismail wasn't Sethos, even if you had to invent it. The last thing we wanted was to have you fall into the hands of the Turks—particularly those of Sahin. He'd been suspicious of Ismail from the start, and he hoped that Ismail would betray himself by trying to free you."

Ramses's tight lips relaxed into a faint smile. "He's a clever man, but trying to stay one step ahead of Sethos is a hopeless job. Using the girl was brilliant."

"If that hadn't worked, he'd have got you out some other way," Smith said brusquely. "Whatever it took."

"He told you that?" I asked.

"He didn't have to tell me. I know him rather well. So. Is there anything else you want to know?"

He had already said more than he had meant to say, and Ramses was looking decidedly uncomfortable. I rose. "Only your assurance that the young woman will be treated well."

"We don't war on women, Mrs. Emerson. She'll be questioned courteously but intensively, and I expect we will get quite a lot out of her; she's an inquisitive creature, I understand. I imagine she'll enjoy being the center of attention."

After a moment he added, "I cannot insist that you refrain from mentioning her to M1—or any of those other confusing numbers—but I assure you she will be happier with us than she would be with them."

"They will find out eventually, won't they? Her father knows she is with us."

"If Sahin Pasha is as intelligent a man as I believe him to be, he will not volunteer any more information than is necessary to keep them from hanging him." He added, with a rather attractive smile, "With any luck, he should be able to hold them off until the war is over."

"May that day be soon in coming," I said with a sigh.

"Amen," said Mr. Smith.

"One more thing," I said, drawing on my gloves.

"Yes, of course. He asked me to give you his regards and tell you he will 'turn up,' as he put it, before long."

"Thank you."

"Not at all." He himself showed us to the door. "If there is ever anything I can do for you, or any member of your family—"

"The kindest thing you can do for us is leave us strictly alone." I swept past him in my best style.

"All the same," I said to Ramses, when we were again in the cab, "I don't think as badly of him as I do of some of the others. Cartright lied to us. Chetwode did not act without his authorization, did he?"

"Chetwode is another military pedant; he wouldn't dare act without orders. They don't think of it as lying, you know. Expediency, necessity, 'whatever it takes to get the job done.' Chetwode fooled me, though," Ramses added, in chagrin. "That air of inept innocence was put on. He couldn't have escaped from Gaza so handily if he had been as incompetent as he seemed."

"He counted on your sense of decency and loyalty to assist him," I said.

"Naïveté, rather. Sahin was right, I'll never get the hang of the business."

I took his hand and gave it a gentle squeeze. "Decency and loyalty have not prevented you from succeeding."

Ramses shrugged the compliment away. "It's over, anyhow, thank God. I'm looking forward to seeing the family again."

"There is one thing I didn't ask," I said.

"Only one? And what is that?"

"Sethos's real name. Bracegirdle-Boisdragon must know."

The lines furrowing Ramses's brow disappeared. "I suppose he must, he admitted having examined various records, which would presumably include a birth certificate. I hadn't given the matter much thought."

"Hadn't you wondered at all? I have. It couldn't be Thomas, could it? After his father?"

"It doesn't suit him."

"Well, but when one gives a newborn infant a name, one cannot predict how it will turn out."

Ramses gave me a curious look.

"As in my case," he suggested.

"Walter doesn't suit you," I agreed. "But no one ever calls you that. William? Frederick? Albert?"

"Robert," said Ramses, entering into the spirit of the thing. "No, something more distinctive. Perhaps his mother was fond of poetry. Byron? Wordsworth?"

The subject entertained us for the rest of the drive. I was happy to see I had got Ramses's mind off the recent unpleasantness. He had done his duty with regard to Esin, not even flinching at that appalling promise—"from the ends of the earth" indeed!—and was more at ease about her. Getting back to Luxor and to the dig would complete the cure.

When we returned to the hotel we found both Nefret and Emerson missing. She had left a message for Ramses, telling him she had gone to the hospital and promising to be back in time for luncheon. There was no message from Emerson.

"Where do you suppose he has gone?" I asked, in considerable irritation.

"To the railroad station, perhaps," Ramses suggested. "I believe he wants to take the train this evening."

"I trust that is agreeable to you and Nefret, Ramses. Did he do you the courtesy of asking?"

"So far as I am concerned, the sooner we leave Cairo, the better."

True to her word, Nefret turned up in good time, to report that all was well at the hospital and that she was perfectly agreeable to a departure that evening. I suspected her motives were the same as mine; I wanted no more encounters with General Murray or any of his lot. We had done our duty and more, we had handed over a very important prisoner to the military, and we had reported (some of) our activities to General Chetwode. They could ask no more of us; but they probably would, if we stayed in Cairo.

"Isn't Father back yet?" she asked. "I made him go with me to the hospital so that I could X-ray his arm and replace the cast, but that was hours ago."

Another hour passed with no sign of Emerson. Nefret suggested we order coffee and biscuits, adding with a rueful smile, "My appetite has become outrageous since Gaza. I suppose it's because we ate such peculiar things at such peculiar hours."

"No doubt," I said.

The minutes dragged by. Finally I heard the unmistakable thud of Emerson's heavy steps, and the door was flung open. A cry of indignation burst from my lips.

"Emerson, how many times must I tell you not to use that cast like a battering ram? And why aren't you wearing your coat? And your cravat? And—"

Emerson glanced in mild surprise at his arm. "Forgot," he said, tossing his crumpled coat onto the floor. "Coffee? Good. How did it go?"

"How did what . . . ? Oh, Esin. It is all settled and she is in good hands. Where the devil have you been?"

Emerson sipped his coffee. Ramses leaned forward, forearms resting on his knees. "Shall I hazard a guess?"

"If you like," said Emerson, rolling his eyes at me.

"Hilmiya."

"Oh, Emerson, you didn't!" I cried.

"I had to, didn't I? What the devil, the crafty bastard did me a favor—two favors, in fact."

"How did you get into the camp?" Ramses asked curiously.

"Walked up to the gate and announced myself," said his father, holding out his cup for me to refill it. "El-Gharbi was not surprised to see me—he had heard of our return. He seems to hear everything. He wanted me to pay him for the damage to the motorcar."

"Did you?" Nefret asked, torn between amusement and disgust.

"No. His people had stolen the thing, hadn't they? I assured him," said Emerson, with another wary glance at me, "that I would speak on his behalf. Exile, to his village in Upper Egypt, would satisfy him and settle my debt."

"Oh, dear," I murmured. "Well, Emerson, you acted according to your lights, I suppose. Go and clean up, it is past time for luncheon."

I followed him into our room, for I knew that if I did not assist his ablutions he would get the cast wet.

"I trust el-Gharbi was properly appreciative," I said, assisting him to remove his shirt.

"In his fashion. He said something rather strange."

"What? Let me do that, Emerson."

I took the dripping washcloth from his hand.

" 'The young serpent also has poisoned fangs.' "

"I beg your pardon, Emerson?"

"Those were his precise words, Peabody. I haven't the vaguest idea what they mean, but it has the ring of a warning, doesn't it?"

"Hmm. Perhaps he was referring to Jamil." I put the washcloth down and picked up a towel.

"The warning comes a bit late," said Emerson. "But that is how soothsayers and fortune-tellers and such individuals make their reputations, by predicting what has already happened. The devil with it, and el-Gharbi. I stopped by the railroad station and made reservations. We will take the train tonight."

I did not wire ahead. We would probably arrive before the telegram was delivered, and Fatima always kept the house in perfect order. The happy surprise I had planned for her and the others was spoiled, however, by the network of gossip that encompasses Luxor. By the time we reached the house, the whole family was on the veranda waiting for us. Sennia darted at Ramses, shouting, "See how much taller and stronger I am?"

Before any of us could stop her, she had thrown her arms round him in one of her gigantic hugs. We always pretended to be left breathless by her strength, but she knew at once that his gasp of pain was not feigned, and began fussing and apologizing. She made him sit down and lifted both his feet onto a stool.

"You've been and got yourselves into trouble again," said Gargery sternly. "Was it that Master Criminal chap? I trust, sir and madam, that he isn't going to turn up here. We've got enough problems without that."

"What sort of problems?" I asked.

"There is no trouble, Sitt," said Fatima, with a reproachful glance at Gargery. "Rest and I will bring tea."

Gargery would not be silenced. "It's mostly these young women, madam. That girl that was working for Miss Nefret has been round saying you promised to find her a husband. She's got a chap in mind and wants you to pin him down before he can get away."

We all laughed except Sennia, who was still fussing over Ramses. "She didn't put it that way, surely," Nefret said.

"She keeps coming round," said Gargery gloomily. "And then there's Jumana. Won't eat, won't talk, won't work. It puts a person off, madam, just seeing that gloomy face. And Mrs. Vandergelt—"

"Enough, Gargery," Emerson snarled. "Can't we have a single day of peace and quiet? No one is desperately ill, no one is dead, no one is missing? Good. Mrs. Emerson will deal with these minor difficulties in due time."

"Thank you, my dear," I said.

The sarcasm was wasted on Emerson. "Good to be back," he declared with great satisfaction. "No use asking Gargery how things are going at Deir el Medina, but I expect Vandergelt will be here before long, with his own list of complaints. Never a dull moment, eh? Sennia, you haven't given me a kiss. My arm is bothering me quite a lot."

Cyrus was courteous enough not to disturb us for the greater part of the day. We were sitting on the veranda admiring the lovely sunset colors, as the calls of the muezzins drifted across the desert in a melodious medley, when he turned up, riding Queenie.

"Figured I'd arrive in time for drinks," he remarked, handing the reins to the stableman. "Sure good to have you folks back. I hear Ramses has had another little—er—accident. I don't suppose I should ask where you've been and what you've been up to."

"No," said Emerson. He handed Cyrus a glass.

It was the answer Cyrus had expected. He accepted it, and the glass of whiskey, with a smile. "Sure have missed you. Maybe you can do something with Jumana. She's just wasting away, poor little girl."

"No, she is not," I assured him. "Nefret and I both examined her this afternoon. She is somewhat off-color, since she hasn't left the house for days, but she hasn't lost an ounce."

"But Fatima said—"

"She has only picked at her meals. That means she is eating on the sly. I prescribed a particularly nasty-tasting tonic."

"She's been putting it on?" Cyrus demanded.

"It's not that simple, Cyrus," Nefret said thoughtfully. "Her unhappiness is genuine. She isn't deliberately deceiving us, but I think—and Heaven knows I am no expert—that her natural youthful optimism is engaged in a mental struggle with her sense of guilt. I honestly don't know whether to slap her or coddle her."

"Put her to work," said Emerson. "Always the best medicine. How are things going at Deir el Medina, Vandergelt?"

"'Bout the same. Found two more tombs. Empty."

"You haven't broken your promise to me, I hope," I said.

"I haven't been in the southwest wadis, if that's what you mean. But if you think I've forgotten what that young villain said, you're wrong. I haven't been able to sleep, wondering what he meant. 'The hand of the god.' What god? Where?" Cyrus held out his empty glass. In silent sympathy, Emerson refilled it. He had no patience with psychology, but this distress he could understand.

Cyrus went on, in mounting passion, "I even went back into that darned shrine—the one where we found the statue of Amon last year. Well, he's a god, isn't he? Bertie and I examined every inch of the darned room. The walls and floor are solid."

"Bah," said Emerson. "Stop wasting time on fantasies, Vandergelt."

"Don't be a hypocrite, Emerson," I said. "We have all been speculating and guessing and theorizing. It is a pretty little problem. Supposing Jamil was not trying to mislead or tantalize us, which may well have been the case, there are a good many gods shown on a good many wall surfaces in Thebes. Deir el Bahri, Medinet Habu, every tomb on the West Bank— What is it, Cyrus?"

"Excuse me, Amelia, I didn't mean to interrupt. You just reminded me. This little piece of news ought to get your attention, Emerson," he added, with a grimace at my husband. "Give you three guesses who has started an excavation in the Valley of the Kings."

Emerson's look of lofty indifference turned to a scowl. "Without official permission? Confound it, Vandergelt—"

"Not the Albions?" I exclaimed.

"Might have known you'd hit it on the head first time,"

said Cyrus. "You're both right. It's Joe and his family, and they don't have official permission."

"And you let them?" Emerson demanded.

"I notified Cairo. That was all I could do, as Joe gleefully pointed out to me. I haven't got the authority to stop them."

"Where in the Valley?" Ramses asked.

"In that southern branch of the wadi near Number Twenty—Hatshepsut's tomb."

"Why there, I wonder?" Ramses said.

"Dunno. It's off the regular tourist track, so maybe they hoped they wouldn't be spotted right away. Can't think of any other reason why they would pick that area."

"Damnation," muttered Emerson. "I had intended to start work first thing tomorrow morning. Now I will have to waste several hours expelling the Albions."

"How do you propose to do that?" I inquired. "You haven't the authority either, and if you lay violent hands on any one of them—especially Mrs. Albion—"

"Good Gad, Peabody, have you ever known me to lay violent hands on a woman? There are ways," said Emerson, stroking his chin. "There are ways."

"Well, I sure don't want to miss that," Cyrus declared. "I'll be waiting for you in the morning. You'll all dine with us tomorrow evening, I hope. Katherine is anxious to see you."

Ramses and Nefret decided they did not want to miss it either. I went along to make certain Emerson behaved himself. Jumana went along because I insisted. Nefret's diagnosis might be correct—it was in keeping with the principles of psychology I favored—but she had confessed herself uncertain as to the appropriate treatment. I had my own ideas on that subject. If my methods were not effective, at least they could do no harm.

Jumana ate very little at breakfast, but I had checked the larder before retiring and again when I arose, and was not surprised to find that half a loaf of bread and a chicken breast had disappeared overnight. It was no wonder Fatima had not noticed anything amiss. The larder was open to everyone in the house, and Sennia had an appetite quite out of proportion to her little frame.

Cyrus and Bertie had been looking out for us and joined us at the end of the track that led up to the Castle. It was a bright, beautiful morning with clear skies; after the fog of Cairo and the rainy weather of Palestine, I appreciated Luxor even more.

"How well you look, Bertie," I said. "The foot is completely healed?"

"Yes, ma'am, thank you. I need not ask if you are in good health; you are blooming, as usual. We had heard that Ramses—"

"The reports were exaggerated," Ramses said with a smile. "As you can see."

"And your arm, Professor?" Bertie asked.

"A confounded nuisance," said Emerson. "Can we get on now? I want to finish this little job, so I can start work."

Bertie was not given the opportunity to ask after the person who interested him most. Jumana had not spoken to him or to Cyrus. She sat slumped in the saddle, her head bowed and her pretty mouth twisted. The taste of the medicine I had insisted she take lingered on the tongue.

We left the horses in the donkey park and proceeded on foot, along paths long familiar to us. I should explain that the Valley of the Kings is not a single long canyon. From above it resembles a lobed leaf, like that of an oak or maple, with side wadis branching off to left and right. The tomb of Hatshepsut was at the far end of one of these branches. We had worked in that area before and knew it well.

The tourists had come early to the Valley in order to avoid the heat of midday. We were not so early as Emerson would have liked, but in part it was his own fault; he had wasted some time playing with the Great Cat of Re, who had come to breakfast with Ramses and Nefret. It had grown quite fat, through overfeeding (by Sennia—she claimed to have been training it, to do what I could not imagine). She had also combed and brushed it every day, so that its fur had become long and silky. Emerson was highly entertained by its antics. As it leaped at the bit of chicken he dangled above it, it looked like a bouncing ball of fluff. (Horus's look of contempt as he watched this degrading performance was equally entertaining.) However, when we left the house it declined to ride on his shoulder and climbed onto that of Ramses.

"Must we take it?" he asked. "You rather overdid the grooming, Sennia, its fur is all over my face."

"His," said Sennia. "Yes, you must take him. What if you were attacked by a snake? I am coming too."

So that caused another delay. I did not want her to see—or hear—Emerson evicting the Albions. He was bound to lose his temper and employ bad language. We pacified her by promising to stop back at the house and take her to Deir el Medina, and distracted her by asking her to help Fatima prepare a very elaborate picnic basket.

Draped over Ramses's shoulder, with his tail hanging down behind, the Great Cat of Re resembled a luxuriant fur piece. Several ladies wanted to stroke him; several gentlemen stared and laughed. Among the latter was Mr. Lukancic, whom I had met at Cyrus's soiree. "Still here, are you?" I called, as we passed.

"Yes, ma'am. What on earth—"

"Another time." I waved. Emerson had not slowed his pace.

The signs of energetic activity were visible some distance off; a cloud of dust blurred the brilliant blue of the sky, and voices rose in one of the chants with which Egyptians lighten their work. The sight we beheld when we reached the spot was unusual enough to bring us all to a halt.

In the background a group of men were digging and hauling away debris. In the foreground, some distance from the dust and racket, was a little kiosk, a sturdy wooden frame with a roof and sides of canvas. Two of the canvas side pieces had been rolled up, and under the canopy, comfortably seated in armchairs, were the three Albions. Oriental rugs covered the ground; a table was spread with various articles of food and drink, over which a turbaned servant stood guard with a fly whisk. Another servant waved a fan over Mrs. Albion. She wore a frock that would have been suitable for tea at Buckingham Palace, and a hat wreathed with chiffon veiling. Mr. Albion had adopted what he believed to be proper archaeologist's attire: riding breeches and boots, a tweed coat, and a very large solar topee. His son was similarly attired, but since he was a good deal taller than Mr. Albion, he did not so closely resemble a mushroom.

One of the workmen came trotting up to Mr. Albion with a bit of stone in his hand. Albion took it, glanced at it, and tossed it away. He then condescended to notice us.

"Morning, folks. Out bright and early, are you?"

"Not so early as you," said Emerson, advancing with shoulders squared and brows thunderous. "You have been told, I believe, that you are in violation of Lord Carnarvon's firman. Close down your excavation at once."

"Who's gonna make us?" Mr. Albion inquired. He looked even more cherubic, his eyes twinkling and his lips pursed. "You?"

"Yes," said Emerson. "Oh, yes."

"Father, if I may?" Sebastian Albion had got to his feet. "Not everyone appreciates your sense of humor. Won't you sit down, ladies and gentlemen, and discuss the situation? Mrs. Emerson, please take my chair. I'm afraid the rest of you will have to—er—"

"Squat," said Nefret, doing so. "Let's hear what they have to say, Father. It won't cause much of a delay and it might be amusing."

"I agree," said Ramses, subsiding with boneless ease onto the rug beside Nefret and crossing his legs.

"Amusing," Mr. Albion repeated. "Yes, sirree, that's our aim in life, to amuse people and be polite. Here, young lady, take my chair. We heard you've been ailing."

Jumana started, and so, I believe, did we all. Such gallantry was not only unexpected but was, in my opinion, highly suspicious.

"No, thank you," she stammered. "Sir."

"I insist." He was on his feet, his face wreathed in smiles. "Sebastian, you persuade her."

"With pleasure." The young man offered his hand. Jumana blushed and ducked her head.

"Sit down, Jumana," I ordered. "Since Mr. Albion is kind enough to offer."

Mrs. Albion ignored this little byplay. She was leaning forward with the first sign of amiable interest I had seen her display. "What a beautiful cat. What is its name?"

"The Great Cat of Re," I replied. "You would call it Fluffy, I suppose."

Mr. Albion chuckled. "No, she gives her cats names like Grand Duchess Olga of Albion. Fond of the creatures. I put up with 'em because she's fond of 'em."

"Now see here," Emerson exclaimed. "I will be cursed if I will spend the morning talking about cats. What do you people think you are doing?"

Sebastian Albion removed his eyeglasses, wiped them on a handkerchief, and replaced them. "As you have no doubt observed, sir, we are clearing the tomb of Prince Mentuherkhepshef. It was found by Belzoni and reexamined in 1905 by—"

"Don't tell me facts I know better than you," Emerson interrupted. Curiosity had weakened his wrath, however; the Albions were so blandly outrageous, it was difficult to remain angry with them. And Sebastian had pronounced the prince's name correctly. He knew more about Egyptology than we had supposed.

"What do you hope to find?" Emerson went on. "The tomb is empty. Ayrton, who was here in 1905, found only a few scraps. The paintings . . . oh, good Gad!"

He whirled round and ran toward the workmen. A stentorian bellow stopped diggers and basket men, and as the cloud of dust subsided, Emerson vanished into the dark opening of the tomb. He was out again in ten seconds, waving his fists. "Someone has been hacking at the walls. There was a painting of the prince offering to Khonsu—"

"Defaced or missing?" Ramses asked.

"Missing. Completely cut out, leaving a great hole. Probably in pieces. Curse it!"

"We didn't do it," Sebastian hastened to say. "We haven't touched the paintings."

"You aren't doing them any good," Emerson retorted furiously. "All that dust and debris floating about . . . My patience is at an end. Stop work at once."

"What are you going to do, carry us out of here bodily?" Mr. Albion inquired. "There's nothing to stop us from coming back."

"Your workmen won't come back. I am about to put a curse on the place. They won't dare go near it after that, and neither will any of the other men on the West Bank."

"You better listen, Joe," Cyrus advised. "The Professor's curses are famous around here."

"That so?" Mr. Albion's eyes narrowed until they virtually disappeared. Then they resumed their normal appearance and a smile fattened his cheeks. "Well, I guess we know how to give in gracefully, eh, Sebastian? It's a shame about those fellows, they really need the work."

That aspect of the matter had not occurred to Emerson. It did not affect his decision, but I could see he was moved by it. He stood for a moment in thought, fingering the cleft in his chin. "It's a new tomb you're after, I presume? That's what every dilettante wants. There are one or two areas I've been meaning to explore for some time. Very promising sites."

Mrs. Albion had been stroking the Great Cat of Re, who politely permitted the liberty. (I had hoped it would hiss or scratch.) She looked up at Emerson. "Where are these sites, Professor?"

We delayed long enough to see the men begin to dismantle the comfortable little tent, and Mrs. Albion lifted, armchair and all, onto the shoulders of the servants. She was extremely gracious, though not to me; she thanked Emerson for his advice, spared a frosty smile for Jumana, and shook a playful finger at Ramses when he rose and settled the Great Cat of Re more securely onto his shoulder. "You really ought to select a more appropriate name for that charming creature, Mr. Emerson. The name of a lovely Egyptian goddess, perhaps? Hathor or Isis."

"I fear that would not be appropriate, ma'am," Ramses replied. "The cat is not of the female sex—uh—gender."

"I may have been mistaken about Mrs. Albion," I admitted, as we walked away. "Cats are generally good judges of character. Playfulness does not become her, however. What on earth were you thinking of, Emerson, proposing other sites for them? You have no right to do anything of the sort."

"Good Gad, Peabody, I expected you would approve of my mild methods." Striding along, hands in his pockets, Emerson glanced at me in feigned surprise. "I am familiar with men of Albion's character; if I had not offered them alternatives, they would simply have moved to some other forbidden area. I can't put curses on every site on the West Bank."

"But the southwest wadis? The Valley of the Queens?"

"The entrance to the Valley of the Queens," Emerson corrected. "There's nothing of interest there. If they mount an expedition to the southwest wadis I will be surprised; it's too far and too uncomfortable. Besides, you heard my condition. They will hire Soleiman Hassan as their reis. I will make sure he reports to me the instant they find anything—which is, in my opinion, unlikely. Why are you looking so glum, Vandergelt?"

"I kinda hoped for more fireworks," Cyrus admitted. "Don't count on Joe doing what you told him, Emerson. He holds a grudge against people who try to order him around."

"Bah," said Emerson.

"They were very polite," Jumana murmured.

"Yes," I said thoughtfully.

We collected Sennia and the picnic basket—and a reluctant but dogged Gargery—and went on to Deir el Medina, where we were forced to listen to another lecture, this one from Daoud. Selim had regaled him and a select audience with an edited version of our recent adventures, and Daoud was vibrating with indignation.

We had to apologize for leaving him behind and promise never to do it again.

"So Daoud knows all about it," Cyrus remarked. His voice was mild but his expression was severe. The same look of reproach marked Bertie's features.

"You promised me, ma'am," he began.

"My dear boy, you must not take it personally. We don't plan these things, you know; most of them just—well, they just happen."

"This one didn't," Cyrus said. "You were in the war zone, I got that much from what Daoud said. Do you have less confidence in us than you do in him?"

"My sentiments exactly, ma'am," said Bertie.

"Of course not," I said heartily. "We will tell you all about it this evening; how's that?"

"Precisely what are we going to tell them?" demanded Emerson, after he had succeeded in drawing me aside.

I had had a little chat with Selim before we left Cairo. I knew Ramses had told him part of the story, and I felt fairly certain he had worked the rest of it out. He had known Sir Edward Washington; he had known a great deal about Sethos; he had been present on several occasions when we had discussed matters that would enable a clever man, which Selim was, to put the pieces together. So I took him into my confidence, holding nothing back. If any man deserved that confidence, it was he.

"Ah," said Selim, unsurprised. "I knew when I saw him clean-shaven that he must be a kinsman of the Father of

Curses. They are very much alike. We do not speak of this to others, Sitt?"

"Except for Ramses and Nefret, you are the only one who knows. We do not speak of it, even to Vandergelt Effendi."

His face brightened with gratified pride. "You can trust me, Sitt Hakim."

"I am sure I can. But now we must work out what we are to tell the others, including Daoud."

I repeated the conversation to Emerson, adding, "You may be sure Selim produced a thrilling narrative without giving anything important away. Anyhow, I am tired of all this confounded secrecy. The more tight-lipped and mysterious we are, the more suspicious people will be. A partial truth will put them off the track far better than silence."

"You may be right," Emerson agreed. "I will leave it to you, then, my dear. What have you done with my field notes?"

I found his notebook in the pile of papers he had brought, and set about erecting my little shelter.

"I must say it looks rather pitiful compared with the Albions's arrangement," I remarked to Nefret, who was helping me.

Nefret chuckled. "Did you ever see anything more ridiculous than Mrs. Albion in her armchair being hoisted aloft by those two poor fellows? God help either of them if he stumbles and spills her out. Mr. Albion would probably have him beheaded."

"What did you think of their excessive courtesy to Jumana? That young man is not still under the impression that he can—er—win her over, surely."

"Surely not," Nefret said. "They were only trying to ingratiate themselves with us, Mother. And they succeeded. I'm like Cyrus; I was rather hoping Father would blow them to bits and perform one of his famous curses."

"Oh, were you?" said Emerson, appearing upon the scene. "I cannot imagine why everyone in this family is under the false impression that I am a violent and unreasonable man. Bring the camera, Nefret; we are about to start on a new section."

From Manuscript H

Emerson stood staring up at the hillside, his hand shading his eyes. He was, as usual, without a hat.

"May I have a moment of your time, Father?" Ramses asked.

"What the devil is Bertie doing up there?"

"Continuing his survey, I suppose. May I—"

"Certainly, my boy, certainly. Something about that new section?"

"No, sir. Something about the Albions. I would be happy to assist in whatever you're planning, if you care to let me in on it."

Emerson's eyes shifted warily from side to side, around, and behind. "Promise you won't tell your mother?"

"I'll try not to. But you know how she—"

"Yes, yes, I do know. But this time, by Gad, I think I'm one step ahead of her. Come over here where she can't hear us."

His mother was two hundred feet away but Ramses let his father draw him aside. "Well, sir?"

Emerson took out his pipe. "It struck me as somewhat strange that the Albions would select that particular part of the Valley. There is no more reason to expect a big find there than anywhere else. Unless they had a hint from someone."

He lit a match and puffed. "A hint such as the fragment of wall painting?" Ramses asked. "Khonsu. He is a god and he has human hands."

"As do many other gods," Emerson said. "But the Albions, for all Sebastian's book learning, haven't much experience, and at the moment they are at a loss as to where to look."

"For Jamil's tomb?"

"I see the idea does not surprise you. What made you think of it?"

"I don't like the Albions," Ramses said. "Any of them."

"I am glad to see you are beginning to trust your instincts," his father said approvingly.

"As Mother would say—" Emerson's scowl made him abandon that thought. "I don't like their behavior toward Jumana," Ramses elaborated. "Their attitude toward Egyptians is characteristic of their class and nationality—bigoted and prejudiced, in other words. After his initial blunder Sebastian has leaned over backward to be polite to her. Nefret thinks it is because they hope to ingratiate themselves with us, but there could be another reason."

His father nodded. "Go on."

"Let's go at it from another direction. Jamil was getting financial support from someone. We assumed it was Yusuf, but there were those interesting items of European manufacture among his supplies. The Albions asked you to introduce them to a few tomb robbers. I don't believe it was a joke. They had been asking around Gurneh, and Albion mentioned that 'Mohammed' had put them on to someone. What if that someone was Jamil?"

"Mohassib's first name is Mohammed," Emerson said.

"It might have been Mohassib, or Mohammed Hassan— or any one of several other Mohammeds. Those two are the most likely, however. Both had spoken with Jamil, both were afraid of him. What better way of conciliating him than to introduce him to a wealthy patron? Then Jamil was inconsiderate enough to get himself killed before he disclosed the location of the tomb. The Albions believe there's a chance he confided in Jumana. An outside chance, but that's what they have been reduced to."

"And Jamil promised that in exchange for their support he would sell them the objects from the tomb once he'd cleared it. My thought exactly."

"If I know Albion, he'd insist on more than promises," Ramses said.

"Oh, well done," Emerson said approvingly. "Yes, he'd want proof of the find, and—a little something on account? Something as fine as the cosmetic jar?"

"Possibly. It's all conjecture, and we can't . . . Father, no!"

"Can't do what?" said Emerson, fumbling with his pipe. He was too late; his face had betrayed him.

"Search their rooms. Don't deny it, Father, that is what you were thinking."

"You thought of it, too, or you wouldn't have been so quick to read my mind."

The accusation was accurate, the grin conspiratorial, but Ramses tried to look stern. "That sort of thing is more in Mother's line."

"We can't have her doing something like that," Emerson said. "It's against the law."

Ramses couldn't resist the grin. He began to laugh. "It's a tempting thought, but not really practical. Even if we found illegal antiquities, we couldn't confiscate them or prove where they came from. Jamil may have dropped enticing hints to the Albions, but they don't seem to know any more than we do."

His father's abstracted expression told him he hadn't got the point across. "This is all conjecture," he insisted. "Logical and consistent, but without substantiating evidence. We can't even be certain that Jamil told the Albions about the hand of the god. It may have been pure coincidence that they chose to dig in that spot."

"Well, we will soon find out."

"Ah. Those alternate sites you suggested?"

"Mmmm." Emerson sucked on his pipe. "None of them has any connection with a divine representation. If the Albions are solely interested in excavation—"

"Ramses!" His mother's voice had considerable carrying power. Emerson twitched guiltily and Ramses turned. She was on her feet, waving some object at him. It appeared to be a large piece of pottery—an ostracon.

Ramses waved back. "We may as well stop for lunch," he said. "Sennia has told me twice already that she's faint with hunger."

"Where is she?" Emerson turned, scanning the terrain.

"Probably in the shelter, investigating the basket, which would explain why the Great Cat of Re has also abandoned us. I must speak to her about overfeeding the creature, it's getting absolutely obese."

"He," Emerson corrected.

Sennia, and the cat, were where he expected. The others joined them in time to save most of the chicken. Ramses's lecture was not as forceful as he had intended it to be; the hurt looks he got from two pairs of eyes, one pair big and black, the other pair round and clear-green as peridots, had a softening effect. Apologetically he offered the cat a piece of chicken.

Sennia had collected a few ostraca too, but the one his mother had found was outstanding—larger than most, the hieratic clearly preserved. He was touched to see how her face brightened when he expressed his appreciation.

"Was this in the fill?" he asked, holding it carefully by the edges. "I'm surprised that any of our fellows would over-look something so large."

"Curse it, Peabody," Emerson mumbled through a bite of cheese, "have you been digging illicitly?"

"How could you suppose I would do such a thing, Emerson? Ali brought it to me. It has been properly recorded."

"Oh. All right, then."

"What does it say?" Nefret asked, leaning over Ramses's shoulder. A loosened lock of hair brushed his cheek. He twisted it around his finger and smiled at her. "It appears to be a prayer—to Hathor, Divine Mother, Lady of Fragrance."

"You can translate it later," Emerson declared, wiping his

fingers on his trousers. "I want to finish that section today."

"I trust you have not forgotten we are dining with Cyrus this evening," his wife reminded him.

Emerson groaned. Cyrus grinned. "I asked Selim too," he said significantly.

"Hmmm," said Ramses's mother.

"Hmph," said Emerson. "Bertie, you haven't told me how you are getting on. Not that I have any right to ask, I suppose."

"Don't be a dog in the manger," his wife said.

"You have every right to ask, sir," Bertie said earnestly. "It's going well, I think. I've got most of the known tombs located now. This is a working copy, of course; I keep the master copy at home and add to it every night."

"Well done." Emerson slapped him on the back. "Now—back to work, eh?"

Not until later that day was Ramses able to arrange a private conversation with his mother.

"Do you really intend to tell Cyrus about Khan Yunus? You know, Mother, that the Official Secrets Act—"

"I do not consider myself bound by any document to which I did not agree in advance," said his mother. Her chin protruded even more than usual. "We must tell Cyrus something. It isn't fair to him to keep him wholly in the dark. Ramses . . . dear . . ." She put her hand on his shoulder. "I know you would rather not talk or think of the affair again, but if you will brace yourself, one more time . . . You have my word that Selim's narrative will not get me in trouble with the War Office!"

"All right, Mother. Dear," he added, with a smile that brought a faint flush to her cheeks.

It had taken Katherine Vandergelt a while to become comfortable with their Egyptian friends. She had had to come to terms with her prejudices, or at least conceal them—his mother hadn't left her any choice! No one but a boor could have treated Selim with less than the courtesy his fine manners and inherent dignity deserved; Katherine's greeting was warm and friendly. She displayed even more warmth toward Jumana, whose pallor and morose expression obviously shocked her, and kept pressing delicacies on her. Jumana, who had not wanted to come, but had been made to, pushed the food around her plate and looked wistful. Cyrus's majordomo had outdone himself—"to welcome them home." The table glittered with crystal, and the silverware shone.

After dinner they retired to the sitting room for coffee. Selim knew what was on the agenda. He had been perfectly at ease up till that time; now he began to fidget and tug at his beard. Stage fright? Or fear that he would forget the lines in which he had been coached by the great Sitt Hakim?

"All right now, Amelia, we're ready," Cyrus said, settling himself comfortably in a deep armchair. "I've been looking forward to this all day."

She smiled complacently and sipped her coffee. "Selim will tell it. Go ahead, Selim."

All eyes turned toward Selim, completing his discomfiture. As he confessed later to Ramses, he would rather have faced a horde of assailants, armed to the teeth, than those focused stares. He cleared his throat.

"I am no storyteller," he began in a voice several tones higher than his usual baritone. "Not like Daoud."

"All the better," Cyrus said with a smile. "We know Daoud's tendency to—er—embroider."

"Start with the motorcar," Emerson suggested, seeing that Selim needed encouragement. "It was a fine motorcar, and you drove magnificently."

Once launched, Selim described the charms of the motorcar in loving detail and dwelled with excessive but pardonable enthusiasm on the perils of the long journey and his skill as a driver. "Khan Yunus is an ugly town, not like Luxor," he declared. "There were many soldiers. The house of the friend of the Father of Curses was where we stayed; it was very dirty. It was there that the real adventure began!"

"About time," muttered Cyrus. "Khan Yunus, eh? What did you go there for?"

Selim glanced at Ramses's mother, who gave him an encouraging nod. He had got over his self-consciousness and was enjoying himself—as well he might, Ramses thought. Never, not even from his mother or Daoud, had he heard such a wild story.

They had been summoned to Khan Yunus to rescue a beautiful maiden—the daughter of a Bedouin sheikh, their friend and ally—from the evil old man who had carried her off, with designs on her fortune and her virtue. It was Ramses who had gone after the maiden and succeeded, after many dangers, in rescuing her. Selim described some of the dangers, which included a duel with scimitars. Ramses covered his face with his hand.

"He does not like to have his courage praised," said Selim. "But it was not over. The evil old man sent men to take her back, and we had to fight them off and escape, in the night, with enemies pursuing us and the town in flames. We stole horses from under the very noses of the Australians! But I have not told you about the ragged beggar, who was a policeman in disguise—and a good disguise it was; he had fleas and smelled bad. The evil old man was a thief, you see, who had stolen jewels from many rich ladies and important antiquities from the Cairo Museum. The beggar was trying to catch him and bring him to justice, but in the end it was not he who captured the villain, it was Ramses."

"It was not," Ramses exclaimed, driven beyond endurance. "It was Father, with—"

"Hmph," said Emerson loudly. "Very well told, Selim. You see, Vandergelt, it was just another of our attempts to assist the police. It is the duty of every citizen."

"How about the maiden?" Cyrus inquired. "You didn't bring her home with you?"

Selim sighed and looked soulful.

"The—er—policeman took her away," Ramses said. He'd had as much as he could stand.

"He was her lover, I think," Selim added.

"Oh, I see. You mind if I ask a few questions, Selim?"

Selim had enjoyed himself, once he got well under way, but he knew better than to risk an interrogation by Cyrus Vandergelt. He got hastily to his feet. "I must go. It is late. Thank you for your kind hospitality."

"Now see here, Amelia," Cyrus exclaimed.

"We mustn't detain him, Cyrus, he has other responsibilities. Jumana, you are excused as well. Selim will take you home."

"But I want—"

"You have been ill. You need your rest."

"I feel much better!"

She looked almost her old self, eyes bright, cheeks pink. The eyes were fixed on Ramses, with an expression that made him want to run for cover. His mother snapped, "Do as you are told."

Ramses went to the door with Selim while Jumana was collecting her wrap. "I owe you for that, Selim," he murmured.

"I only said what the Sitt Hakim told me to. But why are you angry? I know what you did, and if I had done such things I would tell everyone. But," Selim said, struck by a new idea, "we do it to make the men fear us and the women admire us, yes? All men fear the Brother of Demons, and you have won the heart of the only woman you want. When Nur Misur looks at you, it is as if the sun were shining in her eyes."

"I'm not angry, Selim." Ramses embraced him in the Egyptian manner. "You are a good friend—and a shameless romantic."

"And what is wrong with that?"

Selim's grin faded into a scowl when Jumana came out of the house. He mounted his horse and hauled her up in front of him with no more ceremony than if she had been a sack of grain. Ramses heard them exchanging insults as they rode off. Serves them both right, he thought.

When he returned to the drawing room, his mother had taken charge of the proceedings. "Unbelievable or not, that story is what Selim told Daoud. By the time Daoud finishes embellishing it, it will bear little resemblance to fact."

"And I'll sound like even more of a posturing ass," Ramses said sourly.

"Stop complaining," his mother said. "Goodness gracious, I did the best I could! It was necessary to account for our absence in some way. Our friends at Atiyeh saw the motorcar and realized we were preparing for a long desert trip. By the time we left Khan Yunus, everyone knew who we were; they will pass the story on, and sooner or later our activities will be gossiped about throughout Egypt and Palestine."

"It was a pretty good yarn," Cyrus admitted. He lit one of his cheroots and leaned back. "And no wilder than a lot of your adventures. I'm sorry, though, I can't believe in the beautiful maiden. Khan Yunus is only ten miles from Gaza. Need I say more?"

His knowing smile brought a responsive twinkle to her eyes. "Oddly enough, Cyrus, the beautiful maiden is one of the true facts. However, there is no use denying that our mission involved more serious matters. You've known for some time that we have had dealings with the secret service, haven't you?"

"A fellow would have to be pretty durned stupid not to have strong suspicions, Amelia. With a war on, and the way you keep appearing and disappearing without explanation, and your expertise in certain areas . . ." His eyes moved to Ramses. "Well, I'm not asking for details. I just hope to God the filthy business is over soon. You can't keep on taking chances without something bad happening, and we couldn't spare you. Any of you."

"Amen," Katherine said.

"Er—quite," Bertie added.

"It is over," declared Emerson, squirming a little in the warm flood of friendship. "A bloo——excuse me, Katherine—a blooming nuisance too. Now we can—"

"Just one more question," Cyrus interrupted. "You don't have to answer it, but I'm real curious. Was that so-called beggar anybody I know?"

Caught off-guard and at a loss as to how to answer, Emerson turned for help to his wife. "You have met the gentleman," she said smoothly.

"And he's on our side now?"

"Oh, yes. Cyrus, would you think me rude if I asked for a whiskey and soda?"

She looked so smug, her son had to fight to keep from laughing. Trust his mother—she never lied "unless it was absolutely necessary," and this time she had spoken the literal truth. Cyrus had been well acquainted with Sir Edward Washington, but it had not been that gentleman she meant.

⋮

Naturally, Emerson felt obliged to criticize me for encouraging Selim to tell a pack of lies and, with typical inconsistency, for telling Cyrus more than he deemed advisable. We had quite a refreshing little argument about it on the drive home. I had always felt somewhat guilty about keeping Cyrus in the dark—if he was in the dark. He was too intelligent and he knew us too well to overlook certain happenings. I had told him no more than he already suspected, and it pleased him to be taken into our confidence.

He was even happier next day, when he found a new tomb. It wasn't much of a tomb; the offering chapel had been completely destroyed and the burial chamber was empty of all but scraps, but there were several well-preserved paintings.

"That will keep him out of mischief for a while," remarked Emerson to me. "It will take several days to carry out a meticulous excavation and make plans. He can have Jumana to help him."

"Kind of you," I said. "She gets on your nerves, doesn't she?"

"She talks too much. I almost preferred her moping. What did you do to get her out of it?"

"Nothing—unless it was that nasty medicine. I hope there is not a sinister—"

"Sinister, bah! There you go again, borrowing trouble."

"You are right, Emerson," I admitted. "I am so accustomed to having some worry on my mind that it is difficult to realize our enemies have been vanquished and our problems solved."

"Except for one," Emerson muttered. " 'The hand of the god.' What god? Where?"

Sennia joined us for tea that afternoon, so full of exciting news, she neglected the biscuits. "The Great Cat of Re has caught a snake!"

We all looked at the cat, who had assumed one of those Yoga-like positions necessary for the proper cleaning of feline underparts. It looked so silly, with one leg in the air and the other behind its ear, we all burst out laughing.

"A very large snake?" Emerson inquired.

"No larger than this," said Fatima, measuring approximately five inches with finger and thumb. "But it was still alive, Father of Curses, and I do not know whether there will be any dinner tonight, because it is still somewhere in the kitchen and Maaman says—"

"It has probably escaped long ago," Emerson said comfortably.

"Then *you* tell Maaman," said Fatima, thumping the teapot down on the table. "He says he will not cook."

"Oh, curse it," said Emerson. "I suppose I'll have to do something or we won't get any dinner."

"Take the Great Cat of Re," Sennia suggested.

"Not a bad idea," said Emerson, scooping the cat up. Sennia crammed two biscuits into her mouth and went with them.

"Let's go and watch," Nefret suggested. "Jumana, have you ever seen the Father of Curses perform an exorcism? It will be even more entertaining if he works the cat into it."

Jumana shuddered. "I am afraid of snakes. I hope it does not go into my room."

I also declined the treat. I am not afraid of snakes, but I see no point in cultivating them.

One of the men had gone to the post office that morning, so there was quite a stack of letters and messages and newspapers. By the time the others came back I had had a nice leisurely time, sorting the mail and reading the more interesting missives.

"Did you find it?" I inquired.

"Yes, as a matter of fact," Emerson said. He deposited the cat on the floor, where it resumed its interrupted bath. "I hadn't supposed we would, and was preparing an exorcism specifically designed for serpents, but the cat fished it out almost at once from behind one of the water jars. A perfectly harmless Clifford's snake. Ramses took it outside and let it loose."

"I told you I have been training the Great Cat of Re," Sennia said triumphantly. "Someday it will catch an even bigger snake and save Ramses's life at the last second."

"Pure chance," said Emerson—but he said it under his breath. "Anything in the post, Peabody?"

"A nice long letter from Evelyn, and one for Nefret from Lia, and one for Ramses from David . . ." I distributed the missives as I spoke.

"What about me?" Sennia demanded.

"Three for you." They were from the family. They knew she loved getting mail.

"Nothing else?"

I handed Emerson the rest of his letters. "Two telegrams from Cairo. I took the liberty—"

"Yes, of course you did," Emerson muttered. "Well, what do you think of that? Wingate and General Murray request my presence at my earliest convenience."

"I presume it will not be convenient early *or* late," I said.

Emerson emitted a wicked chuckle. "Why do you suppose I made a quick departure from Cairo? We reported to General Chetwode, handed over our prisoner, and assured him and his intelligence staff that they'd seen the last of Ismail Pasha—which is true, since Sethos won't use that disguise again. If they have any further questions they can come to us, but they will get damned few answers. Nothing from Carter or—er—"

I shook my head. "Here is an interesting invitation, however. The Albions are giving a dinner party and dance on Friday. The honor of our presence is requested. There is a little note penned by Mrs. Albion herself, hoping that Jumana will also honor her."

"Me?" Jumana's eyes opened very wide.

"Her?" Emerson exclaimed. "What the devil for?"

"She is one of the family," Nefret said. "I expect they are trying to make up for . . . for any inadvertent rudeness in the past."

"They have not been rude," Jumana said. "They sent me flowers, when I was sick."

"They did? You didn't tell me."

"Many people sent me presents," Jumana said proudly. "Bertie, and Mr. Vandergelt, and Daoud, and an American gentleman I met at Mr. Vandergelt's party. Will we go? There will be dancing. I like to dance."

"I believe not," I said.

"Why not?" Emerson inquired. "It should be a—er—enjoyable outing."

"Emerson!" I exclaimed. "What are you up to now?"

Emerson's sapphirine-blue eyes met my own with a wholly unconvincing look of candor. "I only wish to give you pleasure, my dear. You like such things. It is the least a fellow can do."

From Manuscript H

Ramses knew perfectly well what his father was "up to." Deny it as he might, he was as obsessed as Cyrus with Jamil's tomb. In a way, Ramses couldn't blame him. The words ran through his own head like a litany: The hand of the god. What god? Where? It was beginning to interfere with his personal life. Nefret shook him awake that night, complaining that he had been muttering the words in his sleep. "If you must talk in your sleep, you might at least mumble about me!"

After he had apologized by reciting the epithets of Hathor—"Golden One, Lady of Fragrance, Mistress of All the Gods"—and acted upon them—she settled down with her head on his shoulder and admitted she couldn't get that enigmatic clue out of her head either.

"I've been wondering whether we ought not question Jumana again," she said. "She has a fantastic memory and almost total recall, even for accents. Wasn't it enchanting to hear her imitate Cyrus?"

"It was rather uncanny hearing her imitate Jamil the day we found Mother and Father," Ramses said. "Are you suggesting that if we asked the right questions she might remember something Jamil said about the tomb?"

"That's how her memory seems to operate."

"It's worth a try, I suppose. We might even be able to talk Father out of breaking into the Albions' suite."

"You're joking. No, damn it, you aren't!"

He had told her of his conversation with Emerson. She had scoffed at the time, but now . . .

"That's why he agreed to go to their party!" she groaned. "What are we going to do?"

"Make sure they don't catch him in the act. He's dead set on this, Nefret. I've been thinking about it and I don't believe it will do any harm."

She relaxed against him and let out a breath of laughter. "Well, maybe not. Even if the worst happened—if someone found him in their rooms—he'd talk his way out of it."

"Shout, not talk," Ramses corrected. "What could they do to him, after all? There isn't a man in Luxor who would dare interfere with him."

All the same, he was a little on edge the night of the party. His father had readily admitted he meant to search the Albions' rooms; he had raised the subject himself, overruling Ramses's half-hearted protests and requesting his assistance.

"I will signal you when I'm ready to act. Keep an eye on the Albions. If one of them starts to leave the ballroom—well, you will know what to do."

"Start a fight with Sebastian, for example? All right, Father, I'll think of something. I hope. You will be in disguise, I suppose."

His father grinned happily. "Just the usual, my boy, just the usual. Er—might I borrow a beard? Your mother must have done something with mine, I can't find it. Oh, and if she asks where I am, put her off somehow."

It wouldn't be easy, keeping tabs on three people and fending his mother off, but Ramses thought he could manage it with Nefret's assistance. He only hoped his mother didn't have ideas of her own. She looked very handsome that evening, in a gown of her favorite crimson, the diamonds in her ears sparkling. Nefret was radiant in amber satin, and Jumana looked like any young girl on her way to a dance—eyes shining, cheeks flushed.

The Albions had hired the entire hotel, or at least the public rooms, including the dining salon. That presented no problem to the management, since the convalescent officers who occupied part of the hotel had all been invited. Everyone in Luxor seemed to be there, including the Vandergelts. Mr. Albion's money and his wife's good taste made it quite a splendid affair; the wine flowed freely and the food was excellent. After dinner, when the dancing was about to begin, Ramses edged up to his father.

"Is there any way I can persuade you not to do this?"

"Now, now, my boy, it will be all right, you'll see." Emerson plucked irritably at his tie. It looked wilted. "I am going to dance with your mother and Katherine, and then give our hostess a whirl, and after that I will quietly steal away."

"Have you asked Mrs. Albion? The ladies have dance cards. You're supposed to put your name down for a particular dance."

"Absurd. Dancing should be spontaneous. Joie de vivre and that sort of thing."

He strolled away, his hands in his pockets.

Ramses also approved of joie de vivre, but he had been lectured by his mother and his wife about proper procedure. He'd never been able to see the point of the little cards—appointment slips, one might call them—unless it was to give popular ladies a sense of power, and make unpopular ladies squirm when they saw all the blank spaces.

Jumana was loving every moment of it—the flowers, the fancy dresses, the little booklet and pencil attached to her slim wrist by a golden cord. When Ramses asked for a dance she presented the booklet with an air of great importance and an irrepressible giggle. He needn't have worried about her being neglected; Bertie and Cyrus had signed on, and so had both the Albions. There were several other names Ramses didn't know. She had attracted quite a lot of attention, with her exotic looks and exquisite little figure.

He had allowed himself the pleasure of engaging his wife for the second dance; as they circled the floor, he warned her of his father's intentions. Emerson was waltzing with Katherine, looking as if butter wouldn't melt in his mouth.

"How are we supposed to watch three people at once?" Nefret grumbled. "With everything else that's going on? I promised Mother I'd make sure Jumana is enjoying herself."

"Obviously she is." White skirts flaring, Jumana was light as thistledown in the respectful grasp of a tall American Ramses remembered having met at Cyrus's soiree.

"Mr. Lukancic," Nefret said, following his gaze. "He's very nice. I've got Mr. Albion for the third dance and you for the fourth; suppose I corner Sebastian for that one instead, and you ask Mrs. Albion."

"I suppose I can't very well dance with Mr. Albion. We'll just have to be prepared for emergency action. Be ready to faint or pretend you've seen a mouse if I give a distress signal."

She laughed and nestled closer.

The third dance ended only too soon. As he had promised, Emerson had got hold of his hostess, whose frozen features kept cracking in pain as he spun her vigorously round in waltz time. (The tune was a fox-trot.) When the music ended he led her, limping, to a chair and then turned to give Ramses an exaggerated wink and nod.

Mrs. Albion declined Ramses's invitation to dance. She looked as if she did not intend to move for some time. Nefret had worked her wiles on Sebastian, so Ramses went in search of Albion senior.

He found him in one of the alcoves talking to Jumana. "Don't ask her to dance, this one is mine," Albion said, with one of his jolly laughs. "I can't prance around with the young folks, but we're having a nice time talking Egyptology. She's a clever girl."

"She is," Ramses agreed, glancing at the glass she held. "That isn't champagne, is it?"

"Soda water," Albion said. "You don't think I'd ply a young lady with alcohol, do you?"

The answer to that was a resounding "Yes, if you hoped to gain something by it." Since courtesy forbade honesty, Ramses said, "I'll join you, if I may. What were you talking about?"

"Those sites your pa told me about" was the prompt reply.

"We've just about decided not to do any more digging. The young lady agrees with me that it's a waste of time."

"The western wadis are too far away and too dangerous," Jumana explained. "And there is nothing in that part of the Valley of the Queens."

"Father will be glad to hear that," Ramses said.

The music ended. Jumana looked at her dance card. "The next one is Bertie," she announced importantly. "Will you excuse me, sir?"

"Why, sure. You go right ahead."

Trying to watch all three Albions and fulfill his social obligations kept Ramses fully occupied for a while. Mr. Albion wouldn't stay put; he wandered around the room, talking to his wife and to various other people. Seeing Mrs. Albion head purposefully for the door of the ballroom, Ramses caught Nefret's eye, gestured, and trod on Katherine's toe. Nefret went in pursuit, abandoning her partner.

"I beg your pardon, Katherine," Ramses said.

"Quite all right, my dear. Is your injury bothering you? Perhaps we should sit down."

"What? Oh, that. Well, yes, a little. Not much. It's all right."

He'd lost sight of Sebastian too. What was taking his father so long?

Mrs. Albion came back, followed by Nefret. Her nod and smile reassured him; they must have gone to the ladies' parlor.

He was still scanning the room, trying to locate Sebastian, when he caught sight of his father. He let his breath out in a sigh that ruffled Katherine's hair.

"Let's do sit down, Ramses," she said.

"Did I tread on your foot again?"

"No, dear, but the music has stopped."

Her husband claimed her for the next dance, and Ramses headed straight for his father. Emerson's appearance would have roused his wife's direst suspicions. His hair was standing on end, his tie had come undone, and his smile was reminiscent of that of the Great Cat of Re after a tasty meal. Ramses drew him aside.

"Here, let me fix your tie before Mother sees you."

"What's wrong with it? Oh." Emerson glanced down. "Thank you, my boy."

"Well?" Ramses demanded.

"It went off without a hitch. What did you expect?"

"Did you find anything?"

"Oh, yes."

"Don't do this to me, Father." He jerked the knot tight.

"I can't tell you about it now," Emerson said reproachfully. "But in a word— Oh, curse it. Hullo, Bertie. Were you looking for me? I just stepped out into the garden for—"

"No, sir. That is—did you see Jumana?"

"In the garden? Er—no."

"Is something wrong, Bertie?" Ramses asked.

Bertie passed his hand over his hair. "It's just that this is my dance, and I can't find her. She was with Sebastian, and he doesn't seem to be in the room either."

"They must be around somewhere," Emerson said vaguely. "Damn! There's your mother. Your mother, I mean, Ramses. Am I supposed to be dancing with her?"

"I've no idea," Ramses said. His mother was advancing on them with a firm stride and a look in her eyes that boded ill for Emerson. "You had better report to her, she probably noticed you were conspicuous by your absence."

"Jumana—" Bertie began.

"Yes, right. I expect she's gone to the ladies' parlor. Let's ask Nefret."

Nefret had just returned from the ladies' parlor. "Mrs. Albion has gone there three times! She keeps taking off her gloves and washing her hands. I hate to speculate about why. Is Father—"

"Dancing with Mother," Ramses said.

"Thank goodness!"

"Yes, but Jumana has gone missing," Ramses said. "She wasn't in the ladies' parlor?"

"Sebastian's not here either," Bertie said.

"Oh, dear. I'm sorry, I rather lost track of her, what with . . . one thing and another. Perhaps she stepped out into the garden for a breath of fresh air."

"The Professor just came in from the garden. He said he hadn't seen her. But he wouldn't have, would he, if they were off in a dark corner somewhere."

"There is no reason to suppose they are together, Bertie," Nefret said. "But we'll have a look round."

The gardens were one of the showplaces of Luxor, planted with exotic trees and shrubs. They, too, had been decorated for the occasion; colorful lanterns hung from the branches, and benches and chairs were scattered about. A number of the guests were enjoying the cool air and the scent of night blossoms. Winding paths led in and out of the shrubbery.

"You go that way," Bertie said. "I'll go the other."

Nefret would have been the first to admit she had been remiss, but she couldn't believe there was any real danger to Jumana. Not here, in the public gardens, with so many people about. If the girl had let Sebastian bring her here, she was guilty of nothing worse than indiscretion. Nefret had a sinking feeling she wasn't going to convince Bertie of that. His jaw was set.

"I'm coming with you," she said. "Wait for me."

He had already plunged into the nearest path. She picked up her skirts and ran after him.

They had almost reached the end of the path, where it curved back toward the hotel, before Nefret heard a man's voice, low and intimate, the words indistinguishable; and Jumana's reply, high-pitched and quavering. "No, I am not afraid, but I want to go back now."

Sebastian laughed softly. "Not yet."

Nefret filled her lungs and shouted, "Jumana!"

Jumana came flying out of the shadows. Bertie went flying into them. He dragged Sebastian out into the light and raised his fist.

"Stop them," Nefret exclaimed. "They're going to fight!"

"It looks that way," said Ramses, behind her. "Go ahead, Bertie, give him a good one."

Bertie let go of Sebastian's lapel and stepped back. "He's wearing eyeglasses. I can't hit a chap who—"

Sebastian's fist connected neatly and scientifically with Bertie's jaw, knocking him over backward.

.
.

Thirteen

"Really," I said in exasperation, "I cannot decide which of this evening's outlandish activities to discuss first."

"I can," said Emerson. "Good Gad, Bertie, don't you know better than to fight like a gentleman?"

We had left the party somewhat precipitately. I had known the moment I set eyes on him that Emerson had been up to something, but before I could interrogate him Nefret had run in to tell me Jumana was in hysterics and Bertie was nursing a lump on his jaw and a bump on his head and that Ramses was chasing Sebastian Albion through the gardens and that—in short, we had better go at once. We collected the others, including Ramses, who had cooled off enough to be tractable, and took them away. Since our house was nearer than the Castle, we had all gone there. Having removed coat, waistcoat, and tie, with a glass of whiskey and soda in his hand, Emerson felt in a proper frame of mind to lecture.

"Bear in mind, my boy," he went on, "that there is no purpose in fighting unless you mean to win. Never mind all that nonsense about fair play."

"I'll remember that next time, sir," Bertie said.

"I sincerely hope there will not be a next time," Katherine exclaimed. "Nefret, are you certain he doesn't have a concussion, or a fractured skull, or—"

"He did not fall very hard," said Jumana.

We all turned to look at her. She had wept on Nefret's shoulder—Ramses having refused to offer his—all the way back, but whether from distress or pure excitement I would have hesitated to say.

"I am sorry," she stammered. "I didn't mean . . . But why is everyone angry with me? Why did Bertie want to fight with Sebastian? He was very polite, he only—"

"Kept you there after you had said you wanted to go," Nefret cut in. "Would he have continued to be polite, do you think, if we hadn't arrived when we did?"

Jumana's lips trembled.

"It wasn't her fault," Bertie muttered. "She didn't understand."

"Well, perhaps she didn't," I conceded. "I assumed . . . So I neglected to give her my little lecture. You remember the one, Nefret?"

"Very well," said Nefret, her tight lips relaxing. "I gave her the same lecture less than an hour ago. Evidently it didn't make an impression."

She went to Jumana and lifted her out of her chair by her shoulders. "Have I your full attention now, Jumana? Bertie behaved tonight as any decent man would, coming to the assistance of an inexperienced young girl who is about to be . . ." She glanced at me, and went on, ". . . taken advantage of by an unscrupulous scoundrel. He'd have done it for any girl, Jumana, so don't preen yourself! The only mistake he made was in playing by the rules and expecting Sebastian to do the same. Now go to your room and think about what I've said, unless you want to apologize to Bertie and thank him."

Red-faced and stuttering, Bertie exclaimed, "Oh, I say, she doesn't owe me an apology. It was—well, it was—what one does, you know. Only I didn't do it awfully well. I mean—"

Jumana burst into tears and ran out of the room. Bertie smiled apologetically. "I seem to have mucked it up, as usual. Shouldn't have lost my temper."

"You weren't the only one," Ramses said. He had also divested himself of his extraneous garments and was sitting on the floor by Nefret's chair. "I made an even greater fool of myself, crashing through the shrubbery after him. I'll probably get a bill from the hotel tomorrow for damaged plants."

"One good thing has come of it," I declared. "We now understand the reason for the Albions' politeness to Jumana. That disgusting young man still had—er—designs on her. Your warning to him, Ramses, only spurred him on. Some men, I believe, would consider an innocent girl a challenge."

"And safer than the brothels," Ramses murmured.

"Please, Ramses."

"I beg your pardon, Mother. I wouldn't deny that one of Sebastian's motives was seduction, but isn't it somewhat strange that his father and mother would conspire with him? Especially his mother."

"Bah," Emerson declared. "She thinks the Albions, father and son, are entitled to use any means possible to get anything they want. They want Jamil's tomb. They believe Jumana can help them find it. It isn't difficult to understand why they are so keen. Jamil gave them enough to whet their appetites."

He smiled provocatively at me.

"So that is where you were tonight," I said. "I suspected as much."

"No, Peabody, you didn't suspect a cursed thing, or you would have insisted on going with me, and you'd have been caught in the act, as I almost was."

"Tell us all about it," said Nefret, her dimples showing.

"I have every intention of doing so, if the rest of you have finished chattering. It wasn't my fault that I was almost caught," Emerson went on. "One of the cursed sufragis turned up while I was trying my skeleton keys in the lock. He recognized me, of course, so I sent him on his way with a fistful of money and a few small curses. Once inside, I assumed my disguise."

He paused—ostensibly to sip his whiskey. I didn't ask

why he had bothered with a disguise. A disguise is its own excuse as far as Emerson is concerned.

"You may well ask," Emerson continued, smirking at me, "why I bothered with a disguise. It was a necessary precaution. If I had been found inside the room, by one of the Albions or a servant, the individual would only have caught a glimpse of a bearded Egyptian before I made my getaway, through the window or out the door. In fact, I was not disturbed. I had ample time to search all the rooms, which were interconnected. The loot, if I may so express it, was in Albion's room. He and his wife occupy separate bedchambers."

"That is an extraneous fact, Emerson," I said. "And none of our business."

"One never knows what may be relevant, Peabody. It is possible, though not probable, that she is unaware of Albion's dealings with Jamil. He had a boxful of artifacts, including some fragments of the painting of Khonsu. Jamil must have sold him those and hinted that they were a meaningful clue. The lad had quite a sense of humor. As for the rest . . . Here's the list, as nearly as I can remember. First, another cosmetic jar like the one you purchased, with the cartouche intact. It was, as Ramses deduced, that of the God's Wife Shepenwepet. Second and third, two ushebtis inscribed for the same woman, approximately eight inches high, of blue-green faience. Fourth, and most remarkable, a sistrum of bronze inlaid with gold." He took a sheet of paper from the table beside him. "I did this while you were all fussing over Bertie," he explained. "My artistic skills are not as good as David's, but I wanted to capture the details while I remembered them."

We gathered round to inspect the drawing. The sistrum was a musical instrument, rather like a rattle, played before various gods. It was dedicated to Hathor, goddess of music, whose image appeared here as the head of a woman with long curling locks and the characteristic cow's ears. From this sculptured head rose a long loop of copper wire threaded with rods which were strung with beads, so that when the sistrum was held by its handle—this one in the shape of a lotus column—and shaken, it produced a pleasing if somewhat monotonous sound. All the elements I have described were present in Emerson's sketch, which meant that this object was truly unusual, undamaged, and intact.

"Couldn't get the face right," Emerson admitted. "It's very beautiful. Obviously from a royal workshop."

"And made for a royal woman," Ramses said. "I admire your forbearance, Father, I'd have been strongly tempted to take this. It ought to be in a museum."

"It will be," Emerson assured him, with a snap of his teeth. "We'll give the Albions plenty of rope, before we pull the noose tight. There can be no doubt; Jamil's tomb is that of one of the Divine Wives of Amon, and if these small objects are representative of the contents, Heaven only knows what else may be there."

Cyrus let out a low moan. "I'd sell my soul for a find like that. And if Joe Albion gets to it first, I'll strangle him with my bare hands."

Next day I penned a courteous note to Mrs. Albion thanking her for her delightful party. It was somewhat hypocritical, as Emerson was quick to point out, but in my opinion a certain amount of hypocrisy is necessary in maintaining the social amenities. If everyone said exactly what he or she thought of everyone else, there would be no social amenities.

"Anyhow," I added, folding the note, "breaking off relations with the Albions would be a serious error until we get the goods on them."

We went to work as usual, but did not accomplish a great deal. Emerson's discovery of the artifacts had whetted his appetite and stimulated his imagination. He tried to concentrate on the work at hand, but he would stop from time to time and stare off into space, mumbling to himself. How well I understood! The broken mud-brick walls of Deir el Medina were so pitiful in comparison to golden dreams of a royal tomb.

Jumana had come late to breakfast, looking so woebegone and red around the eyes that Sennia demanded to know where it hurt and what she could do to make it better. Nefret distracted the child by describing the decorations of the ballroom and the lavish menu, and the Great Cat of Re provided an additional diversion by appearing with an agitated mouse in its mouth. With Sennia's assistance Ramses managed to pry the cat's jaws apart and remove the mouse, which he carried outside and released, to the utter disgust of Horus. I hoped that the presentation of unharmed, living prey was not becoming a habit with the confounded cat. Horus at least had the decency to dispose of his in private.

I decided to say no more to Jumana. She had been punished by our combined disapproval and Nefret's tongue-lashing, and after all, she had not committed a serious misdemeanor, only an error in judgment understandable in a young girl. After having been raised in one society she had had to learn the ways of another; and since she had only been acquainted with men whose moral sensibilities were irreproachable, it was not surprising that she should have misunderstood the despicable intentions of Sebastian Albion.

She accepted the tedious task of sifting the fill without complaint and worked steadily all morning. When we stopped for luncheon she sat to one side, her eyes downcast, and Cyrus, kindhearted individual that he was, made an attempt to cheer her up.

"How about helping me this afternoon?" he asked. "You've been at that rubbish dump all morning. That all right with you, Emerson?"

"Certainly, certainly," said my equally tenderhearted husband.

"You were asking the other day about the theodolite," Bertie said. "I'll show you how to use it, if you like."

It was the first remark he had addressed to her, for she had kept out of his way. Her expressive face brightened.

"Thank you. You are very kind."

By the end of the day she had recovered her good spirits.

Whether she had had the decency to apologize to Bertie I did not know, but she was painstakingly polite to him and he responded like the nice lad he was, with no evidence of hard feelings.

Several days passed without our hearing a word from the Albions, to the disappointment of Emerson, who had rather hoped they would notice that the stolen objects had been disturbed. If they questioned the sufragi who had found him trying to open the lock they would know the identity of the intruder.

"The sufragi wouldn't betray the Father of Curses," said Ramses. "You ought to have left your card."

Emerson curled his lip in acknowledgment of this touch of humor.

"Why stir them up?" Nefret asked. "They've abandoned their plans to excavate. Perhaps they've given up on finding the tomb."

"No, they have not," Emerson grumbled. "Selim says they have hired that rascal Mohammed Hammad as their dragoman. He came back from wherever he was as soon as he got the word that Jamil was dead. He's no more a dragoman than I am an opera singer."

"He's a thief," I agreed. "But you may be sure he doesn't know any more about Jamil's tomb than we do. He'd have been looting it before this if he did."

The weather had turned unusually hot for that time of year. Even the nights were still and warm. We were all affected by it to some extent, except for Emerson, who never feels the heat and who can sleep through an earthquake. Never would I relinquish the comfort of my husband's presence, but I must say that lying next to him was rather like being in close proximity to an oven. After several restless nights, I had just got to sleep—or so it felt—when he mumbled loudly in my ear. It was the too-familiar refrain: "Hand of the god . . . what . . . where?"

I gave him a rather sharp poke. He rolled over, shoving me to the edge of the bed.

Wide awake and somewhat vexed, I abandoned any hope of repose. I went to the window and leaned out. The room was still dark but there was a freshness in the air that betokened the coming of dawn. It cooled my warm cheeks, and my temper. I had been standing there for several minutes when I heard the creak of an opening door. It was the door at the far end of the courtyard. I had been meaning to have Ali oil the hinges.

It was light enough by now for me to see dim shapes. There were two of them in the doorway, huddled close together. A whisper reached my ears; one form vanished, the other moved slyly and quietly toward the house.

I saw no need to wake Emerson; it is a laborious process at best, and I preferred to deal with this myself. I waited until she had almost reached her window before I climbed out of mine. She let out a stifled shriek and turned to flee, but I was too quick for her.

"Where have you been?" I demanded, seizing her in a firm grip.

"I—I—" Invention failed; she gasped, "Oh, Sitt Hakim, you frightened me!"

"Where have you been, Jumana?"

"Only for a walk. It was hot. I could not sleep."

"You were with a man. Don't lie, I saw him."

"I did nothing wrong. Please believe me!"

"So you have said before. What precisely did you do?"

"I—I promised I would not tell. I gave my word!"

Exasperation had caused me to raise my voice, and defiance, as I thought it, had caused her to raise hers. A grumble and a thrashing of bedclothes told me that we had wakened Emerson. These sounds were followed by a shout: "Peabody!" He always shouts when he reaches out and finds I am not beside him.

"Here," I called.

Emerson stumbled to the window and looked out. "Is that . . . Oh, good Gad!"

Only the upper half of his body was visible, but Emerson

is a modest man; he retreated, cursing, and began looking for his clothes. I knew it would take him a while, so I pushed Jumana toward her window.

"Go in. You are to remain in your room. If you leave the house without my permission, you need never come back."

She obeyed without resistance, verbal or physical. I thought I heard a little sob. It did not soften my heart.

When I climbed back in my own window, Emerson was still searching for his trousers. "Never mind that, Emerson," I said. "You may as well bathe and dress properly, it is almost morning. We have a serious problem on our hands. Jumana has been creeping out at night—possibly for several nights—and she was with a man. I am afraid it was Sebastian Albion."

"Damnation," Emerson murmured. He ran his fingers through his disheveled hair, pushing it back from his face. "Are you sure?"

"Who else would it be? Unless," I added bitterly, "she has a whole string of them. How could I have been so deceived in her character? I am sadly disappointed, Emerson."

"Now, Peabody, don't jump to conclusions." He sat on the side of the bed and pulled me down next to him. "There may be an innocent explanation. Have you given her a chance to explain?"

"She refused to answer my questions. She said she had given her word. Her word! To a vile deceiver like that!"

"Give her another chance." A horrible idea struck him. In quavering tones he asked, "You don't want *me* to question her, do you?"

"No, Emerson, you are hopeless about such matters. I will give her another chance to confess, naturally. I will leave her locked in her room today and speak to her again this evening, after she has had time to repent."

"And you have had time to cool off," said Emerson, putting an arm round my shoulders. "My dear, I don't blame you for being hurt and disappointed, but—er—you aren't going to starve her, I hope?"

"Certainly not. I will take her breakfast to her myself. Later."

I felt calmer after a nice long bath, but I was not ready to face Jumana. I would be the first to admit that my maternal instincts are not well developed—they had been stunted, I believe, by the raising of Ramses—but I had become rather attached to Jumana. I had had such high hopes for her. To find that she was a sneak and a liar and—and worse, perhaps—had left me not only disappointed, but hurt. Yes, Emerson was right about that. I had believed she had become equally attached to us.

When I went to breakfast, the Great Cat of Re was sitting on my chair, its chin on the table, its large green eyes fixed on the platter of bacon. "This is beginning to be like the house of the Three Bears," I said. "It sits on our chairs, it sleeps on our beds, and now it is about to eat my porridge."

Sennia found this very witty, but nobody else did, including the cat. Ramses's keen black eyes detected the perturbation behind my attempt at normalcy; brow furrowing, he started to speak, glanced at Sennia, and remained silent. It was Sennia who asked about Jumana. I explained that she was not feeling well and would spend the day in bed. "You are not to go in her room," I added. "She needs to rest. Do you understand?"

"Shall I take her a tray?" Fatima asked.

"I will see to that," I replied. "Later. Thank you, Fatima. Where is Gargery? It is time Sennia left for her lessons."

Gargery entered at that moment to announce we had guests. "Mr. Bertie and Mr. Cyrus. You didn't tell us they were expected for breakfast, madam."

"Stop trying to put me in the wrong, Gargery," I said somewhat snappishly. "They were not expected."

"But we are always glad to see them," Fatima said, adding plates and cups and silverware to the table, and bustling out for more food.

"Sorry to disturb you folks," Cyrus said. He did not look

at all sorry. Bliss—delight—happiness . . . The words are too weak for the emotion that transformed his face. The only other time I had seen that glow was on the day he and Katherine were wed.

"What is it, Cyrus?" I cried, jumping to my feet.

"It's for Bertie to make the announcement," Cyrus replied. He was puffed with pride.

Bertie looked round the table. "Where's Jumana? She should be here."

"Oh my goodness," I gasped. "You aren't . . . you two aren't engaged?"

Bertie's boyish laugh rang out. "Better than that, Mrs. Emerson. We've found it, Jumana and I. Jamil's tomb."

Pandemonium ensued. Even Gargery, who had only the vaguest notion of what Bertie meant, clapped his hands and joined in the cries of excitement and congratulation. As the others gathered round Bertie, all talking at once, I slipped out of the room.

Jumana was sitting on her bed, her hands folded and her face smeared with dried tears. Now that I got a good look at her, I realized she was not dressed for a romantic rendezvous. Her shirt and trousers were torn and dusty, her boots were scuffed, and her hair straggled over her face.

"Bertie is here," I said.

She jumped up. "Then it's all right? He told you? I promised I would not, it was to be a surprise, his surprise. May I go now?" She let out a peal of laughter. "I am very hungry!"

Ah, the resilience of youth! From despair to delight in the twinkling of an eye! I could have let her go without further delay; I was tempted to do so, but justice compelled me to make what amends I could.

"First, I must apologize," I said.

"Apologize? To me? Why?"

"For misjudging you. I was wrong, and you were right to keep your promise to Bertie. I deeply regret the injustice I did you and I hope you will forgive me." I held out my hand. She would have fainted with sheer surprise if I had attempted to embrace her, and anyhow, she was very grubby.

"Forgive? You?" She stared wide-eyed at my offered hand.

"I did you an injustice," I repeated. "Shake hands, if you will, and then go to the others."

She did not shake my hand. She kissed it, fervently and damply, gave me a radiant smile, and ran out of the room.

I would not have blamed her for taking advantage of her role as heroine—misjudged, falsely accused heroine at that! Instead she insisted that all the credit belonged to Bertie. It was he and he alone who had deduced where the tomb must be.

"But where is it?" Emerson shouted, tugging at his hair. "Bertie won't say. Jumana, where—"

"We want to show you," Bertie explained. "You'll never believe it otherwise."

"They're entitled," Ramses said, smiling in sympathy. "Lead the way, Bertie."

He led us to Deir el Medina.

Our men were there, waiting to begin the day's work. Ramses called them to gather round, explaining that Bertie had an important announcement to make. The truth had begun to dawn on Emerson by then. "It can't be," he mumbled. "I don't believe it. Damnation!"

"Father, if you please," Ramses said. "Bertie, you have the floor." He added, with a grin, "Make the most of it."

"Oh, well," Bertie said, blushing. "It was an accident, really, you know. I sat here for days with my foot up and nothing much to do but stare at the scenery. I got to know it pretty well. Look up there."

He pointed.

Straight ahead, the walls of the temple occupied the opening of the little valley, with the fields and the river stretching out to the north and the cliffs rising up on either side. The ruined tombs of the workers were scattered along the western slope. Bertie's extended arm indicated the highest point, to the left of the temple. We stared in silent bewilderment for a time. We were all looking for a sculpture—the figure of a god, weathered by time, shaped by the hand of man.

A divinity had shaped it—nature herself. As I have had occasion to mention, the rock formations of the western mountains assume bizarre forms. This might have been a giant fist, gripping the crest of the hill—four regular, rounded, parallel shapes, with a small spur of rock next to them like the end of a thumb. It was a prominent landmark, rising high above the lower, less precipitous part of the hillside, and once the eye had defined it the resemblance was unmistakable.

"There!" I exclaimed in wonderment. "Emerson, do you see?"

Emerson removed his pith helmet and flung it onto the ground. I gave him a warning frown and a little poke. It was sufficient; his better nature triumphed over envy. "Well, well," he said hoarsely. "Hmph. That is—congratulations, Vandergelt."

Cyrus slapped him on the back. "It belongs to both of us, old pal. All of us, I should say."

"No, no." Emerson drew himself up. "We made an agreement, Vandergelt. The tombs of Deir el Medina are yours, and it was Bertie who found this one. Congratulations, I say."

Never had I admired my dear Emerson more. He looked so noble, his shoulders thrown back and his tanned face wearing a strained smile, it was all I could do not to embrace him. Cyrus was equally moved. He took out his handkerchief and blew his nose.

"That's darned decent of you, Emerson. But no more than I expected."

"And no less than you deserve," Emerson said gruffly. "So where is the damned tomb?"

"In that crack between the first and second fingers,"

Bertie said. "It took us several days—nights, I should say—
to find it. Fortunately the moon has been full. We haven't
been inside. We thought Cyrus ought to have the privilege,"
he added, wincing as Cyrus seized his hand and wrung it
vigorously.

"Are you sure the passage is open?" I asked. "I know
Jamil has been in and out of the place, but he is—was—
slightly built and agile and foolhardy."

Naturally the men ignored this sensible comment. Emerson's eyes glittered like sapphires. "What are we waiting
for? Let's go!"

We restrained Emerson while we discussed the best way
to proceed. Bertie explained how he and Jumana had managed it, scaling the cliff and lowering themselves from
above by means of a rope. Emerson was pleased to approve
this plan, though if I had not kept hold of him he would have
started straight up the sheerest part of the cliff.

We all went, of course, including Selim and Daoud. Their
assistance was invaluable, for it was a tricky climb. When
we stood atop the rounded "finger" looking down, I addressed Jumana, who had stuck to me like a burr.

"You did this at night? Really, my dear, was that wise? You
ought to have told the Professor, or Cyrus, of your theory."

Bertie overheard. "It was my fault, Mrs. Emerson. I
wanted to be sure before I told anyone. I didn't mean to tell
Jumana either, but I asked too many questions—about the
terrain here, and whether Jamil had explored this area—and
she wrung it out of me."

He turned to respond to Emerson, and Jumana said in a
low voice, "He would have searched alone. It was too dangerous."

"It certainly would have been," I agreed. "I am surprised
he allowed you to accompany him."

"He said I could not. So," said Jumana coolly, "I told him
that you and Nefret do not let Ramses and the Professor stop
you from doing what you want, and I was trying to be like

you. But you see why I could not speak before. He trusted me, and I had—I had been unkind and unfair to him."

"Ah," I said somewhat uneasily. "So you think well of him, do you?"

She met my eyes directly and with no sign of self-consciousness. "He is a good man. We are friends, I hope."

I hoped so too.

Watching Daoud knot the rope round Cyrus's waist, I issued a final order. "Cyrus, stop at once and come back if the passage becomes too narrow or the ceiling looks unstable or—"

"Sure, Amelia. Lower away, Daoud."

"You shouldn't have allowed him to go first, Emerson," I scolded, as Cyrus's body disappeared into the crevice.

"My dear Peabody, how could I deprive him of a moment he has waited for his whole life? If he died in the attempt, he would die happy. That," Emerson added quickly, "was only a figure of speech. Nothing is going to happen. But—er—well, perhaps I ought to follow him."

"Not with one arm, Emerson!"

"They will have to lower me, that's all," said Emerson, his chin protruding in a manner that made remonstrance useless. "We've another rope, haven't we?"

"It will be a tight fit," Bertie warned. "There's a roughish platform, about five feet square, with the passage going off into the cliff at a right angle. It's partially filled with—"

"Plenty of room," said Emerson, tossing one end of the rope to Selim and trying to knot the other end round his waist.

I said, "Oh, curse it," and tied the knot myself. Then I lay flat on the ground peering down into the crevice as Emerson was lowered.

With the rope anchored and held by both Selim and Ramses, I was not afraid Emerson would fall. I was afraid he would try to crawl into the narrow passage and get stuck like a cork in a bottle. It was quite dark down there except for the limited light of Emerson's torch. I could see very little, and the auditory sense was not of much help either, thanks to the echoes that distorted every sound. The rope went loose and Emerson yelled something, and I let out a small exclamation.

"It's all right, Mother," Ramses said. "He's reached the platform."

"He won't be able to get through the passage," I muttered. "He's twice the size of Jamil."

"He'll get through," Ramses said, passing his sleeve over his perspiring face. "If he has to dig the fill out with his bare hands. *One* bare hand."

I could hear him doing it. Loose rock began falling from the bottom of the cleft, rattling down the hillside. It slowed and stopped. After that there was nothing but silence, until a call from Cyrus brought us all to our feet. Daoud seized the rope and pulled with all his might. As soon as Cyrus's head appeared we fell on him and dragged him out.

"Well?" I cried.

Cyrus shook his head. His lips moved, but no words emerged. Tears ran down his face. His eyes were red-rimmed.

"Dust," said my practical son. He handed Cyrus the water bottle, and then leaped for the other rope as it tightened. With Daoud's help they soon had Emerson up; he hadn't even bothered tying the rope round his body, but was holding on with one hand. We hauled him over the edge and he staggered to his feet, blinking bloodshot eyes.

"There are four coffins," he gasped. "Four. Four of everything, packed into that room from floor to ceiling and side to side. Four sets of canopic jars, four gold-inlaid boxes, four funerary papyri, four hundred ushebtis, four thousand—"

Cyrus began jumping up and down and waving his arms. "The God's Wives," he bellowed. "Four! I never thought I'd live to see this day! If I were struck dead tonight, I'd be the happiest man alive."

"No, you wouldn't," I said, catching hold of him. "You would be dead. And you will be, if you fall off the cliff."

I wanted to take Emerson home; he had ruined another shirt squeezing through those tight spaces, and banged his head, and scraped most of the skin off both hands and cracked the cast. Cyrus was in little better case, but neither of them heard a word I said; they kept shouting enthusiastically at each other and shaking hands. I consigned them both to the devil (they didn't hear that either) and concluded I was entitled to satisfy my own curiosity.

We went down in turn, two at a time for safety's sake: Jumana and Bertie, Ramses and I, Selim and Daoud. Emerson offered to take Nefret, but she said she believed she would wait. The procedure was somewhat uncomfortable—crawling on hands and knees over rough fragments of stone, with dust choking one's mouth and an occasional bat squeaking past overhead, but the sight was so incredible I would not have wanted to miss it.

The opening of the chamber had been closed with mortared blocks. Jamil had removed the upper layers, stacking the stones along the passage, which made the last few feet something of a squeeze. Looking in, I saw at first only a dazzle of gold. It was the end of an anthropoid coffin, inlaid with glass and semiprecious stones. Packed all around it were smaller objects: woven baskets, caskets of ebony and cedar, tattered fragments of papyrus and linen. Jamil had rummaged through the smaller boxes, dragging out anything he could reach.

Cyrus's long patient wait had been rewarded at last. This was another cache, like that of the royal mummies; loyal followers of the Adorers of the God had rescued them and their funerary goods from tomb robbers, and hidden them away in this remote spot. Time and careless handling had destroyed some of the artifacts, but it was still one of the richest finds ever made in Egypt.

We could not even begin excavating the tomb chamber

that day. The passage and the platform had to be completely
cleared first and a method of stabilizing and removing the
objects determined upon. Needless to say, all work came to
a standstill; the men danced and sang and cheered and
Daoud told them all extravagant lies about the treasures in
the chamber. It was necessary to make arrangements for
guards, by day and by night, for the news would spread like
wildfire.

"We might stop at Gurneh and have a word with Mohammed Hassan," I suggested. "A curse or two, perhaps?"

Emerson chuckled. "He will probably cry like a baby.
Yes, I will point out the moral advantages of honesty. If
he had not cheated Jamil, he'd have had a chance at this
tomb."

"It would have been a bit tricky," Ramses said. "Even if
they worked only at night, they would have left traces of
their activities, and we might have observed those signs.
That was why Jamil tried to lure us out into the western
wadis. He wanted everyone away from Deir el Medina."

Since the tomb must not be left unguarded for an instant,
Daoud and several of the other men volunteered to stay until
evening, when they would be relieved.

"I suppose you plan to sleep here every night," I said to
Cyrus.

"Every night and every day till we can get a steel door in
place. Jumping Jehoshaphat, Amelia, you don't know what
this means to me! Katherine! I've got to tell Katherine.
She'll be so durned proud of this boy! And then," Cyrus
went on, grinning fiendishly, "maybe I'll just run over to
Luxor and break the news to Joe Albion. I want to see his
face when he hears."

We sent Selim off with a list of the equipment we would
need, and dismissed the men for the day. A celebration was
definitely in order; Cyrus had promised the greatest fantasia
ever seen in Luxor, but that would have to wait. Excitement
and exertion had left everyone weary, and Bertie and Ju-

mana both showed the effects of several sleepless nights. I instructed Bertie to go home and rest.

We had an early night too. Tea and biscuits and Sennia's excited questions revived Jumana temporarily, but I sent her off to bed immediately after dinner. Sennia would not go to bed until Emerson promised to take her into the tomb.

"Emerson, I absolutely forbid it," I exclaimed, after she had gone dancing off with Horus in her arms.

"Oh, come, Peabody, don't be a spoilsport. Ramses was in and out of worse places when he was her age. I won't take her until we've made sure it's safe." He threw his napkin on the table and stood up. "I'm late. Vandergelt will be there already."

"Emerson," I said. "This is Cyrus's tomb. He is in charge, not you."

Emerson looked uncomfortable. "I suppose I am allowed to offer my expert advice?"

"Not unless he asks for it. He is generously allowing you to participate, which is more than you ever did for him!"

"Hmph," said Emerson, stroking his chin.

"You might quite properly offer him the assistance of your staff," Ramses suggested.

"Oh. Hmmm. Certainly. Including myself?" He gave me a questioning look.

I pretended to consider. Emerson had really behaved quite well, for him. "If he asks you," I conceded.

"He asked me to stand guard with him tonight."

"Then you may go."

Emerson burst out laughing and gave me a bruising hug. "Thank you for giving me permission, my dear. Ramses, are you coming?"

"No," I said, before Ramses could reply. "He won't be needed. Nefret, you might have another look at his injury. In my opinion he overdid it today."

From Manuscript H

Nefret had also noticed that her husband seemed abstracted. He submitted without comment to her examination, but she found no cause for concern. The wound was healing well.

"It's nice to have an evening to ourselves," she said.

"Yes." He was prowling restlessly around the sitting room, picking up a book and putting it down, straightening a stack of papers. Hands folded in her lap, she watched him for a while and then took a deep breath. Her heart was pounding.

"I have something to tell you," she said.

He came to her at once, dropping to his knees in front of the chair and taking the hand she offered.

"I wondered." His other hand came to rest lightly on her waist. "But I didn't want to ask."

"Why not? You had every right."

"No, I hadn't. When did you know? Nefret, look at me. Before Gaza?"

She might have equivocated, mentioned the various factors that made certainty difficult. She met his troubled gaze squarely. "Yes."

"And you risked that? That awful trip, the danger, the—"

She took his face between her hands. "I knew it would be all right. I can't tell you how I knew, but I did. I would have risked it anyhow. I want this very much, but you are the dearest thing in the world to me. I let you go—I let you take the risk—but I'd have died of suspense waiting in Cairo. Oh, darling, aren't you glad?"

"Do you suppose I don't feel the same about you? I'm beginning to understand what you went through, all those times when I was off on some bloody damned job without you. Glad? I suppose I am. Will be. At this moment, I . . . I'm afraid, I think. I can't take this risk for you. I can't even share it."

She had never seen tears in his eyes before. Her heart turned over. He hid his face against her and she held him, her arms tight around his bowed shoulders.

"It's too late to change our minds now," she murmured.

He let out a long breath and when he raised his head she saw again the boy she had loved so long without realizing how much she loved him. His eyes were bright with laughter and dawning joy. "Are you sure you're prepared for this, Nefret? You've heard Mother's stories. What if it turns out to be like me?"

⋮

The house was very quiet. I was alone, without even a cat to keep me company. Many duties awaited me, but for some reason I didn't feel like tackling any of them. Seating myself on the sofa, I found my sewing box and took out the crumpled scrap of linen.

The sitting room door opened. One look at their faces was all I needed. Hand in hand, they came to stand before me.

"We wanted you to be the first to know, Mother," Nefret said.

I had to clear my throat before I could speak. I got out four words before my voice failed me. "Well! Naturally, I am . . ."

"Oh, Mother, don't cry." Nefret sat down beside me and put her arms round me. "You never cry."

"Nor will I mar the happiness of this moment by doing so," I assured her, somewhat huskily. I held out my hand to Ramses, who seated himself on my other side, let out a yelp, and sprang up. He had sat on my embroidery.

We laughed until the tears came; they had not far to come. Returning to his seat, Ramses held up the miserable object.

"She's going to claim she has known for weeks. What *is* this, Mother?"

I wiped my eyes. "A—er—a bib. Babies dribble quite a lot. These blue bits are violets, and these . . . It is rather nasty-looking, isn't it? I think the bloodstains will wash out."

"It's the most beautiful bib I've ever seen," Nefret said, wiping *her* eyes. "And I hope the bloodstains never wash out. You did know!"

"Not until this moment," I said firmly. It would have been the height of unkindness to spoil such a wonderful surprise. "I was making it for Lia's little girl."

"Girl?" Ramses's eyebrows tilted.

"I suppose Abdullah told you," Nefret said with a chuckle. "Did he happen to mention ours?"

"He never tells me anything important," I said. Nefret laughed, and I saw Ramses shape the word with his lips: "Ours." He was still trying to take it in.

I had known, of course, for some time. To an experienced eye the symptoms are unmistakable.

"When?" I inquired.

"September," Nefret said.

"Ah. So the worst is over, and you are obviously in splendid health. If bouncing across the desert in that motorcar and stealing horses didn't bring on a miscarriage, nothing will."

I spoke with all the authority I could summon, which is, if I may say so, considerable, and the faint shadow of anxiety on Ramses's face faded. "If you say so, Mother."

"I do. And," I added, "next time I see Abdullah he will verify it."

From Manuscript H

They told Emerson next morning. It took a while to get his attention; he and Cyrus and the others were already planning the day's activities when they arrived at Deir el Medina. After his wife had poked him with her parasol a time or two he agreed, amiably but in some perplexity, to join them for a brief private conversation in a corner of the vestibule.

They had discussed various ways of breaking the news.

"If I say we have something to tell him, he'll look blank and ask what," Nefret said with a chuckle. "And announcing he is about to become a grandfather is too sickeningly coy."

So, in the end, she blurted it out. "I'm going to have a baby, Father."

Emerson's jaw went slack. "A . . . a what?"

"We don't know yet," Ramses said. "But we're pretty sure it's bound to be either a boy or a girl."

Emerson choked. "Boy? Girl? Baby? Good—good Gad!"

"Take my handkerchief," said his wife.

Emerson indignantly refused the handkerchief; if there were tears in his eyes he blotted them on Nefret's hair as he took her in a close embrace. He turned to Ramses, held out his hand, and then, to the latter's utter stupefaction, embraced him too.

He was with difficulty prevented from rushing out shouting the news at the top of his lungs to everyone present. "A little less publicly, please," Nefret begged. "We haven't told Fatima yet, or Kadija, or Sennia, or Gargery, or—"

"Oh, of course Gargery's feelings are of paramount importance," said Emerson with heavy sarcasm and a smile that stretched from ear to ear. "Naturally, my dears, I bow to your wishes. Good Gad!"

Emerson went directly to Cyrus and whispered in his ear. Within five minutes everyone on the site had heard. It was possible to watch the word spread by the smiles that warmed the men's faces as they turned to look at Nefret.

She accepted Cyrus's hearty good wishes and promises of a celebration to end all celebrations, and then got their minds back to business. "Did anything happen last night?"

"Good Gad," said Emerson, still grinning. "Good Gad! Er—what did you say? Oh. Well, we saw a few shadows flitting about hither and yon, but they vanished when I announced my—our—presence."

"You didn't recognize any of them?" Ramses asked.

"I didn't have to see them to know who they were," his father retorted. "Members of our distinguished tomb-robbing families having a look round just in case."

"They may try again," Ramses said.

"Bah," said Emerson. "It's been over fifty years since the Gurnawis attacked an archaeologist." He added, his face falling, "The greatest nuisance will be sightseers. They will be swarming as soon as the news spreads."

In this he was correct. Following regulations, Cyrus had immediately informed the Service des Antiquités of the find. An enthusiastic telegram of congratulations from Daressy was followed in two days by a visit from that gentleman. It was his official duty to inspect the place and make sure the rules were being followed, and a find of that magnitude happened very seldom. Timber balks and a complex arrangement of scaffolding and ladders had been erected, so it was now possible to reach the tomb from below. They had to haul Daressy up by means of a net. He didn't much enjoy the process, but as he informed them afterward, he would have undergone worse to see the astonishing spectacle.

"My felicitations," he declared, mopping his sweating face. "For once we have got in ahead of our energetic friends from Gurneh! It is a pleasure to know I can safely leave the clearance in your capable hands, mes amis."

He accepted a cup of tea and mopped his face again. "By the by, I meant to ask how it is that M. Vandergelt is involved. I was under the impression that he had the firman for Medinet Habu."

"You are familiar with how it is, monsieur," Emerson said glibly and ungrammatically. "Thanks to the bedamned war, we are all short of hands. We help one another, as professional goodness demands. It was the young M. Vandergelt who in fact discovered the hiding place."

"Ah, je comprends bien," said Daressy, amused. "C'est admirable, messieurs. Proceed, then. I will return from time to time, if I may, not to interfere with your work, but to admire the wonders you will find."

"I told you he wouldn't object," Emerson said to his wife, after they had got Daressy off.

"You left him no choice in the matter," said that lady.

Every tourist in Luxor wanted to see the tomb. Most of them left in a hurry, driven off by Emerson's curses and by the fact that there was not much to see as yet. Cyrus was determined nothing should be removed from the chamber until he had arranged for proper lighting and had made certain that objects like the coffins could be moved without damage.

One group of visitors was more persistent. The Albions arrived, en masse, the day after the discovery. Jumana retreated as soon as she saw them, drawing Bertie away with her, and nobody offered them a chair or a glass of tea. The coolness of their reception would have disconcerted sensitive persons, but that adjective did not apply to any of the Albions.

"So that's how you're going to get in and out of the place," Mr. Albion remarked, eyeing the scaffolding. "Too much for me, but Sebastian would like to have a look."

"Sebastian will have to do without a look," said Emerson. "Good Gad, I have not the time for this."

He stalked off to join Jumana and Bertie at the foot of the scaffold. Ramses lingered, marveling at the Albions' thick skins. Cyrus was unable to resist the temptation to gloat, boasting extravagantly about Bertie and describing the contents of the tomb in loving detail. Mr. Albion's fixed grin remained in place.

"Sounds like a big job," he said. "How long do you think it will take?"

"Hard to tell," Cyrus said. "We'll have to see what's there and what needs to be done."

"Fascinating," Sebastian declared. He looked around with a complacent smile. "I've never observed an excavation in process. Hope you don't mind if we drop by now and then to watch."

Ramses had had enough. "Apparently it has escaped your attention that you are not welcome here," he said. "After what happened the other night—"

"Oh, that. An unfortunate misunderstanding."

"Quite," said Mrs. Albion, speaking for the first time. "I do think, Mr. Emerson, that you owe my son Sebastian an apology."

Ramses caught his mother's eye. He took a deep breath. "I am indeed sorry. Sorry that I didn't catch up with him."

"Well, really!" Mrs. Albion took her husband's arm. "Evil is in the mind of the beholder; isn't that so, Mrs. Emerson? Let us go, Mr. Albion."

Cyrus couldn't resist one final dig.

"No use making arrangements with the dealers on this one, Joe. At the final division, most of the objects will go to the Cairo Museum, and the rest, supposing they are generous enough to leave us a percentage, will not be for sale."

The Albions left, and Ramses said, "You did rather rub it in, Cyrus."

"Enjoyed every minute of it," Cyrus declared, stroking his goatee. "I hoped Joe would slip and make some dumb remark about how he'd already paid for his share, but he's too smart for that. I wonder who else is going to turn up?"

The next to turn up was Howard Carter, who had to listen to a tirade from Emerson about his exploration of the western wadis. "I've been trying to track you down for weeks," Emerson declared indignantly. "Where have you been? What were you doing in the Gabbanat el-Qirud? Why the devil haven't you made your notes accessible?"

Carter was too much in awe of Emerson to protest the injustice of the complaint. "My notes are at your disposal, sir, as always," he said meekly. "I apologize if I offended you."

"Bah," said Emerson. "Now see here, Carter—"

"Father, I'm sure Mr. Carter would rather hear about the new tomb," Nefret interrupted. "Sit down, Mr. Carter, and have a cup of tea."

"Thank you, ma'am," Carter said with a grateful look at her. "I most certainly would. I will be in Luxor for some time—my next project is to copy the procession reliefs at Luxor Temple—but naturally, if I can assist in any way at all . . ."

"You can come by now and then," Emerson said grudgingly. "It will teach you how to conduct a proper clearance of a tomb."

However, the most unexpected news came in the form of a telegram.

"Look forward to seeing you all soon. Fondest regards, Cousin Ismail."

∴

"**I** might have known the news of the tomb would fetch him," Emerson grumbled. "He doesn't say when he is coming. Damned inconsiderate."

"Even more inconsiderate is that infernal signature," I said in some vexation. "How are we to introduce him? The Vandergelts are bound to recognize him as Sethos, but we cannot call him that. What is his real name?"

"Cursed if I know," Emerson admitted. "Never gave it much thought."

"Well, my dear, he will turn up where and when he chooses, as he chooses, and there isn't a thing we can do about it."

He turned up at Deir el Medina, two days later. We had had several other visitors that morning, including the cursed Albions; they came round almost every day, though they did not have the temerity to approach us again. Emerson stormed about this, but there was no way we could keep them away from the site as long as they did nothing but sit in their carriage at a distance and look on. The scaffolding had been completed and the door ordered; since nothing more could be done until we had acquired a generator and electric lighting, Emerson had sent us back to work on our boring village. I looked up from my rubbish dump to see a man on horseback approaching.

He came straight to me and removed his hat. "Good morning, Amelia. At your rubbish again, I see."

He looked well. I observed that first: the healthy color in his face, the upright frame and easy pose. A neatly wound turban concealed his hair, and a magnificent coal-black beard hid the lower part of his face. The tweed suit was not the one he had borrowed from Ramses; it was new and very well cut. In short, he was the picture of a distinguished Oriental gentleman, possibly an official of high rank who had, as his accent indicated, been educated at an English university. Cyrus might be able to identify him as the surly, silent individual who had been his guest the year before, but I doubted any of the others who had known him so briefly would be able to do so.

"A fondness for beards must run in the family," I remarked.

"You could hardly expect me to appear in Luxor without one, my dear. Some sharp-eyed person might notice I bear a resemblance to a certain well-known Egyptologist."

"How am I to introduce you?"

"Cousin Ismail, of course. I rather like the name."

He turned and offered his hand as Emerson came hurrying toward us.

The cordial reception he received seemed to surprise him a little. Nefret gave him a kiss, and Cyrus a hearty handshake, a knowing smile, and an invitation to visit the tomb. Sethos had to hear all about its discovery first; he congratulated Bertie and Jumana, who didn't know quite what to make of him, but who were flattered by his interest. After luncheon we all went up to the platform outside the tomb. Sethos crawled in and out of the passage, and then brushed himself off and remarked, "You've quite a job ahead of you, Vandergelt. I would be happy to recommend a good restorer.

I suspect you may need one, some of the organic materials appear to be in a delicate condition."

"Are you an archaeologist, sir?" Jumana asked.

"I have had a good deal of experience in the field," said Sethos smoothly. He glanced casually at the rock face above the entrance. It was the first time I had noticed the symbol— a roughly carved circle divided by a curving line.

Ramses waited until Bertie and Jumana and Cyrus had started down the ladder before he spoke. "I hope you don't mind, sir. I took the liberty—"

Sethos grinned. "I was about to suggest it myself. The Master's mark may not deter every thief in Gurneh, but it still carries some weight. By the by, are you acquainted with that lot?"

From the height where we stood, the Albions's carriage was clearly visible. It had been there for several hours.

"We know them slightly," I said. "Do you?"

"Albion was one of my best customers. I stopped dealing with him a few years ago, after he tried to cheat me."

"Cheat you?" Emerson repeated. "I wouldn't have thought anyone could."

"Dear me, Radcliffe, was that meant to be sarcastic? He didn't succeed. Watch out for him, that's all I'm saying."

When we parted for the day, Cyrus apologized for not inviting "Cousin Ismail" to dinner. "Got to stand guard tonight," he explained. "But we're expecting the door to arrive in a day or two; once that is up and secured, we hope, sir, to see a great deal of you. I would very much enjoy a private chat."

"Thank you," said my brother-in-law.

I had assumed he would stay with us. He said he had made other arrangements, but would be delighted to join us for tea and an early supper. Jumana's presence prevented conversation of a personal nature, and when we got to the house Sennia was waiting on the veranda.

"So this is Sennia," said Sethos, offering his hand. "I have heard a great deal about you—all to your credit, and all well deserved, I see."

He had a way with women of all ages, and Sennia was no exception. Immensely flattered at the grown-up speech and gesture, she gravely shook hands with him. "Thank you, sir. I have not heard about you, though. Are you a friend of ours?"

"A very old friend" was the smiling reply. "Isn't that so, Radcliffe?"

"You call him Radcliffe?" Sennia spread her skirts in a ladylike manner and took the chair he held for her. "He doesn't like to be called that, you know."

"I had no idea," Sethos exclaimed. "What shall I call him, then?"

"Well, I call him Professor," Sennia explained. "Aunt Amelia calls him Emerson, or 'my dear,' and Nefret calls him Father, which he is, and Ramses calls him 'sir,' and some people call him 'Father of Curses.' "

"Perhaps 'sir' would be best," said Sethos, wrinkling his brow. "What do you think, Sennia?"

I decided it was time to intervene. Emerson was biting his lip and muttering. "Speaking of names," I said, "perhaps you would allow us—your old friends—to use your given name."

"Call me anything you like, Amelia dear" was the smiling and uninformative response.

At least it got us off the subject of names, though Sethos continued to address his brother deferentially as "sir," which made Emerson swear under his breath.

"Do you know Mr. Vandergelt too?" Sennia asked.

"Oh, yes. One might say I know him as well as he knows himself." He left Sennia to puzzle over this enigmatic remark, which the rest of us understood quite well. "I have not met Mrs. Vandergelt, though, or her son."

"Can we have a party?" Sennia asked eagerly.

"We must certainly arrange something," I remarked. "But it will have to wait until the tomb is locked up."

"A wise precaution," Sethos agreed gravely. "One never knows, does one?"

"We are glad to have you here, sir," Nefret said. "You will stay, we hope, for Cyrus's celebration."

"He has good reason to celebrate," Sethos said. "And I understand you and your husband have another cause for rejoicing."

"How did you—how do you—?" Nefret gasped.

"I have my sources," said Sethos. He held out his hand, and when he spoke the mockery was gone from his face and voice. "I wish you joy, Nefret. And you, Ramses. I suppose you'll be returning to England before long?"

"Our child will be born in Egypt, as is fitting," Nefret said. "Do you suppose I'd allow a pompous male English physician to take care of me, when there are two trained women obstetricians on the staff of my hospital?"

"What about you?" Emerson demanded of Sethos.

"I'm in no hurry to leave. England hasn't much to offer me." He smiled wickedly at his brother.

Emerson's face reddened. "Neither has Luxor."

"My dear fellow, I wouldn't dream of interfering with your activities. In fact, I would be delighted to assist in any possible manner."

"Ha," said Emerson.

Nefret turned her chuckle into a cough.

After dinner the men went off to stand guard. Emerson declined, with thanks, Sethos's offer to join them.

"Do you suppose he will ever get over suspecting my intentions?" inquired my brother-in-law, after we had retired to the sitting room.

"Perhaps," Nefret suggested, "if you would get over teasing him . . ."

"I can't resist, Nefret. He's such an easy mark. I was teasing, though, when I implied I would stay on here. I must leave tomorrow."

"So soon?" Nefret exclaimed. Impulsively she placed her

hand on his shoulder. "You will miss Cyrus's party. We want to keep you with us a while longer."

"You really mean it, don't you?" The strange gray-green eyes were, for once, very kind. "I'd like to, Nefret, but I can't."

"You are going back to the war, aren't you?" I asked composedly. "I thought you had promised Margaret this would be your last assignment."

"The job's not finished yet, Amelia dear. I made a quick trip here because—well, for two reasons. I must be getting old; I did want to see all of you. The other reason is more . . . difficult."

"Would you like me to leave?" Nefret asked.

"No. Please stay. Did Amelia tell you about a conversation we had recently concerning my daughter?"

Nefret's eyes widened, and I said, "I considered it a private confidence. I have not even told Emerson."

"Thank you, Amelia. I wasn't quite myself at the time; what precisely did I say?"

"You said she held you accountable for her mother's death, and that she had run away from home. You attempted to find her at that time, I presume. A girl of fifteen or sixteen should not have been able to elude a determined search."

"She was sixteen. But very precocious in a number of ways. Like her mother. I did search, long and hard, without result. I believe she had help, from one of Bertha's former friends—the same one who told Maryam—Molly—about her mother's death. Recently I heard that she had found a— a protector, and was in Egypt. I've been playing with the Turks ever since; haven't had time to look for her here."

"I am very sorry," Nefret said gently. "Can nothing be done to save her?"

"She doesn't want to be saved. Especially by me."

He had not given way, nor would he, but I knew he cared more for the girl than he would admit and that guilt as well as affection motivated his search. I began, "There is a chance that we might—"

"You may encounter her; our Egypt is a small world, in a sense. That is why I brought the subject up. But, Amelia dear, don't assume that because you managed to reform me—up to a point—you can redeem the entire damned universe. If Maryam blames me for her mother's death, how do you suppose she feels about you?"

He rose, rather heavily. "I'll say good night, and goodbye. My regards to Ramses and—er—Emerson."

"Won't we see you again?" Nefret asked.

"Not this time. I have business in Luxor before I leave tomorrow. If you learn anything about Molly, a message to our mutual friend with the preposterous name will reach me eventually. He will notify you of any change in my situation."

"Your death, you mean?" I asked steadily.

"Now, Amelia, it isn't like you to look on the dark side. Who knows, it may be a wedding invitation!" His mocking smile faded and he said hesitantly, "If you should hear from Margaret—"

"I will write her tomorrow," I promised. "Someone must know her current address."

"Thank you." He took my hand. "Turn your back, Nefret."

She let out a gasp and so did I. Sethos laughed and caught me in his arms and kissed me—on the brow.

"You will always be the woman I love," he said. "That doesn't prevent me from loving Margaret as much. You understand, I think."

"Yes," I said. "Turn your back, Nefret."

Cyrus was bitterly disappointed when he learned of Sethos's departure, though the arrival of the steel door, a day ahead of schedule, distracted him temporarily. Selim assured him the men would bend their best efforts to have it in place the following day.

"Then I can send out my invitations to the fantasia," Cyrus said. "Shame Ismail had to leave so soon, I was looking forward to seeing more of him."

"Typical," Emerson growled. "Comes and goes at his own convenience."

"He has other duties," I said reprovingly. "As you are well aware."

We did hear from him once again, however. A letter, hand-delivered, awaited us when we got to the house that afternoon. It contained only two sentences: "There are strangers in Luxor. And my former customer is still in the market."

"I can guess who that's from, but what the dickens does it mean?" asked Cyrus, who had come back with us for tea.

Emerson glanced around to make sure Sennia wasn't listening. He lowered his voice.

"It is confirmation of my suspicions, Vandergelt. Tonight is the last night the tomb will be open. I had a feeling Albion wouldn't give up without a final attempt. He won't get help from the Gurnawis, but strangers, hired criminals, might be willing to attack us if the rewards were high enough."

"Good Lord!" Cyrus ejaculated. "We'd better get over to Luxor right away. Have the fellows rounded up and put the fear of God into Joe Albion."

"I am surprised at you, Vandergelt. One cannot arrest people without evidence of a crime." Emerson smiled. It was not a nice smile. "I weary of Mr. Albion and his family. We will arrange a little ambush and catch them red-handed."

"Hmmmm." Cyrus stroked his goatee. "I like the idea, Emerson. Just so nobody gets hurt."

"And how do you mean to guarantee that?" I demanded. "What if they are armed?"

"We will have your pistol, Peabody," said Emerson, grinning.

"We better have more than that," Cyrus said. "I've got a couple of rifles and a pistol, latest-model Mauser. I only hope I can sneak 'em out of the house without Katherine seeing," he added uneasily.

We had to get Sennia off to bed before we made the final

arrangements. Emerson had sent word to Selim, warning him of our suspicions and giving him his instructions, and Cyrus did manage to get his weapons smuggled out of the Castle without Katherine's knowledge. She would have been deeply distressed if she had known what we were up to.

A little contretemps arose at the last minute, when the men realized that Nefret and I and Jumana meant to accompany them. I put an end to their protests in short order, however.

"So long as you don't bring that damned sword parasol" was Emerson's way of conceding defeat.

The moon was on the wane, but the dazzling desert stars gave sufficient light for us to make our way over the ancient path that crossed the gebel. When we reached Deir el Medina, all was quiet. The coals of a fire burned near the place where our men were stationed; there were only four of them, including Selim. They had been ordered to look as if they had relaxed their guard, and on no account to resist an attack. One by one we descended the slope, and found concealment in the shadows of the ruined tombs.

We waited for over an hour before they came, from the south, creeping along the base of the hill. I counted the dim shapes: twelve in all. The last two carried rifles. Like the others, they were masked, but I had no difficulty in recognizing the rotund form of Mr. Albion and the taller outline of his son. One might have expected they would lead their troops from behind! When Selim sprang to his feet, Sebastian advanced, with his weapon aimed, while one of his hirelings called out in Arabic, "Do not move or we will shoot!"

For a moment I was afraid Daoud would forget his orders. It is not in his nature to submit meekly to threats. However, he remained seated, and within a few minutes our fellows were tightly bound, gagged, and blindfolded.

"Now?" Cyrus whispered.

Emerson shook his head.

Sebastian put his rifle down and began to climb the ladder. Obeying his gesture, five of the others followed. Neither he nor his father had spoken; our people could hear, if they could not see, and the use of English would have been a dead giveaway. Mr. Albion sat down with a grunt, and the other men stood close by him.

Emerson waited until Sebastian had reached the platform outside the tomb. His stentorian voice echoed between the cliffs. "Stop where you are, all of you. You are surrounded by armed men." He added in English, "Drop the rifle, Albion."

"Better fire a warning shot," Cyrus advised. "In case they haven't noticed our weapons."

We were all on our feet, except for Nefret, who had given me her word she would not expose herself to gunfire. Emerson pointed his rifle toward the temple and pulled the trigger.

The men with Albion broke like a drop of quicksilver, scattering in all directions. "Let them go," said Emerson, plunging down the slope. "It's Albion I want."

However, he was too late. I would never have supposed such a round, elderly man could move so fast. The bullet Emerson aimed at his heels only made him run faster.

"Emerson," I said, tugging at his arm. "We had better do something about Sebastian, don't you think?"

Emerson looked up and let out an exclamation.

The men who had started to follow Sebastian up to the platform were dropping to the ground, but Sebastian himself was still there—hanging by his hands from the edge of the platform and screaming at the top of his lungs. Quite a number of people were shouting, so his cries had been lost in the uproar. He must have lost his balance when the gun went off.

"I'll get him," Ramses said.

"Give him a hand, Bertie," Emerson ordered. "You'll need to get a rope round the bloody idiot. There's plenty in the supply shed. I wonder how much longer he can hold on," he added with mild interest.

Nefret and I set about freeing our men, who set about collecting fallen tomb robbers. Some of them had dropped quite a distance, so there were sprains and a broken bone or two, which Nefret treated in her usual efficient fashion.

"Have they got him?" she asked, referring to Sebastian. He was still screaming. "I can't see from here."

"Bertie got a rope around him," Cyrus said. "They don't seem to be in any hurry to pull him up, though."

Leaving the robbers in Selim's charge, we took a silent, shivering Sebastian back to his ma and pa. As Emerson declared, he had not finished with Mr. Albion, not by a damned sight. We all went along, naturally. No one wanted to miss the denouement.

There was no response to Emerson's emphatic knocks on the door of the Albions's sitting room. Fearing that he would wake the poor convalescent officers, I announced in low but penetrating tones, "We have your son. If you want him back you must let us in."

The door was flung open by Mrs. Albion. Despite the lateness of the hour she was fully dressed and bejeweled. "What have you done to him?" she cried, seizing hold of the young man.

"He did it to himself," I replied, pushing mother and son out of the way. Mr. Albion was sitting on the sofa. He must have arrived just before we did, since he was breathless, disheveled, and very red in the face.

"Now you've brought him back, get out," he said.

"This is not a presentation, it is an exchange," said Emerson. "Peabody, my dear, may I invite you to take a chair, since no one else has had the courtesy to do so? Albion, I want the artifacts you got from Jamil."

"Be damned to you!" Albion growled.

Having determined that her son was intact, Mrs. Albion turned indignantly on Emerson. "Mr. Albion paid for those objects, sir. Are you a common thief?"

"Not at all common, madam," said Emerson, with a smile that reminded me of his brother. "I propose not to press charges for armed assault and purchasing illegal antiquities, in return for the objects that were stolen—and for your promise to leave Luxor immediately. Your husband and your son are extremely inept criminals, but I cannot have this sort of thing. It interferes with my work. Come now, Albion, you are a practical man. Admit you've lost."

"Lost?" Mrs. Albion gasped. "Mr. Albion does not lose. Mr. Albion—"

"Is a practical man," her husband said, with difficulty. "All right, then. I'll get them."

"And I will come with you," Emerson declared. "To make sure you don't overlook anything."

They returned with a heavy box, which Emerson handed to Cyrus. "All there. All yours. Shall we go, my dears?"

Mrs. Albion appeared to be in a state of shock. Her eyes had a bewildered look and she kept murmuring, "Mr. Albion does not lose. Mr. Albion . . ."

Was in for a spot of marital trouble, if I was any judge. I sincerely hoped so.

"Just one more thing," Bertie said, in his quiet voice. "Sebastian, take off your glasses and put up your hands."

"Hopelessly, incorrigibly well-bred," said Emerson, shaking his head, as Bertie knocked Sebastian flat.

Cyrus's fantasia was remembered for years as the finest, most extravagant entertainment Luxor had ever seen. The courtyard and the Castle were thrown open; tourists, convalescent officers, Egyptian workmen, and the permanent residents of Luxor mingled in amity, eating and drinking, dancing and singing. It was such a crush I soon gave up trying to do my social duty and was enjoying the sight of Selim and Nefret trying to waltz to the beat of an Egyptian drum, when someone tapped me on the shoulder and I turned to see Marjorie Fisher, a longtime friend who lived in Luxor.

"It's been ages, Amelia," she said. "What have you been up to?"

"Just the usual," I replied. "And what have you been up to?"

She laughed. "The usual. Lunches, teas, visitors . . . That

reminds me, I ran into someone recently who asked to be remembered to you. A sweet little thing with freckles on her nose. Her name is Molly Throgmorton."

I swallowed the wrong way. "Molly *what*?"

"She has been recently married," Marjorie said. "Her husband was with her—a very pleasant but rather coarse American, who looked to be at least fifty years her senior—but she was wearing a diamond the size of a lima bean, my dear, so he must be extremely rich. She said you knew her by her maiden name, but I'm afraid I have forgotten it. Do you know who I mean?"

"Yes. I know who you mean. Where is she—where are they staying?"

"They left Luxor on Tuesday. Is something wrong, Amelia?"

"No. It's just that I am . . . sorry to have missed her. I don't suppose she happened to mention where they were going?"

Marjorie shook her head. "She said she hoped to see you another time. Her exact words were 'Tell her she hasn't seen the last of me.' Rather an odd way of expressing it, but I suppose she meant it as a touch of humor."

"No doubt," I said.

"I am going to break all the rules of decorum and ask Selim to dance with me," Marjorie announced with a smile. "He waltzes beautifully! Come to tea on Friday, Amelia?"

"Thank you. That would be nice."

The festivities were still in progress when we took our departure, leaving Jumana to "cavort with the young people," as Emerson put it. The sounds of revelry faded into silence as the carriage traversed the winding road, and the still, starry night of Egypt enclosed us.

"Vandergelt informed me that the Albions left Luxor yesterday," Emerson remarked. He added pensively, "I must say that the general quality of criminals has sadly deteriorated. Not that I mind—especially at the present time. How are you feeling, my dear?"

He put his arm round Nefret and she leaned against his

shoulder. "A little tired, perhaps. But it was a wonderful evening."

"Life," Emerson declared, in such a happy frame of mind he actually committed an aphorism, "life could not be better. Eh, Peabody?"

"Indeed, Emerson."

Not for worlds would I have cast a shadow on his good humor. Nor was there cause to do so; my fancies were no more than that, idle thoughts of a wandering mind. Yet the words kept going round and round in my head, like a broken gramophone record.

"If she blames me for her mother's death, how do you suppose she feels about you?" . . . "Tell her she hasn't seen the last of me . . ."

"The young serpent also has poisoned fangs."

The Vicky Bliss Mysteries by
New York Times Bestselling Author

ELIZABETH PETERS

TROJAN GOLD
0-380-73123-1/$6.99 US/$9.99 Can
"Wit, charm, and romance in equal measures."
San Diego Union

SILHOUETTE IN SCARLET
0-380-73337-4/$6.99 US/$9.99 Can
"No one is better at juggling torches while dancing
on a high wire than Elizabeth Peters."
Chicago Tribune

STREET OF THE FIVE MOONS
0-380-73121-5/$6.99 US/$9.99 Can
"This author never fails to entertain."
Cleveland Plain Dealer

BORROWER OF THE NIGHT
0-380-73339-0/$6.99 US/$9.99 Can
"A writer so popular the public library
needs to keep her books under lock and key."
Washington Post Book World